MASSAGE WORLD

THE NOVEL

ERIC MADEEN

ANAPHORA LITERARY PRESS

QUANAH, TEXAS

ANAPHORA LITERARY PRESS
1108 W 3rd Street
Quanah, TX 79252
https://anaphoraliterary.com

Book design by Anna Faktorovich, Ph.D.

Edited by Danielle Willett and Dominic Giovannangeli

Published in 2018 by Anaphora Literary Press

Massage World: The Novel
Eric Madeen—1st edition.

Library of Congress Control Number: 2018954819

Library Cataloging Information
Madeen, Eric, 1958-, author.
    Massage World: The novel / Eric Madeen
    266 pp. ; 9 in.
    ISBN 978-1-68114-469-6 (softcover : alk. paper)
    ISBN 978-1-68114-470-2 (hardcover : alk. paper)
    ISBN 978-1-68114-471-9 (e-book)
1. Fiction—Mystery & Detective—Hard-Boiled.
2. Fiction—Thrillers—Crime.
3. Health & Fitness—Massage & Reflexology.
PN3311-3503: Literature: Prose fiction
813: American fiction in English

For Julie, Hunter and Addisyn Madeen

Nonconformity and lust stalking
hand in hand through the country,
wasting and ravaging.

—Evelyn Waugh, from *Decline and Fall*

Under my swimsuit,
a whiteness that has not changed
since my natal day.

—Seishi Yamaguchi, from *The Essence of Modern Haiku*,
translated by Takashi Kodaira and Alfred H. Marks

INGRID SWANSON, LICENSED MASSAGE THERAPIST (L.M.T.),

Shivered in her t-shirt in the back seat of a cab, thinking how Southern California wasn't supposed to be so cold, even in December. The weather always played tricks on you here and was thus extra tricky to dress for. Like this morning's warmth—that had her reaching for the t-shirt—now chased south by a cold snap whistling down from the Aleutians and coming in hard off the bay. To the wind blasting in from half-open windows in front, the cabbie, his name hidden by post-its, seemed oblivious, turning up the happy babble of an excited weatherman talking weather: rain turning to snow by morning, three inches of the white stuff expected. The probability of a truly rare white Christmas in SoCal was tempered on icy roads and walks. Along with the familiar reminders of the need for continued water conservation in this interminable drought, which set off associations from earlier today, involving dragging herself into the mansion after a night of outcalls only to face down a raging unpaid tradesmen, who concluded, "You know what your problem is, Ingrid? You need a man." Then to everyone: "Ingrid needs a man!"

And the cabbie needed conversation. "Why you open this Massage Palace—"

"Massage *World*," she amended primly, then let some silence in, not in the mood to talk.

"Why you opening this Massage World?"

Why? Hovering out there. In no mood to go away. Blood-hungry. Spear tipped. *Why?* "Because," she began, yawning, hesitating, not at all in a giving mood and coming up with "I am a masseuse and massage is what I do and it's time for me to make my move." Warming to talking as a stress buster her answer snowballed into, "The snatch and grab of eighty dollars here and there, and if I'm lucky a hundred with a tip on a good day, is draining me and what with my lack of wheels and reliance on hacks, buses, trolleys and friends… and because I'm tired of sweating out trying to make rent and counting out quarters and dimes across grocery store counters. Because freelance massage is a hard dollar and," the momentum teasing out eloquence, "the body is in pain." She forced a smile for his eyes in the mirror.

Cord wood under an ax, perversion split his voice which cut like a cleaver into his tip. "Pain? I have pain. Down here. Look."

Leaning back in the seat, she said, "And *because* I don't want to spend the rest of my life pestered by jerks like you trying to get me to jerk them off." She leaned forward. "Now would you close the windows. I'm freezing back here."

With the windows closed here came the heat aimed in great gushes that broke her hair and was now getting into her eyes and tickling her cheeks, her neck. From sleep deprivation and playing hard ass all day she felt irritated, like she wanted to fight but, of course, there was no one there with his dukes up and she was a fighter only as much as she was a survivor. She calmed herself by belly breathing. Staring out. The wrap of moonlight on guardrail. Looking at the palm trees that tore across the skyline. A canyon ridge loomed with its ship shape in the night and glimmered with lights which meant houses. And families. And the familiar thought grazing her of how much richer life was supposed to be when you had someone with whom to share it. Cars came up on them, raking light and shadow in webs spinning off the top that was the driver's shiny, shaved head. Three cars. Three knocks of wind on the old Conversion Highway twisting over a rise between boulders then turning into a serpent crawling toward blackness cut with tiny wave curls. He gunned the engine and headlights shot up at the night sky and the image in her mind was of sparklers as the cab bottomed out, scraping a manhole cover, making the construction sound of a power tool slipping. The body was indeed in pain.

No one in the whole wide world could be as lonely as Americans hiding their faces in TVs, bad juju computer/smartphone/iPad screens, and huge, lonely fenced-off houses where she's called to warm them with her hands. (And when the client's capable of handling irony, stinging them with old-world scorn.)

Noticing his sternocleidomastoid, or neck muscle, suddenly bulge from the exertion of an arm rammed straight into steering wheel, she wanted to ignore his, "I said before"—he was from somewhere. Not here. Italian side of the Mediterranean? Photo I.D.—purposefully—

papered over with scrawled up post-its—"I saw your fancy neon sign for Massage Palace and I thought I like that sign—"

"Not Massage Palace," she said, wondering why people could only remember the massage end of it, "but *Massage World!*"

"Anyway," he said, catching her eye in the mirror, "I like your sign."

Signage was everything in the massage biz. If the sign were staid and not bright and blinking then you discouraged the lonely and perverted from queuing up for you know what. (Masseuses should bill the American government, and have the Federal Bureau of Massage down some creaky capitol corridor, compensate for special services rendered, the lives warmed, the lives saved...with touch.)

They descended to her neighborhood and rushed past parked cars and lighted windows of living rooms. In one she glimpsed the figure of an old man clutching a dinner plate as he strode to the kitchen or sofa seat before the television, behind him a large oil painting of sky and snow-capped mountains, which made her think of Sweden, its mountains, and her father with his similar hunker as the dinner-plate man. Her years in America now stretching the distance between her and her mother, father, siblings, and old friends to something that has been stretched too far, like the elastic on old underwear. Her relationships with friends and relatives, comparable to underwear so loose that they fall to the floor. Tossed into the rag bag like her relationship with her sometime lover, Greg.

Hitting a bump and rising a little then bottoming out again, the cab chugged uphill and her stomach and its feeling seemed to drain down deep then chill from a niggling thought creeping in these days like a stray cat that maybe she's not deserving of...love. (Can't get her mind off it.)

She leaned forward and glared at his reflection in the rearview mirror and wanted for about four seconds to cry but instead said, "What is it that you want?"

He was staring at her. They had hit a red light. He turned around. Now that she could see him front facing she saw he was pop eyed. She wanted by turns to both push back against the seat in repulsion and to spring forward with cupped hands held under his sockets to catch them should they pop out, his eyes. "I *want your massage.*"

Such a slippery serpent of a word. A massage could mean the wrong thing to the wrong kind of client, the kind who'd persist through session with overtures, even if the bodywork were given in the most straight-seeming location that had SPA and UPMARKET and CLEAN and SOOTHING and HOLISTIC HEALTH written all over the signage and sundry, as Massage World does. The interpretation all depended on where you were coming from and not necessarily who was giving the massage. A friend of hers, a masseuse with a lantern jaw, acne, huge scaly hands and straggly hair, and a uniform consisting of a sterile white smock, and a studio tinkling with crystals and New Age music, is even tormented by the raging testosterone crowd and their lust monster. She pointed to the road. "Watch where you're going."

All the stress of preparing for the grand opening of Massage World, especially the sheer toil of bickering with tradesmen and chiseling at tiles all day every day so the walls of bathrooms had that *camel-ass texture* (the term of the Egyptian tile setter) had rattled her hopefulness for this new venture and made her truly wonder about her profession and if this is what she wanted. So phallic at all the wrong times this biz. Her biz. The massage biz.

JACKSON COBB

Was in a jet flying toward Tokyo Narita. Throughout the sleepless flight across several time zones he felt moody, edgy about returning to Japan after eight years. Beside him a white South African woman made a grab for his hand at the grind of the landing gear. "Flying terrifies me," she told him in explanation of her death grip.

He let her hold on, but didn't try to calm her by saying, "*Hey, it'll be all right.*" He had his plans already laid out, and he couldn't afford to get bogged down by escorting her into the metropolis while undoubtedly being pestered like he was a tour guide with non-stop questions. Besides, he told himself, she's a stranger. When she drew encouragement from what she thought was his sympathy, she took up an earlier line of query so he quickly opted for saying, "Sorry. Can't hear you." Made a confused face, pointed at his Walkman earphones, and then looked past her—to the lights shaping Narita's runway. False dawn's darkness resonating with his smuggling days long ago, his bowels suddenly felt heavy.

In India—nine or ten years back—he'd dice up an ounce of hash, seal the pellets in a dozen packets of plastic wrap before shrink-wrapping them over a lighter flame. Completely sealed against the bite of stomach acid, the packets were swallowed on top of six 2.5mg tablets of atropine sulfate, which he always feared would give out, his bowels opening like a trap door, at the crucial moment at immigration when the customs official spotted his Indian visa then promptly asked him to unzip his pack. And his trousers practically. He'd acquiesce, not saying a word. In a further show of openness, he'd take a step back and let his arms hang at his sides. *Nothing to hide here.* Or when he sensed weakness in the inspector, he'd make a great show of looking at his wristwatch. Either way, he was always successful, and more successful at peddling his stash at an outrageous markup to drug-starved foreigners in Tokyo's discos and *gaijin ghettos.*

Now, though, that was well behind him, and he was smuggling something else.

Something that didn't even need smuggling.

Money.

In the form of rings on his belt.

Sure, all that he needed to do was declare the amount, as he was exceeding by two grand the ten-grand limit. But since declaration precluded the delicious feeling he felt all around his waist, where the goods encircled him like sharks' teeth gobbling him up, and deeper with that sharp tingle against the drop of his gut, he thus leaned toward the risk and the vibrancy of it, and didn't declare anything.

He knew he'd quadruple his money, the yen having soared yet again and Japanese youth would see the goods—what would very soon be contraband—as *smart-o*. He was certain all those gold and ruby high-school rings he bought for peanuts off Border City's pawn brokers would sell in minutes to trendy Harajuku youth boutiques, who'd turn around and vend them to the dyed-hair and contact lens tinted hip crowd at another four-times markup. Before his sister and partner-in-crime, Bobbie, had dropped him at the airport, he had strung them, all fifty eight rings, on a length of string that he then tied off around his waist. If Japanese immigration searched him, he'd merely tell them what he had told the inspector when the metal detector sounded at Border City International. "Just my belt." "Well," the black woman had said, "you gonna have to take your belt off and put it right in here." She handed him a plastic bowl. He untucked his shirt, untied the jangling snake of ruby and gold now coiling in the proffered container. Those in line behind him gaped. "Some belt," the woman said, curious. "What ya gonna to do with all them rings?"

"Wear 'em," he said.

"Wear 'em in good health then. You may go."

Now wheels hit runway in Japan, jarring the field of heads before him. The young woman beside him relaxed her death grip on his hand. She had been cheerless in conversation earlier, confiding that her job plans involved going *directly* to the hostess bars of the Ginza to "cash in on the strong yen, and be out of here in six months with fifty-thousand dollars. My friend did it. I can do it." She gave Cobb a cadging look but he could only wish her the best of luck. She was dumpy and frumpy, and rich Japanese businessmen, savvy enough to come into money and the trust of a corporate expense account, would allow the mama-san to dump her on their table only once. Cobb knew the game, having drank at several clubs, plus having been employed by a host bar where, after hours, affluent Japanese women waited outside like bandits in hiding, chasing him to the station where he ran to make the last train. They'd pant up from behind, *"I pay for taxi, Jack-san. We go together. No train."* If their aggression were encouraged by their drinking, they might even slip an arm through his own. If he were tired or indifferent to her looks, he'd speak in English, explaining, *"Can't. Against the mama-san's policy. Can't afford to lose my job."* Still holding his hand as the aircraft screamed into braking, wing slats whacking at wind, the woman let it be known again that she was available.

"God, I feel so lost and lonely," she said, fluttering her eyelids with her head angled against her seat so she looked up into his face—her very best innocent-girl-traveling-abroad-alone look strengthened by her touching his arm. "I've never been to Japan. I don't know what I'm going to do."

Cobb had plans. All kinds of things to do. "I'm sorry I can't help you. Tourist information has the scoop on youth hostels. When you're dealing with the Japanese just remember to smile big, speak slowly, and carry a big stick, meaning a pen to write down anything elaborate in simple English." Then he winked before continuing, "Do what you gotta do."

Seat belts were clicking as they were unbuckled throughout the cabin, he bolted down the aisle as soon as he was unfastened, getting a jump on the other passengers, much to the annoyance of a flight attendant waving him back to his seat just as the fasten-seat belt sign flashed off.

At Immigration there were deep lines of Filipinos and Thai, soon to be shivering in tropical clothes, interspersed with Indonesian and Malaysian Muslims in flowing robes and head scarves, their feet in sandals nudging along huge stacks of taped up boxes which somehow were allowed as carry-ons. All miners in a rush for the gold but destined to scrape by as short-order cooks and dishwashers, day laborers, garbage collectors, maids and janitors in pachinko parlors, love hotels, capsule hotels. Cobb himself was a gold miner, having to ask an old Japanese woman for the help she had once offered to give him. *"Whenever you need anything, Jack-san,"* she had said in Japanese when he had left her, breaking out of the prison that was his cracker-box room over her house.

"Well," he envisioned himself as saying, "I need something now."

He remembered her eyes. How on her platelike face they missed nothing in a hoarder's gaze. He cringed at the thought of facing her with his demand.

"What?" she would ask at crunch time, staring. "The yen equivalent of how many dollars?" He saw her, in his mind's eye, leaning back the other way. An inflatable toy losing air. Felt nothing but resentment for her, then for himself for having to stoop so low.

"You're a businesswoman. Consider it an investment."

Here she'd reinflate, her tone rock-hard, her whole person unmoored from that sweet shawl of femininity she clutched around her and ask him, "An investment on what?"

That was just it, an investment on what? How he'd talk his way around that hurdle vexed him all the way through the tedium of immigration and baggage claim.

INGRID

"**I** want your massage," he repeated, lighting a cigarette in the luminescence of his gas jet created the image of two big noses in the mirror. Inhale.

Exhale. A long feminine puff and grip. He touched his hands to his shoulders, his legs, presumably, doing the steering. "I have stiffness." Inhaling. "Here." He had to point there again. "You make me full massage. I no charge fare. Deal?"

She met his big eyes in the reflection of the mirror. Let a moment go by. Just long enough for him to tweak her. "Hmm?"

"No deal," she said—twiddling her thumbs in her lap, thinking about her dog Max, of feeding him and thus ridding herself of that guilt, and wanting to pee (as she couldn't go at the mansion since the plumbers still hadn't finished their endless jackhammering—the rocky soil so hard they had to jack hammer it—and sewer connections, sitting out in the side yard putting two and two together, for over two months)—"deal."

"What!?!" he exclaimed, showing teeth and a ribbon of light that bled violet down his tongue, now sharp with that brand of irritation common to Mediterranean types in the simplest of transactions gone awry.

"No deal. Now you have to take a right—in about a half block, on Pacific Highway."

He shrugged and mumbled, gyrating and grunting through the shoulder roll and hand-over-hand moves required of a sudden turn at high speed. The tires were yelping like banshees. Pistons pinging and panging from sharp acceleration and inefficient combustion. "*I need massage but there's to be no deal.*"

"Oh come on." She glared. "What is it with you? I'm tired and don't want to hear anymore about it. Okay?" He was looking this way and that, avoiding her repeating, "Okay?"

Steering with open hands, splayed fingers, and with his palms slapping up and down, he grumbled, "Huh. No deal. Big deal. *No fucking deal* she says. Like some dame in an old black and white movie."

Like some dame...

He shifted a glance—a frisking glance as searching as a shake down—back to weigh the effect of the insult.

Which was...a broken chuckle. Caught in the throat like a fish bone. Dames don't cry. Her laughter was more like a cough. An idiot's solitary cackle. An index finger curling, infantile, up over an eye to hide this dent of armor. Put on everyday against what she had to make her living off of (alas, the—at least *this*—masseuse's story). Now she could feel tears rising behind behind her eyes. She wanted so much to give herself over to the source, the pain—that tender jelly flood rising up from a smothered soul that pressed at her eyes like a hand. She sniffled for a moment, thinking of that which wanted to gush earlier today in the second bayoneting from a confirming charmer.

"You need a man, Ingrid." There it was again. The reality of it. Some dame who needed to get laid, they thought. To everyone downstairs in the mansion's salon he—a middle-aged righteous unpaid carpenter of this day—had to turn up the pitch of his redneck's version of that reverberation of a black man's snarling R & B voice crowding the microphone with all kinds of extra syllables and growls in there: "Ingrid nee-eeds a a maa-a-n!" Followed by making an unmentionable gesture and saying, "She needs the schlong, man. The big one."

Ingrid took that to mean that she was bitchy and needed a relationship. Well, f-u-c-k them. All of them. Especially this one now bending his gypsy cab through a turn, and her old shrink and his counsel exchanged for the work of her healing hands (a barter arrangement like most that never did work out), in his flat voice urging her to just "Let it out. Don't be afraid to just let it out, Ingrid. Nothing wrong with expressing honest emotion. Come on, Ingrid. Crack it open!

The back end of the cab missed a panel truck by inches. The screech of banshees came again from the tires. She put her hands over her face, fearing a crash. *Nooooo.* "She says there is to be no deal." The plane of his chin jutted out from his neck, signaling a change of tactics after the triumphant fish tailing through in a screech. Which, together with pride, brought a little bobble to the driver's head. "Tell me: you make good massage?" His voice slid down an even lower octave, his right hand making an obscene gesture a la paperhanger. "You do everywhere?"

The madness of lechery raving in his eyes locking onto hers. She couldn't help but notice the saliva bubbling off his lips. His right hand recapitulating the motion. "Huh?"

"I think you're sick. I think you need help. Are you on drugs? What is it? Speed? You a speed freak? Or opiods?"

Now comedic, he turned around to introduce himself, wrinkling his brow for effect in a squinting of eyes, proffering a hand which she ignored. "I'm Nicholas. I go soon for your massage. If good, I bring fares for you to make massage."

"Don't bother." Shook her head. Flung her hands out. *Shoo.* Lying, she said, "I only do outcalls."

"Twenty buck commission you give me for every fare I bring. I do same with Golden Hands and Near East Spa. You know Jack Cobb?"

She let out a long sigh, exasperated. "Don't talk to me about Jack Cobb."

"Why?"

"Why yourself?" She crossed her arms and shivered. Just the mention of his name. Sleaze-ball. Parlor Lord. Jack Cobb. Took over— more like hijacked, no, *Cobbed*—Border City massage parlors. Surely he'd be after her new one, her *palace* soon to open.

The cabby sat bolt upright, as if jolted by a moray eel, his eyes, one second bulging with revelation, the next becoming slits, as if smoking a joint. The snake in the grass sighing, "Ah, yes. Yes, yes. Now I remember. How could I forget?"

"Remember what?" she asked. "Forget what?"

"Ah huh," he said, nodding. "Remember you."

"Remember me what?"

He pointed up at the rearview, at her. "Remember. *You.*"

JACK COBB

Tried to imagine himself saying in Japanese, "An investment on my taking over a massage place called Massage World and cornering the entire Border City massage market."

"*Nani?*" his ex-landlady would ask. "What? A massage place? Massage World? Where? Why?"

He'd shrug. "As I said, Border City. As for why, it's what I do. How I make my living."

"Is that the business you're in, *Jack-san?* A gangster business?"

Jack wondered how she would play it then no sooner told himself that he couldn't see her, instead going through with the meeting with Kobayashi-san (otherwise known as K.), a mafia don ruling substantial quarters of northern Yokohama and Kawasaki, to discuss a human smuggling venture, before going on to memory lane at Yokosuka. Kobayashi had requested the meet through Las Vegas, who then chose Cobb for the job because of his linguistic fluency and years in Asia. The dons of the family in which he affiliated gave him instructions to indulge K. as he saw fit. Cobb knew that K., like most Japanese businessmen, needed not only to see his adversary in person to get a read on his character but actually experience him in the round—through late night hostess clubs and Turkish bath sprees followed by up-at-dawn tee times, where character deficiency, namely selfishness and a bad temper, exposed itself *loud and clear*. In a minutiae of gestures, facial tics, voice inflections, and/or thrown and broken golf clubs, all of which were more often than note lost on the smartphone. Having a fiery temper and a reputation as a *thrower* (of golf clubs) not to mention a selfish streak that ran as cold and deep as Fuji-san spring waters, Cobb knew right now that he wasn't going to play any golf with the honorable Kobayashi.

The potential business involved human smuggling. Less sinister than it sounded, the caper involved helping poor people find jobs in the underworld of developed countries. With only six-month *entertainer* visas, the most beautiful and charming Southeast Asian bar girls, mainly from Thailand and the Philippines, were rerouted, with tourist visas, out of Japan on to Hawaii or the West Coast, including Border City, Cobb's domain, where he washed money through massage parlors he had taken over. Cobb cautioned the higher ups against the human smuggling business with the Yakuza. "*They're too desperate. A new government agency in the Ministry of Finance is hell-bent on collecting collateral, in cooperation with the Ministry of Justice. For several billion dollars of bad yakuza loans, one yakuza property after another's being seized…*"

Cobb handed over his passport and immigration form to the Japanese official behind the counter, telling himself again that he wouldn't see her, old Motoko Ogawa, not out of pride but from fear of rousing the nightmare memories of his dreaded time as captive—in his cubbyhole over her house at her greedy mercy. Already just the thought of her, hair-triggered by the high gloss sheen of Narita terminal, and stepping foot again on Japanese soil after eight years, had busted loose in him that dread he felt all those times he failed to resist her cunning. He tightened his abdomen, shivering against the icicles of gold and ruby doing their shark-teeth chew, trying not to let that squidgy time come loose inside him, leaving him armed with nothing to swing back at his demons.

On the Narita Express clanking over farmland closer to Tokyo, Cobb kept telling himself to stick to business. Not to get sidetracked by the pull of the past. Another voice, though, kept pestering him. It spoke from his *honne*, or deep feeling. That had nothing to do with Las Vegas and parlor schemes, but gave rise to contemplation as he watched dawn's light flutter, slanting through a bamboo grove and strobe through the coach. The slashes of green bamboo were falling away, and there lay the glisten of checkerboards—frosty rice paddies in morning sun.

Sitting near Cobb were a few junior tourists, young Americans, two girls and a boy, on their first trip abroad. Thinking aloud opposite Cobb (in fact their knees brushed) and expressing delight in the simplest of tasks was a hirsute fellow just out of his teens. His plump face was bushy with a beard that grew down his neck, disappearing under his collar, before growing out his long sleeves thick onto the backs of his hands. *He could be in a freak show*, Cobb thought. The younger traveller had busied himself, and begun much too cheerfully for Cobb's liking, making currency conversions, aloud, on a calculator. "If we change fifty dollars," he announced, his feminine voice contradicting his hairy virility, "we'll have this much yen. Look." His two female companions leaned forward to glimpse the calculator screen. "Now, if we change one hundred dollars we'll have this much. Look. So let's just change one hundred then."

Cobb winced. What was one-hundred dollars but a night at the cheapest business hotel, if that? Surely this guy was joking. But far from laughing Cobb was tired. Jet lag and sleep deprivation, together with not being able to shoot his meth, equaled a boxing glove wad of fatigue mashing his brains up against the top of his skull.

"These seats can be flipped the other way so that we can face each other," one of the two girls said, fingering one of her pigtails whose tip splayed over the delicious lump of her breast, sadly hidden by a lime-green ski jacket.

Cobb felt a headache coming on. Worse, his nose was running and he had a fever. Even after he had gone through the hassle of wrestling his beret from his bag in the train's overhead compartment the top of his head still felt icy cold. He couldn't help but attribute the knock down to his coming back to Japan—on massage business no less—after so many years away, and getting into the tangle of his emotions was this prissy group seemingly going out of their way to irritate him. He felt the burgeoning of rage heating up in his chest as they kept chatting nonsense.

"No, Penny," said the other girl, who had a pug nose and a big square face, made more conspicuous by red locks shorn into a bowl cut. "These seats flip back so that when the train changes direction you just have to flip the seat the other way. That way the train doesn't have to turn all the way around." She lifted a shoulder and chanced a grin at Cobb as if to see if he could be drawn into the fray.

He glared and frowned. He made sure to keep glaring until she looked away, blushing.

To distract him from his anger, he thought about calling his new rival, Ingrid Swanson. Pondering a frightful message that he'd give her, he stared out at Tokyo creeping up against the early flare of sunlight. A flock of birds flew up into the sun then dived back down into the canyon between sun-splashed aluminum roofs of warehouses. Then the flock soared, changed directions once, twice—at the same time—then dove below the roof line, disappearing. More buildings and houses, ugly boxes sided with corrugated tin, divided by easement gaps strung together—the last cat's cradle—by wrist-thick electrical wire crossing back and around. If asked why this ugly wire drooped everywhere from equally ugly telephone poles the Japanese would simply say, "*Sho ga nai.*" It can't be helped. Then they would cite earthquakes.

Cobb watched a local train take on commuters then chug away from a station. Buses and cars clogged streets. Then, the tenor of the ape man again assaulted his ears.

Cobb watched him standing there in the aisle, clasping his hairy hands at his chest. "I think there's a water closet in the next car down, ladies!" Then he was off in a determined stride. A minute later, he came back announcing, in the cheerful voice of a real trooper, "Sorry. It's not there. I'm going to check the other car."

He marched back with his next announcement, saying smugly, if not effeminately, "Well, I have news that you girls are going to adore: I'll have you know that I found one water closet three cars down. It probably goes right down to the tracks, though."

Cobb could no longer contain his anger, glowering at the bearded American before snarling, "Then why don't you. And your prissy little diary keepers. Go there together. Then help each other with the wiping while you're at it all right?!"

Tension prickled the air. Aghast, they looked up at him then looked down, like scolded children on holiday.

Noticing the Japanese passengers staring at him, Cobb rose, standing to deliver an extemporaneously composed haiku in Japanese about travellers littering and thus leaving traces of their passing.

"*Koitsura shitsurei de sumimasen.*" Excuse them, he said, they're rude. With that, he bowed deeply then watched the Japanese businessmen disappear behind newspapers and mothers rein in children. Cobb sat back down, looked out the window—at concrete and asphalt and boxlike buildings obliterating the natural. The iron clatter of train wheels echoing off glass and steel, concrete and tin, stress sounds sharpened in the air. Passengers got antsy. Rolling deeper into *Stress City.* Tokyo.

JANICE VERDURIN, L.M.T.,

Felt helpless in the nightmare pull of reality, as she was bouncing and bobbing in the back of a city bus heading deeper into the tenderloin to someplace called Near East Spa, its want-ad—along with another—in her purse. One position, at a spa called Massage World, seemed promising, at least the ad showed no inclination toward the sexual, but Janice still hadn't been able to get through to the manager, Ingrid Swanson. The wordage of the other ad was uncertain, but she had already contacted Mr. Cobb, the manager of the Near East Spa, and in thirty minutes had an interview, which meant, the gruff Mr. Cobb had explained in a tough tone on the phone, that "I want you. To massage me. So that I can see that you. Know your stuff. Okay?"

Earlier Janice had bought a hotdog off a sidewalk vendor. Digesting that and the strain of life, along with creating a new life in a new city where she knew absolutely no one, and that she had to show that she knew her *stuff, okay?* made her stomach burn wildfire up her chest and throat. A no-thank-you cocktail lent a lurch to her step off of the bus and into the traffic noise thrown off of brick buildings. Now a cloud of bus exhaust billowed up into her face and she felt like throwing up. She held her breath instead, then exhaled for five seconds, repeating a relaxation mantra from a New Age hypnosis tape, "I am able and stable, able and stable." She turned her wrist toward a Korean grocery-store window. Time to burn before seven.

To stay warm she walked up the sidewalk, past a Chinese dry cleaners, a noisy bar, a peep show, and a bearded homeless Christ figure of a man wrapped in a ragged blanket. The Near East Spa's integrity slipping the longer she had to wait for some curious interview, along with the pinpricks in her stomach to subside, pain that now pressed like matches against her gut and burned like a flame. It then morphed into a revelation that she didn't quite know how to come to terms with: Any place in such a shitty neighborhood couldn't possibly be a good venture.

She wanted to call this damned Ingrid person again, and swear to god scream if she got her machine again. If only this guy leaning against the phone would clear the heck away with his dirty bib overalls half-assedly pulled over a filthy sweatshirt. "Spare me some change?" he asked, grinning through missing teeth, but his eyes were cool and lifeless under a soiled baseball cap, its bill creased into a crumple like very old paper money.

She held his gaze. "No, no I can't." She continued to stare at him until he looked away. She had shamed him back. That's what you had to do. Otherwise they, the street tribe of panhandlers, drifters, homeless, left their guilt humming in you. She kept walking, looking for another phone, shivering in the wind that sliced through her dress and blew her hair into her eyes. After she had taken so much trouble to do her hair. In the raunchy shared bathroom of that raunchy hotel. For what? but some curious interview on skid row. And what is it with this weather in a *city that's supposed to be warm?* She crossed her arms as a long white car glided like a shark halfway into a tight space and trumpeted two little taps of its car horn. Janice watched a hand extend from the driver's side, yank the lock up, push the door open, and then wave her over. She stopped, her arms still crossed, and bent down to look into the car. She glanced back at another car honking at this old white Cadillac's tail fin cutting into traffic. Some man obscured by shadows and the window glare. It was a white man in his fifties, she saw, with long gray sideburns and big eyes and teeth flashing a smile. He leaned toward the passenger door and pushed it open a little more until the interior light went on. Through the crack came this hushed beckoning, "*Get in.*"

"What do you want?" She watched his eyes look away, saw that his cheeks were mottled from shadow or drink or age or depression.

"Get in." He patted the seat beside him. Then with more urgency he said, "*Please get in.*"

"I don't know you. What do you want?"

He didn't say anything else, closing the door scowling, snapping his head the other way while gunning his Cadillac back into the stream of traffic. Then it hit her.

The dirty old creep! Shrieked, "You're sick!" But he was gone, leaving her cursing under her breath and marching off toward the Near East Spa. She'd arrive early. As if this neighborhood knew the rigors of punctuality.

Now the panhandler was back again. "Just fifty cents, mam. Just need a cup of coffee. Really. Two quarters. No more."

As a rule she didn't give change to panhandlers, concluding the gesture only compounded problems for everyone, but darn it all if she weren't in a jam herself. She was about to say *Just leave me the heck alone* but another impulse overrode her anger and she found herself fumbling in her purse for seventy-five cents which she handed over. She squeezed his wrist once.

Change rattling in his hand, he replied, "Merry *Xmas*, mam!"

"And merry *Xmas* to you too." She walked away, appreciating the X.

"You are one beautiful lady." He called after her three quarters worth of advice: "This 'hood ain't no place for you. No mam."

She came up on the Near East Spa and paused in front of its bay windows framed with blinking Christmas lights. There was MASSAGE and its reflections—in that fractional distillation of liquid air with that gaseous element neon, surrounded by a glowing sheet of plate glass, alive with the swoop of headlights, brake lights, blinkers, and the yellow, red, green of stoplights. The whole scene, mood included, seemed to be right out of a Hopper painting with all its voyeuristic desolation. Peering through these colors at her own reflection, through herself in silhouette, her hair had fluttered out over shoulder straps of a knee-length leather coat and her sharp cheekbones lacked their usual hint of rouge. She noticed four women sitting in the reception area as a headlight glided across the window and a car horn screamed jazzily through concrete night. All were slouching, in various poses of waiting for clients. One over a desk with chin in hands as if she had a toothache. Another two chatting across a whore-house sofa. The fourth wearing a cheap fur over a slip and the lumps of her large breasts were swallowed up in a white wicker chair, the large rounded back, broken by strands of leaves from hanging plants, framing her like a halo.

Gone were short shorts and skimpy sleeveless t-shirts as a uniform for treating clients, Janice imagined, to glimpses of hill and dale and back again for the small matter of tip. *I can't*, Janice thought, *make this scene.* On the verge of fleeing when one woman cast a net with her waving arms, catching Janice in their collective attention which looked fierce at first seeing her. The one at the desk, a cute woman in her early thirties with bobbed blonde hair, sprang from her seat, waving. Janice turned to run. But the bobbed blonde, and the way her arm seemed to reach through the window wanting to wrap itself around Janice's waist, motioned again. She rushed toward the door as the intercom issued an electronic hiccup. "Janice, right? We've been waiting for you."

Now Janice wanted to vomit again. Fought off the bile creeping up her throat by taking a deep breath, then stating, "Afraid I'm early for a seven o'clock interview. With…with Mr. Cobb."

The woman nodded, and said, "No problem." Rattled chain and clicked deadbolts. The woosh of the door. The sting of cigarette smoke. Hating the smell, blinking, Janice stood there directing her attention to an image of a body lotion commercial on a wide screen touching her eye now before she kept scanning the room. More hanging plants. Cheap art. A matador on black velvet teasing a bull already bloody from the pricks of picadors.

"Let's get this door closed, dear," the bobbed blonde scolded her, "before we let in all the cold air." Then in a smiling voice warming as the door closed sbe positioned herself between the door and Janice. "Name's Bobbie. Janice, this is The Officer, Goofy, and Fifi." Bobbie motioned around. Their grins, fortunately, more authentic than their names—*The Officer?* belonged to some buxom woman with a horsey face and angry eyes, clad in a Naval officer's crisp white uniform. Was this an act? Each gave Janice a polite smile, nod, quiet hello.

"Sorry that I'm a little early. Thought the bus trip from downtown would take longer. Got tired of walking up and down the sidewalk." She let an uplifted corner of her mouth and shrug finish the explanation.

"Nice neighborhood, huh?" Bobbie gave her a sympathetic look. "Please sit down, Janice."

Bobbie returned to the desk and picked up the phone. "She just came in. Yeah. Okay." She hung up. "Mr. Cobb will be right out." Bobbie looked at Janice intently. "Been to any other interviews?"

Janice didn't know anyone in Border City. In fact, just this morning she left her parents' home in a Chicago suburb then no more than a few hours ago pulled her two large suitcases, the kind with wheels, off the luggage carousel then over sidewalk cracks before wrestling them up into a bus to get to the flophouse downtown that took half her savings. Just divorced, jobless, newly skilled (certified in massage) in the rigorous marketplace of post-industrial recession, she was the epitome of a young Gen Xer down on her luck. In late January she'd start graduate school in psychology and teach two sections of Psych 110 at the state university here. Still, touching her first pay warrant was two months off. Pressing in closer, the menace of tuition, books, food, toiletries, and the less than obvious purchases that always evaded calculations.

Her best friend in Chicago, Debbie, had urged her to get a student loan. Janice couldn't qualify with her lousy credit record—another corollary of the recession. Her ex and she, facing the bleakness of poverty following their twin layoffs from the same insurance company, worked in one of those low slung mirror-glass buildings out near the airport and had over-charged credit cards and defaulted on house and car payments. David, who was already a heavy drinker, took harder to drink, making good on his (their) suspicions that he was a loser to begin with. Each binge climaxed in text-book verbal and physical abuse of Janice until separation ensued. Janice moved back in with her parents then drifted into the massage trade to get away from her parents, under the influence of friend Debbie, a masseuse herself at a dilapidated Bodywork Center right off the El on Clark near Wrigley Field.

"I don't know if I can do it, Deb. Everyone thinks massage is like, I don't know, edgy, dirty, or like, well, you know."

Now here she was in that nervous, twitchy pre-interview time saying, in answer to Bobbie-the-desk-lady's question, that she had tried but couldn't get through yet at another place.

"You mean," Bobbie asked, leaning forward, "Massage World? Then that would be Ingrid Swanson."

"Supposed to be a high-class place, Massage World," Janice said, hoping to draw her out.

"Quite a spread in the paper anyway," Bobbie said, studying Janice.

Janice asked Bobbie, "Do you know Ingrid Swanson?"

Bobbie shook her head. "Only know of her. Massage is competitive. We have to keep tabs."

Suddenly the door to the back opened on an icy chill. Had to be Mr. Cobb. Or Mr. Severe Eyes. How they glowered at her. His eyes were accented by thick black eyebrows struggling to touch in a sincere—or angry?—expression. His thin face was grasped about the chin by a goatee and pressed by long greasy black hair that hung to his shoulders. He made his hand resemble a pistol that he pointed at her, his deep voice conflicting with his sinewy build. "Janice Verdurin?"

Janice nodded. "Mr. Cobb?"

"Come to my office," he said. "We'll do the interview there."

JACK-SAN

Heard the voice in his head from several years ago, brought back by this return trip to the land of *wa*. As if in a dream it came to him. The past.

"We spend much of our lives pursuing that magical first love feeling. We do anything, even chase the perverse, to get it back." A fellow host at the Tokyo host bar, another American, bestowed this wisdom on Cobb as they set up their drink station for their customers—middle-aged Japanese women, frustrated wives of executives, spending wads of yen from the family finances on their favorite hosts. Cobb himself, along with an Australian surf boy, was in great demand. Just such perversity, the perversity of an older woman and a younger man, Cobb felt between him and his former landlady, a woman who had seen at least thirty more years.

At her living room table, English text open before him, he watched her ballroom dance around the room, one arm held high and the other wrapped around the waist of a ghost partner. The lessons were her idea. To show her appreciation she had cut his rent in half. When he protested, she countered, "You're just a teenager, Jack-san, fresh from the nest. Think of me as your Japanese mother."

She said in Japanese, "Come dance with me, Jack-san."

He patted the text before him. "Ogawa-san, let's get to the lesson here, so I can get ready for work."

"I told you to call me Motoko. Now come. Today I want charm, not English. Charm me as I imagine you charm your customers." She danced over and took his hand then pulled him over to the center of the large room. Up close to her, he smelled, through her perfume, that brooding odor that came off the older women who frequented the host bar, its pungency was that of decay, and no amount of perfume could camouflage it. They danced to some Brazilian tune, but he didn't like to dance as it reminded him too much of work, where a steady stream of horny, frustrated middle-aged Japanese women, "shy" by culture, had no inhibitions of getting right in there for some serious bumping and grinding. Motoko-san led, but he felt too self-conscious. She laughed about his clumsiness. He nodded in the direction of the clock on the richly ornamented shelves. "It's almost four. I have to get to the public bath," he said.

"Take your bath here," she said, stopping the dance. "Come. Let me show you the bathroom."

In the laundry room he watched her kneel in the bathroom near the tub. She always wore a kimono (her late husband had insisted she wear nothing but, and she honored him by continuing the practice). Kneeling primly, her knees swung to the side over the tile and thus showing a glimpse of bare calf, above kimono socklets and the bath sandals she had stepped into, she rested one hand on a pink plastic bath stool while the other broke a stream of water gushing from the tap. "There's a problem with the water heater, Jack-san. The water goes from hot to cold and you have to keep adjusting the tap here. Like this." Her little hand twisted the right tap then the left tap. This way, that.

Watching her there in unexplored, private regions of her palatial old house, fiddling with water, kneeling correctly in her kimono, he felt a rush of warmth, something he didn't feel with the women at the club. He began to strip. She didn't move, but he felt the corner of her eye on him and her head tilt to listen to his jeans coming off, as she sat there, in no hurry, one hand under the water gushing into smaller streams spilling from her palm, the other making adjustments. He pulled off his pants and shirt and socks until he was standing there in the laundry room in only his underwear, which he then took off.

JANICE VERDURIN

S huddered, listening to Mr. Cobb's, "Come to my office…"
Even though his voice was authoritative she intuited that he was jittery, the nervous sort, and rather young for pushing the mister business at her when they spoke over the phone. (Wasn't it up to the other person to add the title of respect?)

Taking a deep breath, Janet thought aloud, "Well, here goes," then crossed the reception area and the exchange of a savvy grin bouncing back and forth between the employed masseuses. "Wish me luck."

Almost in unison they called out, "Good luck!" Bobbie at the desk treated her to a wink and some advice. "Don't be tricked by his bluff. He's just a big pussy cat."

Another masseuse amended, "Or pussy lover?"

Janice studied her expression. Was she serious?

Another voice, the Officer's, trimmed by a whorish huskiness, purred, "No pussy cat. But you have to stroke him *juuuust* right." This brought raucous laughter all around, but from Janice a simple *"Gee thanks, guys"* and a feeling of dread that turned a shade curious as she watched Cobb power walking, already three-quarters of the way down the paneled hall in his loping stride, his black jeans and pointy-toed cowboy boots clopping through trampled burgundy shag. Something jingling. A pocketful of change? No. Keys. A good twenty, thirty of them clipped to a redneck keychain clipped to his belt. With his shoulders pinched together, he leaned into his stride, his greasy locks swaying, leading her deeper in past closed doors of massage rooms and more crude paintings nailed through their frames to brown paneling. Here and there cheap cloth plants, with jagged-edged leaves, sat atop old wooden bar stools. She wanted to bail.

As if reading her thoughts Cobb stopped at the end of the hall, motioning for her to take the turn and continue on ahead, which she did with a look over her shoulder fearing his proximity and reek and that he'd do something wild to her from behind like goose her bottom, his footsteps were closing in loud and close, corralling her still deeper into the parlor past steam-drenched bathrooms and a pair of cedar-paneled saunas. Around another corner the light dimmed, the hotdog she ate burning like wild fire in a stomach that didn't want any of it, nostrils flaring after a thickening stench, something male and musty. Something, Janice imagined, her nostrils groping, like the odor of a male lion in rut. So nasty. *God, what have I gotten myself into?*

JACK COBB

Stood there naked, watching her attention on the faucet waver, he felt he was playing with something huge, teasing her so. Leaving him excited as she continued the pretense of adjusting the tap. Finally she stood and walked past him. Doing nothing to cover himself, he watched her eyes twitch and spark. She moved stiffly with the awareness of his nudity, this white American boy standing naked in her peripheral vision. Speech was a struggle. "*Dozo...Dozo*...Go ahead, turn the knob when the water gets too hot. If you need help, call me."

He nodded and slid closed the accordion style door.

The next day they did the same dance, the rumba, then proceeded to the more intimate dance in the bath. She played with the knobs of the faucet as he stripped just outside the door. She walked past him, voicing her sweet offering of the bath, then patted that which sprang up into her hand and broke the fist she tried to close around it. "How it moves to me," she said in awe, staring.

He sighed, a virgin to the territory, incapable of saying or doing anything until she had turned the corner into the living room, leaving him to go about his bathing. Finishing that, he opened the door for the towel. She was standing there. "Dozo. Please. Let me towel you off, Jack-san, then do a massage. We have some time yet."

She led him to her bedroom, which smelled of her hair, her skin, her body oils. The odor of linen closets and cedar chests. The dead air was charged now with something he couldn't bring himself to resist. She pulled back the covers and had him lie down. She touched him lightly with long strokes. He couldn't bring himself to touch her, but he wanted to. Or wanted her to. He wanted something. "Your heart is beating so fast," she said, resting a hand on his chest, feeding the monster that he couldn't pull away from. Nor could he steer it. He lay back as his skin prickled with a thousand sensations. Her hand pulled away a hand towel she had spread over the heat in his loins. He couldn't make any move to stop her. She started untying her obi and letting her big milky breasts spill out, taking him in her mouth. He exploded in a few gentle bobs. She lay between his legs and lifted her eyes to stare into his. From her mouth came a dripping down the slope of her chin. She was staring at him while he looked at her matronly Japanese face framed by short cropped hair. Her little nose. Her narrow alert eyes. Her milky white breasts hot on his thigh. "Jack-san. You taste. Sweet. The sweet, sweet honey of a young boy." She lowered her head and licked down his scrotum, her little hands pushing up against his buttocks until he raised up to give her total easement. In a baby voice she told him to turn over onto his stomach, her tongue then divulging ancient secrets across his skin as he just lay there, fluttering under her as she'd have him ease up on all fours so she could, lying on her back, burrow up against him, again, day after day.

In bed he had begun to wonder if she were having a heart attack and not an orgasm, what with her age, writhing under him, hissing, the way she did when she soared with the gods, as she put it. Cobb began to feel repulsed at her drawing from their lovemaking an incredible energy that would have her practically swinging from the silk curtains and riding a unicycle across the ceiling. While Cobb himself drowned in guilt and self-hatred, making him want to yank the tablecloth out from under the china and her expensive steak dinners then pull down the drapes, clear off the shelves in a violent crash of her precious mid-Edo Imari dolls and knickknacks. Instead, drawing from his reserve of self control, an attribute he learned over seven years in Japan as a base brat pushing himself out beyond the naval station, he went over to the window and looked out because he wanted out, his back to her, trying his best to ignore her fluttering around like a butterfly, ballroom dancing the rumba with a ghost partner to the same cursed Brazilian tune she kept plunking the stylus on in mad jabs and scratches coursing through the speakers, day after day, all full of the life (his life!) he had given in bath and bed. Her new vitality had caught the eye of an old Japanese dandy in her dance circle. On those days the old fellow's black Nissan President was parked out front Cobb actually felt a pang of jealousy, running by the door and up the rickety old staircase bolted to the side of the house, shaking the shit out of it as if it were some playground equipment, wanting them to feel his wrath, then taking refuge in his little *roku-jo*, or six-mat room.

In retaliation he picked up a sweet doll-faced office girl in Roppongi who looked all of fourteen (perverse for him!) compared to her fifty-plus. Or was it sixty? Alerted by her watchdog's barking, she came out for a snoop, head craning around the corner, watching her Jack-san say goodbye to his new girlfriend at the gate. In the middle of that night Jack Cobb was visited by a ghost.

INGRID

Asked the cabbie, "Remember what about me?"

"Remember something I heard." Again he stabbed a finger at her in the icy rearview. "About you, Ingrid Swanson."

She felt her eyebrows arch, her stomach fall. "About me? What did you hear about me?"

After a moment, chuckling, he said, "That you're a dame. Right out of some old black-and-white movie." Two quick measuring glances back. Two triumphant nods before more mad laughter. Then: "Really: that you're *The Dame* trying to cut into Cobb's turf."

Such an antique word. *Dame.* Inscrutable, she hid its sting from his gaze, fearing, down the street from home, that the jacked-up cabbie would barter her address to Cobb in exchange for more speed or crystal meth or opiodes or massage (traded like currency in the underground) or whatever his vices dictated. So she ordered him to stop well short of her place. "Here's the money. Even Steven. Don't want to see a face that I'm stiffing you or I'll call your dispatcher. Have him stuff his cigar in your ear."

She slammed the door but not before "Just like a dame I'm telling you" burned her ear. She wanted to kick the door and smack the window but had to pee, hit by the urge when standing up onto the street. Had to go so very bad. Running in place, waving, then hitting the window with the fat of her hand she yelled, "Goodbye!" Thirty seconds later, *smack.* "Goodbye!"

The cab didn't budge. After a minute the window lowered. "That your house? You live there?"

"Uh huh," she said. "Right there."

"Then why you no go in?"

"I'm going. Goodbye." Determined, she turned and strode up the neighbor's walk, mind grabbing for an excuse if she were caught in the charade by the housefrau, or part-time housefrau, who like the rest of them on her street pours poison on her with her stares between their full-time jobs pushing paper or whatever it was they pushed besides kids out into the world. Men coming and going to and fro at

Ingrid's place elicited such grunting looks of consternation her way. Never even bothered straightening things out by telling them what she does. Why complicate things? They have their lives. She has hers. Mere neighborliness as a common ground for friendship didn't cut it anymore in SoCal.

When the cabbie finally drove off, headlights dimming up the street, she ran back to the sidewalk then up, turned at her block-strewn path then heard a car engine screaming back down the street. She swung around to see him driving in wild-ass reverse, driver's door cracked open and laying down the goofy shadow of his head which was craning over a snow plow's angling of light and the high whine of engine. He braked before her house and she felt the weight of his gaze schlepped up the concrete stoop of her little two-story Victorian home, dormers and gables blotted by chain link, unshorn palms, scraggly pines and the wreckage of a rusted boat trailer rising like a giant insect out of a tangle of sage scrub and bougainvillea. Through the cab glass refractions came a flashlight beam skittering like the pizza man's across her picture window, then flickering across wooden siding before dancing over and around three numbers screwed to a porch beam as if to lasso them.

JACK COBB

Woke to a tube-headed creature—a ghost?—stomping across the ceiling scape of his room. Horror-stricken, he sucked in his breath. A loud hiccuping gasp. Looked up from his futon, watching the creature, the ghost, *against the ceiling, a towel wrapped around its head, her head, he realized, her face a towering white tube, a bath towel clipped closed with safety pins, backlit by the streetlamp glowing against his window. Nudging him again with her foot, she proceeded to step like a tin soldier toward the door then turn and stomp back through. The worst possible nightmare to wake into, staring at this ghost marching around his apartment. Cackling, she unclipped the mask of towel, untied her kimono, then her hunkered down breasts swinging around crawling under futon covers despite Cobb's protests. "What do you think you're doing?"*

She was trying to straddle him and he pushed her off. Got her to leave finally but couldn't get back to sleep, haunted by the image of the cylindrical head and short legs taking those crazy stiff steps. He was haunted, yes. She was all around him, in the clothes and goodies she had bestowed, her presence (presents!) everywhere, inside and out. She had become a part of him, that part of himself that he loathed, tempted to run downstairs and wrestle her key (his key!) from her to end it once and for all.

* * *

In early November, the Siberian express blew down from Mongolia and Kamchatka. To escape from Ogawa-san, Cobb now and then accepted the offers of the more winsome and glamorous customers of the host club. They'd go drinking then to love hotels. He'd cab back home long after the trains had stopped then tiptoe through the gate, hoping not to wake the dog. The damned dog. Turning into an insomniac, he drank heavily and read until morning, cringing at the sight of her letting herself in to deliver an armful of laundry, neatly folded then put away in his futon closet. His whole apartment was not much bigger than a walk-in closet, and she did nothing in the way of improvements, a ploy to get him to spend more time with her in her glorious rooms downstairs.

His apartment depressed him. Its curtains hung ragged. No water heater or bath or exhaust vent for his gas-powered heater—of the variety that required an open window, which let in great gusts of cold air as he sat there and read, book held in gloved hands, his breath visible in steamy jags, cursing tenants for flushing their toilets through paper-thin walls on either side. Only the distraction of reading kept him from going home to make amends with the old man at the naval base at Yokosuka.

In his apartment that winter or down in her glorious rooms, he read, in Japanese, novels by Mishima, Kawabata, Endo, haiku and tanka by famous poets of past centuries, the literature a sublime distraction from her, even as she fed him hundred-dollar dinners. Then she would grab him by a belt loop and pull him back to the couch when he wanted to bail after eating. "You know how much those steaks cost?"

"I have a cold. Let me go."

"You know how much those steaks cost? Look at me."

"I'm looking. Tell me how much and I'll pay you."

"Pay me with what? You'd have to give me everything in your bank book there."

"So you're snooping in my bank book now?"

"Don't try to confuse things."

"I'm not. I just have a cold and want to go up to bed."

"Cold? Huh. Your real feeling shows in a split second. Japanese know how to conceal their feelings. You're too savage to know how to conceal your feelings. I can read all your thoughts before you start your charade." She guffawed. "Pretending a cold, making a face. Huh!"

"I do have a cold."

"Come here, Jack-san. You have work to do."

* * *

Early one afternoon Cobb was watching World Cup Soccer on her monolingual television when she had a toothache and had to go to the dentist. It was the first time that she had left him alone in her house. After she left he went to her bedroom and poked around, finding in her top dresser drawer a stack of ten thousand yen notes, perhaps two million yen worth. He counted out two hundred thousand yen then shoved the bills in his sock, since he no longer took off all his clothes while they had sex, humping away in shirt and socks, the quicker to get the work done (work—her term).

The next time he visited he was surprised to find her beau there, a short Japanese man in his late fifties who dressed to the nines and sported the most expensive Rolex. She introduced Cobb as her English teacher and sat between the two of them deep in the corner of the sectional sofa, making sure to keep their beer glasses poured full on the big coffee table. When they were drunk she made jokes, lightening the mood, resting her hands on either of their knees as a bar hostess might, or slapping them in fun. The more they drank the farther down his thigh her hand explored. She suddenly had Cobb hold out a hand, comparing his to her beau's smaller hand. The old beau made a joke, pointing to Jack-san's crotch, saying in his terrible English, Beeg. Vedy big.

Cobb knew then where she, perhaps under the old beau's directive, wanted to go. Either hand of hers now in either crotch, wanting to drive the three of them toward an old Japanese custom that would have Jack-san being coaxed to lie in the middle, giving it to her while being corn holed by him. Without saying a word, Cobb stood then and headed to the genkan, jumping into his shoes then heading back up the rickety staircase bolted to the side of the house, giving extra action to his step, wanting them to feel his displeasure. The next day at noon (when he got up) she let herself in, carrying his breakfast on a tray. She asked if she could use his toilet in the mornings, since her toilet had just broke and the plumber couldn't come until Friday. Unable to stomach the image of her, such an old ghost of a person, squatting and evacuating her bowels in his toilet, he refused, telling her to go over in the park.

"In the park?!" she crowed. "You're going to make me go over in the park!?!"

He didn't say anything, eating his breakfast, letting her wind down then head back downstairs.

At work things got worse. The women he had bedded had banded together in an angry pack, hounding him on his way to the station. The mama-san had her rules forbidding her hosts from fraternizing with customers outside work and special host club functions. All the hosts were the mama-san's property in that regard, and she wasn't one to give the store away, having an old woman's miserliness.

On his way to the station, seven or eight women in their forties and fifties would jump out from a doorway, designer bags over their shoulders, diamonds and gold glinting around their necks, fingers, wrists. "Ya!" They wanted to scare him. He hurried on ahead, trying to hear the things they said just out of the range of his hearing. At work notes were passed to him, across the bar or table or while they danced. It was a conspiracy, for each note said basically the same thing: that he was forbidden to continue with anyone but her or else mama-san would be informed of everything.

At a stoplight, the pack caught up to him. Michiko (Cobb remembered the mole on her thigh) said, "Let's follow him all the way home."

Cobb could just imagine the old lady, tipped off by the dog's barking, opening her grand front door, her neck craning out, watching such a troop of women, gaijin groupies as the hosts called them, following him upstairs. Annoyed, Cobb spoke in English: "This is the third night running you've hounded me, ladies. It's getting to be too fucking much!"

"Eigo nante wakara nai," one of them said. (I don't understand English.)

Watching the cars streaming past, tapping his foot (a nervous habit), he said, "I'll say it in Japanese then: Oi omae-ra mikka me daze. Jama bakkari shite. Dandan hidoku nari-ya-gatte!"

One of the older ones said, "Atasha anta no sou-iu kittana-i Nihongo kini-itta ne." (I love it when he speaks rude Japanese.)

"You'll love this then," he said, his anger conjuring up the most vile Japanese. He added a cheerful concluding farewell, "Ja ne. Mata ne. Bye bye." He bowed to their gasps then crossed the street, trotting toward the station.

He didn't even bother going to work the next day, or any day thereafter, not wanting to give the mama-san the pleasure of firing him. Women tightening the tension all around him, he made a decision.

ANNABEL WHITAKER, L.M.T., Holistic Health Practitioner,

W as soaked with sweat and had a headache. Having burned the blue clear out of the sky, high eleven o'clock sun poured liquid fire onto her shoulders. Annabel read aloud the next name on her clipboard list, "Ms. Elizabeth Colladay?"

Nodding in the Jacuzzi was a ragged head with a wrinkly pecan face from too much sun over too many years. Turning, that frozen way that old people do, Colladay tried to shield the sun with her hand while clamping closed an eye so the other took the full force of rays in a hard squint up at Annabel standing over the sunken tub. In a deep no-nonsense voice, heavy with the command of old money, she said, "That is I." The old warhorse of luxury trudged through the water as if moving through a dream. Pushing her straggly wet brown hair to the side with fingers sparkling with diamonds, she bade farewell to her comrades who looked as if they were saluting, shading their eyes above the foam, and watching their friend do that slow motion walk through and up out of water naked toward Annabel standing there with a towel and a glance at a dark bush dripping a thin stream of water evaporating in seconds on the concrete.

A professional at the top of her field, Annabel Whitaker had under her belt two thousand hours of formal training. And behind her a series of rigorous tests and several years of rubbing and tweaking and hacking and slapping bodies of all descriptions. She had made the mistake, however, of contracting here, with the colossal Chateau Spa in north county. After a suave gentleman from Chateau had flattered her over lunch in the main dining room. And promised "a fat salary, insurance, contract that goes with the territory of full-time employment. No more outcall stress if you come to work for us...*now*. Deal's only good today, though."

As if she were born yesterday.

Following an hour bus trip north, she worked out under desert sun all day, massaging rich white bitches and old farts, all from eight a.m. on. Eight one-hour sessions conducted on a heavy-duty massage table complete with facial holes and cushions and pull outs and, you'd think, ship-to-shore sonar, radar, and one of them there boomerang-like antenna that you see on the trunk of ghetto cruisers. Such a big boat of a massage table, what with its heavy-duty construction and tilt and spin adjustability, reminded Annabel of something upon which in another time and place, say Teotihuacan, sacrifices were lashed and fed to the gun god.

She kept telling herself: *lunch soon, lunch soon.* Which was when the spa closed for half an hour. The electricity and water switched off, therapists had nowhere to wash their hands before eating, though. Nor were they allowed to cool off in any of the swimming pools. They were hot and smelly and in need of the toilet and a shower. Under ceiling fans spinning to a standstill in the airless locker room/lunch room, they ate their sandwiches with dirty oily hands and all the good cheer of an undertaker, sitting on benches or outside against the walls surrounding the dumpsters. Still, though, she had this Colladay woman to get around.

Sickly thin, skin hanging loosely on her frame—a sheet thrown over a broomstick—the old woman wrapped herself in a towel then puckered her lips and made kissing sounds to call her little dog, a white toy poodle which she now hoisted to curl around her neck. The dog's paws in each of her hands, she wore the pink belly of the canine around her neck, like a collar, then dripped a trail of water as she stood there.

"Ms. Colladay, my name is Annabel. Would you prefer your massage to be indoors or out?"

"Given the lovely weather we are having, Annabel, I should think that I would prefer my massage outdoors."

They always said that. Now with the Santa Anna condition inland (the wind blowing westerly and hot off the desert), Annabel was dizzy from standing up in the heat all morning and had a tremendous headache, her sinuses tight and prickly. The top of her head was boiling, but management forbade masseuses from wearing hats. Sunscreen, if worn, had to be invisible. But she hadn't had time to apply any protection, imagining management, those silk-suited swarthy macho guys, peering down at her through high-powered telescopes lined up in air-conditioned offices on the Chateau's top floor. Standing on marble all day, Annabel's feet had swollen larger than her massage shoes grabbing hard at her feet. This skinny white bitch was already grumbling.

"My goal in coming here is to lose weight," Ms. Colladay said. "Quite frankly, I haven't lost a pound. My shoulders still feel fat. I hate my shoulders. Massage some pounds off my shoulders, dear Annabel."

Annabel nodded. It was always the same bitch. Always the same flaunting of gold and diamond rings. In their nakedness their jewelry and poodles and Pomeranians were all they had to flaunt. How wrinkly and decrepit these old millionaire war horses looked stretched out naked on their backs with little pads of witch hazel on their eyes. This one, though, was unique in the way she ported her poodle around her neck like a fur collar.

Standing near Annabel's table, Ms. Colladay complained as she set her dog down. "My Florence is not going to sit on this marble floor. I want a pillow for her."

"I'm sorry," Annabel said. "We don't have any pillows here at the outdoor spa."

"I spend over two thousand dollars a day. Surely they can afford to provide a simple four dollar pillow. I will not let you start the massage until Florence is comfortable."

Annabel went over to the phone, mounted to a parasol post at the juice bar, and dialed housekeeping. Enough precious time had elapsed to throw her whole schedule off and have management dock her for a missed massage, and exactly seven minutes later a porter pedalled a pillow over on his bicycle. Out of breath and perspiring, he placed the dog on top of it. "There you go, mam."

Colladay nodded, the triumphant bitch queen.

Angry, she repeated to herself, *Remember, lunch soon, lunch soon.* Annabel massaged the woman's bony back (when she knew she was supposed to start on her legs), digging in with medium pressure opposed to beginning light then gradually working in deep, as was standard procedure. She felt Ms. Colladay's floating ribs through her rough wart-covered skin, and knew it wouldn't take much to snap one. Her headache turned more prickly as the old woman restated her troubles.

"As I said I came to this spa to lose weight. My terrible shoulders need a little more, how should I say, brisk pressure, dear Annabel."

Annabel couldn't tolerate the woman's delusions any longer,

fighting an urge to hit her square between the shoulder blades with her hand opened, or empty, as in karate. She said pointedly, "You're too skinny not too fat. You need to gain weight, woman. You should do something else. You're wasting your time here."

"You don't even know who I am," Ms. Colladay said, surprised. "And you talk to me like that?" She lifted her head and craned her neck around to look at Annabel. In the jelly of their eyes they glared at each other deeply, Annabel pissed off and the white bitch amazed. A moment of intimacy that comes but once a fortnight. "But you know what? I like it. No one tells me I'm skinny. Everybody smiles when I talk. Everyone gives me compliments wherever I go. *Oh yes, mam. Oh yes, mam.* Everyone agrees with me all the time. But you tell me these things and I appreciate it. I appreciate your honesty, Annabel. I do indeed." She closed her eyes, the smile still creasing her face.

Since Annabel was quitting in a few days anyway to go to work for Massage World, she had half hoped to insult the woman but now she felt something akin to affinity with her. She pushed up from Colladay's heel to flex her knee, lifting the frail appendage then swinging it outward then back in, her bones those of a sparrow. A complaining old bird chirping: "I don't know why we have to pay so much here, though. Breakfast is only half a grapefruit. And that silly little Chinese doctor with his needles and pins and the other Eastern European one does nothing more than weigh me, take my pulse, then brandish his prized instruments, his beloved tools, especially that rubber-headed hammer he so loves to tap at my knees. I'll show him reflexes. Kick him in the privates. Huh huh uh. Some checkup. I wonder where he got his license."

Annabel continued massaging her. The old woman held up a hand, indicating the biggest diamond on a spindly finger. "See this rock here, Annabel? It was set especially for me. But it's nothing really. You should see my other diamonds. Much better than the diamonds the other women are wearing around here. Huh."

Annabel didn't know why the lavish pampering didn't take any of the spite out of them, what with all the working out on weight-loss machines, yoga, aerobics, facials, steam body wraps, herbal body wraps, mud baths, low-impact exercise classes in heated swimming pools, and aerobic dance. Plus jaunts in the jacuzzi and sauna and Swiss shower. The professional cooing of the effeminate hairdressers. Visits to the foundation department for makeup. Then back to the hairdresser for a final comb out. Then back to makeup. After they dressed for dinner, around six, when Annabel herself felt that she looked like total shit, the old scallions looked equal to their bank accounts, meticulously made up, adorned in silken splendor, encrusted with the glittering tiara of jewels and sequins, trimmed out with charmingly coiffured poodles and Pomeranians. But hell-bent on having the help see them in all their splendor (as compensation for having been seen at their worst), yelling: "Hi, Annabel!" Meaning: Look at me, Annabel! "Bye, Annabel!"

Annabel kneaded up Ms. Colladay's spindly thighs then around her bony buttocks. "I am happy to tell you, Ms. Colladay, that as of Friday I will no longer be working here."

Her mouth, from the pressure of lying flat on her belly, sounded like that of a carp sucking air, as she said, "Oh?"

"I'll be working in Border City, at a new spa there called Massage World. No more marathon bus rides. No more hot days in the sun. No more rich old ladies chewing on my ear with their grumbling. No more fetching pillows for spoiled poodles. *Huh.*"

Ms. Colladay chortled, turned her neck around for eye contact and the dying fish look. "I like you, Annabel. I really like you." She chuckled, horselike. "Anyway, that is probably for the best, Annabel. You will do well. You are strong and honest—virtues I feel in your hands. One of the women in the jacuzzi said that the black woman is the best. That your touch is addictive. Request Annabel, she had advised. Now I see she is right."

Annabel objected, "Not true, Ms. Colladay."

"True! True!" Colladay exclaimed, turning again to find her eye. "You hold nothing back. Your energy flowing into my tired old body makes me feel vibrant and good. I feel like tap dancing on this table even. Yes. Yes. You've a generous touch, Annabel. You are indeed a top-notch masseuse."

Annabel felt proud, but at the same time the shame from said pride suddenly surged.

"But yes," Colladay continued, "you'd be wise to move on and not let the Italians drink any more of your blood here. You are much too young and pretty to be wilting out here in the desert with us sour grapes. Maybe it is our bad company that draws the refreshing little streams of anger from your magic fingers there. Ohhh, yes, I feel in my heart the life coming in. Mmmm. Luscious. Annoy a masseuse, get a vivacious massage. Huh."

Annabel massaged her back. "When you move on may I still receive your massage, Annabel?"

"Only if you put on some weight first. Right up here where you want to take it off. I want to see a good pound right around the scapulae under here."

Colladay squeezed Annabel's arm. "I like you, Annabel. Be certain to write down the name of your new place of employment."

"Massage World," Annabel said. "How can you forget a name like that?"

* * *

Later, at the end of her shift, on her way to the gate and home, Annabel watched a chauffeur-driven Rolls Royce approach from the side parking lot. In the roomy back seat sat an old gaunt lady. A necklace of diamonds peeked out from a fur collar. Diamond earrings glittered from her lobes. Jeweled barrettes sparkled in her hair. The accouterments of money giving her a queen's grace, she suddenly broke from her rigid pose, poking her head and arm out the back window, waving.

Goosebumps rushed up Annabel's spine.

Tingling, she watched old Colladay, yelling now, then saying something to her gray-haired chauffeur. Unruffled in livery, he brought the Rolls down to tooling speed, Ms. Colladay waving white gloves and crowing: "Annabel! Hi, Annabel! I will gain some weight. Then see you for a massage. What's it called? Massage Universe?"

Annabel corrected her, yelling, "MASSAGE WORLD!"

Nodding, she replied, "Yes, yes, there!" White gloves flapping. "Bye, Annabel! Bye!"

INGRID

Swore, "Damn you!" Max was barking. She thought about running after the cab racing off with her address surely on the way to Cobb who'd be around—when? who knew? She knew she couldn't do anything so she turned back toward the gate where her thighs squeezed themselves together of their own volition to ease the pain of holding it in, while her trembling fingers fiddled with the cold bite of steel latch. Damned gate. There was a cold rustle. And barking. To the barking, but more to herself, she said, "It's just me, Max. Would you shut up?!" The gate screeched closed as she ran up the walkway, making fists to warm her fingers as a porch board howled under foot. She told Max to cool it in his laying out on the welcome mat, the excited barking and squealing and circus-horse door clawing that he greeted her with each evening. She told him through the door to relax, long enough for her to dig down into that little ice bucket of a mailbox after—*Curses!*—the telltale crinkle of cellophane windows on envelopes. Bills.

And more bills. Curses of *fuckah fuckah* could be heard through the racket of Max's baying and her key scratching lock and her business phone's ringing. Figured someone probably wanted a massage, or to talk about a massage. Evenings were always like that. Lots of talk. Little biz. Only one of five lonely-hearts (this was their—or should she say our?—hour, after all) usually committed to an appointment. Her impulse was to ignore the bleating that plowed up guilt with the realization that she had failed that morning to return yesterday's phone messages because she didn't come home yesterday, instead hustling off at dawn for another day of manual labor and swordplay where all through the day and from every angle in the mansion unpaid—and at times drunken—tradesmen came at her in mad lunges, as if to run her through.

"Look out!" Her German shepherd leapt at her, his tongue slurping her cheek in the widening crack of door that issued a blast of heat in her forgetfulness to turn down the thermostat before dashing off yesterday. The house came at her like a mugger over the dog's head, shoving through the crack a hot, damp dish rag heavy with the pass-out odors of massage oil and canine slobber.

She mostly worked out of her house. The deeper she ventured into the house the more saturated it became with massage oil, as if someone had splashed a bucket of the stuff as a mad arsonist dashes out gasoline to the point that a sheen of it was smudged on the armrests of chairs and sofas, and slicked toilet seats (upon squatting it was as if the toilet itself were on roller skates), kitchen linoleum, shelves, and then the knobs of doors, televisions, radios, appliances—all minnows under the grasp. Massage oil going so far as breaking trail over the gray berber starting from the spot where clients rolled off her top-of-the-line Royal Oaks and began their naked or semi-naked prance (dependent on how well-mannered or well-hung they were regarding the drape) busting out of her curtained massage-studio French doors swinging open to cut through the center of the living room (or waiting room) behind the prow of a semi-erection. The path left by their trampling oily feet took on a sharper definition in the hallway before, like a fireplace tool, looping off left into the bathroom while continuing on ahead to the kitchen linoleum where, every now and then, a new client slipped and sprawled ass over elbows on the runner. If he were a wimp he'd scream. Then hobble back with the drama of an injured lineman on Monday night football with hands palming sore spots, face twisted up and bawling for *ellememe*, the attentions of Ingrid.

Worse was the fragrance. From the wholesale house she made the colossal blunder of procuring a whole case of scented—camellia was it?—massage oil. Even though she kept squirting it on them still she had to swear to clients that she'd never again buy such an aromatic blend to fend off their complaints that its redolence ruined their suits and marriages (well, almost), clinging to them all the way home to the Mrs. who, not seeing any flowers, sniffed hard the scent of a mistress. Mistress Masseuse. Ingrid. *La meme*. Who learned to mop off the oil with hot towels as clients lay docilely on her table, happy with the press of hot cloth and steam she had to sell them on at first. "Doesn't that heat feel good? Huh? Better than a shower, right?"

"Mmmmm. Better than a shower."

Most of her regular clients no longer even demanded a shower, where they had tended to dawdle and run up her water bill in this umpteenth year of drought. *Don't be a water hog!* Creating more of those awkward, frozen moments of one client bumping into another in the foyer or waiting room with each pausing to view the other as an interloper. She'd look on with dismay, watching her reputation slide in the eyes of the newcomer, who'd then have to crash the calm of a session with some smart-ass remark: "Didn't know you were so popular." Or, if he were some new jerk thinking he was going to get laid: "I don't like sloppy seconds." If she were caught on the phone or in the linen closet and couldn't give that extra push on a client, to hasten his pulling on socks and shoes, for example, then there might even be a little conversation, some savvy exchange between clients talking over her skills and massage in general:

"I love her feathering." (This offered as icebreaker.)

"Oh?"

"Too bad she doesn't flicker, though."

The new guy would appear confused, as if he hadn't quite caught the drift. "Flicker?"

"You know, butt flicker, with the finger like this." He'd flick an index finger across his palm. "A Korean lady at Tokyo Spa gives great a-hole flicker."

"Is that right. I'll have to try there. Tell me, though: Do they offer the full course?"

The veteran would eye him thoughtfully, then offer sage counsel, "I can only say, friend, with a wink and a nod, that massage is best when you don't know. Even better when the massage place is new, *and* the masseuse is new. So there's absolutely no way you can know."

Perplexed, the newcomer asked, "Know what?"

"Why," the old hand said, "know if she'll be turning the massage down that forbidden alley."

"Forbidden alley?"

"The one leading to release land." (Could there be any other!?)

"Release land?"

"You really are new at this." The veteran looked askance at the newcomer. "Release land," he explained patiently, hands motioning like a football coach, "is that sweet turn that only the best masseuse can finesse into a massage, starting with when she has you flip over on your back for a segue into light powder work. Then, without asking or making any fuss, she'll put aside the powder, get the hot oil back out and start greasing you up. I mean," he said, letting his head fall back so his eyes could drink up the force of this, "greasing you up good." Pause. One, two, no three slow nods of his head, and the clincher: "No finer feeling."

The newcomer would then step closer, lowering his voice, "Does Ingrid here make such a skillful turn?"

Skillful turn: her nudging the connoisseur toward the door and ushering in the newcomer. Fortunately the simple application of hot towels in place of showers had cut back on such encounters: clients comparing notes about her and massage in general in front of her. Now she gets them on their way practically after capping the oil.

Now Max was yelping, skating a few circles on the hardwood which his nails, clicking and scratching, were gradually carving into splinters and sawdust. He stopped, tilting his head to charm her with his cute look. She closed the door behind her with her foot, telling Max absently, "Feed you in a minute, boy." Then she felt a slip stream of fear.

Jack Cobb would soon be witting of her address. She turned and snapped and slid home locks and chains (three of them) with extra care.

JACK COBB

Cut an oppositional figure strutting through the train, wanting to go straight to see the old lady, but at the same time game for distraction to forget about the old lady. In a gray, rumpled trench coat tied off sharply at the waist, complete with gun flaps and sleeve straps and reminiscent of Eastwood in "High Plains Drifter" he fell in with a group of sailors hungry for a new personality to explore. He quickly established himself as a leader, and didn't have to look over his shoulder after they left the station to confirm that the five guys were following him, as he jaywalked across a Yokosuka street.

Jet lag, hovering like lichen, fouled his pattern of speed binges and crash sessions. *Had to get good and drunk then crash*, he thought. He had to eat first, wolf down some carbs to shake the dizziness made worse by Japan's claustrophobic press of concrete and noise. It felt good at least to breathe fresh air out here near the naval base. Memory lane.

Cobb had learned Japanese—from living in Japan through his teens, at the base—under orders from his father, a captain hell-bent on disciplining a rebellious son until the relationship erupted into argument and wrestling matches, with living room lamps and furniture knocked over and broken as Cobb's mother would come home in a drop of groceries, screaming for them to stop, trying to break their holds of half Nelsons and cradles tumbling across the floor.

He shivered seeing the Naval base, the gate and the guards there, frustrating a surprise attack on the old man ("Dad!"). He yawned, feeling tired and in no mood to deal with such emotion. It had been too long. Besides, he didn't have the energy to stand up under a lie and the grilling from Captain Lloyd Cobb, a Naval Intelligence Officer in the Office of Naval Intelligence (ONI), Division of Special Projects.

With a Master's degree in Asian Studies from Columbia University, officers school, then the oath, his father Lloyd Cobb served as an enlisted officer in the Vietnam War, earning a Congressional Medal of Honor for leading a guerrilla platoon forty miles across enemy lines into North Vietnam then freeing thirty-four American prisoners of war from a stinking jungle shithole of a stockade, and then taking a bullet in the shoulder in the process and thus earning a Purple Heart. His successful Vietnam War record, linguistic dexterity (fluency in both Tonkinese and Cochin as well as Mandarin and Japanese, followed later by Mon-Khmer then Korean) and a charismatic daring launched him rapidly up into ONI in Southeast Asia. He had been in on several intelligence ops, including covert/overt with the Khmer-Rouge in Cambodia, then counter-intelligence activities in Laos and Cambodia. Cobb's mother, Emily, now divorced and remarried, was living somewhere in the southwestern United States. With the Cobb children, Jack and Bobbie, staying back with her, she had reluctantly stayed in Japan while her husband did a stint in South Korea. Captain Cobb quickly learned Korean to aid his involvement in monitoring the DMZ then moved back to Japan when Jack turned a rebellious thirteen, smoking cigarettes openly in front of his parents, sneaking beers to quaff with other delinquent military brats. Jack fell in with a gang of base brats. Once Shore Patrol caught four of them, including an admiral's daughter, Jack's girlfriend at the time, whom he later knocked up, spray painting obscenities on base buildings.

Another time the old man came home from work early, turned off the television, and said, "Tell me it isn't true, son."

"It isn't true, Dad."

"Tell me that you didn't jump Mike Peterson's son's motorcycle over a dry dock on a bet last week."

"Can't tell you it's not true, Dad."

"Jesus Christ, over a dry dock? What, sixty feet wide, ninety feet deep, solid concrete—dry dock?" His father exhaled, deflating. Exasperated, he said, "You have a mental problem, son. Some sort of death wish. I'm going to have you see the base psychologist."

"I'm not going to any shrink."

The order was delivered with an officer's glare. "You will go."

"Why? Because I accepted Peterson's dare? Thomas wanted to do it and would have if I hadn't. You know Thomas can't ride let alone jump. Just think of the mess then, Dad, the rear admiral's son scraped off a slab."

"Better him than you. Why did you do such a crazy thing?"

"To save Thomas's ass and win the bike. That was the deal."

"The Petersons are returning stateside soon."

"I know," Jack said. "That's why he backed the dare with his bike."

"What a deal. I never liked that Peterson kid. He's evil." His father was silent then, studying him, then asking how he managed to walk away from such a crash.

"More like rolled away over piled up mattresses. Left shoulder felt as if it were broken. Whole left side is still bruised. Bike landed like this, spearing, and I took some of the shock in my arms before it threw me. Had it cranked to seventy hitting the ramp, had to clear the death pit."

"How did the bottom look sailing over?"

"A gray blur. The far wall looked deadly. Wiethorn took a video of the whole thing, the building of the ramp, Peterson's pledging to give his bike to me."

"How did you build the ramp?"

Cobb explained that they recruited sailors to schlep planks and barrels from a cold shed and mattresses from barracks storage. "They watched from a distance when I jumped, not wanting trouble if shore patrol came. You know, Dad, if you bought me a motorcycle then I wouldn't have to risk my life earning one."

"Earning one? I'll tell you what you earned." The old man took the old spanking paddle from a kitchen drawer then came back and sat down. "Come bend over my knee here, son."

"You're joking. You try to spank me, Dad, and I'm going to take that paddle away from you. Swear I will."

* * *

He found temporary digs in Yokosuka with The Family, a religious cult founded in the Sixties whose proclamations—in their literature—were heavy with exclamation points. Family members didn't work in the formal sense of the word but did *witnessings*. Cobb succeeded in bringing in sailors but loathed the lifestyle, crammed into a tiny two-room apartment with five other adolescent American teenagers. The noise (a ghetto blaster played Dire Straits around the clock), filth (mold caked on ceilings and the scramble of cockroaches), and cold (drafts blew in from everywhere). He quit school then found a job in Tokyo as a foreign male host at a club in the Ginza.

He impressed the Mama-san with his Japanese in an interview down in her little basement host club. She asked him if he knew how to dance. Encouraged by his waltzes with Ogawa, he said that he did. She asked if he could drink. "Like a fish." She brightened. "Good. That's how we make our money. You start tonight." She stared at him then said, "Remember, though, I forbid my hosts to see customers outside of work."

"Sure, sure, I understand," Cobb said.

Cobb used her as a guarantor to secure his working visa at immigration. He lived out of a gaijin house, or rather a gaijin ghetto, having to listen to couples, on either side, practically tearing through the rice-paper-thin walls with their fucking. Two gay guys from Ireland were grunters in their rooting. Then in the room on the left was a young American couple, rosy and winsome Minnesotans, boy and girl fresh from college and now English teachers, a screamer and a dirty talker. Envious, Cobb couldn't stand her high whimper poking through to his room like a saw blade sawing into his solitude. Now that he had enough yen saved to cover key money and a deposit on his own place, he scouted realtors in Tokyo's Shinjuku area. Four turned him down, not having anything to show, or so they said. He knew what that meant, so he then staked out an office from a nearby coffee shop. When a young Japanese man, clearly a client, left with a realtor, Cobb followed, getting on the bus after them, following them off the bus, and shadowing them down a maze of narrow streets refreshed by greenery and money, noting the address of the house they ducked into.

He came back later armed with a gift of Japanese crackers wrapped in expensive paper. He held it in both hands, introducing himself in Japanese, "Excuse me. My name is Jack Cobb." He bowed deeply. "I work in the capacity of a host in the Ginza and understand you have a room to rent."

She seemed amused by his whole spunky display of Japanese and Japanese manners, and more taken with his plight with realtors. She invited him in for tea.

Her house was palatial but gloomy. Laced curtains over her windows made a dark, cold casket of her rooms. As the old lady spoke Cobb felt the hunger of her loneliness, underneath the heavy odors of cooped up decay. She unloaded on him the whole sad story of her life. He did his best to grunt in Japanese to show that he was with her. She, meanwhile, punctuated her speech with courteous reminders of the time. "Is it all right? Will you be late?"

Getting her back on track, knowing that at the end of her blubbering she'd tell him about the room, show him the room, and then maybe even rent him the room; he knew the order. The whole tea service, with her recounting and Cobb's gift of Japanese crackers festooning his saucer, was not only a kind of test for any slackness in his manners (his character!) but a foreshadowing of the unspoken deal that Cobb, on his end if she rented to him, would be expected to hold up: he'd be expected to lend his ears to a little conversation now and then. She went on too feverishly about her hobby, ballroom dancing, between tales of her progeny. "You said you had lived in Taiwan?" Cobb asked. "Fascinating."

"I spent four years there before the war. My father owned a shipping company. My late husband did some business with Taiwan. His company was linked to my father's company. I have two sons and four grandchildren."

Cobb did his best to seem attentive. "Is that right? When I'm married someday I want to have many."

"Oh, you are a nice boy. You speak Japanese so well, so very well. I was so surprised hearing you speak at the door."

Cobb showed humbleness, as good manners dictated. "No, no. My Japanese is terrible. Your English is quite good, though."

She giggled, touched her hands to her cheeks. "Oh, you are just like a Japanese boy. Before I show you the room do you think you could possibly, if it is no inconvenience, give me an English lesson from time to time?"

"Of course," Cobb lied.

"Oh, that's so wonderful. Now let's go up and look at the room."

RYOJI NAKAMURA, LICENSED SHIATSU PRACTITIONER,

Tingled under a delicious rush of anticipation—on his way to massage a favored client. In fact, his hands were sweating already, itching to touch her plum-blossom skin. At the same time he felt sad, too aware that this session with Midori was his last.

A blind Japanese masseur in shiatsu, Ryoji practiced his trade in Tokuyama, an industrial city of 130,000 on the Inland Sea, near the southern tip of Honshu, Japan's main island. A minority in Japan, Ryoji was a *Burakumin*, or hamlet person, one of several living in a special hamlet, or buraku, in Tokuyama.

Marginalized, yet indistinguishable from other Japanese, Burakumin were of the lowest caste, one said to have originated after a medieval war vanquished the defeated into hiding in ghettos throughout Japan. Later, in the more socially stratified Edo Era (1603-1867), Burakumin were called *Eta-Hinin*, or much filth, for their role in human cremation, animal slaughter and as executioners in death penalties, since that association with death was stigmatized in both Shintoism and Buddhism. Historically, Burakumin were limited to *humiliating* occupations, such as animal butchery and industries associated with leather, bamboo, and straw. They also labored as street sweepers, disposers of the dead, grave tenders, and tomb watchers. As for massage, an occupation for "non-human" minorities in the Edo Era, blind masseurs (*zatoh*) ranked second, below local chiefs of ghettos, but above dancers, actors, plasterers, monkey-showmen, stone-cutters, umbrella makers, river boatmen, mountain guards, material dyers, writing brush makers, straw raincoat makers, puppet showmen, and then brothel madams.

As Ryoji trod down a bumpy path inlaid for the blind, he listened to the traffic on Peace Street, the main street of Tokuyama. As soon as the traffic light played a jingle, as signal for the blind, he crossed the street, on his way to his last massage of his secret lover Midori, a young lady of *mizu shobai*, the water trade. In other words, Midori was a bar hostess at an exclusive club for men.   In the cold December wind the odor of noodle broth wafted from his friend's yatai. Ryoji had some time to dawdle so he veered over to the sidewalk noodle stand, swinging his cane back and forth, grinning at Masaoka-san's greeting. "So long I don't see you and soon you'll be leaving."

Ryoji tapped his way over to a bench, ducked his head under the canvas flaps then sat down, sensing Masaoka scrutinizing him, as if memorizing his face to hold in his head for daydream. In a stretch of silence Ryoji shared his friend's melancholy, its weight in the air. The two had grown up together in the buraku. But now, at twenty-five, Ryoji felt anxious, ready to move on to start a new life in a new land.

"At least the weather will be fine," Masaoka said, trying to sound cheerful.

There was Southern California where Ryoji had a cousin, Tadakatsu, who had been sending him various want ads for massage therapist positions. Ryoji's English teacher in Tokuyama read them to him then helped him translate and send off his resume. Only one person, Miss Ingrid Swanson, had responded favorably, writing that she needed a male masseur skilled in shiatsu, to be employed at her soon-to-be-opened, exclusive bodywork spa called Massage World.

Masaoka set a bowl of steaming noodles and wooden chopsticks before Ryoji. As Ryoji slurped down the noodles the two friends played shogi, or Japanese chess. When victory became obvious for Ryoji, Masaoka teased him, as he usually did, by stealing his queen. Ryoji groped for its phantom absence then exclaimed, "Masaoka-san, you thief!"

Masaoka chided, "You have eyes in your hands! I swear!" Masaoka greeted another customer. Ryoji checked his braille watch then groped for his cane, telling his friend he'd see him tomorrow when he'd bring his farewell present around.

Ryoji tapped off the bumpy path then down a narrow side street at the next jingle which played behind him at the crossing. The wind blew hard as he made wide swings with his cane. Hearing a car approach he pushed up against a building. The driver had seen him and passed with exaggerated care. Seeing people always exaggerated everything around blind people, as if they were helpless, which annoyed Ryoji.

Hearing a *sariman* talk on the pay phone at the corner then scenting tobacco at the smoke shop there, he turned left, down a looping, narrowing street. No longer having to calculate the distance to Midori's apartment, he heard, off to his right, a soulful song being strummed on the shamisen. The elderly woman who played the music did little to take the edge off the sadness of this particular song, about a suicide submarine captain stationed at an island just off Tokuyama, bidding a final farewell to his lover. Ryoji heard the low drone of the vending machines just off the street, signaling him to turn toward Midori's apartment building. His right hand felt the block of wall-mounted mailboxes, their metallic tabs nipping at his fingers. His cane bumped the first stair as his hand reached out for the railing. At the first landing, his hand slid off the plaster to the metal of the door. He knocked then heard her light foot falls, then her voice reverberate through the door.

"Ryoji-san?"

The door opened to her fragrance, a mingling of cedar, tatami, and jasmine, which he inhaled deeply. They greeted each other and he slipped off his coat and shoes at the genkan then let her guide him to the table, where he sat down crossed legged. He didn't know how to tell Midori that he was leaving, that he'd probably never see her again. But he didn't want to sadden her now and thus spoil her massage, thinking instead how he would send Midori her present, the two gift wrapped, gold-plated rabbit sculptures stuffed in his coat pocket. Both Midori and Ryoji were born in the Year of the Rabbit, and two *rabbits*, according to the Chinese zodiac, were said to make good chemistry.

"Excuse me," she said, "I have to phone the club."

He sipped hot green tea, listening to her dial then make her excuses. "Mama-san," she said. "I am so sorry. Please excuse me. I am tired and sore, Mama-san. My period is knocking. I ache everywhere. My head hurts, too. I have not been to the hairdresser even. My masseur is here to give me a massage. Can I please have the night off? Yes, he is here now. Yes, I have a fever, too, and am so sore. Please, mama-san. I will come tomorrow. I need a massage and sleep. *Onegaishimasu. Hai. Hai. Domo arigato gozaimashta.*" Ryoji felt the air stir from her bowing. "Yes. Yes. Thank you. Thank you so very much. Tomorrow, yes. Goodbye."

Hanging up the phone, she exclaimed, "*Yokatta!*"

"That is great," Ryoji echoed. "She sounds kind."

"Kind, but greedy," Midori said. "One has to beg for a simple night off. Humiliating."

Ryoji listened to Midori bend over to turn up the thermostat of the electric heater. Then he listened to her undress—she was wearing jeans (he heard the zipper and the flutter of denim), a pullover sweater (he heard the electricity snap in her hair), a brassiere with hooks (he heard the elastic slide around her body and the little links of fasteners parting), panties (the larger cotton kind, heard them slide down her legs). He knew that she liked to strut around naked in front of him, and this never failed to excite him.

"More tea, Ryoji-chan?" She leaned over him to pump the thermos, a bare breast tickling his shoulder (she the cat's-paw, he the rippling water).

His hands gushed with sweat now, anticipating her shape. He had to shift his legs to accommodate the heat there, listening to her getting settled on the futon after taking a courtesy shower, which made her smell wonderfully soapy and clean. She was courteous in everything, Midori. "Ready?" he asked.

"Mmmm."

For over two hours he massaged her steam-soft skin. He finished her legs, resting a hand along the top fringe of her copse, awaiting her signal.

She murmured, "Mmm."

He massaged around her copse and breasts at the same time, then worked his fingers in closer and harder and lighter and harder again in a variety of strokes administered with the dexterity of a cat burglar. Closer, he petted, stroked, pinched, and tickled with ten fingers dancing into the flutter of a hundred as she moaned in pleasure. He felt his sadness rise, constrict in his throat, and gather in his eyes. He'd miss her as he knew he'd never see her again, never again be able to give her pleasure. Bowing over her writhing body as he fondled, he took deep breaths, inhaling her essence deep down, as if to take it with him. Then another odor flitted up, the sweet scent of her menses that his fingers had teased forth. He loved her, felt tears stream harder down his cheeks, tried to stretch the moment of her wet hot clamp of her thighs sandwiching his hand, one thumb massaging her sweet spot, two fingers elsewhere, two more somewhere else, his tongue on her belly and giving attention to both breasts, the ecstatic pitch of her body, the merge of mind, body, soul now clear in her panting "*Iku. Iku, iku...* " I'm going. Going.

Ryoji heard himself whine, a high whimper that he silenced by biting his lip so deep he tasted blood, clenching his face up like a fist and throwing his head back, trying not to weep.

Later, as she lay asleep, he slipped on his shoes at the genkan, and reached in his coat pocket for her present then set the gift-wrapped box, with ritual care, atop the shoe shelf near the door. Then he bowed deeply, whispering, "Sa-yooo-naaaa-raaaa, Midori-chan."

* * *

At home, eating sea bream, rice, and pickled cucumbers with his parents, he became obsessed with the last thing he had to do: track down his older sister who, the last he had heard, labored in the Kawasaki tenderloin for the Kawasaki Gumi, or mafia group headquartered in Kawasaki. For years, whenever she came home at Shogatsu, or the New Year holiday, she had been evasive as to her employer, saying she was caring for a sick elderly woman of some means.

"What old woman?" Ryoji asked once.

"You don't know her, big brother. But she's terribly sick and I help her. She pays me well and is kind enough."

No one in the family questioned her, fearing her loss of pride if they probed. Anyone wearing imported clothes and perfume and French-cut diamonds, that her parents commented on after she left, flying back home instead of taking the train and talking about traveling through Europe again wasn't working as a clothes changer for the elderly. By chance, once in Masaoka's yatai a drunken Tokuyama businessman, living on the fringes of the buraku himself, was bragging about the windfall of a business trip to Tokyo, his speech lubricated with Suntory Dry. Drunk on sake, as he explained, he and his colleagues had ventured into the nether reaches of Kawasaki and its infamous tenderloin. There, at a soapland, the dazzling Turkish bath Ankara Bliss, he stumbled into an old classmate, Nakamura Ranko. "Anyone know her? She's of our town," he exclaimed.

Ryoji forced himself to keep the rage from his voice, saying, "I may want to get to know her. Please tell me more."

"Well, she still wears her hair up in pigtails and looks girlish. She's still more cute than beautiful. Small charming mouth with a quick tongue." He laughed. His laughter seemed wicked. Sinister. Which enraged Ryoji. "Very quick tongue. Noble nose and big eyes, though I didn't remember her as having such big eyes when we were students together."

"Maybe she had the surgery," another customer offered. "Many of them do. Bar hostesses and soapland professionals alike. It's their vanity, understand?"

"Where can I find her?" Ryoji asked, struggling to contain his rage.

"Why? You know her?"

Ryoji swallowed, raised his face to show he hid nothing, and exclaimed, "I want to get to know her." This brought laughter all around. But from the indiscreet fellow more curiosity.

Ryoji felt the man's gaze drill through the steam pouring off the vats of oden.

"I do think you know her. I see resemblance now in your face. You're blood, aren't you?"

"Blood of a soapland whore?" Ryoji laughed the question off as preposterous. "How you insult me." Hoping to bring him around to mentioning the name of the place again, he continued, jovially, "You're not serious. But I do go to Tokyo from time to time and have been known to visit Kawasaki myself."

"In that case," the man said, his voice betraying relief, "ask at the police box just to the right of the Kawasaki Keikyu Station, ask where you can find Ankara Bliss. An officer will help you surely."

"And you recommend this...Nakamura Ranko?"

"Mmm, but ask for her by the name of Junko. And remember what I said."

"About?" Ryoji asked.

The man let out a wicked chortle. "About...you know what."

"You mean," Ryoji asked, disgusted, "about the tongue?"

"Mmmm."

JACK COBB

Watched a straggly group of six sailors pop open beer cans as they stood around him. Cobb took a bite of his hamburger then pushed the plate away, exclaiming, while chewing, "Who here wants to have some fun? Gotta do a little train work to get there, but I guarantee a good time. On me."

On the train the seven of them guzzled beer. Grabbing out more cans from a large sack that Cobb had bought. "Don't spray me when you open that!"

"I'll drink to that." Jefferson, one of the sailors, ripped open a beer can, spraying foam.

Under circular hand grips and across an open six-foot expanse, the seats of the train faced each other and the Japanese passengers glared at the sailors. Cobb stared back, wanting to break the cold hard surface of inscrutability, homogeneity, anger at the barbarians drinking and carrying on so openly and selfishly and thus making their country into something that wasn't their country. Hatred hung like a stink in the air. Relishing it, Cobb, remembering his base brat days, involving trying to escape the confines of the naval station for the larger surrounding culture of Japan, finding himself, though, continuously thrown back. Rejected by Japanese girlfriends under orders from their parents or friends, rejected by roving teenage gangs of Japanese adolescents, rejected to the margins of a karate *dohjo* whose instructor bullied him, in turn inciting his students to bully the gangly adolescent Jack Cobb, making fun of his feet, his hair, his eyes, his big hands and long arms, his way of talking, walking, as a gorilla in parody, mockery that never failed to bring the group—always the group subtracting Cobb—to laughter at his expense, for what but having broken one of a thousand unwritten rules, banished to that no-man's land between cultures. He had become, he realized just then on the train clacking along toward adventure, the barbarian they had seen in him.

It was all wrong, he knew, that each of the sailors took up three seats, slouching, drinking beer, forearms and knees all over the place in complete indifference toward other passengers. But there was something incredibly right, something *real* for him, a reality in the brashness of being bulls in a china shop only half-assed open to them as outsiders anyway. The sailors and Cobb clanked beer cans together then had a race, swilling down whole cans. Spilling. Coughing. Dribbles wiped away by coat sleeves. Laughing bleary-eyed drunk.

"Cheers." They bumped cans.

At the next stop Cobb gave the order and they all poured out of the train in a boisterous pack. Following Cobb's lead they tossed their tickets before the station master seated at the wicket. The station master was a short man, and in contrast to the sailors and Cobb, he appeared very small standing in his wicket shouting at them that they each owed two hundred seventy yen more. He even grabbed the last man through, Dobbs, who merely shook him off then dropped his pants and shot the station master a moon. The short Japanese man ran after them. *"Oi, chotto ma-te! Oi kono-yaroh!"* They rounded a corner and stopped running. Walking down a sidewalk, past Mos Burger and K.F.C., Cobb saw a sandwich board style sign on the sidewalk advertising the Donald Duck English Conversation Lounge, 4F. "A slight detour," he announced, "the very best kind of postmodern rupture." He pointed at the suspicious sign where it said *Foreigners Welcome.* "That's us."

They piled in the elevator, Cobb ordering them what to do, then going over his plan again so they all got it. They mock saluted him before spilling from the lift at the fourth floor, as Jefferson said, "You're going to get us in trouble, man."

"Shhh." Cobb held a finger to his lips.

He counted about a dozen Japanese. At a bar sat four businessmen in concrete gray suits. Pairs of girls sat on high stools at various tables, conversing with each other. Sitting alone was some blind dude, with the most frightful scars over his eyes. He kind of moved his head the way the blind do, intuitively reading the karma that just walked in.

"Welcome to the Donald Duck English Conversation Lounge," said the manager, a middle-aged man behind the bar. He pointed at his nose, to indicate himself, in contrast to the Westerner's patting his chest. "Owner Suzuki Shintaro. You speak English?"

Cobb nodded.

"Then free for you. Coffee free for you too. I *rike* foreigners come because my customers *rike* to practice English. We have happy hour, too."

Cobb ordered seven large bottles of Sapporo, now snatched off the counter by each sailor in turn. Each of the Americans spread open a magazine and pretended to concentrate on reading.

"What you reading?" a girl asked Cobb.

Cobb glared up at her then returned his attention to the magazine.

She spoke in Japanese to her friend, "He scares me."

The friend took this as a challenge. Emboldened, she said, "Where you from?"

He ignored her, reading a news weekly, something about Trump in Japan striking a tough pose on trade. "Hey, this English conversation lounge. You speak here."

Cobb continued to disregard her, delighting in similar annoyances being voiced from other tables.

"Hey, you, we pay money to come here. You no pay anything. And you get free coffee. We need practice English. You speak!"

Cobb glared up from his magazine but just then his smartphone rang. Not wanting to break the pose, he didn't want to answer it. But it kept ringing.

A determined teenage girl glared at him, pointing. "Your phone's ringing!" She was smoking a cigarette and exhaled a stream of smoke in Cobb's face.

Unblinking, Cobb continued to stare, watching her cheeks blush. When she looked away, he returned his gaze to his reading, trying his best to remain indifferent to the ringing.

"I go tell *master*," she said in English, then paused, seeing the effect this would have on Cobb. To top if off she exhaled another stream of smoke into his face.

He did his best not to blink. Unfazed, he watched her hustle over to the bar where someone else was already complaining to the manager.

Then, a businessman slid into the seat beside Cobb.

"He not talking," one of the girls informed him.

"Cat catch his tongue?" He chuckled proudly at his use of the idiom. Then, with the silence dragging on, calling more attention to Cobb's ringing smartphone, the businessman had to point out the obvious. "Your keitai's ringing. You should at least switch it off." Cobb stared at him. Forcing him to slink back to the bar, leaving two more girls trying to pester conversation from Cobb. He wasn't forthcoming but damn it all if he didn't want to answer the phone. Who could possibly let it ring for so long unless it were some sort of emergency?

From somewhere else came a conversation lounge lizard, a

fortyish American man who looked like an old punk rocker—put out to pasture in Japan. He had a mohawk, studded ears and nose, and gold rap chains which were buried in his chest hair framed by the pointy lapels of a double-breasted jacket.   Rupturing the punk/ rapper facade, he addressed Cobb in a high voice, "How are you, sir? Gary Anderson from Minnesota." He offered his hand. Cobb merely stared at it. He had always wondered about such chat house types, the conversation lounge lizards, if they were plants paid off on the sly to drum up conversation. Hell, why else would they want to listen to their tongue be so mangled? Especially while the owner made out like a bandit. All for some lousy coffee. *Coffee's free you know*. It didn't figure. Even more strange was that most of the foreign lounge lizards taught English all day. Where did they get the energy? Unless the Japanese were manufacturing them now. *No more having to depend on overpaid foreign English teachers. No more importation hassles. Get your very own Gary Anderson from Minnesota. Made in Japan. Completely odorless. Demeanor as harmless as pussycat. Oppositional look for frisson.*

"I come here all the time. Great place. Master runs a good show. Where you from? Oh. We're engrossed in reading and not free talking today? I see. You know this so called free talking is very expensive talking for our Japanese friends. The least we can do is oblige with a little English conversation. Coffee's free you know."

Thirty seconds of very heavy silence in which Cobb cut him a razor sharp glare. Gary Anderson sighed. "Okay, fine. But at least if you don't want to talk then switch off that god damned smartphone," Gary Anderson said before slinking away.

The manager stood over Cobb now. "Friend, my customers say you not talking. Your friends too." He pointed around at the sailors seated at different tables.

Cobb ignored him.

"Hey you. What your problem? You no talk, you leave. You with dirty hair. This English conversation lounge. Hey, you!" He tapped Cobb's shoulder. "You no good. You leave! And take that ring, ring, ring with you! Mr. Ring ring ring..."

Cobb continued to ignore him but he wanted more than ever to answer his damned phone. How many minutes had it been ringing? Touching the corner of his eye was the blind dude cavorting over with his white cane, his blue jeans, and his tennis shoes.

"I smell rotten coconut milk," he said to Cobb. "And I hear handy phone that should be answered or cut."

Cobb pretended to ignore him but couldn't help but feel the heavy vibe that the blind man broadcasted. "Cobb," he whispered, covering his mouth with his hand.

The blind man perked up, curious, obviously interested in listening in.

A woman's voice. "Cobb? That you?"

"Who is this?" Cobb whispered. "Oh no, Swan Lake, what in hell? I told you never to call me here. How'd you get this number? You say you have a message for me? Or a massage for me? Which is it? A message and not a massage. Fine. But I'd prefer a nice light powder and a look at your face when the bill comes in for this chat. Let's do talk, though. Suddenly, why, I'm in the mood. Can't stop talking. How's the weather in Border City? Anything you want to ramble on about is fine around these parts, swami. Because we got free coffee coming out the ass and one very curious blind dude hanging his sad moon in on this conversation. How the monster reins. What's he saying?" Cobb turned the smart phone toward the blind man's asking an urgent question.

"You say," he asked Cobb, "Border City? Something about weather in Border City?"

"You say," Cobb repeated to Ingrid Swanson, "something about the weather in Border City? Just a moment, Swan dive. Let me pass you off."

Before she could object Cobb grabbed the blind man's hand then pressed the phone into it, saying, "She wants to talk to you, friend." The blind man looked confused, raising his eyebrows, clutching the phone at his ear. "Haro," he said. "You in Border City? But, but you want to speak to...? Cobb? I see, I see." He handed the phone back to Cobb who couldn't help but blink and shake his head.

"Cobb, listen." She then hollered: "Leave Massage World alone, corn cob ass. Or else I'll have fire breathed up your backside!" A loud click.

The blind man pressed closer to Cobb, saying, "I'm going to Border City. To work there—"

But Cobb wasn't listening, standing abruptly, shouting, "Ten hut." His men stood at attention, facing him, saluting. "March!"

The manager said, "You no come back, Mr. Ring ring ring—"

Cobb interrupted him with a chant that the sailors took up as well, "Ring ring ring...my ding-a-ling... is much bigger than yours... Mr.

Nihonjin!"

They marched out of the Donald Duck English Conversation Lounge in single file, leaving an angry buzz behind them.

RYOJI NAKAMURA

Spent his last day in Japan in an English conversation lounge, one terrorized by foreigners and their rude, heavy silence. He then schlepped around the Kawasaki tenderloin and its reek of cigarette smoke and hair pomade. Which told him *chimpira* doormen were around, those junior yakuza flunkies who wasted their lives away in such *soaplands*. He listened to them scuffling, interpreting it as anxiety at the sight of his presence, the uneasiness the seeing felt around the blind. Their vision weighed on him anyway as he clicked his cane around to Ankara Bliss. He'd been making the rounds for three days now, trying to walk by or pretend to be walking by his sister's soapland when she finished for the day. Her soapland name was Junko. He had telephoned Ankara Bliss, pretending to be a customer interested in Junko. There until seven, as the pimp said.

He killed some time in a coffee shop, then hobbled back by. Stalling, he fumbled with change at a vending machine opposite the entrance, hoping that his sister would stumble upon him. (It had to be her decision to recognize him, otherwise the loss of face—the humiliation—would be too great for her.) He was standing there when he heard foreigners speaking in English. They reeked of rancid coconut. He remembered the stench. The same group that terrorized the conversation lounge with their rude, selfish silence and bad manners, and the one, the leader, Cobb was his name, ignoring him when he tried to tell him that he was moving to Border City, the same place where the call had apparently come from. Ryoji listened to their carrying on, bragging of sexual exploits, as they left Ankara. He instinctively tightened the grip on his cane and felt concern for his sister.

"Who'd you have, Jefferson?"

"Junko, and I done tore that bitch up good. Couldn't fit all the way in her." Then he growled, "But Lord how I tried."

"Gave it to her good, huh?"

"And then some. Little rubber snapped even—"

"Look, that blind dude again."

"Hey, watch it, asshole!

"Look out!"

"Fucker's crazy!"

"Ouch! Shit!"

Ryoji ran at them swinging his cane, missing the first time, the cane biting the air in a whir. Then he cracked his cane against someone, hoping it were the foul talking Jefferson who *done tore up his sister.*

"Fucker hit me!"

Ryoji felt a fist fly toward him. Turned his face away, the blow grazing his ear. Stabbing around with his half cane, he nearly fell over as the grooved knuckles of another fist smashed his cheek. He ducked, flailing fist and cane, hitting nothing more than a glancing blow. Then he lost his legs, kicked out from under him and he fell hard. Clutching his cane, he landed on an elbow and a quick stitch of pain threaded itself like a thick wire up through his arm and around the joint of his shoulder. Around. Down his side. A red-hot coat hanger of pain.

"Look at the fucker squirm!"

"Just knocked the wind out of him."

"Didn't know Jack Cobb knew karate," Jefferson said. "See that flying kick?"

"Well, I'm gonna knock some more wind out of him." Ryoji winced from a kick to his tightened stomach. Gasping air, Ryoji felt his body curl up on the cold pavement. Then a sharp toed boot kicked him in the rectum, no sooner bringing forth spit and bile from his throat. He kept coughing up spit and bile.

"Leave him alone, Jeff."

"Shit, Cobb, what you mean leave him alone? He cracked his fucking cane on my leg!"

"Leave him alone I said."

"But my leg stings like a motherfucker!"

"You'll live," Ryoji heard the one called Cobb say.

"You hear him yell?"

"Sounded like something something my sitar. My sitar."

"Sounded like a spastic."

"What's this fucking sitar business?"

Lying there, on the very edge of consciousness, Ryoji sensed sharks circling.

"God, wonder what happened to his eyes. Look. Them scars."

"Like fucking zippers, man."

"Or saddle stitches that didn't quite close the wound."

"Let's get out of here. Don't want no hassle with cops."

"Shit, just defending ourselves."

"We're gaijin. Come on."

Their voices faded.

Ryoji lay there for a long time then threw away the snapped cane. He listened to it clatter on the pavement then struggled to his feet, holding his stomach and ribs with one hand while the other felt the wet heat of blood pouring from around his torn cheek and swollen eye. *"Kusoh, yanki sailor beat me."* Caneless, he limped over toward the hum of the vending machine. He felt a powerful thirst and struggled to dig coins from his pocket when he heard the doors open and female voices and footsteps spill from Ankara Bliss.

"It's so cold." His sister's voice, with its light timbre, brought goose pimples to where there had just been pain. "I'm going to get a hot tea." She told her friend to please wait.

Coming closer, she perfumed the air with her familiar jasmine which actually brought a smile to his split lip and welcome heat to his gut. He felt his nostrils flaring as if over hot chocolate. In the silence he sensed that she had recognized him, was watching him, stopping short of feeding the coins to the slot. In a whisper, she asked, "Big brother?"

"Little sister?"

He heard coins drop on the concrete and reached out his hand, which she warmed with the squeeze of hers. He covered the awkwardness of his knowing by gushing, "I'm going to America to live. I want to ask you to come along. I'm leaving in a few days. Come with me. I know I haven't seen you in years but please come."

She didn't seem to hear, touching his cheek. "What happened to you? You were run over? By a truck?"

"I fell."

He remembered the sailor's boasting and asked her, "You all right?"

"Mmm. But you." He could feel her looking, and the brush of her fingers on the welts of his face.

He sensed the awkwardness, her not knowing what to say, now that they were beyond the hard fact of his beating and the other meaner truth stood between them.

"It's all right. I've known for a long time. I want you to quit and come with me."

"My owner wouldn't allow it."

"Your owner?" The mention of an owner, how could such a man

own…" He felt the pulse of rage. How could his sister? In disbelief, Ryoji asked, "He will look for you across the ocean?"

"I can't now, Ryoji, if ever—

"After I'm settled, I want you to come."

"Maybe."

One of her friends called to her, saying it was cold.

"Go."

"No, not with you hurt like this."

"Go." He reassured her that he was fine, then told her he'd write when settled.

She hugged him.

"Gentle." He winced, nudging her to step back. "Tell your friends that I am an old customer." He tried to laugh to cover his tears. "Just some old crazy customer." Then he said goodbye and pushed her away. She wouldn't leave. He made a mean face and tried to slap her. There was a pause as he smelled her one more time while feeling the melancholy drinking of her eyes.

"Sayonara," she said, drawing out the syllables to tell him she never expected to see him again. When she was gone he slumped down against the vending machine and wept.

JACK COBB

Couldn't put it off any more, changing trains at Tokyo Station, boarding the Marunouchi line, and getting on the subway, when he should have taken a JR line. Despite knowing he was heading the wrong way, the naughty way, he had fed a one thousand yen bill to the ticket machine and punched the button for the fare that would take him to Nakano. His hand on the ticket itself set off thoughts of her, *that bristle of temptation that tickled him deep down in his gut at the thought of seeing her, just to see what the years had done to her, the deeper rippling of wrinkles, the heavier, silkier sag of old person's jowls. She must be somewhere deep in her sixties now,* he figured, trying to anchor an image hovering behind his eyelids. He felt the haunt of her house (his house where he used to live in that jail cell of a second-floor room). He heard her voice in his head, telling him over and over that if he ever needed her for anything that she'd be there for him. God, how could he ever ask her, an old woman, to help him with anything? Whenever he had money problems, though, there was her pledge turning over in his mind, and now here he was barreling across Tokyo on the Marunouchi, in a subway car with red everything, from velvety cushions and paint job, and cheerful four-color ads and stainless steel poles and shiny chrome fittings and clean plastic handles and straps, which were all heightened by the train's brave roar through dark subway tunnels and the exuberance of Tokyo's richest. The resonance from the thousand times he had gone from her house in Nakano to Shinjuku and environs to work or to play struck him as he was going to Nakano with money problems with her promise clattering on in his mind like a heavy coin refusing to give up its flip on the floor. Memories flooded his perception, lifting him above the funk of his cold and jet lag and general depression when, at the stop for Shinjuku, he tried to put on the brakes (give it up, Jack!), telling himself that she was evil and that he shouldn't venture any closer toward her but instead get off and cut over to the western end of Shinjuku Station where he'd take the Yamanote line down to Shinagawa, then transfer to the Keihin-kyu-koh bound for Kawasaki, Yokohama, beyond to Yokosuka for a definite reunion

with his his old man after having avoided that noise, and turned away
from it each time he stared at the naval station gate and thought about
seeing his father. This new feeling now, which was turning more novel
and wicked the closer the train pulled him to Nakano, had hooked him
so deeply that he just sat there, leaning back against the curled stainless
steel rails at the seat's end until the conductor called Nakano and he
snapped to attention, grabbing his bags, piling out, and then stowing
his stuff in a locker.

Big fluffy flakes of snow fell as he trekked down the labyrinth of
wall-lined streets. The farther from the station he got the narrower the
streets became, looping off and back on themselves, he kept to the
intricately enchanting way that he had devised by trial and error over
countless treks that took him down along the river, morning steam
rising over clear water flowing between concrete moss-covered slopes,
sprinkled with snow, rising, motelike, to grand old three-story houses.
Cobb watched mallards and teal floating together, clear marbles of water
rolling off their feathers as they dove and bobbed fifteen feet below.
Through the railings' vertical bars he watched carp, color bleached by
the current, feed at the surface of a river pool. Hand rummaging in
a plastic bag, downy flakes of snow catching on her hair and eyelids,
an ancient Japanese lady fed them, shaking all over in delight at the
snow, dropping a handful of bread crumbs to the water surface broken
by feeding carp. Mute, she nodded at Cobb across the river and he
nodded back, each savvy not to break the spell of the snow.

He strode along, crossing the bridge then turned left, heading down
another narrow street. Topped off by barbed wire, the high walls on
either side were autumn brown and minutely fluted, the huge blocks
having been scratched by brooms when fresh from the mold. Every
fifteen paces, and under a protective snow-covered hood, a surveillance
camera whirred silently, training itself on Cobb's advancement up this
rich street. *How money separated*, he thought, brushing snow from his
shoulders and arms.

Money. He didn't want her, Motoko Ogawa's, money. Or did he?
He asked himself why he was there then, starting up her walkway then
fumbling with her trick latch under the heavy temple-style covered
gateway. Her dog, hearing him from behind the walls, barked as it
had always barked when she was home, but now the sharp woof, in
the recollection it set off, was like a quiver of arrows hitting a target
one after the other, cracking the protective coating around this part of

himself, his past. A flood of memories hit him just when he heard her voice call to the dog, then call to whomever was at her door. *Donata desu ka?* He wanted to reply, *Jack desu. It's me, Jack.* But he couldn't get the words out. He just stood there, listening to the apparatus of locks, the click and slide of metal, fighting an impulse to flee, when the heavy hardwood door opened and there she stood, eight years of time made visible in the gentler inward sloping of her chin and the darker deeper cracks between the folds of skin around her eyes, all knuckled up, the eyes themselves blazing with the image of him standing before her as if he were on fire, blinking snowflakes from his lashes while looking from her to the bushes beside the door, the bushes that now caught the snow, like during that other rare winter snow storm years ago when she had charged out in her galoshes and winter coat over a nightgown to tie the branches back lest the weight of the snow snap off the spindly ones, as he, a much younger, sprier human being, stood at the *genkan* wanting to help but not being able to help under her orders to stay inside since he had a cold. He remembered her grunting against the snow-covered bushes, digging into them with her arms and body and short neck, down on all fours like a lineman. He slid into his own shoes then dug in to help her, the effort all the years and cultural demons between them felt shoved off like a boat and they worked like a team, one oiled, for once, not from bed work (since that's what it came to be) but something else that trembled between them here and now, eight years hence—that sweet naughty trembling that had been lying dormant fell across the wall like a detective's shadow. *There was no stopping it.*

Now Jack Cobb watched the oaken door open and found himself sniffing the old familiar smell. Of musk. Of dead air. He shivered, watching her standing there. Out of the anger of regret from giving into his weakness he thrust at her a bouquet of chrysanthemum blooms dusted with melting snow. She blinked, flinching, then held up her hands for the flowers, looking from them to him. Cobb quivered himself at the sight of eight years of time exteriorized in an instant on her gray flecked hair, that had, last time, been crayola black. He blinked at her, registering *the bludgeons of time.* But now she was scrutinizing him back.

With an intense gleam, her eyes seemed more like wild animals on the prowl. Prowling over the snow-dusted flowers. Prowling over him. The slackened skin around her eyes themselves and her face in general showed a tired origami of little folds and creases under a thick frost of kabuki makeup that only heightened what was supposed to be hidden. Her flatter nose and speckling gums reminded Cobb of a neighbor's old pug that had lost its teeth and had to gum its food. Her mouth opened, wanting to breathe and speak at the same time in excitement.

Time had reduced her to bony hands and a shallow bow in the shrink wrap of a kimono, starched, tea colored, and much graced with ivory petals. She now did a deeper bow, and came up gasping in delight or pretended delight (Who could tell with the Japanese?), "Jack-san!?" Her eyes brushed him up and down.

He had never called her by name, wasn't about to start now. "Mmm. *Konichiwa.*"

"Jack-san. You are a man. A grown up man now. How many years?"

"Eight."

"Eight years. Really. You are well? You look tired. Your face. Your eyes. They're bloodshot."

"Bloodshot from not having shot," he said in English.

"Nani?" she said. "What was that?"

He fought an impulse to flee and close off forever any emotional entryway permitting her back into his life. He hated himself, hated the weakness in him that had driven him to see her.

"Sleeping well?"

He lied, "Very well. Just arrived this morning. Slept through the entire flight." Another lie.

"Oh, such a long, horrible time to sit strapped in an airplane. But where are my manners? Do come in, Jack-san."

He took off his shoes at the *genkan.* In the living room she sank the flower stems in a vase, which she set on the coffee table. They sat, like old times, side by side on the sectional and chatted, she bringing him up to date on life changes, he pretending to listen while contemplating how to ask her what he came to ask her. When she served tea she asked him if he needed anything.

She read his silence. "You do need something. Tell me, Jack-san. What?" She scooted closer.

He studied her face, the gap of years framed there. The corpse-like makeup job itself magnified like crinkled paint the masterpiece of an old face. *How could I ever have stooped so low?* he asked himself, before standing, and saying, "I need to use your phone."

She nodded, tagging along, saying, "You know where it is."

"By the way," he said over his shoulder, digging out his address book, "it's long distance." Felt good to stiff her with the bill. What a nasty one it would be. Transpacific. And to a cellular.

After he told Ingrid Swanson his plans and she had hung up he shrugged, watching Motoko Ogawa turn tail back for the living room, flustered by his mysterious visit and trespassing on her good nature with the long distance call.

He followed her, then sat back down next to her on the sectional. Time to get to the point. As soon as he did he felt something leave him, then felt a coolness crawl into his soul and curl up like a dead cat.

"How much?"

"About ten or twelve million yen or so."

She straightened her posture, moving back to where she had been sitting. "For what?"

"A business that I want to take over."

"What kind of business?"

"A massage business."

"Is that your business, Jack-san. Massage? Like shiatsu massage?"

"A little different."

She nodded, scrutinizing him. "I see. So it's a clean massage then? Not gangster-style massage, like soapland. Or anything like that?"

He worried that she'd see through his lie, forced himself to shake his head. "No. Clean, healthy massage."

"Wait. It's not a clean healthy massage?"

"No, it is."

"No, it isn't? Or yes, it is?" She continued to stare at him, expert in that Asian way at drawing him out and tying his spiel in knots and at the same time, her quiet begging him to speak, giving her control. Her little eyes, betraying nary a twitch, missed nothing now.

"All right, well, it's like Swedish massage. Do you know Swedish massage? It uses hot oil, which men love."

"Only men go for this massage?"

"Well, no, there are women who like it, too. It's a massage for everyone. Why are you asking me so many questions?"

"So many questions?" she repeated, her little round face framed in her bobbed hair, the hint of buck teeth, gave her the look of a beaver, a beaver chewing into his lies.

Chewing into his spine. He felt weak and hated himself all over again for coming. "Yes, too many questions. Either you're good to your word and will give me the money or you won't."

"True to my word? Give you the money?"

"*Yes, give me the money.*" *Like fork it over now.*

She paused. "If I *give you* the money we'll look at it as a business loan. *Deshoo?*" He sensed irritation, not sure if she were serious about making him pay back the money or simply letting him save face. "You come here, Jack-san, after years of nothing in which you hadn't the decency to call, not even once, nor send a postcard or letter. And you want ten million yen without questions?"

"It's closer to twelve million," he said, slouching back into the sofa and putting his hands behind his head. "But yeah. That's right."

"If I'm going to give you the money there will be questions and more questions. *Wakatta?*" She sounded invigorated, her silken kimono making that vwooshing sound as she got up and ambled over to a shelf and pulled out a notebook. "Now I'm going to ask even more questions." She pumped away and took notes of everything: names, dates, addresses, amounts, collateral, et cetera.

"Now you listen," he said, realizing what brought him back to her was the niggling regret he felt over the years for not cashing in on her pledge she made when he left, "before you fill out my loan application promise me this: that you'll remember where you stand in all this, that you swear to Buddha that you won't try to take over Massage World yourself."

There was sympathy in her eyes, over the coolness of assessment. "You look lonely. Either you don't like what you do or don't trust anyone or both."

"Well, it's what I do, the business I'm in."

"Which is what?" she asked. "Exactly what?"

Vexed by her miserliness, he didn't care now. "I take over and run massage parlors, wash a little money here and there. I do what I want when I want to do it without hurting anyone."

"That is why you look lonely. You have no one."

He quipped, "The price of freedom. I can live with it."

"Can you?"

He shrugged, feeling belittled for giving her a glimpse into him. Felt empty. Felt weak.

Clattering her tea cup back down on the table, she told him that she didn't think he could be trusted with the loan of her money, since he seemed to trust no one but himself.

He saw that she was making a game of it, dangling her lucre then pulling it away. "Promise me that you won't be true to the nature of yourself."

"What nature is that?"

He looked at her beady eyes and felt nothing but hatred. "The nature of a greedy old woman. Who the older she gets the greedier she gets. Who once couldn't get enough of what I so generously gave." He watched her flinch, giving him the courage to add, "If you remember what I don't want to remember." He tapped her notebook on her lap. "Who may be getting too greedy now, wanting to know too much of what isn't her business. Why do you need to know anyway?" He slapped the book then in his anger's next surge grabbed the book and threw it across the room where it slapped the wall.

She imitated his throwing action then squawked, "Don't raise your voice. Remember where you are. We don't shout at each other here. Nor do we so savagely grab and throw things." She imitated his throwing action again.

Jerking his head back, he said, "Excuse my barbarian ways, but you still haven't answered my question."

"Nor will I." Her firm tone meant that she was raging inside. Under an outer show of docility the Japanese woman was rock hard, he realized. While the American woman was soft under an aggressive shell. "Now if you want the money, we'll do the paperwork. And we'll wait. *Wakatta*?"

He knelt and bowed to the floor, exclaiming over and over in mock servility, "*Wakarimashita*." Then sat back down to answer more questions about names, addresses, so on.

INGRID

Stood over the answering machine, Cobb's tone, an anvil of criminal hardness, making her recall the desk vice warnings of infiltrating mafiosi and/or other undesirables. Vice cops took it upon themselves to hassle her—and all masseuses for that matter—when she made her yearly visit to the police department to renew her masseuse license (they refused to mail it). Her massage business fell under Adult Entertainment laws, along with peep shows, strip shows, topless bars, street vendors, etc., and thus required a special City Regulated Permit, as well. On her most recent visit she marched into Vice, hoping to discourage requisite bullying. Standing from their desks behind a counter, grins betraying recognition of her, ol' Ingrid, and the welcome distraction from the tedium of paperwork she provided, Vice cops in their mid-thirties (that most terrible age for any male cop—or any man truly—trying to make his mark) simultaneously rose from adjoining desks and headed to the counter. The thinner and taller of the two explained outright that they'd be stonewalling on the paperwork until they had lectured her wholly on such subjects of illegalities they knew she was committing and the perils of mafia infiltration. "Until we've gone over all the ground, Ingrid, we're not going to renew your license. In fact, we may not reissue it at all, what with your new ambitions. Massage Land? As I understand it's being called. Or is it Massage Millennium—"

She corrected his sarcasm, "Massage World." then pursed her lips to keep her mouth closed.

"What are you trying to do, Ingrid, with this Massage Land?"

"Make a living. Take a step up the ladder. In this free country, the U.S. of A."

"Yeah," the older of the two cops uttered, his eyes gleaming with that smart-ass grin cultivated over countless hard-ass encounters, "make a living. But with your new Disneyland of parlors, Ingrid, I can't imagine a certain element sitting on the sidelines, ignoring such a bold, novel assault on their market." He made his breath wheeze in and out to convey mirth, his choked-back laughter and bushy mustache both cover jobs for a hair lip, his cynicism the toll of an undemanding job. Holding onto the counter, rocking back on his heels, he continued, "When's the grand opening anyway? Got any of them streamers and plastic flags? Lasers? Search lights? Champagne? Television crews? Fireworks?" He thrust out his hands. "Boom! Massage Universe. Boom! Whee!" He gave his partner a look, a cue for him to take over.

"Fireworks," the thinner cop said, depreciating the hyperbole. "Neighbors'll love that, huh, Ingrid? I'm sure we'll be hearing from them."

She struggled to keep her composure. "Whatever gets you through the day, gentlemen. Now may I have my renewal?"

"We've seen it over and over, Ingrid," the taller, thinner, younger cop said, his skinny arms extended to the metallic counter, his fingertips spread and whitened around the nails, supporting his lean upper torso. He was too thin, this one, for beat work, and his light blue eyes had seen only a fraction of what he was now claiming. Not letting go of her gaze, he said, "A masseuse as well-intentioned as you yourself used to be, that is, before your hand strayed from the straight and holistic and slipped down and dirty under the drape." He exhaled a sigh. "We hear everything here, Ingrid. *Everything.*"

"I know what you hear," she said, "and I even hear you listening." She raised a hand to her ear to indicate a telephone receiver. "Which one are you anyway? The heavy breather or the wincing masturbator?"

He ignored her. "We even have it on good authority, Ingrid, that you're no longer requiring your clients to even wear a drape."

"Oh, that's B.S. And whose eminent authority?"

"Can't disclose that," he said, shaking his head.

"Then I don't want to hear it," she said, annoyed. "I came to get my license renewed, not to be harassed by desk cops. You guys are wimps, face it, taking your career frustrations out on me like this."

"You're just like all the rest, Ingrid," the thin cop said gravely. "All the other little innocent finger massagers, marching in hard as nails, demanding respect and licenses"—his voice rose five octaves and sounded bitchy—"'Just give me the damned forms,' they say—ignoring sensible warnings of criminal interventions and takeovers, then waddling back in a month later, as if a carrot had been rammed a dozen inches up the rectum. The tales of woe we hear! And the tears!"

She said mockingly, holding out her hand, "Just give me the damned forms."

The hair lip made his breath wheeze into a chuckle at the expense of his partner, and she treated him to an appreciative wink.

The thin cop didn't say a word, just kept nodding as he twirled from the counter. Perturbed that she had cut his speech short, he went about his business of gathering up the requisite paper that was his job to push, yanking open file drawers, slamming them shut, inking an official seal, then stamping the license as if he were swinging a hammer. The hair lip, meanwhile, leaned an elbow on the counter, remembering what team he was on, and sneered, "Not a wise play to miff Ben, Ingrid."

"Well, Ben miffed me."

"Another enemy you need not, Ingrid."

"What do you mean? You're already my enemies. Every time I come in here you make me feel like a whore."

"Just doing our job."

"Some job."

Ben came then. Holding the papers just out of reach, he gave her a cop's hard glare. "You're not going to make it, Swanson. I'll personally see that you won't, that is, if a certain insidious element doesn't. Now get out of here." He tossed the papers across the counter (they fell to the floor) then pointed at the door.

Once back home, she played back certain messages, jotting down telephone numbers of masseuses who wanted jobs, adding them to her list of candidates, then taking down the names and numbers of potential outcall clients before pulling out another cassette to replace the tape in the machine which she'd save in case Jack Cobb's recorded offer was needed down the road because you never knew which road Massage World would take.

On the back porch she fed Max then stripped and showered in the bathroom. In her nightgown, robe and slippers in the kitchen she microwaved leftover ravioli and prepared a salad then sat at the kitchen table, dickering, between bites, with a new ad that she had been working on:

Grand opening of a grandiose bodywork spa in historic Georgian mansion. New attractive [she crossed out 'new attractive' and wrote young and gorgeous] masseuses offer private [she deleted private and inserted personalized] service from twelve private massage rooms. Six power showers. Four saunas. Whirlpools in V.I.P. rooms. Exquisite lobby with fountain and Greek statues. Barber shop. Nutritionist. Juice bar. Deli. Lounge with card tables and pocket billiards. Olympic-sized pool. Jacuzzi. And more... Let our sensational [she replaced sensational with sensuous] hands take you on a trip you won't forget. [she rewrote this sentence]. Let our sensuous hands play over you like a tropical waterfall. Convenient uptown location. Call anytime: 444-7498. Outcall available too. MASSAGE WORLD. Your world. 5655 Melon Street.

She knew she couldn't afford any therapeutic positioning and had long since field stripped such verbiage, i.e., the lingo massage schools sold, the very same jargon clients didn't buy: manual lymph drainage, reflexology, parasympathetic deep-tissue work, connective tissue relaxation, toxic buildup release, accumulated hard waste emancipation, herbal body wraps, vibrational healing, etc. Only the eager-beavers, upon graduation from massage schools, peddled that crap, then dumped it by the bushel basket for not bringing in any new clientele and paying the bills (the endless bills!). Almost as worthless as technical jargon were the marketing tips and articles generated by trade publications, although her one article about how she, as an L.M.T., distanced herself from both attractive and obnoxious clients was still cited in *Massage Therapist* and *Holistic*.

Any and all advertising had to be spiced up to make it in the massage game, she had learned. To make a success of Massage World she knew she had to stir deeply in the dangerous depths of primal urge, teasing men in a game of seductive hardball, followed by keeping a close watch on masseuses lest they'd succumb to the hand of horny rich *gentlemen* fanning out twenties, fifties, hundreds, in exchange for a wonderland of kinky favors and parlor tricks, any one of which—if acquiesced to—could close the place if Vice were in disguise, playing their shell game. The masseuse never knew who was cop and who was client (a bit of downtown strategy designed to keep the parlors in line). However, she knew that the seductive "personalized," "private," and "sensuous" would bring the law one step behind clients hell-bent on getting off, but she was determined to hire only the straightest of masseuses, her want ad saying so much:

> Masseuses wanted at new 5-star, clean, straight MASSAGE WORLD. Excellent remuneration. Only the legitimate need apply. Call Ingrid for interview. 444-7498. Fax: 444-7499. 5655 Melon Street.

Even though she had already let Max out and back in, he looked as if he wanted to go back out, scratching at the back door then nosing over to her, working his head under her arm and nudging her. "What is it, Max?" Just then he growled and ran to the kitchen window then to the living room window then back to kitchen window, which he stared up at, snarling.

"Someone out there, Maxy? Someone out there?"

Drawing her bathrobe tighter across her chest, she heard nothing but palm fronds scratching at window glass and the grumbling of the water heater over Max's growling and banging on the door knob with a paw. She crossed the kitchen to the back door, flipping off the kitchen light and switching on the porch light. Through the curtain she saw someone, a man, peeking in at her. She sucked in her breath and jumped back from the door as Max leapt up on his hind legs, his paws striking against the curtains and glass until the curtain rod and drapes fell over him. He reared to shake himself free, the curtain rod clanking across the floor. Watching a man turn and run, she struggled to unlock the oily door knob then opened the door with one hand while restraining Max with the other.

"You better run!" she yelled at the figure fleeing down the stairs. "Peeping Tom Pervert!"

She adjusted her grip on his collar when Max bolted free. Not bothering with stairs, he leapt from the porch, bounding upon the culprit turning just in time to be taken down, groaning onto the hard December ground. Pinned under bared fangs, he pushed at the dog's neck, trying to grab at it, but Max kept shaking free, then jutting his face closer, snarling and barking a half inch from the man's face.

"I'm calling the cops," she said.

"I... " he shouted, "I am the cops." He turned his head, trying to keep a forearm between his face and the dog's fangs. "I am the cops," he repeated, his voice firm, without fear, his freckled face stoic as well. "Now call your dog off, Swanson, or I shoot it off."

She ran down the porch steps and looked closer at his face while grabbing Max's collar. She noted in the dim light his orange hair and pale freckly skin of red-haired people. He also had narrow eyes, but she couldn't see the pupils because of the way he was lying. He wore tennis shoes, blue jeans, and his knees were pressed tight together, pointing at the sky, cradling Max in his lap, a dark-blue windbreaker half unzipped. "Why are you nosing around here? Let me see your badge if you're a cop."

She noticed his hand disappear under his windbreaker then emerge with a pistol, a cop's pistol, now aimed at Max's head. His tone was level, steely, "Now I'll ask one more time: Call your dog off. Or I shoot your dog off. On the count of three. One. Two."

"Max!"

"Three." A tongue of flame shot from the barrel, licking Max's careening head now jerking away, eyes closed as if in a snowstorm, then whimpering after the pistol shot exploded like a bomb, the report echoing down the line of houses. She closed her eyes, listening to the crinkle of wind breaker as the killer pushed out from under the body of Max. When she opened them he was pointing the gun in her face.

TRISH TOTT, L.M.T.,

Was the only American masseuse massaging at the Golden Hands. A dive of a parlor tucked into a loft space above some rowdy bar, the Golden Hands was situated under the flight path of Naval jets screaming over on maneuvers at all hours, rattling the floor and windows, and even shaking a brick loose now and then. The dilapidated building itself was on the wrong side of everything, including downtown and, of course, the law. It took up the corner of a waterfront street lined with sleazy taverns, tattoo parlors, trinket shops, and leather-good *crapola*. Just to the south loomed the huge cranes and hulking prows of a shipyard, then more of the same in a junkyard between Golden and a Naval base.

The manager was a crone New Yorker named Margaret. She pissed away her days before an old black-and-white television in an off-stage room, where she took clients' money through a marquee-style ticket window just after they climbed the stairs. Much to the masseuses' annoyance, she enforced a dress code by docking pay for failure to show up for work in anything but white nurselike uniforms, then ivory-colored high-heeled shoes and nylons. Both batty and a battle-axe, Margaret explained to the masseuses that this retro-look, recognized by only the most senior of clients, was what she herself wore when she started out in massage thirty years ago. But whenever the masseuses attempted to circumvent her dictums by going to the sleazy owner Jack Cobb, a paranoid speed freak who came around randomly to empty the till, to ask if he'd please get Margaret to ease up on the dress code, his answer was always the same: "Margaret runs the show here. Not me. Margaret. If you want to work for me at the Near East, that's different. Now you want to work for me at the Near East?"

Of course, no one wanted to work at the Near East Spa, the absolute swamp bottom of the massage business, as ruled by Jack Cobb, pimp king of sleaziness whose temper-tantrums came at you fast and left you delirious, run down, and completely fucked over. Trish kept telling herself that it was time to move on, make a move somewhere. Anywhere. To get the fuck out of this oppressive place with its gloomy light streaming in through dirty windows that some manic depressive had brush stroked black, which did a kind of sausage grinder thing on the light: twisted needles of neon and streetlight bleeding in through black paint, mixing with that from bare bulbs socketed, way up there in the loft space, to industrial-strength cord. Flapping between these ominous cords were cobwebs, monstrous silken wings of the stuff torn out by a long wooden pole that Margaret trotted out whenever the health department sent someone around.

What the place needed was music, but there was none. Just wooden floors braying like lonely hounds underfoot. So it was obvious when the hallway was clear and thus okay to jerk the curtains open and escort a client down to the sauna or shower, past the open ceilings of cattle-car cubicles where drunken sailors hooted when a knotted muscle was undone or groaned primal at orgasm. Even more depressing was an incident with a depressed old man, Frank Johnson, a client who always insisted on Trish. "I want Trish, not Gertrude, not Gun, not Claudia, not Vixen, not Dixon, not Rudolph, but Trish." Indicating finality, he'd nod his head once, his mouth hanging open stupidly, and that was all he ever said, becoming a mute after such a speech. He always wore these strange green sunglasses, their lenses the size of ski goggles burying his eyes. After each session with Frank, Trish felt his depression, massaging out of him a dark cloud of the stuff that'd follow her around for days—to the point that she wanted to push him off on another masseuse.

About sixty years old, Frank's raw meaty face was framed with a good head of gray hair, hair that clumped like pin feathers in the sauna. The sauna. Where she found him that last time looking dead, limbs sprawled as if he was broken over seat and floor, towel undone, genitalia a red hot shrivel, neck contorted, face scarlet from exposure and sagging like a Dali visage over scalding redwood, green sunglasses foggy over invisible eyes—the curlicue of wire earpiece still wrapped into a stranglehold around his auricle trunks and the leather sides adding more cover. She shook him but he wouldn't budge. She ran for the manager who then commanded Trish and another masseuse to fireman carry him under a cold shower (which did nothing in the way of revival) then into a broom closet—despite Trish's protests—where he was stored till the ambulance's quiet arrival at the alley door.

"Don't argue with me, Trish," Margaret said, as they grunted and groaned, stuffing him in against buckets and mops. "I've been through this game with him before."

"What game? You mean he did this before and you didn't tell me?"

Margaret glared at her. "Not now, Trish."

Out of breath from climbing the stairs, an old client came upon them. He was a retired banker, a dapper gent in derby, who often had a cane and wore pinstripes. He was ridiculously out of place on the docks where he had to venture for his weekly handjob. He was also a miser who never tipped. He'd time his half-hour massages down to the minute. The Thai girl, Oi, had nicknamed him *Sticky Shit*, a direct translation from the Thai slang for miser. "What is going on here, ladies?"

They ignored him.

Turkey jowls wagging, cane pounding the floor. "I should say— What in hell is going on here?"

"He *passed* out," the manager explained in her Brooklyn accent. "In the sauna heat." She motioned. "Please go to cubicle three."

The dapper old fellow didn't budge, shaking his cane toward the closet. "He passed out!? Then why in hell are you stuffing him in a broom closet? My word, is he dead? He looks dead."

"No, sir, he is not dead. Come. *Now.*" The manager led him away by an elbow, attributing Frank's state to heat exhaustion.

With Frank packed in the closet, Trish returned to her cubicle, surprised to see on her massage table empty pill jars. She caught up with Margaret. "Suicide. Look. Empty pill jars." The manager Margaret scowled at Trish as if she were responsible, then tried to stop her from informing the paramedics. Now, a month later, Trish was shocked to see Frank standing before her with his gray hair and green shades. "Now, Frank, if I'm to give you a massage you must promise me first: No tricks."

"No," he said.

"No, what?"

"No tricks. I'm all right now."

She turned her head askance, narrowed her eyes, shining on him a studious look. "Don't you dare try anything, Frank. Don't even think of it." She left him to disrobe, dashing off for fresh towels. Returning, she fretted around outside the curtain, waiting for him to undress, recline, then drape himself. She wanted to refuse him her services, but she forced herself to go through with the massage, not wanting to upset the greed of the manager. She snuck a glance through the curtain anyway then saw that he had uncorked a myriad of jars of prescription drugs, pills of every description spread over the white sheet of the massage table. Both his hands were scooping them up and stuffing them in his gulping mouth.

"Frank! Damn you!" She stole from his hands all kinds of pills then slapped to the floor the hundreds of different colored pills that bounced on the hardwood. She got behind him and pushed him toward the door. "No more suicide massages for you, Frank. You're sick. Kill yourself somewhere else. Not here. Never come back here. Never!"

His expression hangdog and guilty at the bottom of the stairs, while a half dozen masseuses and Margaret at the top of the stairs watched on. White socks and shoes in hand, he stood there barefoot and wouldn't meet Trish's eye. She told him that he had big problems as he just stood there shaking his head and repeating, "No, no, I'm all right. I'm all right now."

She slammed the door and ran back up the stairs, casting a glance at the sheep in their stupid uniforms, all bunched together like school girls at some international school, faces bobbing angelically around the matron, Margaret, who was standing there with her hands on her hips.

"What are you staring at? Where were you when I needed you?"

"Oh, Trish," the Columbian woman said, holding out her hands. *"Tu eres muy fuerte."*

Trish walked past them. They followed her to her cubicle. In the hallway a few men in their mid-thirties—always in their mid-thirties, most clients—stood wrapped in bath towels trying to piece together what happened. Margaret shooed them all back to their sessions then came to look in on Trish, who was slipping off her high-heeled shoes and uniform. "I won't be needing this anymore." Stripped down to her black underpants and brassiere, she handed the cotton dress to Margaret, who with one hand closed the curtain and with the other grabbed at the dress.

Draping it over a flabby arm, looking Trish up and down with envy and awe, she said, "You leave, Trish, there's no coming back."

"I understand that." Trish slipped on a white t-shirt then a purple turtleneck. She took down her black jeans then pulled them on going over to the opposite corner where her armor lay in a heap. Her lover Elizabeth had bought her the protective gear and made her promise to wear it. Wishing Margaret would go away, Trish untangled her one-piece black leather suit, stepped in each leg, slipped her arms in, then zipped it up.

"With your red hair," Margaret said admiringly, "you look good in black. Now what is that contraption you're putting on? You look like Darth Vader, Trish."

"Don't try to charm me. I'm quitting, Margaret."

"Don't burn bridges, Trishy."

"Why not? I enjoy a good fire." Trish slipped her head through her black and rainbow-colored roost shield, an injected-molded chest protector which seemed more appropriate for motocross but again, Elizabeth insisted and had even picked it out at the accessories shop. Having stepped into the plastic-over-tempered-steel shank of her black motocross boots, she bent over to snap closed the white reverse-cam buckles. Grabbed up the black air gloves out of her helmet, along with the keys, then picked up her white pumps and crammed them in her big side pockets. Stomping out, she put on her helmet, a black Vetter, against Margaret ranting at her side. *Nobody quits on me like that. No notice. No remorse. It just isn't done. Jack isn't gonna like this—"

"Fuck Jack. Fuck you, too, Margaret." Trish held up a middle finger as she approached the stairs.

Margaret gasping, "*I have never heard such talk. My word—*"

"Oh, B.S." Trish stomped down the back stairs sideways, as if she were in ski boots, hearing a rack of pool balls breaking over The Stones' *Start Me Up* which was cranked on the bar jukebox below. She kicked open the door then kicked it again, leaving it open. Someone was there. She shuddered. Seeing Jack Cobb her fear turned to anger. Passing him on the back stoop, she said, "You're an asshole."

Cobb, still walking, taking the step up, replied, "And you no longer work here."

"Duh, I already quit."

Cobb, not bothering to turn around, said over his shoulder, "Thank you for saving me the energy of canning you. Retard."

Trish continuing down shot back, "*Fucktard!*"

Cobb shook his ass at her then continued up.

She then turned the corner into more darkness, striding the narrow passageway between brick buildings on the way to her Harley, drilling her eyes into the darkness and December fog blowing in off the harbor, praying Frank wouldn't grab her in a bear hug. Or that she wouldn't stumble over his corpse. Under the tent of the foggy streetlight at the end of the passageway, she scanned the parked cars looking for her hog.

She turned up her leather collar against the cold wind, glancing up, one last time, at the creaky New-England style placard—of a pair of golden hands oddly pressed together like praying hands.

She mounted her motorcycle then turned the key and electrically started 1200 cc's, walking the hog backward then steering toward the street to head to the Blood Jet, a lesbian bar in uptown. She wondered how the experience would have been, massaging Frank to death, his life leaving him under her kneading chopping hands now feverishly working clutch and throttle of an engine howling under her thighs, her body bending like a crossbow, then coming up over the gas tank. She shuddered at the thought of his corpse at the end of session, if and when she would have even noticed his skin turn cool. She gunned the bike higher, popping it into third, front end rising, falling, a roaring bouncing off storefronts, tearing a hole through the night.

JANICE VERDURIN, L.M.T.,

Felt disgusted entering Cobb's office. *What a mess!* Gun-metal gray filing cabinets stacked high with ragged newspapers, motorcycle and guns and ammo magazines. Diet Pepsi and beer cans were tipped on their side and styrofoam cups and ashtrays were strewn across everything, spreading out from the central clutter of an old roll-top desk, the sliding top itself propped open with a broken yardstick.

Cobb proceeded to clear the mess as it trespassed on the massage table set up diagonally, like an ironing board, across the middle of the room, whose walls pressed in with posters of topless girls astride choppers sloppily Scotch taped to the paneling.

"Sit down." He nodded, indicating a folding chair facing his desk chair. "While I get things set up. Now, massage oil," he said, as if his thinking aloud were meant to prepare her for what was to come. He looked toward the desk. "I know I have some cooking here. Somewhere."

Janice knew this was the time to make her move. "Mr. Cobb, may I please use your phone?"

Cobb stopped what he was doing long enough to look at her suspiciously. "Can't it wait?"

She stood, crossed to the phone on his desk. "No, I'm sorry. It can't. Just one quick call."

Cobb, perhaps seeing that she was determined, stepped aside. She felt him studying her as she dug through her purse, held in such a way as to prevent Cobb from seeing the classified ad bearing Ingrid Swanson's number. After she dialed the number and Ingrid had answered, she told Ingrid to please wait a moment, then covered the receiver and looked at Cobb to relish the sting. "I'm terribly sorry, Mr. Cobb, but I may have to run along to another interview."

INGRID

Jumped from the pistol report shearing off ribbons of silence around her ears. Her stomach felt as if it was in her throat, as though a hand was closed tight around it, as she watched him lower the pistol to push at the slumped body of Max. She couldn't bring herself to rush after him nor go to Max, bewildered, she instead watched him roll out from under the carcass and spring to his feet in a twirl with his pistol held high, commando style. When rage set in she ran at him, swinging one fist then the other. He dodged her first blow then caught her by the forearm, twisting her arm back hard until she fell over. She lunged back up, but was stopped by a pistol barrel aimed at her head.

"*Freeze.*"

She remembered the ice in his voice, this Mr. Freeze cop fuck, looking from the hole of the barrel up into the holes of his face, his mouth a dark slash of sucked in lips. Nostril wings fluttering, opening the dark holes of his nostrils wider, darker. She wanted to stuff her thumbs in his nose and rip apart his face. Rake his eyes of anger. Tear the scruff from pumpkin brows, his unkempt hair. Tear it all out like weeds. And knee him in the balls for good measure. She took a step closer to him and heckled, "Dick nose."

A wrinkle fluttered up his nose, around his eyes. Extending his arm, his pistol barrel felt icy cold tattooing a circle into her forehead. Her eyes felt like buckets of anger trying to get beyond the shadow of the pistol to pour themselves into his eyes. "I know you, dick nose. I worked on you in an Old Town hotel room. You tried to get me to give you a handjob. Kept pulling twenties out from under the pillow and stacking them up. 'Now I'm telling you, Ingrid, this is the last twenty that I'm going to give you.' Remember?"

"Wrong guy."

"Not wrong guy! Not wrong guy! When I threw your money in the air and walked out, you made the same pissed-off face. Remember?" She looked at him with disgust. "You're a sick and dirty cop. One who knows what a wretched vice caper gone bad is like. But you're going to pay for shooting my Max." She jabbed a finger up into his face.

His eyes were little hammers pounding back at her. His freckled cheeks quivered, as he pressed the icy barrel harder against her forehead which made her back off. Out of the corner of his mouth came a mumbling, "Massage World'll be Up Your Ass World if you don't listen—"

She tried to bat his arm away. "I don't want to listen—"

Closing her eyes to a den of lions roaring into microphones and bad concert feedback in her ear, Ingrid sucked in a good long breath, lifted a leg, then stomped a foot, before doubling over. "AiiE-E, aiiE-E." The report now a drill bit melting into liquid silver which was trickling deeper into her head, a scratchiness going round and round. Grasping after the wounded sense, she felt K.O.ed as her eyes widened into a stupid stare as he loped off through a hedge of eucalyptus obscuring his clearing of the fence in a scissor-kick blur. Pursuing him dumbly, as if sleep drunk, she shook off the shock, branches snapping against her face, as she heard a car door slamming faintly somewhere that couldn't have been that far away from her. Zig-zagging back to Max in a confused hunker as if dashing under chopper blades, she knelt over him. With her masseuse fingers probing down into the warm wet hair of his head, index probing one neat little skull hole, the entry wound, then three fingers slipping into the bigger exit wound spilling warm worms of brain. She sat down on cold, hard ground (ground that Max denuded when he was a puppy, all paws and play), his bullet-torn head in her lap, sighing then giving herself over to a hurdle of sobs, tear-soaked eyes blurring porch flood lights that kept flicking on and pouring over trellises and vines and the shape of neighbors clamoring like sharp black cutouts along her fence, touching her with their giant shadows.

Someone, some man, kept repeating: "You all right there? All right there?"

She shouted, a corner of her mouth snapping the word off, "Fine!" In her anger she wanted to add a little something, a barb of some sort to get back at them, all of them, for their years of scorn. When police sirens began echoing down the row of houses followed by red siren lights feathering up through trees, down the slope of roof, across high sharp gables of second floor dormers and shutter slats, these surreal fish of red lights, she tried to wrap some sense around the voices mumbling along the chain link.

TRISH TOTT

S wung her Harley into the parking lot of the Blood Jet, tires cutting through gravel. She knew who was there already by the bikes parked around. The Ducati M900 Monster belonged to Kathryn, a butch from New Jersey. (She had let Trish ride it once and Trish thought it turned like shit, handling in general, well, like a monster, with too much head shake.) The cute little Honda CRM250 next to it belonged to Kathryn's lover, Chelsea, a femme from Border City who grew up down the street from Trish. In fact, they used to sleep over at each other's house, sharing the same bed after slow dancing to Motown singers. Then there was the dirt bike contingent, half a dozen Suzuki 125s, not to mention the larger rice rockets whose owners engaged in a constant teasing dialogue with Trish and whoever else owned an *inferior Harley*.

Crunching over the gravel in her boots, Trish took off her helmet and unzipped her jacket. She pushed open the door, looking around the smoky room for Elizabeth, not sure how to give her the news. The room was crowded and narrow, like a train car, with three pool tables aligned end to end where women leaned over their shots or hugged and talked. Jasmine, a femme from Detroit, played the air guitar, or rather pool cue, her thumb strumming above the handle of the stick. She sang along with the lead singer of Heart on the jukebox. Trish made her way over to the bar, saying hello to Tara from Tucson. "Trish, you look down."

"Bad day." Trish kept walking, nodding to Cynthia, a two-hundred pound bull dyke who taught Women's Studies at the state university. Trish managed a smile that Cynthia saw through.

"What happened to Trishy?"

Trish shook her head. Cynthia nodded, knowing not to press.

Trish dropped her helmet and air gloves beside a bar stool, lifted off her chest protector, unzipped her one piece suit, slipped off the top so it hung free behind her (as if she were in a ski lodge), and ordered a beer and a kamikaze from Nina, who squeezed her hand. "Cheer up."

Larry came over then. She was a passing butch named for her

resemblance to Larry of the Three Stooges. Larry was bald in the front, her hair growing back long and brown and curly as a clown's. She wore baggy gray pants held up by red suspenders. "Trish, I gotta tell ya. Just moved my shop if you still want your scooter welded." *Scooter.* Big ol' Harley called a scooter. This made Trish grin. "I'm now on Hastings and Worth. Come by Saturday and I could take care of that front fork." She traced a straight vertical line in the air. "Weld it off so you won't hear so much as a whimper. Change the outer chamber fork oil, too. Give you a great price."

"Thanks, Larry," Trish said. "I may just do that."

Stephanie on Trish's left stood to make room for Elizabeth, Trish's lover, who sat down next to Trish, putting a hand in her lap, stroking her thigh. "Saw you come in. Hey, what's wrong?" Trish shrugged.

"Come on. Don't do me like that. What is it? That Margaret ragging you? Or is it that creep Corn Cobb again?"

Trish didn't look at her. "I quit, Liz. That old crazy guy Frank Johnson tried to commit suicide on me again. Didn't want to take him but I knew Margaret would have made me. Just couldn't handle it. The whole sucky place."

Liz hugged her, stroking her shoulder. "It'll be all right."

Worried, Trish cared about Elizabeth and didn't want their relationship to deteriorate to one of those one-sided affairs where one lover was doing everything. *Maybe I should get out of massage*, Trish thought, but then knew that was futile. Massage was all she knew. She had embarked on a venture once in the gay community (not to mention a massage business catering to the sisterhood). Through friends she established contacts with individual clinics in Ciudad de Frontero that administered a one-day injection treatment for AIDS patients suffering from tuberculous Pneumocystis Calini and/or other opportunistic infections. To round up clients she ran ads stating how the treatment method and drugs hadn't yet been approved in the U.S.A. Her first group was comprised of twenty straggly AIDS patients, all gay men. They took the trolley down to the border then crossed the bridge to the clinic for their injections. Then the U.S. approved the drug and Trish changed her business. Under the aegis of the Mexican clinics, she advertised a twenty-four hour I.V. drip treatment. AIDS sufferers flew in from around the country. She met them at the airport then led them down to the border and across to the clinic, staying overnight then guiding them back the next day. Often they had to spend the second night at her and Liz's apartment, which got to be too much. Gaunt, weak, barely able to sit up on the sofa, pus oozing from open sores, they looked awful. Trish worried about staph, and about Liz getting staph. It wasn't fair to Liz. To make matters worse, in each group there were always four or five patients who didn't want to make the final payment, saying they felt no different after the treatment. Trish had to threaten lawsuits and sundry, shrieking at them to get them to pay. When they didn't, she had to rely on Liz. She hated that, having to rely on anyone. To end her frustration she started full-time at the Golden Hands. Now, Elizabeth was saying something about a new place opening.

"Some big spa in uptown near the hospital. Just saw an ad in the weekly. They're calling it Planet Massage. Massage Planet. Something like that. I'll get you the number. If that doesn't work I'll take care of you. You know that." Liz moved closer to embrace Trish.

"Don't," Trish said. "Don't even say that." Not in the mood for pity, that fast-food of emotions, Trish jerked her shoulder back so Liz's arm fell away then downed the rest of her beer, swung off the stool, then began suiting up in her armor.

INGRID

Wasn't in the mood to answer any stupid questions but the cop kept asking them, following her up the porch steps asking, "How do you know he was a police officer?"

"Because I've seen him before. I'll see him again too, if not in person then in a photograph at the police department."

"Why the police department?"

"Duh. Because that's where he works. Only logical, right?" Ingrid tapped a finger to her temple.

The officer questioning her was an overweight Latino in his late thirties. His beer belly told her he enjoyed life. He rolled his eyes, then cast a foreboding look in the direction of his partner, not sure what to say to forestall any potential embarrassment for them if she charged into the precinct raving mad. Ingrid let the screen door snap closed before he could follow her in. She yanked an old Army blanket from the top shelf of the living room closet then went back out. The officer repeated a question, his pen poised over a pocket notebook as she shook out the blanket and let it fall over the corpse. "Where did you say you saw him first?"

"At the Purple Sage Hotel in Old Town. I went there on his request to give him a massage. He had a scraggly red beard then, I think. Kept offering me money, asking me to do something extra." She knelt down to tug wrinkles from the blanket.

"Did you do it?"

"Of course I didn't do it."

"What did he look like again?"

"I told you. Shaggy red hair in need of a cut. Freckles. Cold eyes, maybe blue. Pudgy nose. It was after I called him dick nose that he pulled the trigger. So we know he has a temper, true to type in that regard. Know him? Probably works in vice." She scowled. "A red-headed dick."

"No one I know like that in vice. How tall again?"

"About six feet. Well-built. Probably works out."

"Now I need to know what exactly happened in this hotel room."

"What hotel room?"

"Where you said you saw him that first time. What did he do?" the officer asked, inclining his head as if to drink in all the juicy details.

Ingrid didn't say anything, looking away, crossing her arms.

Her whole career evolution as a masseuse: one big problem. Sweating out the slumps. Dealing with the jerks. Such as her old landlord and his lowered eyes staring holes in her blouse—as his voice slid a dangerous octave, offering to barter rent for massage but *more than massage*, catch his drift? Happens in the massage business. Usually all at once.

When the ads in the weekly don't hit home and the phone stops ringing and people you just meet make that fiercely confused face when you tell them you're an acupressure specialist: "Acupressure? Like air pressure? Like *acutire pressure* at the gas station? I don't understand."

"It's like finger pressure," she'd explain, "that gets right to the point. See, I'm a deep tissue specialist."

"Say what!?"

"You know, a kind of physical therapist but specializing in body work."

Here the brow wrinkles under the brain's feverish massaging away of euphemism until the light bulb goes on and they get it. "Oh, I got it. *You're a masseuse!*"

"Do a little dance, make a little love, get down tonight..."

A Swede by birth, Ingrid used to wonder what it was that gave Americans such a hard-on about massages. She often wrote off their curiosity and jokes to lingering Puritan ghosts and ambiguity she had to work when business was bad: their not knowing if you're parlor or therapist. Whore or healer. What do you do? What don't you do? Do you do it all? Here draw one of those jagged comic-strip circles, as if around the word *POW!*, around MASSAGE, and for a kicker add *The Magnetic Fields of...* Massage was a loaded word. Sliding signifiers sliding trombones all over the place.

Determined to go the therapeutic route she used to stress in her ads the benefits of massage. How it soothed pain dysfunctions. Eased pelvic disorders. Cut down on recurring injuries. And, of course, aided movement functions for the elderly. Et cetera. But the phone didn't ring and she starved. So she tried laboring for a shifty chiropractor who insisted on paying her only after the client's insurance compensated him. Somehow, mysteriously, the insurance money rarely came through. If and when it did the pie was sliced pretty thin. She ended up working for some rip off spa who took the lion's share of the fee. Plus, she had to tolerate horny clients who abandoned her for cut-throat colleagues hard after return clientele. Not to mention pushy-greedy managers and dirty politics. Frustrated, she quit to go back out on her own.

Needing regular clients, she did her best to give a massage the way they liked it. Deep or light. The way they liked it. It's a question of survival. But that giving of release, that receiving of tip or "happy ending" was all going to change at Massage World. No more release, no more, no more, no more. Massage therapists, in interviews, were told just that. *No release. No happy endings. In other words, no handjobs. This is going to be a clean spa.* At which point she would glare and not blink, *Understand?*

She told them not to listen to the clients' clamor. To put their hands over their ears against the constant hoopla of men going on about how they can get almost anything anywhere nowadays.

Client: *Geeze. Offer even a holistic health practitioner a little extra and get yourself fellated.*

Masseuse: *Is that right?*

Client: *Sure. Sure it is. I'm not lying.* Despite his head shaking, as if denying the veracity of what he swears to be true.

Men are such sneaks. You never know if they're telling the truth. Or if such a quip is a ploy. A kind of ticket for a reserved seat in the theater of lust. Their having said that means she, as a good sport, should, well, naturally accommodate when it came to...that. A constant source of strain: that.

What did it—*that*—make her?

When she was a straight masseuse insisting on the drape, she always had to do battle with those stinker clients. The ones who ripped the towel from over their buttocks or waists then bundled it up under their head as pillow. Hands up there or reaching around to block her hands from snatching the towel back. The same with the second towel she'd drape over them. Any struggle—even the slightest game of tug of war—had them demanding their money back.

Since her good intentions were subverted by a market that determined her stroke patterns, she went hungry. Until she told herself, don't be silly. We're born that way. Why the fuss? Just let the client take off the towel. For that matter a vice cop told her if no extra money changed hands then no law was broken while a little good will was earned. The only way to get a client to come back around was to give him release by hand to help him totally relax. No extra charge. No questions asked. Though if there's a little tip in there, why, even better. The competition does it. You must do it. And not just for dirty old men but professional people, too. They want it. They need it. Just as they need to sob through an hour session sometimes. Just as she needed to—but couldn't—sob on this cop's shoulder. Lonely people or all people need release. It's the release they're after.

Release. And its downsides. Men staring deep into the jelly of her eyes, deep into that truth space, as they whimpered. Charging an emotional toll that makes you feel like outlaw and whore together. In other words, like a dame. A desensitized dame in an old black and white movie. The hollow feeling of having no one to belong to.

People, neighbors in particular, think you're a prostitute. A *pross*, as the vice dicks say. What with so many entering the fray. Some masseuses evolve into pross, tempted over to the other side by men offering wheelbarrows of money until even esteemed holistic health practitioners are going over to the other side giving who knows what out of their living rooms. You sometimes have to (stress: *have to*) remind yourself that a complete massage nowadays means sexual release (at least to the loyal and lonely male client) and is not considered an act of prostitution among certain practitioners and clients. It's expected and it's performed as part of the massage, and no dialogue is needed until some jerk wants you to take off your blouse so he can touch your boobs. A jerk you have to tell yourself a hundred times not to blame because after all you had to send out, in a business slump, some sort of sexy signal in your ads. There was no taming the lust monster.

Pushing his hands away, "No."

"Then I won't come back to you. I get too turned on. Too frustrated."

You have your dignity. You draw the line there. Letting clients paw you is too much. Too humiliating. As is the client, deluded by the release you have given him last session, coming back a second time dropping his pants right off. "Have ten minutes, that'll make it ten dollars, right?" Wanting only that, he humiliates you who were trying to be nice, giving a good service. You then explain how his ten minutes would rob you of a valuable time slot, throw your schedule out of whack. You get frustrated to the point where you don't like men anymore. Frigid, you are no longer turned on sexually by anyone, male or female. You feel like an outsider. *A dame.* You become an outsider. A pariah dame. You don't want to have anything to do with men.

Sexually you stay well away from them; their encroachments disgust you. You become someone who has no one to belong to. Dancing in your head. All those crazy characters charged up in motel rooms. Little boys. Running in circles. *Do I have a big one? Can I see your...? Can I play with your... Can I? Can I?*

You don't say a word.

"Talk dirty to me."

You don't. You say only, "Use your imagination. Think about what you want to think about. Or think about nothing. Lean back. Close your eyes. Make believe."

But he insists on pawing you. Wedging his fingers deep in your crack. You spin away. Warn him. Slap his hands when he does it again. Suddenly he rolls from the table, grabs you, throws you on the table, starts ripping off your clothes, saying that you led him on. You kick and scream and claw and roll off the other way. A cat after mouse, he chases you around the table. You run outside, waiting, wondering what to do. Finally he emerges. In a wide arc you walk around him, as if in a knife fight. You try to go back in, but he blocks you. As if it's his house. You run around back and go in after a baseball bat, lay in wait in your studio.

A businessman with a reputation to protect, he keeps trying to look in, worried that you're calling the police. He decides to head you off.

From the window, your head just above the sill, you see him on his cell phone calling the police himself, reporting you, then pocketing his cell quickly, obviously without leaving his name, then making a b-line for his car.

The investigation begins. You're scared. Your phone is tapped. You see each client as a cop. Each session ends in a chill, "Is that it? No release?" Release could mean jail. More of your business cards found in the bushes out front. Thrown there by clients afraid their wives will find them.

Fewer repeats. Business goes south. You can't go on like this. For peace of mind you have to quit massage. Or maybe just massage special friends. Or regular clients. But most of your clients have given you wrong telephone numbers to prevent you from calling them. They don't come back around. You have no other skill. You continue in massage, driven by a dream of opening your own spa. The dream spa. Massage World *warmed by classical music of violins and cellos. Holograms of nature scenes. Waves and beaches and sunsets and wheat fields blown by wind. Smells of oceans and forests and cut grass. Sounds of waterfalls roaring and lightning thundering. Fish swimming upstream and jumping. Rain sprinkling a lake.*

...A cop staring you hard in the eye: "Tell me everything he did in this hotel room, mam."

"I told you already! Even when I identify him, you'll probably do nothing. Right? That's how it is with cops. Now why don't you concentrate on this crime, instead of trying to get off on what didn't happen in a hotel room? See those neighbor boys over there? That cluster of parents?" She pointed to their gathering along the fence. "Start with them. Ask them if they saw anything. Do a little police work. You may want to ask if anyone saw an unusual car parked on the street. Find out what kind of car. You know, police work." She wanted to push him to get him going.

The officer questioning Ingrid spoke to his partner, who had been circling the draped corpse of Max and staring at the mound under the blanket, as if that would solve the crime. "Johnny, go ask them if they saw anything."

Then the phone rang. Ingrid dashed back to the protective cover of her house. She picked up the receiver, saying, "This is Ingrid."

"Ingrid, I've been trying to reach you for a few days now. Could you hold for just a moment though?"

Ingrid stood there, listening on the phone to Janice someone saying something to someone. But her words were muffled.

She came back on, apologizing. "Sorry about that, Ingrid. My name is Janice Verdurin, an L.M.T. from Chicago. Just arrived today. What I need is an interview. As soon as possible. Please."

"I'm sorry," Ingrid said, the woman's panicky tone irritating her. "My dog's just been shot."

"Your dog? Who would shoot your dog? That's terrible."

"The police are here. I can't talk. Please call at another time, Janice. This is a terrible time. Really." Ingrid set the receiver in its cradle then looked to see that the door was closed.

Ingrid closed her eyes and repeated the word fuck three times under her breath.

Part of her tension came from a six-inch stack of contracts and building code booklets and pamphlets of lease and zoning laws and loan applications, standing neglected in a corner of her living room/ waiting room. Her junior partner Ermae had promised to take care of all of it, fine print included, but hadn't. And Ingrid didn't have the time or patience. Then the health and building code inspectors came around every other day to the mansion, dealing her more paper from their deck of ordinances. Legal blackjack. Worse than everything, though, was having to fence with enraged contractors yapping for money. Just today the electrician told her, "Before the weekend, pretty lady, I want to see the green of your asshole. Come Friday, I start ripping out the wiring."

"Wiring of my asshole?" she asked, humor the last weapon in her arsenal.

"Yeah," he said, grim-faced, "that too."

Just after that the painting contractor threatened to pull his crew unless he saw some money before the weekend. Problems kept jabbing at her from all sides. She started to head back out to talk to the cops but then realized that would do nothing. She thought about calling Erma, but she picked up the phone only to set it right back down. (Sympathy at this point would also do nothing.) She used her anger as encouragement to confront the beast, a part of it anyway, sitting down at the desk, and grabbing the letter opener, slicing open envelope after envelope, then unfolding and flattening out a crisp half inch stack of invoices and bills. In a ledger she noted the account and how much was owed, then found her savings passbook and figured that if she combined the last of her savings with the money from the outcalls tomorrow, she'd have just enough to pay the painters who, like most of the workmen, would have to wait until Massage World had opened and profited before receiving their final payment (something that enraged them to no end). Concerning the opening, she knew she'd have to open early, in only three days. Tomorrow she'd phone the newspaper to reword an ad. Then phone a few more masseuses to line up interviews (which she had no time to give). The thought of this and the cops knocking at the back door now just as the phone rang again brought back all the anxiety she had given away in an Indian sweat tent over a holistic Sunday in the desert. *Three days were simply not enough time.*

JANICE

Wanted to scream when her plan backfired. Enraged, she had an impulse to call Ingrid Swanson again, reach through the phone and strangle her. How could she hang up like that? And what was that about her dog? Her dog was shot? Who would shoot a dog? Despondent, she closed one eye, curling her lip, deploring Mr. Cobb's lording it over her as he stood there, one hand on a hip, the other wagging an upturned finger for her to relinquish his chair.

"Now it's my turn to use the phone." They shuffled around, switching places. He grabbed the receiver and pressed a button. "Hold all my calls, Bob. Yeah, going into a session." As if stoned and angry and horny all at the same time in anticipation of her trial massage, he turned his maniacal gleam on Janice as he spoke on the phone. "Yeah, I'll be all alone with Janice for a while." He had the guile to wink at her. "I will." He hung up, never taking his eyes from her. "You called Ingrid Swanson. Why?"

Janice didn't say anything.

"Is that who you called? Her place won't last, Janice. You heard it here first. She has no experience. She's just a freelancer in over her head. I'll bet she's closed within a month. There are a million things that can go wrong in this business. And they usually go wrong in the first month."

She crossed her legs, watching him look down then back up to her face. He asked where she was staying.

"At the Berkshire," she lied, not wanting to tell him the truth lest he could track her down.

"You could move in with Bobbie. That's if I hire you and not another girl who's a bit more experienced. Bobbie has an extra room. You wouldn't have to worry about rent."

"I'd rather stay alone. But I don't know if I want to work here yet."

"Can you afford not to work here?"

"Sure," she stammered. "Sure I can."

A wrinkle fluttered across Cobb's brow and he waved an arm as if to wave away the lie. "I'll speak with Bobbie if we work things out. She could arrange it starting tomorrow if you'd like. But now let's talk about the Near East Spa. We're the oldest spa in Border City and my masseuses make more than any other masseuses anywhere, even those in Vegas who do nothing but outcall." He took out a cigarette and lit it up, for some strange reason cupping his hands around the lighter flame. He inhaled deeply, the corners of his mouth digging back into his face as if to free some food caught in his gums.

"How much do they make?" Janice asked.

He took his time answering, blowing a ring of smoke at the ceiling. He then knit his brows and stared her dead in the eye: "My masseuses make a minimum of three hundred dollars a shift. Now you, Janice, look good. You're young and pretty and innocent. Clients won't be able to get enough of you. With a little training from me and Bobbie you'll be clearing half a grand a night. Easy. And then some."

After two night's work, Janice thought, *I could be out of that stinking hotel and into a nice apartment.* But her instincts told her that Mr. Cobb wasn't honest. She sensed menace in him, violence lingering just below the surface, remembering the chill he delivered to the reception area. "What's the catch?"

"No catch." He dragged deeply from his cigarette, held like a joint between his thumb and index. He even kept the smoke deep in his lungs as if it were indeed pot, then he exhaled another thin stream of smoke in a kind of whistling noise. Stabbing out the butt, he stood and began undressing, repeating, "No catch. Provided you know how to give our house massage." He jerked open the pearly western-style snaps of his shirt, which made popping sounds. "We're known for a special medical massage."

"Yeah," she said. "I'll bet."

"It's true. Doctors from all around send their patients to us." He pointed to a file cabinet. "That there cabinet is packed with letters written by medical doctors attesting to their patients' needs." He pulled off his t-shirt next, revealing a narrow chest matted with black hair, in which some kind of dog tags hung on a chain. He shook his head and his locks danced, then he sat back down and had the nerve to ask her to pull off his cowboy boots, heavy slippery things that fought like marlin in her hands. Finally she removed them, practically falling over backward in the process, then tossed them, in a show of disgust, to the floor. He was so kind as to do his own stinky black socks which, peeled off, revealed foul-smelling feet tinged a sunfish yellow high on the arches. She had to turn her face away. "*Yuk.*"

As he stood and unbuckled his belt Janice didn't know what to do. She turned her face away again, but felt herself sneaking glances, out of the corner of her eye, as he yanked down and stepped out of his black jeans, using a foot to clamp down on a cuff so as to free his legs without having to bend over. He dropped the jeans across the back of a chair, ignoring the change that fell from a pocket and rolled around. He lifted off his dog tags then dropped them on the desk. "You could say," he said, "that the Near East Spa specializes in this kind of medical massage for our housebroken clientele." Then off came the jockeys; Janice recognized the gray stripe (her ex wore the same brand).

Buck naked, he handed her the plastic container of massage oil, dripping hot water from a heating tube. "Use this," he said, then climbed up on the table, reclining on his back, shifting, stretching out, shifting some more, before getting perfectly settled, his whole long thin body twitching from toe to knee cap to elbow to shoulder to chin. All in anticipation of her touch.

"I see you're comfortable," she said. "Now where's the drape?"

"We don't need no fucking drape between practitioners," he snarled. "I've my license too, you know. But when customers come in, make sure you drape 'em. Then let them take off the drape. That way we know they're not the law."

The way *law* vibrated in his throat, Janice thought, with that little extra twang, and the choice of word itself, pointed to nothing but lawlessness. "What kind of medical massage is this again?" she asked, fumbling with the hot oil, squeezing some into her palm, trying not to look at his penis which she found herself glancing at anyway as it tried to spring from an entangling thatch of black hair, hair that criss-crossed and disappeared in the pale white of a taut stomach before thickening again up from his belly button to grow solid across his chest, the hair. She tried not to look at his penis rising, pointing straight up at the ceiling now as she spread hot oil across his chest. His skin and body hair felt rough and thirsty, drinking in the oil. She squeezed more oil into her hand, the plastic bottle making that farting sound.

With his hands behind his head, he lifted his head up enough to give him the optimum view of her hands playing across his woolly bodyscape. He was either looking at his penis or at her. Her hands were trembling. She did not want to look at him, and thought of Debbie instead.

"If you're worried about the stigma," Debbie had advised, "just do what I do: shame management. The massage gurus should offer a course in it. Quite simple really. All you need to do is be fully open with people. Tell them what you do. That way they have nothing on you. No dirty suspicions or mistrust of where the money's coming from. Instead I get a kind of envy from women for having the nerve to do what I want to do. And this kind of heightened interest from men. A kind of wide-eyed 'Oh really' look, right? People find me intriguing."

Intriguing. Huh. Ever since she started in massage Debbie's aura was more like a kind of *I-don't-give-a-shit-we-only-go-around-once-up-in-flames exuberance.* Which made Janice wonder what she did and didn't do in sessions. "I don't think I could do it, though." Janice half hoped Debbie would tell her she could.

Debbie's shrug peaked Janice's interest, had her trolling harder for support. "If I did do it, I don't think I could like tell people. I mean, I'm not as bold as you. I could see my father's face: Dad, I got a new job. As a masseuse. He'd like give me his stoic look then throw me out."

"You have to look at it as a temporary thing," Debbie cautioned. "The masseuses getting fucked over are the ones who get stuck in it for the long haul. I make it clear to people that I'm by no means a career masseuse."

"But, Deb, as I said, I couldn't tell people—"

"Then don't fucking tell people. Use grad school for validation. Let them file you there. Do massage on the side. Use it to learn about people. You'd be surprised at what clients blab in session. The intimacy brings out all kinds of dirty little secrets. You'd have thesis material aplenty."

Janice closed her eyes then rubbed her knuckles over them. "I don't know."

"At least try it. Maybe start at the Massage Bar at the airport. Can't be any worse than wiping asses at a nursing home. I see you shaking your head, Janice Verdurin, smiling your sly Janice smile. I know you. Now don't say another thing. Just take some of these books home. Read. Then we'll talk."

Debbie slipped a stack of holistic health books on massage into a paper bag then sent Janice on her way. Janice read everything and even completed "hands-on" classes in a three-month intensive program, culminating in a certification as a licensed massage therapist and her placement at a massage dive in Evanston. This, this news of her new profession, trickled into the gossip channels around her parents' Melrose home. Then finally fed into the ear of her mother. Gravely Catholic, Janice's mother laid her daughter open with a guilt trip. "I'll not have a"—she jumped over whore or slut or whatever to—"for a daughter." Eyes big and poking at her. A very long sad shake of the head and deep silence. Then she said, "Maybe you should leave early for school before your father finds out. I won't lie to him."

While mom was a part-time cashier at the local supermarket making union scale, father was foreman of a machine shop over in Cicero. A Vietnam War veteran, French Catholic, and a fourth-generation American, he didn't have much use for words, and like most of the reticent he was suspicious of the garrulous (any explanation in defense of her new profession would be met with a shake of the head and newspaper block out). Janice interrupted her mother to explain that there was nothing wrong with massage. And that's all she did, massage.

"Relax, sweet Janice," Mr. Cobb was saying. "You know clients can sense any tension coming through your hands. That makes them tense. A massage should be a relaxing experience."

She ignored him, saying, "Strange."

"What?"

"Starting on the front like this. What kind of medical massage are we doing here?" She spread more oil across his chest then kneaded the greater pectoral muscles.

"A simple prosterate massage," he said.

She felt a crispness in her upper lip. "A *prosterate* massage?" Maybe he meant to say *prostate*.

"Generally," he said, shifting his arms so they lay alongside his body, "you should try to sneak up on the penis but I hate the word penis. Sounds too much like...puny." He raised his voice two octaves, saying, "*puny wuny penis wenis went to the market.*" Then shook his head, sneering, "so let's call a spade a spade and a cock a cock, all right? A word with balls." He paused, his nostrils flaring as he bared his teeth, saying with finality, "*Cock*, with a capital C." He raised his hands. "Now here, give me your hands." He took her hands in his own then set her hands on either groin. He guided her hands around his cock, which she stared at now. "Do it now," she heard him say, "and you'll have no hesitancy in doing it later." For his wiry build, he had a large penis, now arching over, in slow motion, toward his belly. "You do under here, too, the prosterate here." He used his feet to help arch his back and buttocks above the table, steering her right hand down a path that started at the base of his testicles and reached to the bottom of his crack. The authority in his voice, the grip of his hands on her hands, the taboo area into which he was leading her, his hardening penis, it all made her feel too weak to fight him now. With his hands doing the guiding, there was a certain detachment, a coming out of herself she felt as he gradually eased her other hand over his penis. "That's the motion. Uh huh. Good. Feather down on it then back up and down. That a girl." He took his hands away and encouraged her. "Keep going. Sneak up on it with your grip, as if your hand were a slaughter snare and my cock a hare. Yes. Grip it like that now, ever so much more tightly closes the slaughter snare. Yes. Keep going. Yes, make love to it with the hot pussy of your hands. Here." He handed her the bottle of oil that had been leaning on its side against his thigh. "Reload. Grease it up good now."

He locked his hands behind his uplifted head again, taking it all in. "Uh huh. That a way. Grease it up good. Yesu, yesu."

Squeezing more hot oil into her hand, she glanced at him. He was staring at her, his eyes glazed over, giving her a look of stoned lust. It took her a moment to pull her gaze away from the intensity burning in his eyes. She felt something then. A flash of something that she'd never admit to. She forced herself to recall Debbie's coaching her to imagine the penis as a sausage or a cow's teat. Rubbing the handful of oil down around his testicles and up his penis, which had thickened but remained curved, she was unable to trace the exact source, if it were a high school friend or some perverted boy in the neighborhood chiding another boy meant more to offend the girls, a boy's voice anyway ringing loud in her head in some hazy adolescent memory about such a bend, how *too much beating the meat* (that was it) in the formative years lent a curve to cock, as she heard it said. "Yes. That's the stroke." Since he had released her wrists, his voice was doing the work of his hands, guiding her with its surprises—*her hand as slaughter snare*, which she tightened around him growing still harder in her hand.

"Jerk me with a little more pressure. But increase the pressure slowly. Remember that you have to sneak up on cock. Yes!"

"Oh!" she gasped, feeling her head snap back, startled by a blob of his semen shooting all the way up to his chin, then slashing across his belly like a Jackson Pollack painting, more and more, after but a mere tightening of her hand.

"Keep jerking! Keep jerking! Harder!" He whined, kicking his legs out straight, then bending them, then straightening them, like a frog. He kept coming, his eyes scrunched shut in pleasure. "Ahh! Keep jerking!"

Finally, he lay still. Janice didn't know what to do, holding her hands out before her. "Find a towel and mop up," he ordered, shaking limp hands over his belly to indicate what needed to be toweled off. "Mop up all this prosterate juice."

She found a stiff hand towel on a chair and took a long moment to wipe her hands. She then tossed the rag onto his belly. "*Mop up* your own *kumquated* self, and don't forget your chin," she said, then sneered, "I'm not your maid. Mop up your own...*prosterate* juice." She laughed, mixing delirium and disgust, which an edge of guilt chopped down to a series of raving chuckles. *Oh, god*, she thought, *what have I done? How low have I gone?*

"What are you laughing at?" He glared at her, his eyes hard under knitted brows as he toweled his stomach off then rolled off the table and began dressing. "What's wrong?"

"You must think I'm some sort of virgin idiot."

"Why?" he asked, incredulous.

"This whole dirty charade." She made a jerking off motion with her hand.

"What charade?" he asked, pulling on his jeans, taking care not to catch any pubic hair in his zipper since he hadn't bothered to retrieve his underwear fallen to the floor behind the chair.

"The charade of this so-called *prosterate* massage," she said, feeling feisty, wanting to rupture the artifice he had so deftly created.

He snapped up his shirt then tucked in its tails. "I know the whole thing sounds crazy, and many of our girls were suspicious during orientation, but you wouldn't believe how many men have prosterate problems. As I said, I got files and files of official letters from all kinds of doctors. I swear I do."

She mocked his twang, "I swear I do." Then she rebutted, "Where? I want to see these letters."

"As I said, right in them there files there." He pointed to one then the other of the two filing cabinets on either side of the desk.

"Well," she said, "open them up and let me see."

"Can't." He shrugged. "Lost the key."

"Lost the key? You can't be serious."

"I do have one letter on the wall there. From one patient's physician. It's like all the others."

"Where? Let me see."

He nodded, reciting the Charter of the House, the guiding lights of the Near East Spa: "The prosterate massage is our specialty here and it's all done by prescription. Now unless Bobbie or whoever at the front desk tells you otherwise, assume that every client is coming in for a prosterate. But he alone has to undrape himself and indicate he wants an extra, or prosterate."

"A prosterate?" Janice asked. "Or hot oil handjob?"

He looked at her with what she was coming to recognize as his dumb look, mouth gaping, chin jutted to the side, eyes wide and staring. "Prosterate," he said, annoyed. "We... are... a prosterate... house. That... is... our thing. Prosterate. Patients come from all over the southwestern United States. All the way up from old Mexico and over from New Mexico." He nodded again, as if it were all set straight now.

"Why don't you put it in the window then?" Janice said, "and learn to spell it right, all upper case: Capital P-R-O-S-T-A-T-E." Janice drew a line in the air, as if to underline it, then said, "House of."

He turned his dumb look on her again. Then he shook his head and made a silent whistling sound. "Put it in the window, she says. Huh. Put it in the window. That's lunacy. Now if you don't believe me, just lift up that wall calendar there and read the letter. Go on." He pointed to a motorcycle calendar to the right of the light switch. He kept his arm raised, his finger pointed, until she had worked her way around the massage table and a stack of old phone books and had lifted up the calendar.

Much as fire does to the part of paper that it hasn't burned to ash, time had done to this precious letter, singeing the sheet and yellowing the missive's frame of Scotch tape. In an uneven font, or old Underwood pica, dated more than four years ago, without official letterhead, seal, or anything else validating, it read:

Dear Near East Spa:

My patient, Mr. Raymond Springer, has been under my care for several years. Mr. Springer has a severe prostrate condition requiring weekly manual manipulation of the muscular and glandular tissue surrounding the urethra at the bladder, in addition to a more dexterous manipulation of the posterior rugae on up to his scrotum, penis, and pubic symphysis. I recommend your using a heated massage oil and starting with light pressure, or fingertip "crabbing," or "feathering" if you will, working toward a light medium pressure until patient experiences a full release of prostrate juices (a creamy white fluid resembling semen) through the male genital duct, or urethra. If you have any questions concerning any of this, please feel free to call me at my office.

Very Sincerely,

Dr. Milton Lademere, M.D.

Full block, flush left, and sloppily typed, with typos x'd out instead of whited out or corrected with erasure tape, the letter was signed in a wild, illegible hand, making Janice conclude that the massage therapist who had probably cobbled it together, with the aid of an anatomy text, a manual typewriter, and Cobb's general direction, had gotten that part right, i.e., the physician's illegible scrawl. Besides the major error of misspelling prostate as "prostrate," the letter made her wonder who in this enterprise was literate enough to produce such a forgery. Surely not Cobb himself. Still, such an earnest attempt by such a left-field outfit to legitimize something illegal was both puzzling and bizarre. Why go to such great lengths to justify giving, or selling, a handjob, an extra that she presumed was almost S.O.P., or Standard Operating Procedure, at such a dump?

"Who wrote this?" Janice asked, turning a bemused grin on Cobb.

Sitting down and pulling on his boots, he snapped, "It says right there on the fucking letter who wrote it. Your questions are starting to piss me off. You don't have the job yet, you know. Another girl's coming to interview tomorrow."

Ignoring him, wanting to see how he stood up to her challenge, she pointed out that the good doctor had offered neither phone number or address.

"I can get you his phone number," he snarled. "That'll be no problem. I'll get you his fucking phone number. All right!?"

Because he was looking up at her as he struggled with his boots, she could see a solid tangle of webbed veins in the bloody whites of his eyes. Something wasn't right with him, but she couldn't put a finger on it. "Please do," she said.

"I'll have it for you tomorrow when you come to work. But remember to call him on your own time. Not on my time. Your time. Now, about the dress code. Wear something..." He paused, looking her up and down. "That shows off your charms. And remember the three no's: No perfume; No dirty hustling; No forgetting to upsell at the outset. And no fucking around. And no forgetting to fork over every penny to me or Bob after each massage. And no forgetting that all monies are split 50/50 right down the middle, and that includes tips." He made a slicing motion across an outstretched hand.

"That's at least six no's," she pointed out. "You said three." She waved three fingers.

"Tomorrow there will be seven."

"Maybe I won't come tomorrow."

"Fine. Fine. If you don't show tomorrow I'm hiring the other girl. I know she wants the job. Maybe I'll hire her anyway."

"Maybe you should just do that then," Janice said, and walked out.

"I will!" he yelled after her. "God damnit I will!"

Like hell you will, she thought, knowing there was no other girl and the job was hers if she wanted it.

BOBBIE COBB, L.M.T.,

Gave the desk and its responsibilities to the officer as soon as Janice left. She strutted down the hall and around to Jack's office. "Well," she asked, seeing that her brother was in pensive mode, sitting back in his chair and staring at the wall, "how was she?"

"Let me think this through," he said, leaning forward. "Properly." He opened a desk drawer and took out a syringe and a foil wrapper of methamphetamine.

"My little brother has gotten to the point," Bobbie said, glissading toward the folding chair, "where he needs a shot to think."

"Let's just say," he said, letting her roll up his sleeve and tie off his arm with a blue bandanna, "that it *speeds* up the process."

She ignored the pun, Jack's lousy attempt to cheer her past her disapproval, watching him dip a white-stained teaspoon into a glass of water then sprinkle the drug onto the spoon. He heated the bottom of the carbon-blackened spoon with a lighter flame then handed the spoon to her. Then he drew the contents into the syringe.

"What are you going to do over there? Shit. They catch you holding, especially in Japan with your record. The Japanese don't fuck around, Jack, not when it comes to drugs. You know that."

"Yeah, yeah."

Cobb's people in Las Vegas got a blistering report from Kobayashi in Japan. They now wanted him to do a trip back to apologize. Prop up the old mafia don's face and all that. But the human smuggling business was dubious, and had little chance of succeeding. Too much media generated heat on the heat.

He handed her the syringe. "Here you go, Bob. Do me up."

She eyed a purple worm of vein rising on his forearm, stuck him, then pumped in the contents of the syringe. He had a tissue ready to soak up the blossom of blood.

Jack shook his head, bunched together his eyes, nose, and mouth, the latter of which he puckered, sucking in air. "Ohhhh, I love it going in. Love it going in."

"You sound," Bobbie said mockingly, "like a homo, Jack. *I love it going in. Love it going in.*" Shee stuck two cigarettes into her mouth. She lighted both then handed him one, saying, "The girls think that beneath her winning smile and cover girl facade that this Janice of yours is too prissy. That she won't fit in. And that you shouldn't hire her. At least not here. That she's capital T's. Trouble and Tease. And probably better suited for the Golden Hands, or better yet, ship her off to Japan. They'd love her there."

"No. I want her here."

"You like her? I thought you would." Bobbie blew a stream of smoke out the side of her mouth. "We were talking, Jack, the girls and I. Any Asian girls you bring back should come here—"

"No, they're going to Golden first to be broken in, as I said."

"Why, damnit?" She raised her smoking hand and pushed her face at him, eyes glaring. "You know their English is going to be terrible."

Cobb guffawed. "As if they even need to speak period."

"You got your period, Jack?"

"Oh come on. Massage is a physical thing. Not verbal."

"Bullshit. Problems come up all the time. They always do, even with the Latinas and Europeans."

"I could always enroll her in applied linguistics classes. She'd go in for that kind of self-improvement in a minute. Then let her supervise the newcomers."

Bobbie scoffed. "In any case, Miss Priss is going to Golden Hands. We don't want her. Tell me how she played, though."

Jack leaned back in his squeaky chair, putting his hands behind his head, casting his gaze to the coffee-colored splotches staining the drop ceiling. "Mmm," he said (the *Mmm* a souvenir brought back from Japan). "She acted as if it were the first handjob she had ever given, which turned me on. I came in a snap and all the way up from my toes. But I get this funny feeling about her. The minute she stepped into my office, she insisted on using my phone. Turns out she called Ingrid at Massage World. Pleaded for a job but it sounded as if Ingrid had hung up on her. The whole thing seemed staged."

"She mentioned to me too that she wanted to work for Ingrid," Bobbie said. "And she does act naive. As if this is all some kind of *neat* adventure."

"All a front I bet," Jack said matter of factly. "She's a spy for Ingrid." He held up his hands. "It all fits."

"A spy?" Bobbie ventured, wanting to draw him out.

"She didn't buy your letter. She wants the doctor's number so she can call and confirm the prosterate business."

Bobbie stumbled on his habitual mispronunciation of prostrate, suddenly remembering he once told her he was employing it as a neologism, countering, "If she were a spy, why would she push this letter thing? It doesn't make sense."

"Maybe it's an elaborate con." He leaned forward, took a deep breath, and seemed to shake all over as the drug dug in. "She plays up her prized innocence, does this so very well. She has to know that's what we're looking for."

"She's not a cop, is she?" Bobbie gave him a searching look, inflating a cheek and partially closing an eye.

"A cop would never jerk me off like that. Come on, Bob. I tell you she's a spy for Ingrid. The more I think about it the more it fits. Her calling Ingrid in front of me and asking her for a job, then pretending to be a hard sell on the letter thing." He counted off on his fingers.

Bobbie said, "It's either a clever con, or your drug-induced paranoia. When are you going to get off that shit anyway?"

Jack ignored her. "You'll find out either way what she is. I already told you that I need eyes and ears at Massage World."

"No way, Jack. Don't lay your satanic stare and medieval plots on me."

"Why not? You're the only one I'd trust. We both know there's not enough market for another house. One that big. Randy told me the place is immense. With our Oriental friends coming, where we gonna source clients? I don't want Vegas breathing up my ass." He held the cigarette near his mouth, preparing to take a drag. "Our survival depends on taking out or taking over Massage World A.S.A.P."

"Taking out? You sound like dad. And Trump threatening to take out North Korea. *Take them out. Take them out.* Yeah, we'll take them out all right—after I risk my ass undercover. No thank you. I'm happy here."

Cobb leaned back heavily in his chair, as if she were hopeless. "Don't you get it? There won't be a here if we let them do business. Call Ingrid and set up an interview. Once you've infiltrated, find the soft spots. Divide and conquer as they say. *Not* sabotage and bail. Clear?"

Bobbie shook her head. "No. Not clear. The whole thing sounds ridiculous. If Janice were a spy for Massage World, then she'd certainly recognize me if I got a job there."

Jack said, "Tell her you were tired of my antics and quit. She'll buy that, especially after we stage a sacrifice circle in a day or two. You'll object when it happens then storm out, yelling that you've had enough. *Comprendo?*"

INGRID

Went up to bed at about 4 a.m. Unable to sleep she lay there, a battlefield of emotions, staring at first light framing the shades at around 5. She rose, called a taxi, and dressed. Downstairs she sipped coffee in the kitchen and stared out the back window. Under dew drops and army blanket Max's shape was clear enough.

In the garage she found a pick and shovel, yanking them free from a tangle of rakes and hoes, their wooden handles making that sharp cracking sound against concrete. Out back she started digging Max's grave near the back fence when she heard the taxi horn. Trying to ignore everything, including the weight of her neighbors' disapproval of her being out here at dawn picking into their sleep after the mysterious shooting late last night broke into their slumber as well, she swung the pick's sharp point at the boulders that sent sparks flying with each swing, she kept telling herself to keep digging.

She heard the cab horn again and decided to ignore it. She had to bury Max before doing anything. Swinging the pick into rock set off another flash of sparks, as the handle tried to jump from her hands and electrocute her elbow and upper arm at the same time, leaving her twisted over and cursing a mere handful of stones, which she then kicked from the little scooped out hollow of earth. Breathing jags of breath in the cold dawn, she slammed the pick down, asking herself why Max was dead. She groped down from this wretched point where pressure from cops and neighbors and tradesmen felt as if she were being violated from both sides, but in the same hole what with one minute the darker side of massage tendering a sleazy offer tinged with threat and the next a wayward fringe of society, in the form of a deranged cop, threatening her life and taking her pet's should she proceed as planned. Then there was the social thing.

What was America's problem? What kind of Victorian slash Puritan ghost lingered here? When she told people in cocktail talk what she did for a living they gave her a dirty look. Worse, meaningful relationships with men were nearly impossible. With Greg, she rarely got turned on, as if her job of touching men's bodies every day had left her numbed sexually. Other masseuses said the same. Not only was her sexuality sacrificed but her social identity too—to the point where she couldn't tell people she was a masseuse and had to hide behind the camouflage of the more PC appropriate "therapist," or "technician." But Americans, curious to the point of rudeness, were unable to tolerate ambiguity. On those occasions Ingrid tried venturing into society, with the help of a rich client or a friend in her theater group who was in other words an artist (who knew the way through the loop holes the upper classes left to ensure their rejuvenation), some doddering accountant ass had to spoil her quest by insisting on her telling him exactly what she did for a living, wanting so earnestly to wrestle her to the ground to extract that one word as if armed with a tax form, his pen hovering over the occupation slot. He kept sticking her with questions, asked in earnest, as if she were an insect to be stuck with pins, each one aimed like a dart under a squinting, assessing eye: "Now what kind of therapist are you exactly, Ms. Swanson?"

"Well, I'm, uh, um, a kind of physical therapist. A hands-on body worker. Which is sort of related to chiropractic, acupuncture, physical therapy, that sort of thing."

"A hands-on body worker? The PC term for a masseuse, you mean? Are you?" he asked, his voice lowering four notches below the belt.

"Am I what?"

"A masseuse?"

"Me?"

"Yes, you." He widened his eyes and leaned in close, pointing a sharp finger at her chest. "I'm asking you if you're a masseuse, Ms. Swanson. Now answer the question."

"Well, kind of."

"You're kind of a masseuse?"

"All right. You win. I'm a masseuse. Now are you happy!?"

"You're a masseuse!?" Dumbfounded, then triumphant, he practically spilled his martini while throwing his hands up and dancing a jig. "A masseuse! A real life masseuse!? Hey! Look everyone. Look what I caught!"

Gasp. "You mean"—waves of cool shock directed her way—"Ingrid's a..." They couldn't say it, this word, a word she first heard as a child in her family's sauna where everyone massaged each other then ran out nude into snow drifts back in Sweden, which she left in the nineties when her father died and she finished school. At seventeen, she knew the time had come to leave the nest, venturing to London to polish her English. For work she stumbled onto an apprenticeship in massage at a hospital, joining a four-person masseuse staff the hospital employed, massaging bed-ridden patients to keep their muscles limber. Two years later, bitten by wanderlust, she immigrated to America. In Southern California she made the rounds at hospitals, inquiring about a massage position. But no one knew what she was talking about.

"You want to work in massage!? At a hospital? We can give you a job as pantry help but we don't hire people for massage. We don't do that here. No, no."

Finally, she found a masseuse position at a seedy parlor in SoCal, then realized she could make more freelancing. She worked out of a friend's place, inconveniently located in a bad part of town. Clients always complained, saying the house, an old gothic Queen Anne, looked haunted. They'd say on the phone, "Isn't that the haunted house? Oh, I remember you." Then they'd hang up, since men always wanted a different masseuse and a special something extra.

Joanie, her friend, worked days as a beautician. Her husband, a construction laborer, had been laid off and lounged around the house, *haunting* the Queen Anne all day and did nothing in the way of clean up. Dogs and cats slept on furniture. Dishes and trash piled up everywhere. Ingrid always had to clean the living room that clients had to pass through on their way back to her studio. She'd polish the hardwood, dust, straighten up, fan out the magazines on the coffee table, and keep the bathroom and its hallway clean. She also made a huge point of keeping the bedroom doors closed, thwarting a view of the litter boxes and dog turds and once, the husband, Tom, lying there spread-eagle naked, masturbating his brains out while giving her the big eye as she gave him the finger in return and slammed the door.

To get himself through the day he tormented her, making a point of opening all the bedroom doors then riding his bicycle around, leaving tracks over her freshly polished floors. Then at noon he'd pedal off to the convenience store and return with a twelve-pack of beer. Halfway through it, empty cans kicked around up and down the hall on his way to the bathroom, he'd start jumping around with his basketball, getting his hunting dogs barking and worked up. He liked to dribble the basketball down the hall then stop just outside her studio door, dribbling faster and faster, dogs barking then yelping when their noses got smacked. For five, ten, fifteen minutes he'd dribble, harder, faster, the ball's impact jostling plaster and floor and client, scaring off that rare kind of client just starting to be faithful. Business abated so much that Ingrid had to move on.

She found a cute little cottage through a classified. The location confused clients, though. One wrong turn and clients were lost down a one-way street that stretched down through a canyon for a country mile before offering a turn. It took them at least twenty minutes and several tricky turns to get back to Point A. Ingrid learned to give meticulous directions then have clients read them back to her. But men being men, they'd say, "I know how to find it. All right!? Now I'll see you in twenty minutes."

"Wait!"

Click.

She never saw half of them.

A bigger problem was the landlady, an old spinster snoop from Germany who lived opposite of her. She loved to speak in German with Ingrid whose mother tongue was Swedish. To discourage the old landlady Ingrid spoke back to her in Swedish. "I'm Swedish, remember? Not German." When Ingrid avoided her she suspected that Ingrid was a witch and called her four or five times a day. "Why don't you ever open your curtains like Europeans do? I want you to open them so you can see my nice little garden."

"I'm a nudist," Ingrid lied. "I love nothing more than to walk around the house nude and I don't want anyone looking in at me prancing around in my birthday suit."

"What's that witch's mask you have there hanging on the gnarl of my eucalyptus?"

"A gargoyle's mask I bought at a flea market," Ingrid explained.

"I don't believe you."

One day a stray cat meowed out on the stoop until Ingrid set out a saucer of milk. In the process of lapping up the milk the cat had spilled some, leaving a silvery stain on the concrete. Coincidentally, on the corner stop sign someone, some street gang of local punks, had spray painted a satanic sign, which, as the landlady deduced, was of the same silvery color as the milk stain on Ingrid's stoop. "I think you're performing witchcraft on me. All those men you have coming and going there are part of your coven."

"I told you I'm a masseuse," Ingrid explained. "Those are my clients."

The old lady called the police who then came around, chuckling about the old German lady's senility. But Ingrid had had enough. One day on her way to place her massage ad at the office of the weekly newspaper she felt a strong feeling draw her in the opposite direction. "Turn the corner and you will find what you need," her angel told her.

She turned the corner. There was a quaint little Victorian with a sign wired to its fence saying, *For rent or lease. Perfect for both business and residence.*

BOBBIE COBB

S tabbed out her cigarette in an overflowing ashtray, indifferent to the mess of gray flecks sprinkling her brother's desk. She mocked her brother, saying, "*No comprendo.*" Sighing, she went on, "I'm tired of your warped little schemes, Jack. Your games and perversions. Your sacrifice circles and fucking the help. I have to hear about it all day. From the girls you do and the girls you don't do. I have to pretend sympathy. It's too fucking much. I'm exhausted."

He ignored her. "I want her to move in with you."

"Janice!?" Bobbie sneered. Narrowed her eyes. Watched the speed pump up her brother, deepen his voice, intensify his expression, enliven his tongue and give him a determined look, character lines between his eyebrows and under his cheeks burrowing deeper as if his brain were sucking at his face. "Janice? Move in with me? You've lost it completely."

"We need to keep her hemmed in." He tapped the tips of his fingers together. "Make it more difficult for her to contact Ingrid. And in the off chance that she is straight, this will bring her around faster."

"Hemmed in, hemmed in," Bobbie mocked. She shook her head violently. "No way! Anyway, if I go to Massage World, then who will do my job here?"

Silence.

"You see?! Your plans are always filled with holes, Jack."

Another expression washed over him. His vocal chords issued something between a hum and a grunt. He began rocking back and forth, his lips curling into his mouth as if he were blowing a fife. He chortled, speed flitting debauchery into his eyes that now he appeared capable of seizing her by the lapels. *That meth is intense*, she thought, wondering if in his mood swings he were here with her now, if he hadn't injected too much this time. He stared at her, the half grunt caught in his throat turned over and over into a low hum. "She will," he said at long last. He kept rocking, grunting, humming. "She will."

"Who will!?"

On his speed-injected roll he made a smartass expression, bobbing his head, shaking his shoulders, his brain a mass of crystalline tubes through which blue flames raced, pushing out dots of sweat across his face that looked as if a blow torch had just passed over it, so sweated up now. "Our foxy Janice Verdurin." Showing an idiot's pride, he grinned, head still bobbing and sweating, eyes twitching from the salty sting of his perspiration. Then he stopped, pointing a finger. "But not yet. Not yet. She's too strong willed for regular training and not yet ready to manage. That is, if she's straight. In that case, we'll let the clients break her in. Yes, that would be best. Let the clients break her in. She'd feel more in control without us heckling her into anything."

"Then I should call Randy," Bobbie added, impressed with her brother's mind when it was *on* like this.

"Yes, set up Janice's first massage with Red. To cover ourselves if she is straight. Have him do his just-out-of-the-hospital-and-haven't-gotten-off-in-months sob story. If she doesn't buy that, have him garnish it with a mention of a prosterate problem, which got him hospitalized in the first place. Maybe he could produce a doctor's letter. She'll think this ridiculous at first then take comfort in the lie. They always do, even if deep down they know it's bullshit. Have him top his stories off with a C-note that you'll pass to him. How she handles that will tell us something. She may just see his bit about the prosterate as substantiating my line."

"Prostrate," she corrected, matter-of-factly, fleshing out sibling rivalry.

Jack made his angry face at her trying to jam up his thinking with grammar. "What!?"

"You said, as you always do, prosterate. It's pronounced, prostrate."

"Prostate, prostrate, prosterate. What's the *dif?* You sound like that Janice bitch now."

Bobbie grinned at her younger brother's glare, at the tremors of disgust jolting his face, as if his expression were the visible signs of an itch that his face, sweat streaked and thought provoked, was scratching after. He always looked as if he were throwing a fit after he shot.

"You know," he said again, as if to extract revenge for her little correction that threatened to bring him down from the ether, "she didn't buy your letter. You, the big writer in the family, couldn't even fool a hick Midwesterner."

Bobbie ignored him. "What do you think we should do about her suspicions? Have Randy pose as Doctor Lademere?"

"If she insists on calling him, you mean?"

"It'd just be on the phone," Bobbie said. "I'll coach him on doctorspeak, five-syllable Latinisms, all that."

He waved a hand. "Oh, come on. Red can only play so many parts. You speak of him as if he has the range of Robert DeNiro, for Christ's sake. You're also forgetting that she has half a brain. She'd see through his bluster in a minute."

"But," Bobbie asked, "if she does insist on calling him?"

Jack said, "Say we can't find his number. Say we can't find his number. Anyway, she's probably a spy, so it doesn't matter." He waved both hands at her, to dismiss such banter as ground already covered.

He was never so animated than when he was high. Bobbie knew that the way he was all jacked up with energy, making gestures, making faces, mind racing ahead of thoughts going off in all directions, but with a certain brilliance in the chaos of his thinking, a certain clean line of logic that tap danced and skittered, like cocaine under a razor blade, ahead of her own thinking, only came about when he was high. She didn't like to admit it, but her brother was smarter than her at such times. But only at such times. Those times were too often now as she suspected he was burrowing too deeply into addiction's heartless shell. "And if she objects to jerking off Randy?" Bobbie ventured.

"Then I'll have him bust her for something. When I bail her out she'll be indebted. Then I can steer her sweet ass in the direction of bigger money."

"The Japanese kind? The Chinese kind?"

Secretive, Cobb waved a hand, and said only, "Perhaps."

"But what about the spy thing and Ingrid?" she continued.

"Your little mind, big sister," Cobb chided, "is like a pitbull when it gets a hold of something."

"And your mind can't keep a hold of anything," she retorted.

"Let me tell you this. Let me tell you this. I just sent Red over to poke around at Ingrid's. If she's giving any Swansong massages there he'll bust her. Close her ass down. If that doesn't work, I told him to keep pinching her, pinch her sweet ass out of business before she's even in business."

"Oh how that dirty drug brings the slyness out."

"Then give me another shot," he said, turning his hands upside down and moving all ten fingers at once, like an overturned crab. "Then give me another shot. Then I gotta go."

"Jack, as we've been talking, I've been thinking. Only under one condition will I play along with your ploy."

"What's that?"

"If you get off that shit." She flung a hand at the works he was preparing with the care of a jeweler.

He handed her the syringe. "Don't know if I can do that, Bob. Just don't know. Tell you what, give me a blast and let me think on it. Let me think on it."

"See? As I keep saying, you've gotten to the point that you can't think without it. And more and more you're saying everything in duplicate. Like Donald Trump. Everything in double. But for some reason it only bothers me when you're jacked up like this."

"I say everything twice because it takes that many times to get through to certain people," he pontificated, nodding, cocking his wayward eyebrow at her, a teasing look that reminded her of their father, a man of precise diction who, when he'd treat them to a kernel of wisdom, gave his eyebrow the same bend. "When I am in good company," he said, "I have no need to repeat myself. Anyway, the only reason you want me to quit is because you can't handle my out thinking you when I'm high. That something so illegal and dangerous gives me that edge drives you crazy. Your blushing tells me that I'm right."

Even though she was aware of the press of heat on her cheeks, Bobbie said, "I'm not blushing. Now make a bigger muscle, wimp. I swear you're wasting away to nothing." She jabbed in the needle, pumping in the meth.

"Oh, I love it going in—"

"Oh, I love it going in," she mocked. "You know the needle is symbolic of the phallus. I think you're a latent homo, Jack. I keep saying it."

He stood, buttoning his shirt sleeve. "I can't handle your pecking at me anymore."

"Where you going?"

"Told you, *fishing*."

"Which means?"

He ignored her.

"What's the code? Help me Jack. Fishing means going to Golden Hands?"

"Mmmm," he said. "Maybe meet Red first then take a look at Massage World. But perhaps not in that order." He held out a hand. "Just give me my god damned coat."

She tossed his leather jacket at him, exclaiming, "*That order*, as if you have an order, Mr. Disorder."

He ignored her, going through the pockets until he found a thick wad of bills. "Good, got my dough." He counted out a thousand dollars then put it in an envelope then in another pocket. "Have to pay off Red. Later, Bob," he said and stomped out the door.

"Just who in the hell do you think you are?" Bobbie yelled after him.

"Jack Cobb," he said over his shoulder, adding, "Future Lord of Massage World."

JACKSON COBB

alked into Barney's, looking around for Randy "Red" Gudsikes. Crept up behind him playing solitaire on a bar table. He grabbed him, saying, "Yo Red."

Gudsikes started, cursing at the scare. "You're late," Gudsikes said by way of hello.

Cobb glared back at his cop friend in his customary windbreaker, jeans, and running shoes. "You're right."

"Where you been?"

"Fishing," Cobb lied. Cobb went to the bar and ordered two bottles of Bud, then returned and handed one to Gudsikes before sliding two quarters into the pool table, then pulling the lever to release the balls which clanked into the tray.

"Saw our friend Ingrid," Gudsikes said. "Your cabbie pal was right on the address."

"Yeah?" Cobb glanced up from his business of racking the balls. "You talk?"

"Talked to her dog first. Sonofabitch shepherd caught me looking in on her, digging on her jugs flopping around under a bathrobe. I fled but she let him out. Fuggin' thing jumps me off the back porch. Fangs salivating over my face, wanting to make dinner of my nose." Gudsikes made his hand into the shape of a pistol, one pointed at his temple. "Got it right here."

Lifting the rack from the triangle of balls, Cobb looked up, said, "Yeah?"

"Fucking shepherd croaked right on my chest. Had to fucking shake its corpse off then find Swanson in my face. Calling me Dick Nose and shit. Bitch remembers me from a sting operation a few years back. Couldn't get her to take from the flash roll in some motel and she lost it. Just now told her to back off. She don't hear too good. Had to squeeze one off to get through the ear wax, right. Believe me, she ain't had near enough."

"Fucking A," Cobb agreed.

"Fuck away," Red said. "Bang away all you want."

"But," Cobb added, "can't give pussy a black eye."

"Unh unh," Gudsikes seconded, "can't give pussy a black eye." Gudsikes became pensive. "You know what bothers me, though. I have to go into Massage World undercover. And get Swanson to accept some money—up to a grand, the chief says—for jerking me off. The chief is breathing fire up my ass, with a deadline and all kinds of pressure."

Cobb sank a bank shot. Looking up, "So what's the problem?"

"Obvious," Gudsikes said. "She's going to remember me."

"So," Cobb said, "you need a disguise."

"Any ideas?"

"Let me think on it. I'll think on it." Watching some bearded woodsman and a square-jawed fellow at the next table caught up in a game of eight ball, Cobb took out an envelope stuffed fat with a thousand dollars in small bills then handed the loot, a week's wages, to Red after he circled the table. "Tomorrow or Wednesday we may be in need of your services to break in a new gal."

"At The Near East?"

Cobb nodded, remembering Janice Verdurin. "A babe, too. Kind of virginal still."

"I'll be there with my crab apples," Gudsikes said, grinning.

Cobb scowled, remembering that time before his family moved to Japan to join his father at the naval base there. The three kids, Gudsikes, Jack, and Bobbie, had collected a bucketful of crab apples from a grove near the railroad tracks. They all had laid down in the grass and Gudsikes suggested playing doctor. Gudsikes and Cobb took off their clothes first then Bobbie followed. She was thirteen or fourteen then and two years their senior, perhaps giving her the courage to pull off her shirt then shorts and underpants and lay back under Dr. Randy's orders. Gudsikes squeezed her breasts then petted the light fringe of pubic thatch before performing a more aggressive exploration with his fingers. Jack held back, watched as his sister writhed and squealed under his friend's touch. Gudsikes said to Cobb, "Instruments, please." Cobb passed him the bucket of crab apples. Gudsikes grabbed a handful then began pushing them up Bobbie who winced then cried when a stream of blood poured out. Gudsikes ran off shaking and looking back, face twisted up in fear's grasp, then running faster. Jack, not sure what to do, ran home. He grabbed a roll of paper towels and a tray of ice cubes then ran back to Bobbie who was weeping in the grass, her underpants balled up and sandwiched between her thighs to staunch the flow.

Gudsikes sank a stripe then cued up his next shot.

"You fool," Cobb said, pushing him away. "Now look out. I'm stripes."

Gudsikes looked bewildered then pissed off. "*Fuck.* Thought I had the big ones."

Cobb drilled the eleven into the side pocket, then banked the thirteen into the corner as Gudsikes heckled him.

"Beat your cheating ass anyway. I'll bet you a bucket of crab apples." He let out a burst of lonely laughter.

Circling, Cobb looked over the table. Cued up, sank the fourteen, then lined up a shot at the black ball. Sinking the eight, he threw the cue stick onto the table and headed out.

"Where you going?" Gudsikes asked.

Over his shoulder, he said, "Fishing."

"Like hell!"

Then Cobb had an idea. "Just thought of something, Red. For your disguise." Gudsikes looked confused. Cobb clarified, "So Swansky won't remember you."

"Got the big ears on," Red said, holding his hands up to his ears. "Go ahead."

When Cobb finished explaining, Red grinned, said, "I like it. I like it a lot. She'll never in a million years see through it."

Driving to Golden Hands in his beater, an old Dodge window van, bumper pasted with stickers falsely proclaiming him as a *Border City Native*, Jack Cobb, when he was alone, liked to reclaim his higher mind, dumping the guise of renegade massage-parlor pimp and ungovernable speed freak manager (a role that even Bobbie had bought) and think in Japanese, his mind dictating an ideogram through his finger scrawling on a pant leg. He relished reading Japanese literature in Japanese, and loved the older writers of the New Sensationalists beginning with the Meiji Restoration, and then his favorite, Yukio Mishima. He directed his right index finger to trace on his thigh the ideograms visible behind his eyelids. He traced the first half of a modernist master's famous haiku, beginning with the katakana for "Naita" then the hiragana "no," then the second line, starting with the horizontal strokes then vertical, the near diagonal last, his father's stern face flashing to mind in his ordering (everything was an order with the old man) Jack to memorize ten ideograms a day, every regimented day, demanding him to scratch them out before dinner, until Jack had learned one thousand more than the standard two thousand chosen by the Japanese Ministry of Education. Through his fingers now came the stunning ideogram for "gekai" (four squares making one square over a house-like structure that looked ready to take flight) then a particle in hiragana. His fingers stopped halfway through the poem, leaving his mind to savor the image without delving into the more literal translation that would impose if he continued. Shuddering, he uttered the words in Japanese, "Naita no / soko gekai nite... The very bottom / of a night game."

He drove on, repeating the phrase until a weather warning was forecast on the radio. A weather nut, Cobb turned up the volume and fine-tuned the frequency: A series of tropical storms waiting off the coast threatened to pound the city with four to six inches of rain turning to snow on the morrow. "In light of the marathon drought, we need every drop of that rain, folks. Hear anyone complaining you know their tourists."

Welcoming the tension of a storm, Cobb pushed in a CD of The Doors and cranked the volume, driving hard down Milestone Boulevard under towering trunks and crowns of glorious eucalyptus, singing along with Jim. "You know it would be untrue / If I were to say to you." He honked at two streetwalkers, curb crawlers as he called them, strutting down the pavement before a gas station. Basketball-sized buttocks bulging from miniskirts, purses swinging from shoulders, they waved at Cobb's blaring horn. He shouted out the window, "I may be back for you!" Then he added his siren song, "For an exciting new career in massage!"

He felt good. Invincible. *Light my fire. Light my fire.* Banging the three-in-the-tree down into second, not bothering to signal, he swung into the right lane to avoid a line of cars backed up at a red light, which he knew would now flash green. Punching the accelerator, he drove through a red light, singing along, feeling splendidly in control, striking a farmer match to a cigarette, and then hanging a left on Park. With the accelerator pressed harder, deeper through the turn, he ground the shifter back into third to drop the slack. He felt like he could do no wrong, as he sang along with Jim all the way down to the docks and the Golden Hands Massage Parlor, parking in the back alley, front bumper jarring a dumpster.

So as to arrive unannounced he was going to slip under the beam that tripped the alert signal upstairs but there was someone, some bitch coming at him all wrapped up in motocross gear, walking like

Frankenstein. She lifted her visor then said she quit. He called her a Retard and she countered, calling him a Fucktard. *Bitch*!

Without batting an eye he told her she was fired, etc. This and her whining retort which he countered by shaking his ass at her showed that he had won the exchange. Chuckling, he took the stairs two at a time.

On an authoritative walk he went twice around the massage cubicles huddled like roofless shanties in the center of the loft space, giving a little extra action to his heels to tear up the silence, the exercise a simple reminder to the masseuses cowering over their clients in their cubicles that there was a boss and here he was.

He knew they knew. He didn't have to say a word, just let his boots do the talking, strutting down the center aisle of the cubicles, door curtains billowing before him, no masseuse so much as daring to poke her head out for a peek at him as he more shouted than sang *Light My Fire*, hearing masseuses shushing their clients' questions as to who the hell was that. "Don't ask."

"*C'est moi*," he boomed, "*Jacques!*" Then a jet flew over, rattling the building. Cobb threw his arms out and made a noise deep in his throat to imitate its roar, running down the aisle between the cubicles up and back again and around before half circling around to the office off the top of the stairs, yanking out his key chain then shoving the key in the lock. He threw open the door of Margaret's little claustrophobic burrow and its acrid smell of the aged. The gist of Cobb's modus operandi expressed in the dictum *To surprise is to control*, he took by surprise to maintain control, watching her, Margaret Manager, spring from the couch, afghan clutched to her chest.

"Snoozing again, Margaret?" He stomped across the wooden floor. "Didn't even hear the alarm, huh?"

Groggy, irritated, her hair was mussed and the sides of her face sleep sagged and patterned with the loops of the afghan, she snapped, "You always burst in here like a madman, Jack."

"How's biz?"

"For Christ sakes thought you were in Siam still."

Margaret wasn't up on her geography and, by Cobb's design, Cobb's schedule. "I'm obviously back now," he said, grabbing the box of envelopes off the top of the little refrigerator, then rifling the money from each envelope after checking that the amount squared with the number of massages and the gain (both penned in Margaret's griffonage across the back of each envelope). He held the bills pulled from each envelope between different fingers, half curling them there in a kind of stadium vendor's trick.

Margaret cleared her throat then brought him up to date. "That crazy Frank Johnson tried another suicide massage on Trish. The floor of her cubicle was just covered with pills." For emphasis, Margaret lifted up the folds of the afghan, as if they were wings. "All kinds of pills." Widening her eyes, she flapped her arms again. "All colors. All shapes. A dozen prescription jars and caps lying among them. Pills across the floor. Across her table. Went in to see her afterwards, just now, standing there in her underpants and putting on her gear. Said she's quitting. Not coming back."

Cobb interrupted his counting. "I know. Tell me about her."

Margaret sighed. "She's pretty. A redhead. Fiery temper fitting to redheads. American. The one you were worried about, the one you thought was snotty."

Cobb studied Margaret through squinting eyes.

"Oh, come on, Jack. You know. The biker bitch, the lezzi redhead."

"Oh. *Her.* Couldn't see her face cause she had a helmet on."

"Probably going to that new place," Margaret said. "Just saw another ad for it." Her voice rising, mimicking the copy, *"Only one week until the massage of your life. Massage World."* Then she shifted, exclaiming, *"Your world."*

"Fuck world," Cobb sneered, then had an idea. "Listen, Margaret. When this Frank guy calls for Trish again, make sure to tell him exactly where she went. Have him do his suicide number on her there."

"Where?"

"At Massage World."

"I'm sure he'll be calling for her. He's always calling for her."

"Then be sure to tell him that Trish is now gainfully employed at Massage World. Give him explicit directions how to get there. Help him fill his prescriptions even. Chauffeur him to the pharmacy if you have to. Whatever it takes to get your Frank Johnson to do himself there."

"Where?"

"God damnit! *At Massage World!*"

She jerked back her head. "You don't have to shout."

With his pockets packed with wads of bills, he stomped across the floor toward Margaret, a finger motioning for her to move, toward him, and fast. "Get up."

"I'm going to throw your little toy away," she threatened.

"Get up," he repeated, a hand already on the cushion under her.

She shook her head in disgust, threw the blanket aside and stood, brushing the wrinkles from her white nurse-like dress.

He tore off a cushion, pushing it to the floor, then dug into the couch, slipping his hands under the back rest. He pulled out the 38 pistol by its muzzle, checked the clip then shoved the barrel half down his pants. He zipped up his leather coat to cover the bulge.

"On a mission, Jack?"

He ignored her, stomping back across the wooden floor.

She wore a grandmotherly expression. "Where you going?"

"Fishing, damnit!"

"Fishing? What!?"

He slammed the door behind him and ran down the rickety back stairs leading to the alley, wanting to take a look at Massage World.

INGRID

W as still trembling, having just buried Max under some stones and not much dirt, before cabbing to the mansion. She ran up the walk and the stylobate steps, across the peristyle, past the fluted columns of Massage World. Her hand shook, taking three tries to thread the skeleton key in the lock.

She was the first one there as usual. The smell of fresh paint greeted her, along with ladders rising to a regal balcony and a grand stairway swirling down to giant sheet-draped statues of Androgeus, a skillful wrestler, and Hermes, the god of commerce, invention, cunning, theft. The sound of peanut shells crunching under her feet seemed to echo as she strode over a half-acre of vinyl and newspaper protecting the checkerboard floor, her eyes going back and forth, searching for illegal immigrants from Mexico. She had set up an office in a sauna where she now played back messages, jotted down numbers and names, returned calls, set up outcalls and interviews with masseuses. She looked around as she talked, remembering the old Mexican man she had thought was retrieving his possessions from a massage room (from what the landlady said she rented out as storage rooms). He was so unlike the others scrambling through to the back saying *No Ingles* to her *Stop right there!* She never knew where the migrant workers fled.

Sometimes in the morning she'd catch one or two men sleeping somewhere then roused them out clutching their hobo's bundle of belongings. Once Ingrid watched an old Chicano fellow waltz in, reeking of beer, singing mariachi, giving her a sloppy grin.

Nodding, she grinned back, hoping, despite an obvious language barrier, to learn what he thought he was doing in her mansion. He motioned for her to follow him into a sauna, where he pantomimed sawing the sauna benches a certain way so he could open them like a trap door. He proudly showed off the Hardy-Boy hinge work in the sauna, opening the trick door to darkness below. Neck craning, Ingrid sniffed dry dirt. Then she had a carpenter nail closed the funny trap-door business the next day, but still she was worried that there were more such mysterious entrances.

JACKSON COBB

Was headed to Massage World. He drove back up Park, sailing through another light just as it flashed green, encouraging him to belt out, along with Jim Morrison on the CD, a snatch of *The Crystal Ship*.

He turned left on Orange then took a quick right on Melon, passing stately old mansions then the towering structure of the hospital. He turned off the music, peering from the passenger window to a construction dumpster ahead on the left then, in a front window, the burning red neon letters: *Massage World 5655*.

Will be my world, he thought. Behind an iron-rail fence rose a fricking mansion, with palacious columns, balconies, French windows, and a majestic entrance. He switched off the engine, punched off the lights, rolled down the window, lit another cigarette and stared, letting schemes, like pachinko balls, clatter through his mind. On his thigh he traced the Japanese ideograms for "mine" (*jibun no mono).*

Seeing someone, Cobb sank down, peeking over the wheel to watch an old man totter toward him on the moonlit sidewalk, toting a plastic-handled shopping bag. He stopped against the fence, the points of which glowed like spear tips in the moonlight. He did some trick with a bar, jimmying it out of something, creating a gap that he slipped through. He replaced the bar then walked around the north corner of Massage World.

Fifteen minutes passed before someone else came along. A young woman humming as she swished down the sidewalk in the moonlight, in some kind of tent dress, judging from its shape. Under a fluffy cap her dark hair frizzed out and her makeup seemed thick. Judging by her features and complexion, Cobb thought that maybe she was Latina. She appeared to be solidly built, broad shoulders clear in the dress. She too looked both ways then did the thing with the bar, slipped into the yard, walked around the palms, oleanders, and lesser bougainvillea before disappearing around the corner where the old man had gone.

Cobb himself looked both ways then eased open his van door, snuck out, gently closed the door to the point that the interior light switched off in a gentle click. He went over to the fence and shook a few bars before finding the one that gave. He slipped through, replaced the bar, walked around the trees toward the house, and peeked around the corner. The woman was standing, her dress hiked up, pissing on a shrub the way a man would piss on a shrub. She was a man, he realized, a transgender.

Cobb remembered driving up Worth one day and seeing about a dozen people like her walking on the sidewalk in full camp, recalling an article in the daily about a roving gang of Mexican transvestites, and how they had been robbing and harassing people in the park. Captivated, Cobb studied her profile and the moonlit arch of urine.

She finished, turning toward the house and a screen-like grate. Cobb cleared his throat to alert her to his presence, as he walked closer, fingering a wad of bills in his pocket, pondering how to word a proposal. She gasped, holding up her hands, saying, in a pissy English voice, "What you want? Who you are?"

"*Hola,*" Cobb said, getting the mothballs out of his Spanish. "*Habla Ingles?*"

"Yes, I speak *Ingles*. Now what you want?"

"*Adonde va usted?* In there?" Cobb pointed to the crawlspace grate at the base of the house.

"Why you ask?"

Cobb touched his chest and jiggled his hips side to side. "*Yo le quiero.*" He had to bite his lip to keep from laughing.

"No more room. You go." She crossed her arms, not budging. "I tell you to go." She pointed in the direction Cobb had come.

Cobb pulled out a fifty and handed it to her. "I'll give you fifty more if you show me the way in. *Entonces mucho mas.*" He reached out to touch her cheek. "*Tu eres bonita.*"

INGRID,

When stressed, was having more and more trouble relaxing. She sensed that something was different in the mansion without being able to put her finger on just what. It had to be the illegals. Like stray cats that kept getting in the yard, and there was no keeping them out. The landlady ignored her complaints as day by day their clutter grew back up, stacked to precarious heights, into which, up high in the salon, someone had stuffed, like a diving board, a single fold-up massage table left over from when the mansion was a spa in the nineties. Big in the nineties, a Sit Sauna had half blocked the landing and resembled a deep freezer, the hole on top for one's head filled one morning with the scruffy face of a sleeping Mexican who Ingrid woke then chased out.

At the foot of the sculptures, and pitched over clotheslines tied off at outlandish junctures, old blankets and bolts of canvas had formed tents. (Ingrid would cut them down one day then see them pitched back up the next.) In fact, the entire salon area had resembled an antebellum salon fashioned into a makeshift hospital that took in Civil War wounded. Up to one's knees ran the litter of food tins, soda plastic and cans, fast-food wrappers, newspapers, Spanish-language magazines, porno centerfolds, busted crates, half-crushed boxes, empty cigarette packs, match covers, and towering over one's head plastic garbage bags full of broken treasures loaded into stolen shopping carts.

Having trod through the first time behind the landlady in bleached blonde pigtails and day-glow pink bicycle pants, Ingrid and her junior partner Erma commented on the mess. Money counter she was, the landlady took care to accent the positive with her flashlight beam, opening the door of an old massage room, flashlight beam splintering into a thousand bits of light strewn across ceiling and walls. "This was our mirror-ball room," she explained, going on about the celebrity photos on the wall, all clients of hers back when she ran the spa way back in the nineties.

It was all so old, Ingrid thought. But the old place had its charms. Ingrid agreed to the deal. Money changed hands, leases were signed, and licenses were applied for. For the business to be considered a spa, however, they had to follow the adult entertainment laws that massage fell under, which meant they needed an on-premise barbershop (which they decided to install)—or a doctor, chiropractor, acupuncturist, or holistic health practitioner—as stipulation to frustrate the happy-go-lucky plans of just anyone wanting to open a massage business.

As refuge from the tedious details Ingrid liked to give herself over to manual labor, now chiseling past the soreness of her muscles and taking satisfaction only when a whole clean tile snapped off. She cursed bits of tile flying into her face as the painters announced themselves downstairs in a drop of paint cans hitting the floor in a hollow thud. Then, a few minutes later, Erma Debaggio arrived with her husband Johnny. A junior partner and friend of Ingrid's from their days together at Magic Spa, Erma was a complex person, having a Master's in chemistry yet was totally new age. In other words, a Millennial hippy, retro all the way.

Into crystals, herbology, tarot, incense, palmistry, and eye readings, Erma had dragged Ingrid to the Indian sweat tent thing in the desert where Ingrid had tried to give away all her anxiety only to have it return now—with interest. Ingrid regretted recruiting Erma who was proving herself too flaky (call it *crystally*), arriving later each day with one excuse or another. Or calling to say she had a load of laundry going or the truck wouldn't start. And bringing this jerk, Johnny, some cowboy hillbilly loser drunk boyfriend.

Erma bade a cheerful, "Good morning," standing in the doorway, watching Ingrid work.

Without looking away from her tools, Ingrid nodded, listening to Erma's husband walk through the rubble, wondering if he were drunk already.

"Had trouble getting Johnny's truck going," Erma explained.

"You need another chisel, Ingrid," Johnny advised. "I've been telling you that for weeks."

At that moment Ingrid's chisel failed to make a purchase and went skittering, the hammer head glancing off her knuckle and nearly crushing her hand. She winced, sucking in air then licking a spot of blood from the gash.

"See!?" Johnny crooned. "It's that chisel. What I tell ya, Ingrid?"

"You all right, Ing?" Erma asked.

Trying to ignore them, Ingrid snapped off three whole tiles in as many blows. She was tired of having to put them to work each morning. They knew what had to be done but just stood there watching her work. Had they no conscience?

"Johnny," Erma said, "I think Ingrid is doing quite well."

Johnny lit a cigarette. "Tell ya, with a new chisel, she'd be doing much better."

Louder hammer blows punctuated the silence between them, as did Ingrid kicking around in the rubble in the tub where she felt caught, trapped in their attention.

Erma said, "After going to the pistol range last night we took a look at a new truck."

"A good used truck anyway," Johnny corrected.

Everything about the guy irritated Ingrid. Unclipped nostril hair. Neck beard growing down to his chest hair. Long greasy ponytail. The way he smoked: holding the cigarette prissily, his lips making a popping sound when he inhaled. Ingrid couldn't understand what Erma saw in him. Now he slouched against the jam and intoned in his desert hillbilly accent, "Hell, get me a decent truck and we'll be here on time."

Ingrid let her arms drop to her sides. "What's the point of coming in at all, if you're just going to stand around and watch me work all day?"

Just then the foreman of the painting crew came down the hall. He entered the bathroom, demanding back pay, taking a pencil from behind his ear to make a show of formally writing down, on the back of a scrap of sandpaper, what she would say. Ingrid explained that he'd be paid a week later than scheduled. Having covered the same ground each morning this week, they had to go over it again.

Johnny slinked away on the heels of the painter, mumbling something about going out for a new chisel. Erma said it was time to get to her sanding, something she lost herself in every day, as if she were trying to sand away her frustrations: Johnny's drinking and his carrying on around the place as if he owned it and doing absolutely nothing in the way of help at home or at the mansion.

Ingrid went downstairs for her thermos then saw Johnny instructing the painters in their business, telling them to "*roll it out more so the drops don't show. Gotta roll it out better than that, son.*" He stared at their labors, while lighting one cigarette off the butt of another. Inhaling deeply and squinting pensively, he said, "That won't do, friend. Gotta roll it all out smooth like I said. Baby's bottom is what we're after here.

We got over two hundred fricking grand sunk in this place. More money than you'll see in your lifetime. So let's get it right, son."

"I thought you were going out for a chisel," Ingrid reminded him, heading off a scene with the unpaid painters.

"And here I go," he said, slinking off.

Four hours later he returned staggering drunk, starting in on the painters again. "I tell y'all that paint ain't rolled out right."

Two young men doing the rolling exchanged glances as if saying—"What's with this jerk?" Erma merely hid in her sanding, feverishly scraping at cabinets.

"Let me take a step back so I can see it all straight up like Jack Daniels," Johnny said, then tripped. "Ohhh shit!" He landed, sprawling onto a pile of drywall scraps. Regaining his feet, he brushed at his chalk-streaked jeans, crooning, "Fellahs, that simply won't get it done roun' these parts."

Ingrid couldn't help herself. "Listen, you drunken...hillbilly... asshole: *Shut...the...fuck...up!*" She stepped closer. "The only time I saw you try to do any work was the time we rolled up that carpet, but you couldn't even bend over. The other time was when you started chiseling tile. You swung the hammer a few times, then swore a few times, then ran off to the nearest bar. Then came back like you are now, hillbilly drunk."

"I'm not drunk. Told you I was out gettin' y'all a new chisel."

"Okay, where's the chisel?"

"Fuck you, Ingrid," he slurred, his head wiggling in that way common to drunks. His lip curled sheepishly. "Fuck you."

The painters stopped their work, poised on knees, stilts, and step-ladders. Their rollers and brushes as quiet as kittens in their hands. The only sound came from Erma grinding away at the cabinetwork, dumb in her stupid sanding.

Breaking the tension, a businessman walked in. "Knock, knock," he announced, standing near the door, his hands adjusting an expensive wool suit coat.

"Can I help you?" Ingrid asked.

"I saw the sign and need a massage, but..." He looked around, holding up his hands to indicate disarray.

Ingrid told him to come back for the opening on Friday, handing him a business card.

"I will do that. Some time in the afternoon. Champagne and

massage. Two of my favorite things. Cheers."

"Where's this chisel you promised me, Johnny." Her anger sharpening her wit, she held out a hand. "Hand it over then drop your drawers and bend over." She chuckled, as did the painters.

"I said, fuck you, Ingrid." He looked down, his expression pouting.

"Pull them down," Ingrid ordered, stepping closer.

He shrieked, "I said *fuck you*, Ingrid!" He kicked at a pile of drywall scraps, raising a cloud of dust, then nearly fell over, bringing more laughter down from the ladders. "I put so much fuckin' work into this place and you treat me like shit!" Johnny started for the door, then veered, dipping a shoulder and circling. "Honey, you comin'?"

Erma kept sanding, sanding and sanding at a feverish pace.

"Honey, you comin'!?"

Erma sped up the rhythm of her sanding, sawdust cloud billowing up around her head.

"I said, 'hONey, YOU coMIN'!? BItCH, coMIN'!?'"

A sob pulled at her shoulders as her sanding ground to a halt. She swung around, throwing the sanding block down, jumped up and down, tears springing from her face. "No, fuck you, Johnny! I ain't comin'! I ain't comin'! Hear me?! I ain't comin'! I ain't comin'! I ain't comin'."

Her voice hoarse, hurt clear in her eyes, she wept, then buried her face in her hands. Johnny did a tortured dance, whipping his arms back and forth as if they were rope, shaking his head and stomping his feet. "Fuck fuck fuck." Arms behind his back, he did a little tap dance, chanting, "Fuck fuck fuck." Voice escalating, "Fuck fuck fuck. Fuck your booty." He bent over, picked up a sharp chunk of scrap wood, then flung it side-arm style at the new drywall, in which it stuck like a martial arts star. Throwing up his arms he puffed out his cheeks and looked like a puffer fish, but was actually mimicking a bomb exploding, arms thrust out, exhaling. "That's what I'm going to do. Blow up this whole fucking shit hole. Take back every lick of work I put in."

Looking mean, one of the more muscular painters jumped off a ladder, chest and biceps bulging under a white t-shirt. He strode toward Johnny. "We've heard enough from you, friend."

Lunging, Johnny took a wild swing at the painter, who ducked then caught Johnny up in an arm twist behind his back, using the hold to escort him outside.

"Let go, fucker! Don't let me go in three seconds and I'll be back around. With a sidearm. Swear I will. Blow the shit out of you. Blow the shit out of this whole shit ass dump of a massage fuck!"

The painter pushed him away then faked a chase after Johnny running off like frightened sheep, Erma following until Ingrid cut between her and the door, catching Erma in her arms. "Let him go, Erm."

"Oh, Ingrid," Erma bawled into Ingrid's sweatshirt. "What am I gonna do?"

"Forget him, Erm. Go back to your precious sanding. Lose yourself in your work. It's what I'm doing to forget about Max."

"What happened to Max?" Erma asked between sobs.

Ingrid described the shooting, the red-haired vice cop, his threats, the struggle to bury Max that morning.

"If this cop said something about Massage World," Erma said, "then he'll be coming around. We'll get the creep then, Ing."

Anger swelling, Ingrid didn't say anything but hugged Erma tighter for the thought. Stood there patting Erma's back, knowing she was right—that they'd get the red-haired creep cop.

COBB

Watched the she-male or he-she back off, holding the bill in such a way as to study it in the moonlight. "What your name?"

"Jack Spratt. Yours?"

"Juanita." Juanita held the fifty up to an ear and rubbed the folds together. Satisfied, she shoved the bill down a neckline plunging to the bumps of breasts and bra. *A pre-op transgender woman,* Cobb thought. *Or a hormone queen in high drag.* In either case, he accommodated her, saying, "Lady, it's the real thing. As I said, there's more if you show me the way in." He went over to the grate and kicked it lightly. "Now where does this lead?"

Juanita's tone softened. "Why you want to know? Who you are?"

"A night man and admirer," he said. "Who likes you so I followed you."

Cobb watched Juanita checking him out. "You *macho,* and handsome."

"And I have *dinero.*"

Juanita touched her breasts with the heels of her hands. *"Dinero* help me become more of a woman." She made a guillotining motion across her groin, causing even Cobb to wince. She moved closer to Cobb, looking up into his face, one hand spreading over his crotch, the other grabbing his jacket lapel. "You come with me, Jack?"

"Where?"

"Under house to secret place. There secret door in floor, our home under stairs, between walls. We move walls. We sleep here. *Eet* too cold camping in canyons. You come, Jack?"

"After you, Juanita. After you."

Without hesitation, Juanita reached down and pulled off the grate, got down on all fours, and swiveled her head to instruct Cobb to slide the grate to where it had been, then fearlessly crawled and disappeared into the darkness. Cobb wrestled the grate back in place then followed, the powdery dirt cold and hard under his hands and kneecaps. The space smelled like rotting wood and dry crawl space dirt. He reached up just over his head to feel gritty floor joists then crawled after the *shushing* of Juanita's dress, biting his lip when the spangles of a bottle cap had dug into his palm.

"Where are you, Juanita?" Unable to see anything, he crawled deeper under the house, in the direction of her cackle, changing direction after pulling sheets of spider webs from his face and spitting them out of his mouth. "Let me hear your laughter. Say something, Juanita." He felt for his lighter. "Where is this trap door? Juanita!?"

Then dim light spilled down as she pressed up against a trap door twenty feet away. Cobb crawled toward the light, hearing footsteps overhead. In the pool of light Cobb poked his head up, smelling sterno and kerosene. He saw the shapes of men sprawled around, staring at the newcomer as if he had emerged from the sea. Then on another side were a few others, sitting with their backs to the wall before a lantern burning on an overturned crate. They looked at Cobb as Juanita explained his presence in rapid Spanish.

"*Buenas noches*," Cobb said, extending a hand that they ignored.

The spoke quickly in Spanish to Juanita, who started singing to block them out.

"Time to go, *amigo*."

Cobb pulled out his piece, aiming it at the floor. "I'm not going anywhere, friend." *Fucking macho assholes, maybe I'll have to aim it at them.*

Cobb felt Juanita pulling him away. "This way, Jack."

They walked under staircase creases that wound up high out of the lantern light when he kicked something, a dead flashlight battery skittering across the floor.

"Shhhh," Juanita warned.

Juanita led him down a space narrowing into a hallway about four feet wide. "We see into all these rooms for massage." She ran her hand across exposed studs. "We see through the mirrors." She pointed to a hole where drywall had been chipped away, revealing the blackened side of a mirror whose paint had been scratched off.

In the split second Cobb hunkered closer to squint through the back of the mirror and he had a déjà vu moment that left him gasping: *watching Janice Verdurin through the same mirror he had torn of drywall then scraped off the paint with a razor blade. His arms crossed, he stood there, staring at her, his chest in flames from the pain, working on some businessman asshole he had given her to see which way she'd go. The wrong way, he saw, his penis in her hands, his hand reaching back around her ass somewhere he couldn't see slipping into the tight space his hand where Cobb had just been himself as she smiled down at him the same way she smiled up at him when they made love. She was enjoying it. The whore! He banged on the mirror, yelling for her to stop. She continued jacking him, casting a startled glance back toward the door then around the room. "Janice!" he yelled, pummeling the mirror. "Janice!" She then fixed a gaze at the mirror his fists were banging, mouthing the word, "Jack?"*

"Jack." Juanita pushed him away from the mirror. "What *ees* wrong with you? You shaking there. You loco?"

"Huh? Oh, nothing. *Nada.*"

"Too dark now. But I take you in for short time. We go through secret door. Okay, Jack? But no turn on lights."

"Lights?" he said, still shaken from the vision, then attributing it to the speed he had injected.

"*Esta bien, Jack?*"

"Yeah, bien, bien," he said, composing himself. "Tell me," he asked, scheming, "do you have any *amigas*? Like yourself? You know...?"

As if scorned, she looked at him suspiciously. "You don't like me, Jack?"

He grabbed her hands. "I like you. I like you. But I need you and your *amigas* to help me with something."

"What?"

"Some simple fun."

"Just fun?"

"A lotta fun." He dug a wad of bills from his pocket. "Where are your friends, Juanita?"

"Y por que?"

"I want them here." He waved the money, watching the shadow of his hand on the back of the drywall and on the eyes of Juanita hypnotized by the money going back and forth. "I want them here as soon as possible."

"I go to Frontera and get them, Jack. We do banzai cross."

"I want you to show me every little peep hole."

"Si, si, Jack."

"I want you to show me all around this place. Back here. On the other side. Everywhere." He tapped the wall. "Now here's a hundred for the tour. Another hundred for your friends in Frontera."

Juanita rubbed the bills together again.

"Call it crossing money. There'll be three hundred more after we have some fun. Right in here." He tapped the wall. "In Massage World."

INGRID

Under stress liked to eat, and as such had just wolfed down an old piece of pizza the painters had left behind in its delivery box. Just after midnight she slipped off her shirt and bra to take a G.I. Joe, or a sink bath, aka upper-body scrubbing. Having half bathed and half changed, she dashed to her now ringing phone.

"This is Ingrid. Hello? I can hardly hear you. Who is this?" A sinking feeling. "Is this you, Cobb?"

"You sound like quite a businesswoman: 'This is Ingrid.' Well, Ingrid, this could very well be your most lucky day, not only because we have a fine connection bouncing off satellites but—"

"Lucky day? What are you talking about, Corn Cobb?"

"That's Mr. Cobb to you, Swan River. But listen. I got an old lady here in Japan staring me down for calling you at her expense. Anyway, I'm looking at what could very well be your salvation."

"What are you talking about, crazy corn on the Cobb?"

"I may, though I'll hate myself for it since it goes against my instincts, Swan Song, be a nice guy and buy you out instead of taking your ass over."

"Taking my ass over?"

"But I don't know," Cobb continued, "the way the old girl's looking at me now, Swanny, I don't know if she's good for the hundred and change."

"Hundred?" Ingrid asked. "Hundred what?"

"Hundred thousand banzais," Cobb said. "Hundred thousand K, as in clams. Hundred fricking thousand, Swan Lake. Don't make me draw you a picture or I'll lose it and hang up, all right?"

"A hundred thousand dollars for what?"

"What else? Your Massage Country, of course."

"I told you I'm not selling," she said, then snapped, "And it's Massage World!"

"Then you're basically saying," he said calmly, ignoring her tedious correction, "that Massage Country's mine for the taking? Try to be a nice guy and—"

"Go fuck yourself, Cobb." She cut the line. Closing her eyes, belly breathing, which did nothing to reduce the dread of unimaginable horrors heading her way.

JANICE VERDURIN

H ad just gotten off the phone with Ingrid, the Massage World interview was all set for tomorrow, when Cobb burst into the Near East Spa. A black girl of about sixteen trailed after him. His goatee heightened his wickedness, as did his eyes sickling back and forth communicating, *THINGS IN ORDER? WHERE'S THE LOOT?!* His greed, his masculinity (nothing was ever enough for Cobb) by turns vexed Janice and tongue-tied her. She could never really stand up to him, though, without hesitating and stuttering, like now, when she wanted to tell him off for throwing the door open and exploding into the room. And with a minor who he had been screwing from the first trial session, or interview even. This new favorite's name was Darlene. But what Darlene didn't know was that she was about twenty minutes away from being *sacrificed*, as Cobb had told Janice, *to keep the troops in line.*

INGRID

Was near the fountain, under shadows thrown by the statues of Androgeus and Hermes, where she had assembled her staff of massage technicians. They sat on the fountain or against it as she lectured. "As you can see on the chart here there are seven basic types of postures. I want all of you to not only memorize them but also assimilate them into your massage repertoires. Eventually you'll be able to do a quick diagnostic while you're giving your client a tour of the facilities, that is, before you even go into a session. Watch how he or she moves. Listen to what he or she reveals about their career or what have you. Does your client work at a desk and need a lot of neck and back work? Does he work with his hands and have any pain anywhere? Then align the massage with the job and body profile, making sure to tell the client that your assessment is done in order to give him the best possible customized massage. Again, it's crucial to explain why you're asking the questions because many clients are paranoid about questions and especially paranoid about giving you their names. So explain as you're taking mental notes that everything is strictly confidential. If they don't want to give you their name and information that's fine too. At the end of session when you're seeing them to the door make sure to give them our business card, even though they'll probably toss it in the bushes so the wife doesn't freak out as to where hubby's been. Any confusion so far?"

In Ryoji's fixed grin Ingrid read confusion. "Ryoji, do you understand all of this?"

"*Hai.* I mean, yes, yes, I understand."

"Even though you'll be doing mainly shiatsu, Ryoji," Ingrid continued, "listen to my explanation of each profile so that you can at least get an idea of the concept."

He nodded. "*Sank you, sank you.* I listen."

"Now, the most common type of body profile, as Nitya Lacroix has it in *Massage for Total Relaxation*, is the first one here." She pointed to the flip chart, a photograph of a man with his arms crossed, neck shortened, shoulders lifted and hunkered together. "This body profile is called The Guard. As you can see, he's protecting himself from what he may be perceiving as unwanted feelings and/or stress. He's not conscious to the fact that the pose has tension built into it, tension that is not released when the stressful situation passes. For this type, concentrate the massage on the neck, shoulders, back, and chest muscles to alleviate the upper body tension. Here are the strokes to use." She flipped the page of the flip chart and explained each stroke.

When she was on the profile, The Victim, illustrated by a photograph of a slouching woman, Annabel raised her hand. "Ingrid, I see myself in various photographs there. At times I see myself as a Warrior, all ready for battle, and at other times I'm a total Stoic, carrying the weight of the world on my back without so much as a peep. I guess what I'm trying to say is that it may not be so easy to pigeonhole a client into one of the seven categories."

The insight was intelligent. A holistic health practitioner, Annabel, Ingrid knew, was her best technician. "Good point. I was going to address that later, Annabel, but let me just say that we all know that the complexity of human psychology cannot be clearly reduced to seven simple postures and their accompanying psychological profiles. I'm offering these profiles as rough guidelines. With all my years in massage, I can diagnose almost unconsciously. When I see a Stoic slash Warrior, for example, I know to do a mixed bag of strokes, and then I may even do some crossover moves into Superman and Intellectual if the body isn't responding to type, finally settling into the stroke patterns the client responds most favorably to, both audibly and physically. Then at the end of session I'll amend the client's file with a note—for example, *Definitely more Warrior than Stoic.* The completion of the following session may have me deeming him a Total Warrior. Ensuing sessions will have me going right into Warrior mode then." Now Trish had her hand up. "Trish?"

Trish nodded, and said, "What if the client won't go along with any of these programs? I know that when I was at the Golden Hands, sometimes giving a Warrior the appropriate Warrior massage just wouldn't go. He wouldn't have any of it and wanted nothing but light powder work followed by you know what."

This brought laughter all around. A warrior, Ingrid felt a sudden buildup of tension in her jaw. She knew she had to make the speech and worried that it'd fall flat, since it contradicted her own experience as a freelancer. "Yes, and I was going to address that too, better now than later since you brought it up. Now, the first rule of Massage World forbids giving and/or selling handjobs. Again, handjobs are absolutely forbidden. I assume that's what you are referring to, Trish? Good. There are a number of reasons why, foremost is that massaging the genitalia is considered a sexual massage, which is against the law. Undercover vice officers will surely be around offering you the moon to get you to do just that. Don't. You'll be arrested. The media will report your arrest, given the scale of our enterprise here. Then the ire of the neighbors will be on us. They're already mumbling their suspicions across their hedges. Any time that you're even tempted, and I don't care if Tom Cruise is there begging for relief, just think of the repercussions: jail; humiliation; ten o'clock news; pickets; petitions; angry housewives; religious fundies; court injunctions; and then, maybe, Massage World's demise. Just from," she chuckled, "greasing the meat." Feeling uncomfortable, she looked from masseuse to masseuse, making sure she had established eye contact with each. "So don't grease the meat. That goes for you, too, Ryoji."

A blind man's pose, head inclined that certain way. "Pardon?"

"No greasing the meat," Ingrid said. Laughter fluttered about until Ingrid cut it off. "Now, I'm serious: If I catch any of you giving a sexual massage you're fired."

JANICE VERDURIN

Wanted to ignore Cobb's order for her to start preparing a sacrifice circle for Darlene. She loathed Cobb for the hold that he had on her. And since he had returned from Asia with his Thai playmates he had gotten much worse in every way. He tossed hair from his eyes, scowling. "Who was that on the phone?"

Since Bobbie had thrown a fit and quit, Cobb had Janice assume Bobbie's responsibilities. What he wanted her to do, he had said, was sit there "primly" at the front desk, receive clients, schedule sessions, answer the phone, keep the books, and give an occasional massage. "And of course keep me informed of everything."

She told him who called, saying, "Just some guy who wanted only *to talk* about getting a massage."

He squinted, pissed off. "Why didn't you close him?"

"Can't close everyone," she said. "When I told him the prices he lost interest."

Cobb grunted, grabbed the log book then began tearing out those pages where a masseuse had *menstruated*, his word, about some lunatic on an outcall wanting to grab ass and everything (but for nothing), crumpling up the pages and throwing them at the wastebasket. As he read, he mumbled, "As we all know Darlene's repeats are through the fucking roof. Start preparing a circle for Darlene."

Janice glanced at Darlene, who didn't know what awaited her. Darlene couldn't be over sixteen, woolly hair done up in little pigtails, cheeks rouged up to beat the band. Cobb liked them young, drawn to the young Thai girl, Joom, for the same reason. Darlene hailed from the Deep South and was probably a runaway, and certainly a prostitute (hence the sacrifice circle). She had long red fingernails, the polish sloppily applied, and a gorgeous face. The other night when business was slow she climbed up into the bay window in her mini skirt and did a sexy dance on the sill, singing an old Archies' song, swinging her bottom back and forth, clapping her hands. "Honey. Oh, sugar, sugar." Cars skidded and honked out in the street from near accidents. Men streamed in, pointing, "I want her," demanding a session with Darlene, booking her through to closing. After Darlene finished a session in about twenty minutes (when the client had paid for an hour), she'd strut back out, high assed and beautiful, no less of a sashay in her hips after gobbling up a half dozen men. "Who's next? Oh, hi, honey. Oh, honey, honey. Sugar, sugar. Come on back." She'd get behind them and push playfully. "Gonna give you a *nos* massage."

On her first day, before heading back to the lion's den, Darlene told the masseuses sitting around in front, "Mr. Cobb's gonna teach me massage real good."

Later that same day, despite the masseuse staff's protests, Cobb sent her on an outcall to massage the absolute worst of clients, an old lecherous traveling salesman whose bag of tricks was filled with pornographic paraphernalia he called artwork. Worse, was his filthy tongue. Darlene, however, waltzed back in after the session, saying, "That gentleman, I tell y'all, is a sweetheart. So *nos* that he asked me to come back tomorrow. Wants me to do some kind of plastic wrap massage. We got any that plastic stuff?"

Janice watched Darlene who was beaming now, obviously misreading the reason for the sacrifice circle.

"Y'all gonna have a circle for little ole me?"

"What am I going to tell the clients?" Janice asked Cobb. "She has seven sessions today, starting at five. In fact, she's backed up through Saturday."

"Reschedule them with someone else," Cobb said.

"*Great*. They'll love that."

"Call 'em then, and explain."

"You're not serious," Janice said. "You know men don't leave their real numbers."

Cobb shrugged, answering a call on his cellular as he headed back to his office. Wherever he was, as far away as Thailand or Japan, he called her at odd hours, asking, "Tell me in a hurry, Jan, tell me who's with Barb in 4. Give me the full name. Now, who's down at six-thirty? Who isn't wearing a dress? Who was late? Who's cheating me?" When he intuited that something was amiss there his old van would skid to a stop out front and he'd dash in, stomp down the corridor, opening doors on either side, poking his head into massage rooms. Totally unpredictable. Masseuses never knew when he'd crash from a speed high and turn paranoid, barging into their sessions, wielding a mood as sharp as a dagger. "I smell sex. Is it you? Better not be god damnit."

Then slam the door. He stored a box of envelopes in a locked cabinet in his office. On the phone to Janice, "Jan, get the box, tell me how much is in each envelope. Okay, now read me the log. Who's under quota?"

But now, for the sacrifice circle, masseuses began assembling in front. A frizzy brunette, Connie, a veteran of these things, pointed out to Janice, "Ever since she did her little dance the other night I knew it would be a matter of days before her head rolled and we were drinking champagne."

They brought three bottles from the break room refrigerator and passed out the paper cups. Cobb burst in from the back, stimulating fear and a collective breath drawn. He told the dozen masseuses, "Let's all sit in a circle here. One big happy family. Jan, take the phone off the hook."

Masseuses knelt on the carpet in their dresses. The uninitiated glanced around furtively. Sacrifice circles were always tense. Cobb started by talking about everyday things. "We gotta get our linen counts down. We're using too much cloth, gals. One table sheet must, not should, *must* get a practitioner through an entire shift. Just brush the pubes off after every session. Towel costs are piling up as well. Two or three towels are plenty to get you through a shift. Some of you ninnies are using two or three per session. Just hang them on the rack in the sauna after the client has showered unless they reek noticeably. Keep rotating towels through the sauna after each session, and maybe even make a little speech about the towel coming straight from the drier, all folded up and toasty warm, held up to the client's face after having just come from wiping the oil off another's arse, but of course what Joe Blow doesn't know won't hurt him, but what he should know are the little things like toasty warm towels being proof positive of the Near East's commitment to superior service. Next problem is going over the allotted time. You're all guilty here, girls. If a client pays for a half hour, he should be the hell *outta here in a half hour.* Wrap up the session in nineteen minutes on the nose. Right when the timer sounds. If he's not a regular but rather some putz who just wants to hang around, maybe jerk off other putzes in the sauna or shower, tell him all the saunas are broken or time's up or anything. Just get 'em the fuck out pronto. Move 'em up. Move 'em out." He drew an invisible circle with his hand, like a football coach signaling to keep the clock running. "Now let's uncork the bubbly."

Corks ricocheted off the drop ceiling then bounced around on the floor. Cobb poured sparkling wine into paper cups. "To our happy family at the Near East Spa. Cheers!" Cups were tipped together, wine drunk. Another bottle poured around. "Okay," Cobb said, "now let's go around. Everybody say how they like it here."

Laureen, brushing back thin red hair from a freckled forehead, said, "I like my job at the Near East Spa. I'm happy to be working."

Toni, the popular African American masseuse, lied, "I'm glad to be supporting myself by doing something I enjoy."

Joom, the young new Thai masseuse, said, "Me like massaging American men. Me like American men!"

Everyone laughed. When their turn came they lied. Said any little cliche but the truth which was that they were poor and needed the bread.

Most of them being path-of-least-resistance people, Janice felt a certain superiority over her colleagues, what with her grad school ambitions.

Cobb pointed at the new girl Darlene. "Okay, next item. Darlene there the other day went on an outcall massage and gave a sexual massage. She had sex with a client. Then she did the same thing here on the premises. In fact, several times. Therefore Darlene no longer works here. Darlene is fired. Darlene, go get your things and get out." He pointed at the door.

At this sudden turn of mood, Darlene wailed, burying her face in her hands. Fear was a big animal breathing in all the air in the room, leaving the women gulping and sweating and those who wore tight collared dresses pulling at their collars and fanning their faces. The Thai masseuses and Toni started to comfort Darlene but Cobb motioned them away. "Anyone so much as pats her back they join her."

Darlene stood, sobbing. "Just getting my bag."

Janice ran back and got it, handing it to her, saying, "Probably best to leave this dump anyway."

Cobb ignored her insubordination, repeating his dictum, "A session should never go any farther than a *prosterate*. Remember that. 'Cause I'll catch ya. Like I caught Darlene. Clients backed up now till Sunday. Jesus. Cops'll have us busted and closed down. All it takes is one simple blurb in the paper to keep clients away for weeks. They don't want to be caught going to no whorehouse. We're selling massage. Not... you know what. And I'll say it one more time: Darlene, kindly get yours the hell out of here. And watch it going out. Or you might find the door knob up it."

Janice watched Toni and everyone else, looking down, looking away, and didn't like what she was feeling, this severe trespass on decency that the maniac Cobb was doing. Who was next? Janice remembered when he once fired three-fourths of his staff. Then he went out in his van to pick up their replacements off the street where he found Darlene. Cobb looked at his clipboard. "Now let's get to the next item. Missy and Beth, where are you?" One overweight woman in her early forties, Missy, with long brown hair and large breasts, and a tall thin woman, in her late twenties, with a librarian's mousiness in thick glasses, big ears and braided hair, both touched their chests, swallowed largely, and held their breath. In professional mode, Cobb knitted his brows and spoke in a deep voice, "The log indicates that both Missy and Beth have failed to draw sufficient return clientele, which is forty percent as you all know. Why is this?"

"Why is it forty percent you mean?" Janice asked, snickering.

"Duh," Cobb said. "Why is it that Missy and Mousy failed to achieve forty percent? Well, I'll tell you why: it's because they're not giving the house massage. It's simple." He banged the side of his clipboard on the floor for each word. "If you don't... administer... the prosterate... then you won't make your quota. But if you're too ambitious like little Darlene up over ninety percent, doing everything from *half and halfs* to peanut butter and jellies, then you're history as well. Too high a risk either way." Cobb shook his head, looked around, holding up his hands, and asking, "Questions?"

Janice herself never had enough repeat clientele but had learned to cook the books. She'd write in names like Mr. T. Smith, under Wednesday. Or: *Tom Smith*, the following Wednesday. Then on Friday, she'd write Thomas Smith in again. Then Mr. T. K. Smith on Monday. Then Ron Snyder maybe twice a week, like that, careful not to have too many or too few *repeats*, keeping her quota just over forty. The few masseuses Janice liked, such as Colleen and Toni, she cooked the books for as well. Envious, the half dozen street tough prostitutes among them sneered at Janice's deskwork job. Janice hated the shitty middle person role. Hated Cobb even more for his making her do the calculations, figure out the percentages, and thus serving as an accomplice hatchet person of sorts in his ruthless firings. That Beth and Missy stood up and left with dignity gave her little mollification.

INGRID

C alled on Bobbie when she raised her hand. To Ingrid, Bobbie was a paradox as she seemed at once too loose (a bra-less strutter of her stuff and raunchy raconteur of dirty jokes with both masseuses and workmen puttering around) and too ambitious (she showed a wily inquisitiveness in asking Ingrid about her and everyone else's background while making it clear that she was very much interested in putting in "*boocoo* hours" and doing the reception/ schedule/desk work as well. ("As I told Erma, I've worked as a receptionist, secretary, and masseuse, Ingrid. I'm perfectly capable of juggling all three at Massage World.")

"Bobbie?" Ingrid pointed to her.

"I have a question."

"Go ahead."

"Some men, especially older men, have prostrate conditions and—"

"You mean *prostate*," Ingrid corrected her, softening the severity of correction with a wise grin.

Bobbie blushed but continued unabated. "Yes, some men have a *prostate* condition that requires massaging. I assume we'll be permitted, then, to give prostate massages."

"In all my years in massage," Ingrid countered, "I've never had a man ask me for a prostate massage."

"I've had several," Bobbie countered.

"And what did you do?" Ingrid shot back.

"I put the client at ease," Bobbie said, "by giving him what he wanted."

With a Mona Lisa grin, Ingrid stared at Bobbie and challenged, "Which was?"

Bobbie didn't hesitate, proclaiming, "A prostate massage."

Ingrid pressed on, taking a step closer to Bobbie, asking, "Did the client ejaculate?"

Bobbie stammered, "Um, no, not that I know of anyway." She crossed her arms and lowered her chin (a typical guard defense).

"Well," Ingrid said, "it sounds suspicious to me."

Bobbie sounded both irritated and childish as she asked, "Why?"

"Because the prostate is in the criminalized zone," Ingrid explained. "Under the drape and out of bounds." Then Ingrid threw the challenge back. "That's why. Men will say anything to get you to massage there. This prostate business sounds like such a thing."

"I thought the same, Ingrid," Bobbie said. "But clients have shown me legitimate letters from medical doctors prescribing just such a massage."

"Curious," Ingrid said, foreseeing obvious problems with Bobbie. "Where was this now?"

"In a holistic health center in Hayden."

"Well," Ingrid said, "if any client comes in with such a letter direct him to me first. Okay? Now, Erma wants to talk about some other diagnostic measures."

In her knee-length suede boots, white pants, and pink and white striped shirt complementing her rosy cheeks and big brown eyes, Erma, Ingrid's junior partner, took the floor then and lectured on palmistry and eye color analysis as a diagnostic of character type and therefore massage style. Ingrid could not help but notice a curious response to Erma's new-age magic show when Bobbie, perhaps a little piqued about the prostate standoff, directed a roll-of-the-eye sneer at Trish, who replied with a grin, then a lowering of her head to cover choked back laughter, implying that Erma was too *crystally* for them.

Then Ryoji got up, introduced himself and bowed. In his serviceable English he talked about shiatsu, using Ingrid, lying supine on a mat, as a model. Following that, Annabel had everyone follow her into a massage room, the savannah room, which was done up with a photo motif of wallpaper which consisted of green grasslands and zebras, giraffes, and elephants. Using Ryoji (the only man) who alternately giggled and winced, lying on his stomach on a table, she demonstrated how to save one's strength by using one's body to apply the bulk of the pressure in a back massage. Then she went through the different strokes as Ingrid cued them, calling off each stroke from the house's guidebook, starting with calming, then circular, complete back, cross-over, cupping, deeper, effleurage, feathering, hacking, hand stroking, invigorating, kneading, pummelling, releasing, rhythm and sequence, soothing, spiralling, squeezing, stimulating, tapping, and lastly wringing.

Mid way through the session Bobbie, much to Ingrid's annoyance, excused herself and left, saying that she had an appointment, something about having to do a shift at a massage bar at the airport.

"But you're going to miss this," Ingrid said, disappointed. "You'll also miss my talk on illegal strokes."

"No such thing as illegal strokes," Bobbie snapped, strutting by Ingrid, fixing her with a hard glare. "That is if you want to make it in this business."

"Something tells me," Ingrid said, "that we're going to have problems, Bobbie, you and me." But before Ingrid could tell her not to come back Bobbie had strutted across the salon, leaving Ingrid both angry and puzzled. Angry, because she had challenged Ingrid's authority. Puzzled, because there was some truth in her words. Of course Ingrid wanted Massage World to be successful, but damnit all she had to maintain her determination to make it go straight. She'd simply fire Bobbie if there was any more back talk or bad talk.

JANICE

Had finished her trial massage with Ingrid and was waiting in the break room at Massage World, surprised to see Bobbie Cobb strut in as if she owned the place. "Didn't know you worked here."

Bobbie scoffed and said, "Massage World's ten times better than the Near East. Look, Janice." She pulled from a sweater pocket a donut-sized roll of bills banded by a thick rubber band.

Janice gaped. Such a donut of money would end all her problems. Curious, she remembered that Bobbie had been sacrificed in a Cobb circle for not making her quota. Had Bobbie changed? "You made all that here?" Janice asked her. "When?"

Bobbie looked at her watch. "One more to go before the end of shift. One shift. Seven hundred dollars." She opened the refrigerator, took out a can of diet soda and popped it open.

"How did you make all that money, Bobbie?"

She quoted an old commercial, "The old-fashioned way."

"The prostate massage?"

She ignored the question. "Feels great to be out of that stinky Near East shit hole, though I could have killed Corn Cobb for sacrificing me."

"Tell me, Bobbie, really. How did you rake all that in?"

Bobbie gave her a coy look. "*Oh, Janice.*" She slogged down some soda. Wiping her lips, she said, "Gotta go. Have an hour with a company president." She widened and narrowed her eyes a few times and rubbed her fingers together. Then turned, nearly colliding with a red-haired masseuse entering the break room. "Oh, Trish," Bobbie said. "You have a client waiting in 4, some old dude. Seems harmless. He already paid for a half."

Trish nodded. "Thanks. Start right on him."

Ingrid Swanson came in then and she and Janice sat at one of the folding tables. "We have a lot to cover. First a short-hand orientation of company policy, to be followed to the letter of the law. Masseuses must give only straight massages and follow city-imposed dress codes.

Shirts must be sleeved, mid-riffs and belly buttons covered, collar bones covered as well. Skirts or shorts must extend at least four inches from the crotch, and don't be surprised if Vice or myself comes around with a tape measure. They're sticklers for these regulations. Fingernails are to be clipped short, for obvious reasons. And what am I forgetting? Oh, and hair has to be clean and stylish, which you obviously won't have any problem with. I do like your hair." Ingrid gave her a warm smile. "I liked your massage, too, Janice. You'll fit right in, if you want the job."

Just then a woman's scream, a terrifying scream, tore through the mansion. Ingrid and Janice exchanged a troubled expression. Ingrid stood and ran out. Janice dashed after her through the salon, past men carrying cue sticks down the back corridor heading in the same direction. Between the sound of skin slapping, a woman's voice shrieked, "I hate men! I hate men!"

Eric Madeen

RANDY GUDSIKES
BORDER CITY POLICE DEPARTMENT
INVESTIGATOR'S REPORT

IN THE MUNICIPAL COURT, BORDER CITY JUDICIAL DISTRICT
COUNTY OF BORDER CITY
AFFIDAVIT FOR SEARCH WARRANT
No. 19643

I, Randal R. Gudsikes, do on oath make complaint, say and depose the following:

1. I am a police officer and detective employed by the Border City Police Department. I am assigned to the Vice Unit of that agency.

2. I believe the there is substantial probable cause as required by Penal Code sections 1524 and 1525 to search the following premises:

MASSAGE WORLD, a massage parlor, contained in a three story stone mansion opposite Sherman Hospital in the 5600 block of Melon Street. MASSAGE WORLD is surrounded by a spear-like fence and then a brick wall on the west side of the property. Semi-circular balconies extend from each of the second and third floor windows. The roof, of the mansard variety, could prove hazardous if scaled in the event of a raid. Under the front portico hangs a large red neon sign that reads, MASSAGE WORLD 5655.

3. Assigned to the Vice Unit of the Border City Police Department for approximately six (6) years as a Vice Detective, I have investigated prostitution crimes and assorted activities of more than fourteen (14) unlawful "massage," "modeling," and "escort" agencies and related "fronts" profiteering from crimes of prostitution. It should be dutifully noted that I have investigated more than seven (7) organizations unlawfully operating under the aegis of massage parlors, spas, motels, or other "front" businesses providing prostitutes to paying customers. In

addition, I have labored as an undercover POLICE OFFICER posing as a customer/john, and I have conscientiously conferred with fellow undercover POLICE OFFICERS who have also posed as customers of prostitution businesses or who have pretended to be employed by prostitution businesses. FURTHERMORE, I have rigorously prepared and participated in the serving of several search warrants for prostitution businesses conducted under miscellaneous "front" business categories and have meticulously scrutinized the evidence seized thereunder. MOREOVER, I regularly interview and interrogate PROSTITUTES, including those "employed" by so called "outcall" agencies, and I have arrested over four hundred (400) persons for prostitution crimes and/or related offenses against the state. As a result, I have become an expert in the trade's arcane usage of jargon, coinage, and street slang sundry. What is more, I have given expert opinion testimony in the interpretation of such language concerning pandering and pimping in the Border City Superior Court. IT SHOULD ALSO BE DULY NOTED that I have testified as an expert in the interpretation of outcall prostitution records in the Border City Municipal Court.

4. My in-depth training and varied experience have taught me that many, if not most, of the criminals who violate laws pertaining to pandering, pimping, keeping a house of ill-fame, keeping a disorderly house, and soliciting prostitution (Penal Code sections 226(h), 266(i), 315, 647(b)) irrespectively, operate "front" businesses which may appear to be legitimate by the public, but which under closer analysis prove to be vehicles used to conduct prostitution. I know first hand from my many experiences over six (6) years that the owners of these "businesses" and their "agents" maintain lists of both customers and prostitutes. The "client list" serves as a ready and reliable source of identity verification meant to deter infiltration by law enforcement officials. The lists of prostitutes are essential in the coordination of liaisons between "johns" (male customers) and prostitutes. My experience has also shown that many of these "businesses" survive in good part through repeat and/or established customers (more later).

5. To get down to cases, the following describes my on-going investigation into MASSAGE WORLD as a highly suspect house of prostitution.

In early February, D. MAYFLOWER, #3795, of the Border City Police Department Licensing Division, informed me that an anonymous male called to complain that his recent MASSAGE WORLD massage went beyond the bounds of propriety. "If you want everything," the anonymous male caller said to MAYFLOWER, "then ask for 'Erma.'" (The term "everything" refers to oral copulation which is indisputably equal to sexual intercourse.)

I hastened to obtain the latest issue of a local publication and found ten (10) massage ads for MASSAGE WORLD. Each ad employed distinctively sexual terminology and a different masseuse name. The language pointed more toward the sexual than the holistic, with the following ad (actual copy attached) being a case in point, "Let my soothing, sensuous hands take you on a trip you'll never forget. Come to me for just the right touch to *release* [sic] your tensions. Erma. Now at MASSAGE WORLD. 444-7490."

I called MASSAGE WORLD and arranged a session with "ERMA" at 1535 hours. The massage was to be thirty (30) minutes in duration for forty ($40) dollars. At 1535 hours a white female with curly brunette hair met me in the salon. She wore a simple short yellow blouse that exposed her belly button (against penal code 4317). She didn't seem to be wearing a brassiere. Her white slacks were tucked into high suede boots, and she was chewing bubble gum. "Hello there. My name is Erma." ("Erma" was later positively IDed as DEBAGGIO, Ermine Denise.)

"Erma" led me past four unkempt, shady men slouching around a pool table and juice bar and making unseemly jokes. Said individuals snickered as we walked past. One of them, nodding in my direction, made an obscene gesture (repeatedly jerking his hand around the region of his crotch) as the others hooted and cat called, imitating Ms. DEBAGGIO's stride, which, needless to say, was undeniably seductive in nature. We walked down a hallway past several numbered massage rooms on either side. "Erma" directed me to the FOREST ROOM, which smelled of moss and bark and green leaves and roots. In short, it smelled earthy. She punched in a CD of African tom-tom music pouring from Voss speakers and everything was going too fast at this point.

"Erma" told me to take my clothes off. She said that she would be right back. I did as "Erma" instructed. I stripped then lay on the massage table naked. "Erma" returned and closed the door behind her then dimmed the lights. The beating of the tom-toms became more intense, so loud that "Erma" seemed to be chanting, "Do you... prefer powder? Or do you... prefer oil? Oil? Powder? Powder? Oil?"

"Oil."

"Oil," she chanted. "Oil. We've struck oil. Texas T. Black gold." "Erma" massaged my back. Kept squeezing oil into her hand and applying it to my back with warm, soothing strokes. "Erma" chanted questions to me about my profession. I told her that I was a graphic artist for a large graphic design firm.

She asked about my clients and how I composed my designs, whether they were for print media or television. I was unprepared for such in-depth questioning and now think that she interrogated me so rigorously because: 1) She wanted to determine my salary so that she would know how much I was capable of "tipping" for additional services; 2) She wanted to determine conclusively that I was not a law enforcement official; 3) She was bored with her job and simply wanted to pass the time.

When I said that I compose my designs on a computer, she asked me what kind of computer. I feared I blundered when I said, "A simple Dell." "A Dell!?" she said. "Not a Mac? Not an AVAX?" She asked me what software I used. I told her I didn't know. That the technical department handled those decisions. "You don't know something as basic as software?" She then went over to turn down the music and turn up the lights, glaring at me all the while. I repeat, she did not take her eyes off me. In fact, she looked as if she had just seen a ghost.

"You're not a cop, are you?" Her eyes grew wide as sausages.

"Why?" I asked.

She chuckled, chewing her gum. "You seem just dumb enough to be a cop."

I retorted, "I'm no cop, but are you?"

"You're a funny guy," she said, then turned the music back up, turned the lights down, then spanked my buttocks, telling me to roll over onto my back—"like a good boy."

Lying on my back now, I felt "Erma's" hands on my stomach just above my penis. Then her fingers ventured deeper under the drape as she bent her torso over my head, her crotch brushing the top of my head. (I could see, at this point, the underside of her breasts under her blouse; "Erma" wasn't wearing a brassiere, in violation of Penal Code 1314.) The beat of the jungle drums and bongos reached a crescendo.

"Erma" giggled. "It looks as if you're pitching quite a tent there, sir." (I had no idea what she was talking about at this point.) "You know," she said, we're not supposed to touch the penis. But I can see that... someone's would like to be touched."

"Oh?" I said.

She said, "When you get your massage license at the police department they tell you about a hundred times that you're not to touch the penis." Her hands grazed my genitals while she worked another kind of pressure between my scrotum and thigh. She slipped an oiled finger between the crease of my buttocks then made a dialing motion around my anus in what was, in essence, a probing move of my sphincter (firmly tightened against access, I repeat, firmly closed).

"The Oriental places do it as part of their massage. It's supposed to relieve tension."

"Do what?" I asked.

"Massage the penis, dummy. What do you think I'm talking about?"

"I don't know."

"*I dunno*," she mocked, then massaged down my legs, away from the groin. "Most clients ask for powder instead of oil. They get all hot and bothered and ask for extras. I promised myself, though, that I won't do one little thing that can give me AIDS."

The conversation proceeded as follows:

TRISH TOTT

Walked into room 4, saw her client lying there, his behind properly draped, his face buried in the face hole of her massage table. "Sir," she said, touching his leg. "What kind of pressure do you prefer?"

He didn't respond. She gave his calf a playful pinch. "Sir? Your wake up call." Still nothing. She shook his back and felt cool skin. Then, she gasped, clapping her hands to her chest which was thumping wildly. Trembling, she didn't know what to do. Standing there with her hands on her cheeks then wrapped around her stomach, backing up one step at a time, whispering, *"Frank. Frank. You didn't."* She recoiled even more before finding the courage to rush over to him, to touch his back, his cold back. Lifting his head by the scruff of his neck, she confirmed that it was Frank, knew he was dead, then shrieked and screamed and slapped his back twice.

She ran into Ingrid at the door, pushing past her and her questions and confusion. "Who's dead?"

In the break room, Ingrid crowded her. "Frank," she told her.

"Frank who?"

"Frank," she hissed, disgusted, angry. "Frank Fuck Head!"

Ingrid's face was in Trish's face and her hands were grabbing Trish's arms. "What happened?"

Trish shook Ingrid's hands off of her shoulders. "Killed himself. Go see for yourself."

Ingrid blanched. "Wait here. Sit down. Don't move."

Trish snapped a heel against the floor then extended her arm across the table, raking it against the napkin holder, cutlery basket, and salt and pepper shakers all of which sent sent crashing to the floor. Then she knocked over chairs, then threw the chairs, and flipped over tables, screaming, "I hate men! I hate men!"

* * *

Officer: "What exactly do you mean by extras? I've never heard that term before."

Suspect: "Nothing that could give me AIDS."

O: "Do you give extras?"

S: "I don't know. Are you a cop?"

O: "You already asked me that. If it'll help, I'll have you know that I got a ticket the other day."

S: "Well, I charge twenty for a handjob, forty if you want me to take my clothes off."

O: "Damn. I only have an extra ten."

S: "I'll give you the special introductory special for ten."

O: "You will?"

S: "I will indeed."

O: "But that would break me."

S: "I don't want to break you. Better wait for next time. Don't tell anyone here what I've done or said. Some of them are really straight, like Bobbie, for instance."

O: "What about Ingrid?"

S: "Ingrid will do just about anything for a tip, but I heard she doesn't really have the touch like I have the touch, at least that's what clients tell me."

O: "I've heard that she doesn't give massage, that she only manages."

S: "If the price is right she'll accommodate. But, shhhh. Hush, hush. Cheerio."

At the end of the session I asked "Erma" to explain the difference between a powder and an oil massage. She demonstrated by lightly encircling my penis with her finger and thumb. Then "Erma" asked for the forty (40) dollar fee. I paid her with two tens, one five, and fifteen newly minted singles then vacated the premises immediately.

* * *

Gudsikes had prepared two sets of reports, and now as he walked down the hall he saw that the Chief had finished reading the first set and was waving him in.

Gudsikes entered the room, thick as it always was with cheap cigar smoke. He sat in a chair before the desk. "Well?"

"You can't be serious, Red," the Chief said, eyeing him suspiciously. "What?"

"Oh, come on. These reports read like a creative writing exercise out of *Police Academy.*"

Gudsikes couldn't maintain his composure any longer and grinned. The Chief laughed deep and hard, holding his belly. "*Quite a tent you're pitching there.* You're too much, Gudsikes."

"Thought you'd appreciate it, Chief, given the circumstances."

"You should have been a comedy writer, Gudsikes. My word. Why I never..." The Chief, chuckling, quoting another line, "'*I had no idea what she was talking about at this point.*' My god, what an imagination."

Gudsikes was happy that the spoof had done its job of softening up the Chief's gruff exterior, so as to prepare the way for the real McCoy, as Gudsikes now handed over the toned down version to the Chief. "Read away. I'll be at my desk when you're done." Gudsikes himself grinned as he left the office, less at the humor than at his confidence that the ploy would work as the comic draft serving its purpose of lending authenticity to the *real* draft.

* * *

Later, Gudsikes heard footsteps and looked up to see the Chief charging toward his desk then dropping the stack of paperwork angrily before him. "In all seriousness, Gudsikes, your reports are a joke. A postmodern farce."

"A joke? A postmodern farce?" Times like these Gudsikes hated Jack Cobb, hated him for making him fry on the rotisserie. He now felt the hot press of tension all over his body. Sweat poured from behind his ears and down the back of his neck. His hair even prickled so much that he wanted to scratch his head all over then flail out and push the noise of the Chief away.

"For starters, Detective, you seem to be a little out of touch with reality. Halloween costumes, sexism, racism, and involving a sister at that, homophobia, essentialisms, objectifications, and general white noise to beat the band."

"Beat the band?" Gudsikes said. "What band? Say what, Chief?"

The Chief drew his head back until his chin disappeared in his neck. A wave of anger washed over his face as he leaned over Gudsikes' desk and so close to Gudsikes' face that for the first time he noticed little black pimples—or were they moles?—around the Chief's eyes. His hands spread across the blotter for support, frankfurter breath of mustard and onions billowing into Gudsike's face. "Listen, Gudsikes, your whole scenario, as laid out in this mess of shit you call reports is seriously deluded. Your quotations and descriptions are too filtered."

"Filtered?"

"*Sifted.* Or how about just plain tainted? The white-male consciousness of Randal R. Gudsikes writing at a white heat." *Jack was going to pay* boocoo *for this*, Gudsikes thought, fumbling for a defense. "Come again, Chief?"

A big shake of the head, a bull raging, complete with nostrils flaring and a hand waved angrily through the air, he said, "Oh. come off it, Gudsikes."

"Come off what?" Gudsikes sneered. "But let's turn the sensitivity around for a moment, shall we?" Gudsikes, a white man, stared up at the Chief, a black man, who was staring down at him, the awareness of their racial difference like little knives prying up and poking at the larger differences of worldviews. Fingers jabbing like stilettoes, he continued, "If you wrote the reports up your blackness would be evident, right? Then what about the issues of vamping and solicitation that I was doing my job to elicit?"

"I don't have time for this," the Chief said, taking a step away, but only a step. Knowing he had to deal with it, the Chief stood there, half turned away, watching Gudsikes out of the corner of his eye. A look of pure hatred.

"Time for what?"

"Time," the Chief said, "to go through and reference each offense. But god damnit give me that." He snatched up a report:

"**...**She poked me with a single finger, saying some nonsense word in a babyish voice, like describing a bouncing ball. 'So big now. *Boing, boing...*'
and

'...lifted my left arm and placed my left hand on her left breast. I... I...'
and

'IN SUMMARY, IN CONCLUSION...based on my extensive experience, special training, and the facts recited herein, I believe... beyond the shadow of a doubt...that grounds for the issuance of a search warrant exist as set forth in Penile Code section 1524.'

Gudfuck, see that all the b.s. is edited out. Maybe you don't get it.

Let me spell it out: the fearless leader Swanson has to be indicted or else they're right back in business. Got it? Now go get it!"

INGRID

Feared bankruptcy. Business was dreadful. As the recession deepened, tradespeople, four of them already, filed liens against Massage World. And the landlady had jacked up rent again. Everything was going wrong and now Bobbie had called a meeting in Ingrid's office upstairs, breezing in with Erma then sitting down as if she owned the place.

"The whole staff wanted to come to this *pow wow*, Ingrid, and discuss our problem with return clientele. As in we're not getting enough. I did a little research on the computer." She handed Ingrid a stack of printed out pages then pointed to the names of clients and the frequency of their visits circled and connected in red ballpoint. "It averages out to only a ten percent return, as you can see. We need at least forty. Now, here are the estimates of what you owe."

Ingrid knew already that returns were insufficient, but what bothered her more was that Bobbie was crunching the numbers on her own time and steering Erma around at will. Since the masseuses were hired as independent contractors, they made their money only if they gave a massage, with Ingrid taking fifty percent. She knew what Bobbie would say next.

"It's a question of release, Ingrid."

"At least you're no longer calling it a *prostate* problem," Ingrid said.

Bobbie was all business. "All the men are asking for it. They say they won't come back or tip if they don't get it. Outcalls the same thing—clients wanting their money back. We're talking basic survival now."

Erma, sounding conniving, said, "It's true, Ingrid. Massage these days includes release. Just about all of the clients are bitching."

"Let them bitch," Ingrid said. "That doesn't change my policy one bit. Understood?"

Bobbie rolled her eyes. "Okay, let's talk about something else. The first thing callers ask is '*Who's working?*' When they hear the same old names they hang up."

"This is true," Ingrid said. "Men always want a different technician.

What are you proposing?"

"Hire a dozen new masseuses," Bobbie said. "Keep changing their ads and shifts and names around. Each masseuse should have at least three first names for not only her classifieds but also for a list we'll keep next to the phone. Whoever's on desk will simply read from that day's list of names."

Ingrid thought such a shell game wasn't right. It could, in the end, annoy a client when he'd learn that Victoria was none other than old Sharon. But it also wasn't right that clients so shamelessly violated the premise of goodwill by hopping from one technician and spa to another—after each tech did her utmost to give a great massage. Ingrid had no choice, however, and told Bobbie to go ahead and try her shell game, to hire the new masseuses and do the trick with the names and so on.

Bobbie's next proposal, which Ingrid also agreed to, was to issue coupons that gave massage credits and to sell massages as gift coupons in coordination with various health clubs. Feeling her base of authority weaken with each concession, Ingrid also gave the nod to hiring a telemarketer at a ten percent commission on each massage sold. She couldn't help but dislike Bobbie, however, for coming up with such cunning ideas: display ads and a logo and promotional programs with flyers and sales staff and seminars that encouraged technicians to coax clients to extend their sessions. Great ideas, these. But they begged a niggling question: "What do you want in all this?"

Bobbie motioned to the papers she had laid on Ingrid's desk. "I'm a hard worker. Don't mind at all doing extra work." She paused, hands in her lap, looking down, the pose of a good girl.

"What is it that you want, Bobbie? You know that we can't afford to pay you anything above what you make on your massages."

"I'd like a stake in the business—"

Ingrid uncrossed her arms then raised her hands as if to push her away. "Oh no. There's just no way. I put in eight months of hard labor, Bobbie, then there's several thousand dollars thrown in, and you just want to waltz in here—"

"Listen to her first," Erma said testily. "It makes more sense then doing nothing and going bankrupt."

"All right, I'm listening."

"I'm proposing that you give me the title of assistant manager." Bobbie waited for this to settle on Ingrid.

Titles were cheap. Raising a hand from the chair, she said, "I'll do that. Consider it done, Assistant Manager Bobbie Johnson."

Bobbie continued, "Let me hire and manage the masseuses. If we're not making quadruple what we're making now, then you don't have to give me anything. But if my work and ideas pay off, then I want to come in as a partner." She held up a hand to silence Ingrid. "*Buying my way in*, the more money I give you the more my share in the business increases. I'll lay it all out on paper."

Ingrid felt intimidated by this woman's superior ambitions and business savvy. She didn't know what to think other than that she knew she had to try something before a combination of factors brought ruin. "Maybe. One big fat maybe dependent on several things. First, the stipulation that any potential share of the business will not exceed ten percent. Before we can even talk, though, I'll need a more extensive resume from you, plus five references, two from former landlords, three from former employers. A TRW too. Then I'll need to clear all this with someone else before we proceed even an inch."

"In the meantime," Bobbie said, "we can at least go ahead with hiring and advertising. I'm sure you agree. Let me add that I don't mind the extra work if things don't pan out. I hope they do, though, since my own survival depends on Massage World's survival. I know we can make it go."

"No need for speeches, Bobbie. I'm going to the desert this weekend for a much needed rest. I'm giving Erma final approval on everything you do." Ingrid looked at Erma, noticing Erma's eyes skipping off again—whenever she looked at her these days Erma wouldn't meet her gaze. Something wasn't right with Erma, her sheepishness, trailing behind Bobbie as if on a leash. "I'm trusting you, Erm. You hear me? Look at me. All right? You're in charge. Okay?"

"She understands," Bobbie said.

"I'm asking her."

Erma nodded meekly, and looked away as if scolded.

RANDAL R. GUDSIKES, VICE DETECTIVE, B.C.P.D.

W atched with apprehension as the Chief power walked back to his desk. Rapping the surface once with his knuckles, he boomed in his baritone, "You keep telling me you're on it but I haven't seen shit. Maybe you're in over your head and balls, Randal."

"Pardon me, Chief?"

"Time's running out, Guddy. As I said, you have only one more day to nail the big gun, the one with the masseuse's name. What's her name? Swanson. Right. You still haven't given me diddly on one Ingrid Swanson, and we can't move an inch until you deliver some very well written paper on one bitching Ingrid Swanson before I can send the troops in. Mayflower in licensing is all over me, itching for the collar."

Gudsike's face felt like a dishrag, squeezed and twisted. There was no nailing Swanson, he knew, without complications. "I told you she doesn't give massage, Chief. Made that quite clear in my reports."

Used to getting what he wanted, the Chief was confident, if not arrogant. "Offer her enough she will. Go up to a grand. It'll be legendary, Gudsikes." Gudsikes flinched as he raised a hand, cutting a banner headline, finger and thumb a few inches apart: *THE THOUSAND DOLLAR HANDJOB THAT BROUGHT DOWN MASSAGE GALAXY.*"

Gudsikes shuddered, then corrected him. "It's called Massage World, Chief."

Eyeing him, the Chief blew out a puff of air, turned over his palms, and held them out expressively. "I don't give much of a shit, Gudsikes, if it's called Massage Yo' Ass. All right? Just get me Swanson."

Stomach turning, Gudsikes feared Swanson. Surely, she had it in for him since the whole dog thing—from when he shot her dog in her backyard. *Shit.* How in the hell could he get into a session with her without being IDed?

"You look as if you just turned five shades of white, Red," the Chief said, studying him.

Too fidgety to sit down, Gudsikes paced between the rows of desks, keeping his gaze glued to the floor as he walked up and down, ignoring his colleagues' comments. "Red's in pacing mode. Look out."

He was fretting the guise. What could he possibly wear? Of course she'd remember him. She was practically standing over him when he blew out the beast's brains! Whatever he donned had to be elaborate, like a little house around him so that she couldn't see his red hair. It seemed impossible. How could he get into session with her without her recognizing him?

He sat down, grunting and groaning, looking up at the ceiling and scratching his hair. Then he began sketching mindlessly on some scratch paper, his subconscious pushing out a wiry little out-house structure as doodle. *Jesus. About what it'd take.* He started sketching frantically. The big one appeared out of a knot hole in the out-house. Rembrandt protruding. He sketched an arm, his arm, as a protuberance connected to the body of the out-house. A hand, his hand, holding a wad of bills, a thousand dollars, held out to Swanson. Her image appeared, looking apprehensive but comely with *Playboy* cartoon curves. Shy about taking it. Shy in her glance at Rembrandt. At which his other hand pointed. A bemused but grinning face, Gudsikes' face, poking out of a face hole. Over his head a cartoon balloon with the blurb, his blurb, no Eastwood's blurb: "Go ahead. Make my day."

Ridiculous! An outhouse to cover himself to get him into session with her! He stood up so fast that he knocked his chair over. *Damn!*

God damned Cobb. Maybe he'd have an idea...

He crossed for the door on his way out to call Jack, but there was the Chief cutting him off. He caught Gudsikes down the barrel of a pointed finger. "Get me Swanson, Red." He raised his hand then lowered his sights again. "I want paper on her by tomorrow, son, or else your ass is grass and out on leave. Now get outta my face."

GET THE MIDAS TOUCH AT MASSAGE WORLD

by Dee Pressed

A rumor circling in the uptown district has it that the new five-star massage parlor, Massage World, is considering adding another massage to its menu. The new massage, *The Kevorkian*, in memory of the late client who recently allegedly gulped a rainbow of pharmaceuticals and perished in session, would cater to the terminally depressed, or anyone in dire *knead*. The author of the Kevorkian, purportedly a fiery Harley-striding Border City Native, was unavailable for comment and is said to have taken a leave of absence from her staff position at Massage World.

On a lighter note, it has been two months since Border City has seen the opening of Massage World, which, in line with the new massage craze storming the country, features a *wonderland of amenities* (a phrase lifted from brochure copy) situated in a handsome landmark mansion on Melon Street across from Sherman Hospital. No longer does one have to brave the mean streets of of the South, Southeast and East Border City and then fret about being seen ingressing a seedy massage parlor bearing a nominal link to the Near East—and "acupressure" (opposed to acupuncture—can you dig it, yes I can).

"We're straight and clean and represent the new breed of body-work centers opening across the country," says the owner-manager, Ingrid Swanson. As for massage going mainstream, Ms. Swanson explained that at no time in our country's history has the body been in so much pain. "The body is in intense pain right now, and Americans are the loneliest people on earth—certainly the most touch-starved. The dissolution of the nuclear family, the war between the races and sexes, sexual harassment, phone sex, and the whole Internet and Skype thing, sex without the fluids in this time of AIDS, jackhammer sex without tenderness, acquaintance rape, intense media coverage of child molestation, mediation of the imagination, and, of course, the dirty sex wars playing out across our land, so on and so forth, all add up to a collective fear of initiating touch. Massage, on the other hand, helps reconnect the body and mind, for a liberating, healing experience." Swanson added that body types and pressure preferences are continuously upgraded on computer so that each massage is client tailored.

One enters Massage World through a stately gate before proceeding up a pillared portico. The salon space is bathed in a soft yellow cathedral-like light streaming down from the stain glass windows and chandelier. Adding to the deliciously kitschy enchantment are the black-and-white checkered floor, canonically god-sized Greek statues (one of Hermes, one of Androgeus) hovering over a peeing-boy fountain at the salon center. The click of billiard balls echo off a huge table in the rear of the salon where clients hang out and flirt with Swanson's stunning staff of massage technicians—n*ot masseuses* (Swanson is firm on this point). "The word masseuse conjures up the old days of parlors and prostitutes which is not what we're about at all."

INGRID

Felt refreshed from a weekend in the Cocotillos. At nine sharp Monday morning the door of Massage World opened to Elton John blasting. Ingrid stood there and stared, felt depression flood through her to the point that she couldn't do anything but reach for the door to lean upon, watching a couple dozen people reeling. Dancing on the juice bar with their are breasts jiggling. Bare breasts straddling a supine fat belly on the pool table, then people leaping off from halfway down the stairs clinging to a hanging plant. Looked like some wild eyed Chicano swinging toward Androgeus. Letting out a war cry climbing up to stand on the statue's precarious shoulders, then swinging back to the stairs, giant chess piece base left wobbling.

I remember when rock was young/Me and Suzie had so much fun/holding hands and skimming stones/had an old gold Chevy and a place of my own.

Some big guy was swinging someone around in a wheelchair.

But the biggest kick I ever got/was doing a thing called the crocodile rock/while the other kids were rocking 'round the clock/we were hopping and bopping to the crocodile rock.

A drunk falling in the fountain in a splash on his ass, transvestite Chicanos bare breasted stripped to panties covering bulges there, splashing old storage space guys in rags away from the fountain, dancing jigs in locked arm steps with four Asian girls doing the jitterbug through London Bridges falling down and squealing.

Well, cry rocking, stomp and shout/and when your feet just can't keep still/I never knew me a better time/and I guess I never will/Oh lord Mama those Friday nights/with Suzie woman dressed in tights...

The pool table was a forest of beer bottles, and a young woman's big bare breasts bobbing up and down giving a massage to a fat slob sprawled out on a swimming pool lounge chair cushion someone had thrown over the felt. Straddling him, not giving him a massage, but rather fucking him in total abandon.

La...la la la la la. La la la la la... But the years went by and rock just died/Suzie went and left us for some foreign guy/ long nights crying by the record machine/dreaming of my Chevy and my old blue jeans...

On the juice bar, topless, bobbed blonde hair, doing a go-go dance. *Bobbie!* Crossing to the barbershop to punch buttons and more buttons across the stereo until the music stopped, Ingrid then roared in Swedish then in English and back and forth until she shouted, "Everyone get the hell out of here god damnit! Except Bobbie! You, up to my office now!" The fellow doing the wheelchair tricks clicked the heels of his cowboy boots together, thrust out a hand, long greasy locks swaying. "*Ya vol.*" Putting a kink in her anger, she realized she had been speaking in Swedish, summoning it back up, "Get the royal fuck out of here! Bobbie, upstairs. *Now!* Bring Erma wherever the hell she is."

"Not here." Bobbie sat on the bar slipping her t-shirt on.

"Bring her anyway!" Ingrid ran up the stairs to her office.

A minute later Bobbie burst in. "I'm not even going to try to explain, Ingrid, but here." She tried to hand a wad of bills to Ingrid, but Ingrid refused the money, shaking her head, watching as Bobbie lay the bills on the blotter then give them a Las Vegas spread.

"What's this?"

"From a very wealthy man. We helped him celebrate his birthday. At Massage World. Over twelve hundred dollars. All yours, Ingrid. Get that jerk ass plumber off your ass."

Bobbie didn't know the half of it. Ahead of the plumber was the linen company manager coming today to strip the tables of his sheets and the showers of his towels. Then utility bills, not to mention the phone company threatening disconnection and the newspaper accountant screaming for his. Doing some quick addition, Ingrid surveyed the twelve hundred, skimming over the random denominations of the bills, fives, tens, twenties, a few stray fifties, four or five hundreds, all mixed together in the shuffle that could keep them in linen, phone calls, and advertising for another week.

Ingrid didn't touch the money, afraid to be lured into playing

Bobbie's game. But she didn't tell Bobbie to get it the hell off her desk either, listening to her reefer burping voice (as if smoke were hoarded in her lungs as she spoke), "I want to introduce you to someone. Who can turn our business. All the way around."

"You have a pronoun problem, Bobbie. You're not part of *our* anything."

At that moment the greasy haired guy had come in, as if on cue. "This is Dr. Dick Pierson, Ingrid. He's not only a doctor but a holistic health wizard and marketing genius. Just listen to his ideas then tell me you're not spellbound."

"I recognize him as the smart-ass comedian," Ingrid retorted. *"Ya vol* yourself."

He ignored the barb, extending his hand which Ingrid didn't want to shake but shook anyway just so she could give its greasy massage oil grip straight back to him while addressing Bobbie. "Jesus fucking Christ, Bobbie, I come back to work on Monday morning after a day and a half away to find transvestites swinging from the rafters and you dancing naked on the juice bar and some slut grinding away at some slob on the pool table."

"It's not what you think, Ingrid."

"What the hell am I supposed to think?"

"Well, I told you it was Mr. Simms' birthday. And there is twelve hundred dollars." She pointed to the loot still spread across Ingrid's blotter. "Plus, there's six hundred more. So that's almost two grand for your precious day and a half in the desert."

"You took in six hundred? How?"

"By hiring the new masseuses, all of whom are great. And doing this and that."

"I can imagine the *this and that.* I saw the pool table action, Bobbie."

"It's not what it seems."

"Well, it just doesn't *seem right.*" Ingrid covered her face with her hands then rubbed her index fingers against the throb of pain over her eye sockets. "Not right at all."

"That's eighteen hundred dollars," Bobbie continued. "Net. Tell me that you even grossed a quarter of that last weekend."

Ingrid couldn't tell Bobbie that and remained silent, face still buried in her hands.

"And tell me you're not just a bit relieved at getting that snarling-ass plumber off your back. Soon all of them... the painters, carpenters, tillers, carpet baggers, will all be the hell off your back...for good."

Ingrid sighed, studying Bobbie leaning back in her chair, not in the least bit agitated by what was supposed to be a scolding, if not firing. "It just doesn't feel right. It all feels wrong."

Bobbie leaned in, asking an aggressive, "Why?"

"I don't know you. Judging from your go-go bash downstairs I feel that I don't want to get to know you. You and your fat man and whore and comedian here and ethnic contingent playing ring-around-the-rosy. Were those transvestites or what? And the Asian girls, you hired them?"

Pierson waved a hand to cut off Bobbie's attempt at explanation, glaring hard into Ingrid's eyes as he spoke, "The Asian girls as you call them are from Thailand where I hired them. They're highly qualified massage technicians in the fine art of Wat Po Massage. Have you ever heard of Wat Po Massage? I didn't think so. Now, the Mexicans...I don't know where they came from. But I don't have anything against Mexicans. Do you? Good. Now I have a proposition: How would you like it, Ingrid Swanson, if I got Massage World on national television?"

"Have I met you before?" Ingrid asked. "Your voice sounds familiar."

He took advantage of her curiosity, pulling up a chair, and sitting down. Pierson's head wobbled as he spoke, causing his greasy locks to dance across his shoulders as he tried to sell her on his spiel. "Listen. I talked to a scout for the Ellen Show, as in Ellen DeGeneres, told him the set up here, about this special one of a kind class I'm going to give in the pool here."

"Which pool?"

"Our pool."

"What do you mean by *our*?"

"Okay, the pool at Massage World, all right? Now would you believe it? They're going for it."

"Who?"

"Ellen!" His foot stomped the floor. "*Here.* Massage World is going to be on national television."

She didn't know what to say. Only by refusing the money and media agentry could Ingrid maintain at least a semblance of control let alone self esteem. But such control would result in a failure to pay the bills. *The fucking bills!* Which were like swords stabbing at her. She realized, as Bobbie and Pierson pushed their oily silence at her, that she didn't have a choice but to let them do their circus act. At least for now.

She'd have to get closer to them, though, to see what their game really was. "What kind of doctor are you anyway?"

"Just a doctor doctor."

"Now what in hell does that mean?" she asked, put off. "*Just a doctor doctor.*"

He shrugged. "A general doctor, like that."

"You mean a general practitioner?"

"Jesus," he said, standing up and kicking at something invisible, "what do I have to do, show you my fucking license or what? We're talking the Ellen Show and you—"

She held out an open hand, while her other hand rested on her hip. "Can I see your license, doctor?"

"I don't think this is going to work out between us," he said. "Good luck with your business. Bobbie, get the money there and let's go."

Ingrid thought this a bartering ploy, until Bobbie obeyed.

"Wait," Ingrid said, grabbing Bobbie's hand trying to scoop up the bills. "Would you just wait a second?"

* * *

Ingrid couldn't believe it when the Ellen Show crew trooped in. Technicians, in baseball caps and jeans, porting video cameras, tripods, lights, and spools paying out cord everywhere. Pierson gave a self-defense lesson for senior citizens in the swimming pool. "The water'll serve as a cushion. Just fall right back." During videotaping a sound technician sat in the lifeguard's chair and held a microphone pole over the action in the shallow end. Up to his waist in water, Pierson demonstrated defense moves with a volunteer, a gray fox in his seventies who he beckoned to attack him with a rubber dagger. Pierson ducked then grabbed the man's arm, twisting the bony appendage behind him in slow motion. All very nice.

Then Pierson instructed sixteen elderly men and women to pair off and imitate him. From various angles the cameras shot the action of a line of elderly women thrusting daggers at a parallel line of elderly men (the program's cut away image before commercials). Subsequently, the show's host who Ellen must have sent gave American viewers a tour of Massage World, after introducing Dick Pierson as "Manager" (irking the hell out of Ingrid who didn't get any air time). Pierson gave his best knitted brow look, pontificating, "Massage World is the upbeat, upscale health spa of the new millennium. A total time out from the stresses of postmodern life."

The host leading the tour said, *"At Massage World clients are given tailored massages according to their needs, and can choose from one of a dozen massage rooms all done up thematically. Take a trip to the Orient, Egypt, the heart of Africa or the Swiss Alps, or time travel back to the seventies in the Disco Ball Room."* The next shot had her, the host, up to her chin in a bubble bath, Trish feeding her caviar and crackers, Ryoji giving her a neck-and-shoulder massage, Annabel tilting a champagne glass to her lips. Her eyes closed, the host purred, *"Nothing like the pampering of a VIP Massage, huh folks? Followed by a sauna, whirlpool, and power shower. A little more champagne, please..."* Cut away to a turbaned barefoot Sikh (actually Dick Pierson) in white pajamas teaching a yoga class in a carpeted corner of the salon, the blonde host in a half lotus and gi, then a shot of Bobbie as Hari Krishna playing some hookah-resembling instrument hooked under her toes, sweet notes resonating with the yoga class ambience, and a shot of the Greek statues and bubbling fountain, then the cutaway shot of old women trying to stab old men in the shallows of the swimming pool.

DETECTIVE RANDY "RED" GUDSIKES

Followed Bobbie and Jack's dictum—*Need about a dozen, Ran', so keep on truckin'.* Randy Gudsikes combed the streets of southeast Border City. His old Dodge Colt's headlights lanced through the darkness as he screeched through a U-turn then drove back down Thirty Second street. The closer he crawled toward the Friday deadline the more of a funk he was in. By turns anxious and afraid of having to face down Ingrid Swanson to get her to massage him, he feared she'd ID him, despite the costume.

He found welcome distraction in sight of a whore strutting down the sidewalk just past an old clapboard church, along a hedge of bushes under a streetlight.

What Gudsikes liked about her on the first pass held true on the second. She dressed nice, in a sexy cowl neck over a dark skirt and ankle boots, the complement of reddish stockings thrown in. She also understood marketing, merchandising herself as a piece of ass that was hard to get. Playing the tease out (a skill transferable to the massage room) she all but ignored him. Even better was her winning shape: tall and slim but generous of ass and breast that weren't jiggling for the crowd but left to follow the natural rhythms of her body that now had him slowing to steer toward the curb.

"Fucking Colt," he swore, embarrassed to be pulling up to such a class act in his beater and angry at Jack for not letting him buy a new Mustang. (Anything new stirs envy and curiosity, went the Cobb dictum.) He rolled the window down and watched her not missing a stride. A pretty lady. Big eyes. High cheekbones. Hair moused down with whatever that pomade shit that black chicks caked on. *"Whatch you want?"*

Her sass made him semi-hard. The worst thing that he could do now was be bold, since such a whore needs to be in control. "I'm a little shy."

His hesitation stopped her. He watched her walk over to take a better look at him, bending over to give him a seductive look. "*Whatch your name?*"

"Timothy."

"Timothy? Donna." They shook hands.

"Like Donna Summer," Gudsikes said. "You know you look like her."

"I don't either. You a kidder. Now you want a date or just talk? 'bout the date, I catch everything." Meaning, she would gulp down all of his ejaculation.

With the ice broken, she went over and climbed in the passenger seat. Driving up the street, Gudsikes hadn't figured her for a crackhead and was surprised when she pulled out a long, thin glass pipe. "Gonna crack it up a bit here, Timothy. I date better when I'm high. You see. Let me just dig this pebble out here." From her purse she pulled a rock out of an empty makeup jar the size of a film container. Slipping the *pebble* into the bowl, she clicked her lighter then drew hard and kept drawing, the flame licking into the clear glass stem.

In the dark interior Gudsikes was transfixed by the glow, the long tongue of yellow and blue flames mixing in the glass stem. The silky threads of smoke doing their magic carpet ride into her sucking lips he imagined going down on him. She kept sucking, the pebble a little orange coal disappearing under the jet of lighter flame as she kept gulping it down, as if she were chugging a tall drink. Then she held the hit for the longest time that Gudsikes wanted to snatch the pipe away from her. Break it in his fists then slap her back. *Enough already! Now would you stop smoking that shit!* Cocaine crashing into her bloodstream and brain she gave him a cross-eyed look over crack-puffed cheeks. A full minute later she, with eyes crossed, exhaled a long stream of crack smoke into his face.

She coughed a few times then a few more times. "Oh shit," she said before she shook all over, giving him nervous glances. She seemed on the verge of collapse. Or vomiting.

"You all right?"

O.D.ing, she didn't answer, but panted and shrieked. He cut down an alley. No other choice but to dump her. Her hands pressed against her face, she moved her head in crazy circles, up and down and around in the motions of a mental patient while issuing a primal plaint of fear. The quiet suspicion that she was dying crept up on him until he swore under his breath, *Jesus fuck*, and swung his head around to check for traffic. For pedestrians. For witnesses. He drove farther up the dirt alley along dilapidated wooden fences falling away from ramshackle houses under bone white eucalyptus, potholes jostling the Colt as he turned around, headlights swinging past garbage cans and a flattened roll of rusted iron mesh. When he heard her fart and smelled crap he knew she was gone or almost gone, her head back against the seat and her eyes mere slits. *Damned whore.* The decision raked sweat beads across his chest and down his temples, neck, and back. He reached over and snapped opened the passenger door, giving her shoulder a fierce push toward the weeds. All he could hear was the crunch of rocks as he glanced at the bending of straight sharp lines of fence cracks as he kept driving. But out of the corner of his eye he could see some damned piece of clothing.

Her bag strap. It was looped like an ammunition belt across her chest. It had snagged on the door handle and she was swaying like a sack of potatoes, ass scraping rock and snapping weeds and her legs were bent like rubber at the knee folded across the dirty gray of the floor mat. Half in half out. Another pothole whacked a shock up through the wheel into his hand as his other hand pushed at her legs. He had to keep pushing at her legs, like throwing balls of socks into a trick drawer that kept throwing them back until he jerked the both of them up by a handful of pointy toes, her legs springing all the way up above the seat as the brooding smell of shit poked back at him.

Somehow she had managed to slip off a shoe somewhere, the ball of a bare heel was in his hand now pushing up against the back of her thigh, her head flopping over to cut him a corpse's haunted glance just when a wild patch of weeds rushed up thrashing at the door, grabbing at her like a car wash sea monster.

The Colt laid down rubber and kicked stones fishtailing out of the alley. Hell-bent, Gudsikes unleashed a string of firecracker curses.

Oh Jesus Christ motherfucker sonsofbitches all. Turn down Archibald street. *Fuuuuuu-ku!* Jam up Thirty Seventh. *You haven't...* Fly in swoop onto Birmingham... *done anything...* and now you're cool again... back in whores up to your armpits biting the tit that bit you, bastard. *How dare the bitch O.D. Practically taking a shit on my lap. Did herself.*

He saw one whore seeing him then her breaking from the pack. Hungry. Tongue flicking already. Another whore bait. All tittied up and no where to go. And what is that some kind of thrift shop teddy top shit mildewed up her ass. Too much of a whore for Bobbie and Jack. Should be a movie.

Bobbie and Jack. Fuck 'em if they can't take a joke. You dating? I was thinking about it. Yeah? I'm a little shy. Don't want to be rushed, huh. Dat's cool. You're not a crackhead, are ya? You kiddin'? You're not a cop, are ya? Now you're kiddin'.

He couldn't stop the nervous laughter.

She shook her ass around the front of the car then climbed in, waves of fear sloshing through in her little darty movements and glances, as if wolves were in the cab and snapping at her. He was going to head straight to Jack with her. No fucking around. "What I really want is a massage," he said. "I'm gonna take you to this place called The Near East Spa."

"A massage? What place? I don't give no massage. I give head. And whose shoe is this?" She held up the dead whore's ankle boot while staring at him.

"Cinderella's. Now what's it fucking to you?" He grabbed the shoe from her then tossed it in the back seat, reminding himself to burn it later.

"Tell me you not the maniac out here *slautrin* us." She stared at him out of the corner of her eye, a searching gaze.

"Actually, if you must know..." He left her stewing in a good minute of silence.

"Know what? Tell me."

He gave her a hard-assed look. "I'm a cop."

Her back reeled hard against the passenger door and seemed to shake all over, as if shocked by his proclamation and literally shocked—electrified—by the dead whore's aura she was brushing against. He pulled out his wallet and flung it open, flashing his badge.

"Oh, god, no, please don't tell me you bustin' me. Do anything, Officer. Just blew a cop down on Forty Ninth. He caught my ass hustling. Do you the same, Officer. I suck a sweet cock, Officer. Catch everything. I don't want to go to jail, please, sir." She started to lower her head over his lap. Gudsikes pushed her away—hard. "Not a blowjob or a bust I'm after."

She snapped back up, swiveled farther around in her seat, eyes narrowing in anger more than fear. "*Whatch* you after then?"

"Talk."

"Talk?"

"Talk about your new career."

"New career?"

He reached over and popped open the console, taking out his forty five to lend weight to the orientation. Her eyes, enormous, stared at him. Fear never failed as a branding agent.

INGRID

Sighed in frustration, watching Dick Pierson waltz into the salon singing *My Way* the day after the Ellen Show feature aired. He was wearing surgical garb, three days of whiskers, black cowboy boots (scuffed white at the toes), and a stethoscope around his neck. Near the stairwell Janice Verdurin hung upside down from an exercise bar, her long brown locks dangling, her cheeks rosy and puffed up like a hamster's from the blood flow. "I hope the guy singing there isn't who I think he is."

Pierson strutted over to her. "Jan, you're so lovely. You turn me upside down." He knelt and tried to kiss her.

She protested, body swaying, trying to push him away, which made her body sway so much she squealed, thinking she'd spin over. "Get away, pig!"

He persisted, catching her and giving her a kiss until it melted her resistance and she wrapped her arms around his legs and kissed him back. Then he helped her dismount, bleary-eyed as she stared up into his eyes.

"Now, Jan, I want to try something. Close your eyes. Keep them closed. I'm not going to touch you."

"Why should I?" she protested.

"Do it," he ordered, waiting for her to close her eyes, then he bobbed his head toward hers. She jerked her head back each time he bobbed in for a kiss. "As I thought," he said, "there is something between us."

She opened her eyes. "What? What is it?"

"Something big. Now I'm going to close my eyes and stand still here. I want you to pucker up and move in as if you're going to kiss me, but without touching me."

His head bobbed back each time her lips neared his. "How did you do that?" Janice asked. "Could you feel my lips?"

"What's between us is doing that, Jan. Here, give me your hand. Come." He led her to a back massage room. Three hours later she stumbled out, eyes gleaming, hair mussed, clinging to Pierson, which irritated Ingrid all the more what with not being able to get rid of the guy. On the contrary, he was always there.

That night, making her rounds before locking up, Ingrid caught them out by the swimming pool, lying under the canvas cover and staring at the star riddled sky. Ingrid had to shoo them out, waiting on the steps until they left hand in hand. Next morning, though, there they were on the front steps, leaves and twigs clinging to their clothes and hair, dreaminess on Janice's pretty face, her dark eyes glassy, love-struck, her hands clasped over her heart. "We spent a romantic night together under the stars. In the park. Oh, Ingrid."

"Yeah, oh, Ingrid," Pierson grumbled. "Let's get this place opened up, oh Ingrid. We need a shower. If you trusted your employees with a key for Christ sakes we wouldn't have to sit out here like bums freezing our arses off."

Ingrid paused, staring at him. "A shower? A key? What are you talking about, Dick?" Since the Ellen episode aired, Pierson's arrogance was intolerable. "You know, Dick, not one client said that the Ellen thing had anything to do with his coming to us."

He ignored her, only returning her stare with a cool disinterest. Or was it hatred? Whatever it was only served to stir up her emotions that she tried to ignore. Running up the steps past them, she went to open up. Pierson was bad news that only got worse. An hour later Ingrid was checking the thermostat control on the saunas. Opening one sauna door she saw both of them in there naked. Sitting on a towel spread over the first tier, leaning back against the second, Pierson winked at Ingrid and lifted his arms, stretched out along the top tier, into a conductor's gesture. As if to present to her the spectacle of them naked and in love in her sauna. Janice, kneeling between his legs, stopped bobbing her head long enough to turn and look at Ingrid, Pierson's erection in her mouth poking at her cheek.

"I don't mind if you want to stand there and gawk, Ingrid. I wouldn't even mind if you wanted to administer in this fine art of oral massage. *But Jesus Christ close the damned door.* You know how much it costs to heat a sauna? We got bills coming out the ass and for all intents and purposes it seems you don't care, standing there with your thumb up your arse, gawking and taking mental notes of my training session with Janice on oral massage." Pierson pointed to the door, swinging his hand back and forth. "*Close please.*"

Flabbergasted, Ingrid couldn't move. Could only exhale a series of "Huh, huh, huh, huhs," which sounded like the disturbed breathing of someone being socked in the stomach repeatedly. Pierson's eyes were huge, and she realized that he was mocking her own eyes, the way he jutted his face out and gaped back at her. Ingrid cut an angry glance at Janice. A dingbat in love, lashed to Pierson's penis with strands of her slobber, she gave Ingrid a messy grin and giggle. *How innocent she had been! Now what a spell this Pierson had her under!* Ingrid couldn't believe the transformation, felt rage at their audacity, snapping, "We got clients walking around and... I... Just get the hell out of the sauna! I'll leave the goddamned door open as I please!" She stormed off, then when she was ten paces down the hall thought better of it, stormed back, and kicked the sauna door closed.

Pierson was evil. Her life was going to hell. She didn't know what to do about it when a few days later Ingrid heard a car pull up. From the barbershop window she watched both Janice and Pierson climbing out of a cab, the taxi driver she recognized as that shaven headed guy who had hassled her and drove off with her address that night Max was killed. They untied the trunk. Unloaded boxes. Schlepped everything in—pillows, pots, and pans in clothes hampers, hangers of clothes grasped by curled fingers under hanger hooks dangling down their backs, elbows pointing at sky, running right through the salon to the storage room.

Ingrid ran behind them. "You can't stay here, Janice. Janice! This is not a hotel!"

Janice tittered, a girl in love. The massage technicians sitting around the desk defended her. Pierson confronted her, "What are you going to do, Ingrid, throw our employee out on the street?"

"Would you please please please stop saying *our*?!"

"Only," he said, grinning, "if you would please please please stop misquoting Hemingway."

"Ingrid," Janice said, "I'm moving in. Only until Dick and I find our own place. If it bothers you that much, I'll sleep out by the pool. Just do my toilet here."

Ingrid replied, "Oh gawd. Do your toilet here?" From all the anger building up Ingrid couldn't help but laugh. That or cry. The image inspired by doing her toilet...one of Janice squatting.

Then of course everyone else had to chuckle or smile at Ingrid's outburst of hysterical laughter and throw in their two cents.

Annabel said, "Why not let her stay?"

Trish, who was back after her leave, chimed in, "What could it hurt? Besides, we have plenty of toilets if that's all she wants to do."

Ingrid argued, "But it's not just her." Ingrid nodded toward Pierson spinning Janice around a few times before a heavy make out session in front of all of them, leaving Ingrid cringing, saying, "It's *him*. Here." Ingrid couldn't fathom what Janice saw in Pierson, writing the attraction off to perhaps her perception that he had some kind of sleazy appeal.

But before she could force a showdown the new shift of therapists trooped in en masse. Each of them was odd in some quirky or shady way. All of them were dubiously hired by Bobbie.

Half an hour later complaints poured in, beginning with a distinguished Armani-clad businessman confronting Ingrid at the front desk, complaining of Goofy, a tall gorgeous blonde. Strange, forgetful, illegal in braless lace, purple pumps, blow-you lipstick and a mini, Goofy always forgot what room she had, waltzing in on another massage therapist's client after scaring her own off with her tricks. "They tell me you're the manager. Hear this: I refuse to pay for the session. This...masseuse, massaged nothing but my left calf muscle. For twenty-five minutes. Kept telling her to massage other parts of my body. 'Yeah,' she'd say, 'but I don't want to hurt you.' She kept massaging just the one leg muscle. 'What's your name?' she'd ask. I'd tell her. Two minutes later: 'What's your name?' I'm sorry, mam, but your Goofy is just too Goofy for me. Good luck with your business."

Ingrid pulled Goofy aside, chastising her, but was met with a stupid hangdog grin and not much else. "Great, Goof. You just scared away another client. Happens again you're history."

Goofy babbled, "Sorry, Ing. Thought my client was in the Mirror Balls."

"That's Mirror Ball Room," Ingrid clarified, then went to Bobbie to complain, telling her to fire Goofy.

Tossing hair from her eyes, in a kind of fuck-you snap of the head that communicated pure insolence, Bobbie defended her, saying, "Goofy is a fine masseuse. Just give her a chance."

"Oh come on, Bobbie," Ingrid said, exasperated all over again.

Problems multiplied and it became herculean to deal with. Like cutting off one snake head only to have eight crop back up. This old regular client from her freelancer days, a professional man rushed up to Ingrid in a huff, unloading, "Lying on my stomach waiting for her. Finally comes in, hear her taking off her clothes, can't quite believe it, watch her stripping, then this, this Goofy asks *me* to give *her* a massage. I said, 'That's your job. That's why I'm here.' She said, 'No it isn't. I am the client.' Then she said, 'You are the masseur. Now give me my massage, monsieur masseur.' I've had a helluva hard day, Ingrid. You know my work. Stress ulcers and the rest. Legs, back, killing me. I needed a massage but get a strip show and games. No thanks."

Ingrid asked about the massage fee.

He just laughed, "Huh," shook his head once, and made a beeline for the door while Ingrid went the other way, hunting Bobbie down, but was instead confronted by some distinguished older man saying he was an M.D., "an internist," who had made the mistake of buying some vitamins for "the masseuse Maria and her toddler boy you see running around here all the time. The kid's anemic but she, the mother Maria, is not forthcoming with the sixty dollars the vitamins cost me. So you'll have to pay. I understand you're the manager. Tried to get it from the mother but she tried to pay me off with her body just now in session. Nothing doing there. Don't you people know about AIDS? Anyway, pay me the sixty and I'm gone."

"Can't do it," Ingrid said, studying his face, which seemed sincere. Another log on the fire: another Bobbie hire, Maria, wanting to service a client in exchange for... vitamins. "You'll have to get it from her."

"Mañana, mañana. All I'm getting from her."

Ingrid held up her hands to communicate that it was out of her hands, walking away, trying to ignore his ranting after her, "Your Maria... Huh. Your Maria just came into the massage room, dimmed the lights, unzipped her one-piece suit and was quite naked underneath. She pulled the towel off me and tried to climb up on the table. I jumped off, asked her if she knew about AIDS, why she wanted to do something crazy like that. Is this place all right? I never know from the paper which places are clean."

Ingrid started to tell him that Massage World was clean but... couldn't. She could only say at the stairs, "Not my problem," leaving him at the banister ranting up after her dashing upstairs that he needed "the sixty or else."

"Are you threatening me?"

"I don't make threats to the police."

"Do what you have to do."

If she didn't get there first. Each time, though, that she had the urge to bring the cops in she recalled that tall, thin, desk-cop twerp

Mayflower, his warning about the mob infiltrating. How did it go? "Don't come to us with a carrot up your backside when they do." But were they mob, Bobbie and Pierson?

Ingrid recalled how they both had weaseled into managerial positions behind a little money then had stopped giving her any money at all. Now she was making nothing. In fact, she was losing money. Losing clients. Losing control of everything. And with paranoia creeping in, she was all but losing her mind. Clients, distinguished men of means, were storming out of terrifying sessions!

At the log book now she checked some things. Saw that Charming Kevin was available and that he was four hours over and felt her stomach churn. Another nightmare. She wanted to have it out with Bobbie but that meant she'd have to leave the desk to Rochelle who was playing grab-ass with slackers at the pool table.

Rochelle herself was another eccentric Bobbie hire. Tonight she was done up as a squaw doing fire dances in mad lunges and shrieks tearing through the salon. Last night she played Charlie Chaplin in a bowler hat, old black suit, cane, and magic-marker mustache, doing pantomime and tricks for the slacker crowd cheering her on in the salon. "Give us some more of that." "Yeah, more of that ol' whore house piano!" Which had been played by none other than Pierson. Before that she did a wild-west period piece, done up in saloon skirts and petticoats. Ingrid was enchanted at first, watching the men's cheerful expressions and the stare of their gleaming eyes as if in a pleasurable trance, robust catcalls, appreciative applause. In some way she felt proud for helping to provide such a complimentary show. But that was the problem. The song-and-dance acts distracted from the business of massage. At night's end there was nothing in the till! Then there were the rumors that circled the salon that managed to touch her managerial ears in conspiratorial whispers, which then fed a burgeoning paranoia streak in Ingrid not knowing what to say to Trish, only telling her in hushed confidence that Rochelle also liked to perform in session. Trish made a fierce face, reflecting the gravity that her mind gave the rumor. "Maria told me, Ingrid, that Rochelle's client told her that he had liked her powder massage so much that Rochelle felt encouraged to experiment by massaging him with her long hair, letting her locks tickle up and down and around you know where, Ingrid. She's going way too far."

Then Annabel knocked and entered Ingrid's office, perhaps intuiting the nature of the session, saying in a voice just above a whisper, "We have to talk, Ingrid. Now."

They unloaded a bushel basket of complaints regarding Goofy, Maria, Rochelle, Suzanne, Kevin, Bobbie, and the rest of the sorry crew from hell. "They're all too much, Ingrid. Whatever they are, they're not serious massage techs. Clients are telling us all kinds of things. A gay guy informed me that Goofy offered to solve his problem, telling him that she could teach him not to be gay anymore. Goofy actually invited him to her apartment for sex. Then there's Kevin."

Charming Kevin. Another Bobbie hire. "We need another masseur," Bobbie had argued. "Think of it as a P.R. ploy to put a damper on certain suspicions." She hired a blond pretty boy, a real smooth talker who held court in the salon for hours. To try to get some work out of him during the promotional campaign, Ingrid steered several female clients his way. At first, they liked his massage so much they brought friends around. Then he went too far, too fast. Out by the pool Ingrid overheard talk, one woman or another going on about having to slap his hands away. "I know, isn't he a little devil?"

The number of female clients dwindled.

No matter for Kevin. He had a loyal following of men, mainly older and moneyed, coming around. His biggest fan was a company president, a refined gentleman named Norman who now came every day for Kevin's massage. Ingrid worked out a special deal with technicians who brought in their own clients, renting them the massage room by the hour as a safeguard against their giving the massage out of their own home and eventually giving the middle finger to Massage World. But the plan backfired with Kevin. Stiffing Ingrid for interminable sessions that ran four, five hours, he owed Ingrid fourteen hundred. She nagged him but each time he found a way to slip by her, saying he didn't have it on him, patting his pockets. "Tapped out. Sorry, Ingrid. Catch me tomorrow."

"Can you believe that guy?" Annabel asked, handing the log to Ingrid. "Look."

Noting when the session started then the time now by a glance at her watch, Ingrid calculated that the cute little shit was doing another four-hour mega-session with Norman. Perturbed, carrying the log book at her chest, she ran downstairs, asking Erma if she'd seen Kevin.

"Just saw Pretty Boy," Erma said. "He and Norman came out of a sauna in nothing but towels."

Knocking on his massage-room door, she said, "Kevin? We have to talk. Open up. Knock, knock."

Two minutes later he opened the door a crack. Shirt buttons undone, belt unbuckled. "Yeah?"

"Kevin," Ingrid asked, "did you just take a sauna with Norman?"

He shook his head emphatically. "No, Ingrid, we did not just take a sauna. We just took a jacuzzi. Before the jacuzzi there was the sauna. Like that."

"Kevin—"

"It's okay, Ingrid. No big deal." He closed the door, locking it.

"It's not okay, Kevin. You owe me fourteen hundred something dollars and I need the money. Need it now, Kevin. You know my situation. Who's putting you up to this? Bobbie? Pierson? Who? I hope you're not paying them."

When he didn't respond she thumped the side of her fist against the door. Thumped it again. "Little shit!" Then ran upstairs to look for Bobbie to have it out over Kevin. Not finding her, on her way back down she gasped then had to clamp down on her lips to keep from screaming at Tess was pulling a pair of pantyhose over her head, stocking legs hanging down right and left, then opening the door to a suit, cocking her head quaintly, "Would you like a massage, *monsieur*?" She twirled the stocking legs before her and rocked back and forth.

The suit looked her up and down. "I'd better go." Over Tess's shoulder to Ingrid at the landing, he said, "Maybe I'll come back when you have more serious masseuses." He turned and fled down the stairs.

"*No mas*, Tess. You're fired."

"You can't fire me, you didn't hire me. Bobbie did. Unless you want a fight." Tess raised her fists and hit at the air. "I'm pretty tough, Ingrid."

I don't believe this is happening. Where the fuck is Bobbie? "Bobbie!" she yelled out as the phone rang. On her way to the desk Ingrid passed Suzanne who was sloshing in from the pool, dripping water all over hell and back. Ingrid looked over her shoulder, doing a double take in disbelief of Suzanne's skimpy crocheted bikini as full of holes as a macramé plant holder. Also in the losers' circle of Bobbie, Suzanne was a hari krishna or playing the part of one in this great collective act to scam her out of business. Caught between the phone's bleating and long, wet, black pig tails, a thick neck festooned with Krishna beads and what was worse (a cluster of herpes vesicles resembling a bunch of grapes in miniature on her upper lip), Ingrid played traffic cop, turning her back on the phone, stepping in front of Suzanne and stopping her with an extended hand. "You're supposed to be working, Suzanne, not swimming."

Suzanne quit singing her mantras, looked at Ingrid, rolling her big brown eyes in a dopey way. "I wasn't swimming, Ingrid. I was in the *jacuzzi*. I'm sure."

If Ingrid had a pink slip she would have written up Suzanne, but she could only tell her to go home. "Don't come back until you're lesions have cleared up." Wagging a finger, she continued, "And don't let me catch you traipsing around here in such a swimsuit."

"My herpes aren't the contagious kind, Ingrid, and...my swimsuit I made myself. You hurt my feelings." She looked on the verge of tears.

Ingrid lurched toward the phone but it had stopped ringing so she headed back upstairs. In her office she paced, trying to sort things out. She felt as if she could trust no one, realizing without a shred of doubt that Bobbie and Pierson were doing a damned fine job of starving her out, blockading her business with their parlor tricks. She hadn't taken in a dollar in the last three days and had a total of seven dollars to her name, her inheritance from her father all poured into Massage World and now gone. Then, the following day, she realized they were doing the same to those faithful to her, the technicians she hired, and when Annabel cabbed back from three failed outcalls, her face creased with worry lines that told Ingrid right away that she was thinking miserable thoughts.

"Unfolding my massage table in his living room. This pudgy bald creep. 'How we going to do this?' he asks. 'You want me on top or what?'

'On top? I'm here to give you a straight massage, nothing else.' 'A massage?!' 'What did you expect?' 'A good fuck.' 'Listen, I said on the phone that it's a straight massage.' 'You all have to say that on the phone.' 'Either a straight massage or forget it,' I said.

'Let's just forget it then.' I told him, 'Pay me for my taxi fare.' 'I'll do no such thing.' 'I'm not leaving here until you pay me—'

'Wanna bet. '

He grabbed my arm, Ingrid, he grabbed me like this, pushed me hard, at the door. At the next two places no one home. The fourth an old lady spoke through her chained door. 'That a card table there?'

'It's my massage table. I'm here to give a Mr. Cotthaus a massage. He your husband?' 'No one ordered no massage here,' she said. 'But

I called the number... ' 'Not my number.' *Who would do such a thing? Pull such a prank? I spent sixty two dollars on taxi fares and didn't earn a penny from massage. Need to be reimbursed so that I can make rent. I'm serious, Ingrid.*"

Holding her chin in her hand, a finger stroking up and down from a corner of her mouth to the fleshy part of her chin, Ingrid watched Annabel. Sensing she spoke the truth and that the outcall shenanigans had Bobbie and/or Pierson's fingerprints all over it, Ingrid couldn't help but suspect that there was indeed a starvation scam afoot. She could only sympathize with Annabel. When that didn't placate her she quoted house rules—that taxi fares were covered by practitioners who were hired as independent contractors, whose profits were split with the spa. How much they made depended entirely on how many massages they gave.

"I know all that," Annabel snarled with a hand on her hip, and a defiant look not quite at Ingrid but not quite away from Ingrid either. "Just great, Ingrid. Just great."

Ingrid raised her shoulders and held up her hands. "What do you want me to do?"

"No more outcalls for me." Annabel left in a huff, nearly running into Trish spouting her litany of problems, "Big problems, Ing. Suzanne is on desk and we're talking major herpes. She's down there in nothing but a crotched bikini and pool water dripping over everything. Then who marches in but the Officer taking over the phone to line up her appointments she says she's gonna give out of my massage room again. All the other massage rooms are full. The Thai girls pushed Ryoji out of his room. I don't know what to do anymore, Ingrid."

"Back me up," Ingrid said. They ran downstairs. Ingrid shouting, "Suzanne, you're fired! Now get out!"

Suzanne stood then pirouetted around the desk. "I want to scream! I want to scream!" Which drew the full attention of the slackers. One in rap chains and a football jersey hanging down to his knees had to imitate her, pirouetting himself and saying in a girlish voice, "I want to scream! I want to scream!" They all had to laugh, of course, which embarrassed Ingrid but not enough to keep her from grabbing Suzanne and giving her a good shake. "Stop it now!" She handed her clothes and purse over. "I'll see you to the door and then I never want to see you again."

Back at the desk a metal head came in, some kid slurring drunk and reeking of gin. "Officer here? Have my session with the Officer."

Ingrid wanted to draw him out. "You like her?"

"Like her!? Love her!" In anticipation he swiveled his hips as if they were doing it already.

Ingrid didn't even know her real name. Lanky, breasty, short frizzy brown hair, the Officer was supposedly a genuine United States Marine Corps officer, so everyone called her the Officer. In her first week on the job she wore her officer's uniform, saying she was only interested in massage as a side job. During her second week the Officer dressed like a streetwalker in heavy makeup, spider-leg eyelashes, and smelt like she sprayed herself with a bottle of perfume. Between sleeveless stretch tops that exposed her belly and mauve stockings over spike heels, she wore mini-skirts shrink wrapped over a behind that betrayed no shame, grinding across the salon to uproarious catcalls from the pool-table brigade, the rapidly expanding contingent that now spent nothing and did nothing but be there to make the bad moments worse. Ingrid's attempts to throw them out were met with indifference. They hung out all day belching, farting, scratching, flirting, and swatting and pinching at the bottoms of masseuses strutting through. Obnoxiously whooping it up over the tedious mimicry that the Millennial crowd was so good at, which only pointed at their weakness in the creativity column.

"Listen, Officer," Ingrid said, shifting a step with this supposed superior officer to hold her eye, to stay in her gaze so as to deliver firmly to the clutch of her mind. "You're going to have to tone it down. Dress and makeup both."

The Officer scoffed, sneering, looking away which prompted Ingrid to shift around as she was committed to standing in the net of her attention. "I work for Bobbie, not you."

"You work here," Ingrid said. "And here we're getting tired of your commandeering the phone and working dubious clientele listed in an even more dubious little black book. You should hear yourself."

Ingrid grabbed up an imaginary receiver, saying into it, "'Ted? The Officer. I'm here at Massage World now. The new place in Uptown. At four? I'll be hot to trot.' Then next: Bill? It's me, the Officer. Yeah, at Massage World. How does five sound? Light my fire at five? You're on.' Then: 'Charlie? You guessed it. Yeah. At Massage World. How 'bout something that sounds like six at six?'"

"What are you doing, Ingrid?" the Officer growled. "Monitoring my phone calls? I don't believe this."

Ingrid, glaring, said, "And I don't believe you have paid me a cent for the room, which Trish is scheduled to use tonight. You owe me nine hundred dollars, Officer."

"Wrong. I owe that to Bobbie."

"But—"

She was already leading the metal head to his massage. Afterwards, Ingrid did a little inspection of her massage room. On the floor, laid out like a mattress, were large decorative pillows bearing the clear impression of one long reclining body. Clearly the Officer's imprint, Ingrid deduced, picking up the middle pillow and sniffing the odor of sex strong in the fabric. Obviously they had just been fucking. Ingrid threw the pillow against the wall then ran to the desk. She picked up the phone to call the police (who else could she call?) then remembered her pride and the desk dick closing that door. *Don't come waddling to us, Ingrid, with a carrot jammed up your ass when they infiltrate.* Wasn't that what he said? She slammed down the receiver, then looked up to see an old crazy client wobbling through, soaking wet from the jacuzzi where he had the habit of jumping in with his clothes on. Dressed in loud, oil-stained plaid pants and a black-and-white striped shirt, he dripped water all the way across the salon to the juice bar while chanting an idiot's babble of, "Chia Chia Chia, Betsy Betsy Betsy, Chia Chia Chia, Betsy Betsy Betsy..."

Ingrid couldn't take it anymore, exhaling a long sigh, stood up screaming, "*Would you shut up!?*"

Suddenly, a violent quiet fell across the salon. And she felt herself at the middle of it, feeling the heat of some fifty people staring. "What are you looking at!?" she screamed, twirling around, jutting her face out, staring back, and fixing her eyes on some thin scruffy kid fit with scarecrow rags. He fidgeted with the pool cue in his hands, directing his attention to what his fingernails scratched at, some small imperfection in the wood, lifting it closer to his eyes, focusing, to wait out the storm of scolding. "Tell me what you're staring at!?" They all said nothing. All eyes were lowered in embarrassment at her loss of temper, but kept flicking at her their curiosity in glances and their retaliation in a soupçon of sneers. Expressions, though, became as smileless as beasts when she walked up to one then another slacker in a stare down she, as manager of Massage World, inevitably won.

Striding away from the spectacle she heard things, though. First, like a faint wind stirring through the salon, whispers touched her ears.

The whispers became louder and chased her up the stairs. The roar of purposeful laughter which licked her back with fire, burned her face with shame and stung her mind with the revelation that Massage World was obviously no longer in her grasp.

* * *

The next day after a sleepless night in a massage room Ingrid awoke to the Doors on the stereo. All of the speakers were switched on so that *The End* blared through the entire mansion. She sat alone at the desk, her face in her hands, cursing over Bobbie's scheduling when she heard the door open. She flinched at the odd sight of a heavily bandaged man in a wheelchair. His face looked that of a mummy. Eyes, nose, mouth dark slashes and dots of shadow. His wheelchair was caught in the threshold, one wheel on the salon floor and the other down on the pronaos step, he pumped at the push rims with one hand and tugged at the door frame with the other.

"Just a moment. Let me help you." Ingrid ran over, grabbed the lower wheel and helped pull him in.

The mummy head spoke in the foyer. Straining, breathless, "Name's Thornton. Larry Thornton. I am troubled by your lack of wheelchair accessibility I'll have you know."

"Sorry. I'm Ingrid. How can I help you?"

"If you would be so kind as to roll me into a massage room."

"Before I can do that, Mr. Thornton," she said, closing the door then getting behind the wheel chair, "I'll have to roll you over to the desk."

Giving her control of the chair, he held up his hands. "As you please."

Ingrid parked him opposite the desk chair then sat down, asking him the routine questions (how he heard about them, if he were having any pain and where, etc.), while noting how his bandages ended at his wrists, his lip didn't move as he talked, and he clipped off his words in a seemingly aristocratic affectation. How he seemed a little creepy, the way his eyes bolted back and forth deep down in the cave of bandage gashes—that had a square shape as if from the poke of a giant screwdriver head. "A Mr. Temarias, of Mr. Temarias After Shave referred me. He is a close friend."

A fine reference behind him, the mummy suddenly became

much more human. Technicians fought like tigers to go to Temarias when he called. Temarias ordered three technicians to work on him simultaneously. Then tipped extravagantly.

"If you are not busy," Mr. Thornton said, "I would most appreciate your massage, Ingrid, instead of taking my chances on the draw."

Down to her last dollar in her pocket, she felt visited by the heat of temptation but said, "I don't give massage, but let me see who's available." She scanned the list beside the phone, her index finger leading the way straight down.

"You are a masseuse?" he asked.

She looked up from the list. "A massage technician, yes." Then back down. "Let's see..." Ingrid herself didn't usually work the desk this early. But Bobbie had called in with the flu. Then Fifi did, too. Then Maria. The Officer. The masseuse flu. Ingrid's pencil point paused at "Goofy." No, she couldn't turn over someone freshly referred by their best client to Goofy (and Goofy was in session for another half hour anyway), then farther down the list her pencil paused at Trish. No, not Trish (she was booked through the afternoon). That left only Kevin and his tricks. "Do you have a preference, Mr. Thornton, as to masseuse or masseur?"

"I prefer the touch of a woman," he said through the mouth gash of his bandages, "if you would not mind."

At a nervous impasse. That twitchy time of a business deal that begged to get around the frustration of obstruction for the simple purpose of closure. They stared at each other. "We have a problem."

"And what might that be?"

Refraining from explaining why (because she feared Vice would attempt entrapment), she said, "I don't give massage, and there is no one else available but a masseur, who is quite outstanding really."

He shook his head. "If it'll sway you, Madam Ingrid, I am most appreciate of a woman's massage and will pay the royal sum of five hundred dollars for your massage—"

She cut him off. "No, I'm sorry. I don't give massage."

"Five hundred dollars for one hour's work, Ingrid." He pulled a stack of bills from a brown paper bag he had stored between his thigh and the clothing guard of his wheelchair. Tapping the stack, "As for the five hundred, here." He handed her the bills (she took them, as if only to look). "I was just awarded two and a half million from the insurance firm of the cowboy trucker who flattened my chauffeur and me in my limousine. Five hundred dollars, I will have you know, is entirely within my means."

She stared at the five hundred, seeing all kinds of things (rent, square meals, cab fares, toothpaste, rags). Fingering the stack of twenties, she looked around the salon for eavesdroppers on this near break of policy, clarifying, "A one hour massage, right?"

"That is correct," he said. "One hour, no more." He held up a finger, kept holding it up, to add one more menacing thing. "But I'll need for insurance and tax purposes an itemized receipt, with your name, signature, and date and time of massage."

She thought about his request, concluding it didn't seem unusual for someone looking so unusual. "For insurance and tax purposes? Okay. First tell me if you're in any pain."

He held up his hands. Waved them. "None. No pain whatsoever. Only my head and arms are bandaged, to protect the scabs, from where I flew into the plexiglass partition. You need only ignore my arms and head in the massage, Ingrid."

She nodded, filled out the receipt, handed it over, then said, "Okay, we're in business. Now let's go." Pushing the wheelchair determinedly, fearful that a tech would come upon them, she said, "Wheeling you back to three, our Egyptian Room."

MOTOKO OGAWA

Felt lost, jet lagged, and culture shocked. Fatigue came down harder, and she felt like hands were squeezing the top of her head. When the light flashed to signal an available bank teller at Sanwa Bank in Border City, she wanted the Japanese teller (now busy with a Japanese businessman) not the blonde American girl. Surely there would be a language problem. Americans were too short-tempered. Only her sense of *gimu*, or obligation, to Jack-san had her stepping forward, tensing, stammering, not yet sure what to do with the duffel bag—set it on the floor (no, too many criminals in America) or plop it down on the counter. She settled for clutching it to her chest. "I have special probrem." She looked at the girl through the bars of the teller counter at the downtown bank. "I want change money."

"What denomination?" the teller asked.

"Yen to *dorrars*."

The young lady flinched when Motoko told her the amount. "Would that be in cash?"

"Cash," Motoko said.

"You have a bank check then?"

"No, bank check. Cash. I have all cash..." Motoko lifted the duffel bag, resting it on the counter. "Money here."

"Do you have an account with us?"

"Account in Tokyo, Sanwa Bank, Nakano office." She produced a passbook and passport and slid them through the slot.

The teller said that she had to get managerial approval. When she came back, she explained the exchange rates, and Motoko began crunching the numbers on a calculator. Figures squared, heads nodding, Motoko pulled bricks of yen from her duffel bag then slid the stacks of bills to the teller. The manager, a middle-aged woman in a pink dress and gold earrings, breezed over to help with the counting, picking up one of the bundles then tearing off the paper looped around the bills. "All this cash," she asked, softening the question with a smile, "you carried from Tokyo?"

"Mmmm," Motoko said. "From Tokyo."

"Are you sure you want cash in return?" the manager asked, leaning into the question aggressively, as Americans do. "We," she emphasized, lifting both eyebrows and nodding, "could give you a bank check, you know."

In Japan in her generation everything was in cash. Motoko Ogawa knew no other way. "*Sank* you. But cash *prease.*"

"What size bills?"

"All hundred *dorrar biru,*" Motoko said.

"All hundreds?" the manager asked, the disbelief in her tone startling Motoko.

Americans were too direct in their expressions. "*Prease. Hundreds onri.*"

"That's one hundred thousand dollars in hundreds," the manager calculated, shaking her head. "We'll have to go into the vault. Take us about half an hour. You're not in a rush?"

"Rush?" Motoko said. "What mean?"

The manager said, "You're not in a hurry, are you?"

"Mmm, hurry." Motoko looked at her watch. "*Prease* hurry."

INGRID

Noticed that Mr. Thornton was a rather well-built man. And surprisingly, for all the wrapping, didn't need much help hobbling up onto the massage table. Ingrid parked his chair against the wall then saw, in the moment between his underwear coming off and her throwing the drape over him, that he was hairless. His underarms, chest and pubic rim showed a mere stubble of indecipherable color, as illuminated by the Egyptian Room's holograms of pyramids and camels and turbaned men and veiled women silhouetted against hot orange sunsets. But a freckle blemish glowed over his white skin, giving it an additional hue.

She turned on a CD of sitar music. Hand hovering over the accessories she asked, "Hot oil or light powder?"

Stretched out on the table he said, "Powder. Oil would make a slimy mess of my bandages."

Halfway through the massage she shepherded the drape around against the impropriety of a trespassing glance as she had him turn over onto his back. "At this point, Madam Ingrid, I must tell you that when your hands come to the junction of my thighs and scrotum that I desire a change up. Put the powder away and get out the hot oil."

Pinched, his voice also seemed bandaged—too falsely eloquent in trying to get her to give him a handjob. Wasn't that what he was doing? Suspicious, her intuition kicking in, she followed the spray of freckles ending under his neck bandages, then she imagined them continuing up onto his face, a face she envisioned by reading his bone structure. His nose. She knew that pudgy nose. It was extra fleshy, making his nostrils seem squeezed. She nearly jumped back against the wall registering it.

He sat up, gasped, "You act as if you've just seen a ghost."

She tried to laugh. "More like a mummy. Maybe it's the sitars, the whole ambiance. I never really liked this room."

"I imagine I do look a sight in my bandages," he said, pointing with his arm. "But could you please hand me the paper sack on my chair there."

She couldn't speak. Couldn't move. She just kept nodding until a surge of anger hit her hard at the recollection of Max. His bleeding head in her hands propelled her away from the table. She felt the sack, but didn't feel a gun so she handed it to him. He poured out its contents on the sheet. "Five hundred dollars." He slapped the bills against his other hand. "My request is unusual. For that I am all too willing to compensate you with an additional five. All for a simple penile massage. Here." He nonchalantly tried to hand her the stack of bills.

"What's that for?"

"I guess you didn't understand. Okay. In layman's terms, Ingrid, a handjob, albeit one lubricated with hot oil. Now here. Take the money. Five hundred dollars. For a simple penile massage. Not implant, hah hah. But massage. Now here."

"No! I mean, yes. Not yet, I mean. You just keep the money. At least until you're satisfied. First let me get a different oil. In the other room. You lie still. I'll be right back..."

"Wait. Where are you going?"

Ingrid ran through the salon, flew up the stairs two at a time, then knocked on the VIP room where Trish was in session.

I, DETECTIVE RANDAL "RED" GUDSIKES

Lay there, fingering my bandages, listening to eerie sitar music, my eyes transfixed by holograms of pyramids, nomads, camels.

Swanson breezed in out of breath and nervous. Apologetic, as if covering her agitation. "Sorry I took so long. Had to go upstairs. First, I'll massage down your chest. Close your eyes. Breathe deeply."

Things were going too fast then suddenly too slow when a damp cloth was thrust onto my face, pressed over my nose and mouth by a firm hand. The sharp reek of industrial-strength chemicals made me shudder and convulse.

Delirium. Nausea. A distant voice said, "*You bastard. You slimy cop bastard.*"

Tried to get up, rope cutting into my chest. Eyes half opening to a flash blinding me. Tried to scream through a gag's bite but could only whimper. Squinting, spied SWANSON and TOTT (previously identified as Trish TOTT, Massage License 36740), moving in a slow motion blur through back lighting and my chemical asphyxiation that was equal to attempted murder.

Too obscene, too offensive, for any decent person to repeat.

"Get that gag off him." "Gag or rag?" "Thing's soaked with spit." "Loosen the ropes." "Yeah, good idea. Don't want ropes in the picture. That could implicate us."

Playing opossum, I closed my eyes, holding my breath to escape the fume rag TOTT now removed from over my nose and mouth. "Okay," TOTT said. "He's under." "Still can't believe I'm doing this."

I felt like Gulliver wrenching up against the tug of ropes, twisting from the cart. But dizziness struck and I fought a temptation to vomit and pass out at the same time.

The last thing I heard: glass crashing against my head, TOTT saying, "*Later, asshole.*"

I felt icy cold, coming around in the chill of March wind. Knew I was outside in winter weather. The crowns of the portico's pillars giving me my bearings.

The tree tops were blurred overhead against blue sky, delirious, hearing TOTT and SWANSON's laughter as they pushed the cart—*me*—away down the concrete stairs. Each stair the cart bounced down was a club smashing against my back.

The cart crashing down faster, I rolled nude, bound, gagged, speeding farther from SWANSON and TOTT's carefree laughter and high-five congratulatory slapping watching with glee the cart—me!—pick up speed.

Strapped to the cart, I shivered all over and felt adrenaline shoot through like a lethal injection. I tried to scream and rip free from the blades of rope lashing me as bougainvillea thorns raked over my toes, my shins. It tore deep into my thighs as the two accomplices laughed and slapped high fives. Thorns raked clean up through my scrotum (see attached photos), tearing through bandages, skin and hair (see attached photos).

The impact of the cart crashing into the fence put out my lights...

—I don't know. I don't have it in me to understand why the two accomplices did to me what they did.

I was unconscious for several days.

JANICE

Felt her eyes glaze over. She was trying her best to follow her client. "Injuria non excusat injuriam will most certainly be considered non vult contendere, an exigency pertaining to extenuating circumstances in desuetude dictum. Corpus delicti is hitherto mere conjecture and wholly nonsequitural in the matter of compounding a felony or compounding a misdemeanor. Estoppel permitting, immunity is to be invitum and in camera after mitigating circumstances transcribe themselves into volente non fit injuria."

Her legs dangling from the massage table, struggling to stay awake, Janice couldn't find the thread in the babbling of her client, a yuppie lawyer sitting fully clothed in his three-piece suit in Massage Room 8, the Alpine Room. His face had reddened as he spouted legal terms, and his voice broke as if adolescent.

In his nerdy tone he scolded her, "What I want is for you to listen. No one listens to me at the firm. *So open your eyes and listen!*"

"You sure you don't want a massage?"

"God, no." He made a face as if disgusted.

Janice looked at him. Meager of build. A thin, fragile face. A weak chin which he caressed as he spoke, playing lawyer. His nose twitched under the weight of steel-rimmed lenses. A military cut made him look too boyish and proper. The opposite of Jack in so many ways. She loved and loathed Jack, and his daring, his aura of total irresistible outlaw prick. Who made her put off grad school another year. Can you believe it? Him!? While this lawyer guy was all convention and hesitation, hemmed in by bookishness, all flattened out by legal language. A bore. Pontificating to an empty courtroom.

"Vicinage and liability and subornation of perjury will be considered quid pro quo should the case come to plea bargaining where misdemeanors may be weighed against misfeasance, pain and suffering against official malice aforethought. Without divestiture, immunity will most assuredly be gratis, de minimus, id est, in the bright light of the fruit of the poisonous tree doctrine..."

INGRID

Was reading the alternative weekly newspaper. On page seven she burst into laughter at an hysterical shot of Gudsikes, strapped naked to the cart like an accident victim in ragged bandages, badge glinting on his forehead where they taped it, a tiny black square censoring the image of his...*thang*. The caption ran, *Letting it all hang out, one of Border City's Finest enjoys a break in the rather gray weather as of late to sun bathe nude on Melon Street.* The headline was a scream:

UNDERCOVER(S) VICE DICK GETS EXPOSED

By Dee Lighted

Ingrid read the article, then felt tense, nervous, fearful from the last paragraph:

...Border City Police Department Chief Samuel Hibler refused to comment on the case, other than saying that "the whole mess is turning into one nasty massage war, of which this is but one little battle."

A clunk resounded through the salon. Someone was thumping the clacker. Ingrid put the paper aside then crossed the salon. She opened the door to rain sounds and smells and a little old Asian lady in the frou-frou of a flower-patterned kimono. A pixie cut over a heavily made up face, she looked up at Ingrid with a cheerful gleam in her eyes despite the weather. Clutching a duffel bag and umbrella before her, she asked, "You Ingrid?" She introduced herself to Ingrid and bowed and said that she was from Tokyo. "Your weather like Japan." She motioned to the rain. "Now can we talk? Can we talk business?"

A little too comical. Or surreal. What business? Curious, Ingrid invited her up to her office. There, Ms. Ogawa said, "I know your country different from my country. So I speak direct."

Ingrid was nodding along. "Please. Go ahead."

"I want to buy your spa," she said, and as if her hands were holding Massage World, "then make present of it to friend."

Had Ingrid heard right?

"I would *rike* to buy Massage World."

Ingrid leaned closer, turned and tilted her head, giving the older woman a sidelong stare, asking, "You're saying you want to buy my business?"

Motoko nodded.

Ingrid said she had heard about the Chinese buying up America but not the Japanese. When the attempt at humor failed Ingrid apologized, saying she didn't really want to sell.

Motoko shrugged, as if she knew something Ingrid didn't. In a sing-song voice, she said, "You never know."

"I do know," Ingrid said. "We just opened. I think I can make it go."

Motoko lowered her voice, looked down at the duffel bag on her lap. "I offer you one hundred thousand *dorrars*. Money here. Now—"

"You have one hundred thousand dollars?" Ingrid stood and walked around the desk as the Japanese woman opened the bag and dug out bundles of dollars and laid them on Ingrid's desk, motioning to the large mound. "One hundred thousand *dorrars*. All hundreds. Cash. For your Massage World."

"I don't understand. What? Why?"

"*Presento* for friend."

"Presento? Which friend? Who? Present for whom?"

"*Secreto*. I no can tell you. But if you don't want money, okay. I go now."

Ingrid fought an urge to tackle the little old Japanese lady as she fed stacks of bills back in her duffel bag then zipped it up in a hurry. There was something exhilarating about the sight of so much cash. "Before I go back to Japan, Ingrid, I come back one more time. I invite you to Japanese restaurant. We talk."

The Japanese lady didn't register Ingrid's refusal, said, "*Sank* you, Ingrid-san." She bowed. "I go now."

* * *

Ingrid lay on the recamier in the salon lounge. Too charged up from the sight of all that cash, she got up and paced. She wanted to do something. Not play pool, shaking her head at some guy asking her for a game. Cigarette dangling from his lips, he wore three days of scruffy growth and a dirty thermal-underwear shirt under a faded flannel with sawed-off sleeves. "Can I at least use your phone?"

She pointed toward the pay phone.

As he spoke into the receiver he drooped his head and raised his shoulders. In his trying to make a phone booth out of his body, it gave him the curious look of a vulture, which led Ingrid to come up behind him on near tip toes, pricking up her ears to catch his whisper, "She's here now. I'll see that she stays here."

Ingrid should have recognized his uniform: the law posing as the lawless, and was about to ask him who was here, when the front door crashed open and a column of cops charged in wearing dark-blue windbreakers stamped POLICE in white block letters. Immediately, Ingrid recognized the lead cop as the ornery fellow she had irked in the Licensing Division. Getting his revenge, he held a badge and paperwork out before him and shouted, "This is a raid! Nobody move!"

Cops spread out with fire-drill urgency. Four ran upstairs. Five dashed through to the back. All of them pounding on doors. "Police!" The began ushering out scared clients in bath towels and frantic technicians into the salon whose expressions asked, "What gives?" Three cops in the salon dumped the contents of the desk drawers onto the floor. Another poked like a horticulturist into some potted plants—"Where's the grass?"—then bent down behind the juice bar, turning over cartons while singing an old John Denver song. "Take me home..."

ANNABEL

Remembered Colladay despite the old lady contending, "I didn't think you'd remember me, Annabel."

"How could I forget Ms. Colladay? Little white toy poodle. Diamonds the size of the Ritz. Chauffeured limo." Annabel was currently massaging the rich old lady she had met at The Chateau, recalling, through her fingers, her aged skin. A gunny sack stuffed with chicken bones, which felt sharper from her having lost even more weight. Her spirit was also sharper, pricking Annabel with a complaint about The Chateau, "I will never go back there, Annabel. Not a decent masseuse to be found since you left. The help has gotten more snooty, grumbling about wages as if to extract more of a tip. For the thousands we pay who wants to hear such grumbling?"

"I know, Ms. Colladay. Now just relax and enjoy the massage."

"I always enjoy your massage, Annabel. I was just telling Martini. You remember my driver—"

Suddenly there was a pounding at the door. Annabel snatched her hands from Colladay's body as if it were shocking her. Colladay hooted at the shout of "Police!" As the door knob slammed against the wall she hooted again. Two cops bumped shoulders as they charged in.

"What in heavens!?" Colladay clutched the towel up around her. "The Keystone Cops!"

"Nobody move!"

Colladay scolded the two officers ushering her out into the salon, then asked after *her* Martini. A portly cop with pork-chop sideburns and bell bottom blue jeans. "Something tells me we've found the owner of the double-parked Rolls."

"And her chauffeur." Draped in a towel, standing where they put him—in a corner next to a potted plant.

"Here's your corner, lady. Don't turn around—"

"I said don't touch me!"

The pork-chop cop made a joke, "Maybe I should strip search her."

INGRID

Knew it was all over when she saw the mean desk cop glaring at her. The tall, thin Mayflower from Licensing, the one who pledged he'd bust her, was there now doing just that, giving the orders, pointing and shouting. "As you apprehend, corner, and confiscate, keep your eyes open for a secret ledger. Guddy swears it's here somewhere."

Another flurry of officers trampled in, flashing badges andrunning through to the back. "Police. Open up." They took over the desk, phone, barbershop, and juice bar. Two officers rushed back into the salon from the pool area with three male clients dripping wet from the rain or the jacuzzi or pool hustled in ahead of them complaining to Ingrid, "What's going on?"

Gruffly, the cops said, "No talking that's what. Your corner, pal. Don't move." Cops asked for names, jotting them down in pocket-sized pads. They dumped the drawers of filing cabinets and used their shoes to kick open and leaf through the files all while mumbling about a secret ledger. "Guddy swears it's here." Drawers of papers were dumped in cardboard boxes. One cop sat down at the computer, voicing a curious theory about the "high probability of the secret ledger being hidden right here" as he booted up the system. Tea canisters from the juice bar were dumped across the bar top. Noses crinkled up. Tea sniffed. "Where's the grass, girls? Guddy swears it's here." In tears and handcuffs, Annabel was led out. Mayflower smacking warrants— search and arrest—into Ingrid's hand. Gleeful, he couldn't contain himself behind a shit-eating grin. "Remember my pledge, Swanson? Before I arrest you, help me, though. Looking for your secret ledger, dear."

"What ledger?"

He shrugged. "You don't want to cooperate? Fine. Going down hard either way. You're looking at serious time." He rambled off reasons, held like old grudges. *For insulting me. For making folly of the department. For hanging Red Gudsikes out to dry.*

A tall muscular cop ushered Trish and an older woman out into the salon, holding them by the arm. Both Trish and her client had nothing on but the towels wrapped around them, disappointing Ingrid. "Found this one," the cop said, pointing to Trish, "lying atop this one, getting all kissy face."

"Huh." A grunting voice, "See any muff diving?"

"Unfortunately, no."

"You're all assholes!" Trish snapped. "This is typical patriarchal testosterone overload. You don't own my body. You filthy pigs!"

"Let's not go calling each other names now—"

"Asshole!"

"Say it again and I'll start stacking 'em."

"Stacking what?"

"Stacking charges."

"*Asshole.*"

"That's assaulting a Police Officer as well. I'm placing you under arrest."

"Stupid cop. Nothing but blatant male oppression. I was just giving her a massage."

"Without any clothes on yourself? That's illegal, too, lady, but I haven't made up my mind whether I'll charge you with that yet."

"Listen, you don't own my body. I'll do whatever I want with my body. Behind closed doors, who am I hurting? Besides, we're lovers!"

"Cuff this one, Wilb. I've heard enough. Let her wait outside in the rain as she is. Yeah, in just the towel. Let her cool off in front of the cameras."

Two more cops strode in from the back hall, leading four transvestites, the same ones, Ingrid remembered, who were swinging from the plant holders. Singsong voices (this was all a game to the cops, Ingrid thought) announcing, "Look...what...we...found."

Four Mexican transvestites in handcuffs were cursing the cops as they were led out to a paddy wagon in a mishmash of vile curses switching from one language to the other like something electrical. "*Chinga tu madre mutha fucka. Americano peeg!*"

"He-shes. Caught 'em passing around this joint. Size of a stogie. Look." One held up a cigar-sized joint rolled out of newsprint. "Guddy was right about the grass. They were trying to scramble through a trap door in the floor while holding onto it—"

His partner arched his eyebrows and grinned, interrupting with his two cents of fun, "A trap door under the massage table. Imagine getting a massage and seeing through the face hole one of them there creatures crawling in." He made his face express the worst kind of terror in a silent scream. Serious again, he said, "Huh. Grabbed this one by the ankles as he was crawling out. Little fucker. Turned around quick as an animal entering its lair and snapped. Bit the shit out of my hand. Right here." His holding his hand up before his eyes invited other eyes to examine the wound.

"Have to be checked for HIV."

"Start the timer."

"Three days, they say, right?"

Expressionless as sharks, the cops closed ranks around the rugby scrum of pre-op transgenders. Perhaps intending to kick them like curs. The transgenders covered their heads, cowering, their eyes huge and bulbous like soldiers sheltered in fox holes with bombs whistling overhead.

A lieutenant or cop of higher rank spied the violence about to happen and rushed over, calling them off with, "Make sure they get their own paddy wagon. Do we have a special one for...the third sex? How many we got anyway? Straight to the pig pen with the lot of 'em."

Another cop came in summarizing, "Jesus Christ, quite a fun house. A real Mad Hatter's tea party. Grass, he-shes, fornicating Chinese, and lesbian lovers getting it on...how I'll never know. Where's the grass? Where's Ingrid? Oh, there's Ingrid. Well, Ingrid, I can only say that you made two very major mistakes: pissing off Mayflower in the licensing division and pantsing Red Gudsikes for that weekly rag."

Another cop chimed in, "Quite a pornographic frame job of brother Guddy, Ingrid Wingrid. You don't embarrass the Border City P.D. and live to tell about it."

"Ted, you see the media circus out front?"

"Fucking cameras up the ying-yang."

"Up the what?"

A short cop announced to no one in particular, "Bagged me a lawyer here. Or he says he's a lawyer. I'll park you here, Mr. Lawyer."

To the nerd-looking fellow who had been practicing law with Janice, old lady Colladay said, "Lawyer, you're hired. Now earn your retainer. I'm bailing out everyone—"

The young lawyer lifted his chin, caressing it, pontificating, "A writ of habeas corpus due to extenuating circumstances will be in order, notwithstanding the seizure of said property being invalidated along with the search warrant of this property."

As he spouted legal jargon Ingrid sensed that he probably wasn't a lawyer but a college student at best, at least one with lawyerly ambitions. A cop had similar suspicions and asked to see his ID. "Says here he's Warren Barekette. Age nineteen. Lawyer my ass. What a fricking comedy club—"

Ryoji's girlfriend, Midori, had just arrived the other day from Japan, and seemed not to know what to make of the turmoil and was separated from her man by a cop leading them by the elbow. The two lovers clad in nothing but bath towels were announced by their apprehender, a swarthy cop leaving nothing to ambiguity by paraphrasing Shakespeare, "Just caught these two Chinks doing the double backed beast."

Ingrid winced, a quarter of her staff caught in the buff, watching the two Japanese exchange looks, one seeing, one not seeing, that were by turns incredulous and painful. This *Welcome to America* for them, Ingrid snickered in her thoughts, like a trip to another planet. She'd pay money (if she had any) to hear their exchange interpreted.

"Ryoji-kun. Nan de? Ano omawarisan wa anata no heiya kimashta? Ga chong, ga chong! Nandeshoo? Futsu?"

"Ie, ie, ie. Midori-chan, wakaranai. Honto ni. Tokubetsu yo. Hajimete. Honto. Gommensai ne." Much deep bowing on the part of Ryoji.

At each new capture led out into the salon and any fresh pandemonium Midori's eyes grew large and danced in fear and shock. Both of their mouths drooped farther open. She assumably told all of what she saw to the blind Ryoji who stuttered his comprehension in a machine gun-like "Eh, eh, eh, sou? Honto ni? Okama? Eh, eh, eh, sou? Ingrid-san mo? Shinjirarenai. Eh, eh..." Both of their faces were enlivened by scores of new wrinkles—*How 'bout that? Wow!*—at this American excitement that every friend and family member warned them against. Just as quickly the thrill turned to pure dread when two cops came over. "So this is Nakamura. Hold out your hands, young man. You're under arrest."

Now Colladay was growling, "Martini! Martini! Don't you be pushing around my Martini! Imbecilic cops."

The young Mayflower strode deliberately back over to Ingrid, staring at the floor as if measuring his words. The nervous type, he kept coughing as he spoke, shifting around, twitching his nose as if it weren't drawing enough air, like an old school teacher tortured by chalk dust over too many years. "Chance for you to talk, Ingrid. Go back where it's quiet if that'll help." His hand grasped her arm with a firm pressure as he led her along. Trish and Annabel were cutting their eyes at her with the squint of spiteful, mediated suspicion that she was on her way to make a deal that'd get her off at their expense. Back in Ryoji's Oriental Room, Mayflower pointed at the futon. "Is that where they do it?"

"Yeah, that's where they do shiatsu, if that's what you mean."

He gave Ingrid a dubious look, repeating, "Is that where they do it?"

She didn't say anything.

He sighed loudly, as if he were fed up, when she didn't answer. "Then explain the spots on the futon, Ingrid."

"Just...candy stains," Ingrid blurted, without thinking.

"Candy's stains? Who's Candy? A masseuse?"

"I said candy stains not Candy's stains." She chuckled at the absurdity, continuing, "But if the masseuse who used this room was named Candy we'd have a perfect pun." Of the blotchy spots in the futon's center, she said, "Come to think of it, they do look more chocolate colored than..." She wanted to say menstrual but found it too penetrating and crude so she let her voice trail off then rise into a guffaw of disgust. "Oh gawd. I don't believe this. Anyway, you're not going to find anything."

"Huh." His whole body jerked as if from the shock of high tension wire. "Eight arrests already. Pimping, pandering, assaulting a police officer, solicitation, marijuana possession. And them there...candy stains. I call that something." He knitted his eyebrows but one refused to cooperate, giving him the cunning look of a used car salesman. "In a minute you'll be number nine. If you tell me one thing, though, Ingrid, I may just cut you some slack." He stepped toward her, held up his hands, not to tell a fish story but to wall in the conversation. Taking her into his confidences, his voice descended down to an aggressive whisper, where everything would be all right if she cooperated. "Tell me where the secret set of books is, Ingrid. Guddy swears they're here."

She watched the dark hole of his gaping mouth and seductive raising of eyebrows—once, twice—then scoffed, looking away, looking back hard into the brown marble of his irises that blinked at the angry gaze she drove into them. "There is no secret set of books." She glared until he looked away, then looked down at her shoes, said meekly as if to some illusive witness, "I don't believe this."

He squinted at her and his head tilted as if hit by a force not his own, the menace of promise back sharp in his tone, "Last chance."

"Nope." She shook her head. "Nothing doing."

"You're under arrest." He read Ingrid her rights, unclasped his handcuffs, then cuffed her hard, the metal pinching the skin of her wrists so hard that she had to suck in her lips to keep from shrieking for him to loosen the damned cuffs when he jerked her back out into the salon, leading her out in the drizzle to the cold assessing eye of the cameras. Janice trailing along nonchalantly in her pony girl outfit of derby hat, white tights, red jacket, and black heels. (Pierson had turned her into a clothes horse). Hands-free conspicuous, she kept asking in her midwestern drone turned valley-girl whine, "Like what did you guys do? *I don't believe this.*"

Ingrid cringed. Three TV news crews jacked into three different minivans backed up to the curb, bearing television channel logos and spilling cord and equipment and harried technicians running around like eager-beavers. (On the five and ten o'clock news, scanning shots of the mansion. Ominous close ups of the lighted neon sign *MASSAGE WORLD 5655* as cut-away teaser replayed along with images of Ingrid, Erma, Trish, Annabel, and Ryoji hauled into custody over the shoulder of the lovely Channel 7 female newscaster.) Ingrid watched her, the newscaster, now hold up the microphone then run a hand over her hair to sweep away rain drops, and turning to give the camera a shot of her sincere eyebrows arching. Her determined, lovely face became the focus against a chaotic backdrop of cops taking their sweet time, exchanging wise cracks and rolls of the eye, maximizing humiliation of Ingrid and the staff and sundry before neighbors and media in vindication. But then a van was pulling up. Dick Pierson's van. Only it was newly painted white and shockingly emblazoned with *Massage World* painted in big, bright red letters over the Massage World telephone number. Even more of a shock to Ingrid was a second van, a brand new full-sized white cargo, that pulled up behind Pierson's van. It too was white and spangled with the Massage World logo and telephone number. *What the fuck was going on?*

Through water-streaked van windows she recognized Dick Pierson and saw several passenger shapes. Blurred heads, shoulders. The cop was pulling her along and everything seemed to be moving slowly. Pierson's stepped out splashing into a puddle, Walkman headphones doing little to stop the sway of his long greasy hair. Seemingly indifferent to the fiasco, he slammed the driver's door closed then slid the back door open. Kevin handed him a box of something. Reading the label design, she saw that it was a case of Dom Perignon champagne which Pierson hoisted onto his shoulder as Kevin climbed out. Beautiful Kevin, in dungarees and moccasins, head held high for the cameras. Next, Ingrid saw Rochelle dressed as what she was, in black thigh-boots under a black mini-skirt that practically showed panties, with raccoon-faced rings of silver mascara looping around her eyes, an inch of blush on her cheeks. Climbing out of the van after her was Tess in her glorious culottes over espadrilles, seventies curls in her beautiful brunette hair fresh from the curling comb. Then swaggered out the Officer, in full uniform of spotless Marine Corps whites, lending a note of officialdom to the ensemble.

From the second van, the new van, came Bobbie, in hip-hugger blue jean bells (more seventies retro) clutching a key chain. Last out were the Thai girls in jack boots and hot pants hugging shopping bags brimming with bright packets of chips and pistachios and party hats and plastic glasses peaking out. Squinting around the bags they clutched in the drizzle, they crossed through the spectacle, not registering their hand-cuffed colleagues with so much as a flicker of surprise. Eyes darting from them to the big bold italicized red logo type of *Massage World* emblazoned on the vans as if on a commercial jetliner's fuselage, Ingrid stared at Pierson, bellowing at him, "Who in the fucking fuck gave you permission to do that paint job?"

Kneeling under an umbrella held by an assistant, a cameraman hoisted a video camera on his shoulder then made panning shots, back and forth. Then he gave the signal, dropping his hand for the newscaster to begin, "*At the new upscale massage parlor, Massage World, you get more than just a massage...*" A cop prompted Trish up into the paddy wagon. She spun from his grasp, yelling toward the camera something about everything being wrong. "*The wrong people they got.*" Hands cuffed behind her back, she jutted her face out in the direction of Dick Pierson and Bobbie and their entourage. "*The cameras should be pointed there. At them...*" One cameraman shot Pierson motioning toward his headphones with his free hand, making an idiot's face (*Can't hear you, can't hear you*) against the champagne case on his shoulder, pointing his load and face toward Ingrid, giving her an incredulous look, saying, "Bad girl. Too bad you're gonna miss the party, Swan Song." Bobbie sneered, "Caught greasing the meat, huh Ing?" She struck her index fingers together as if they were flint. "Shame, shame." Rain drops splashed silver bullets on the black street. That and attendant noise snipped into the live broadcasts:

> *...A scene of pandemonium on Melon Street in uptown. Five masseuses from Massage World... into custody for alleged prostitution activities... result of a full-scale undercover vice sting... panning out before us... a successful raid... months of investigation."*

Ingrid watched the camera swing back to the paddy wagon. Watched the cop grab Trish and try to hoist her up. Her feet on the bottom stair, shins against the top stair, elbows flung out against the door to obstruct the cop's efforts of shoving her in, she bent over, cuffed hands behind her grabbing up the towel. "You got the wrong fucking people I'm telling you you got—" Mooning the camera, her white ass split by her crack the cop palmed around her cheeks until she fell hard into the paddy wagon, the newscaster leaned harder into her broadcast, saying, *"Officer Mayflower...leading the raid...the Border City Police Department...could not sit idly by...watching our city...turned into another Las Vegas."* Shoved up and in, Ingrid sat beside Trish sobbing at the end of the bench. "Just not fair." Trish banged her head back against the panel. "Would you stop!" Ingrid tugged against the cuffs, elbowing her, shuddering against her. "It's a fucking war. A god-damned massage war. That prick cop chief had it right."

"Now it's our turn, Trish said.

"Our turn for what," Annabel scoffed. "To go to jail?"

"To retaliate." She saw Ryoji, through the narrow door, carted off in a squad, looking devastated, head bowed in shame. As if he were ready to disembowel himself if he had a knife. Caught naked with his girlfriend from Japan with candy, or rather menstruation stains, on the futon. Ingrid winced and sighed at the same time. The paddy wagon started rumbling away. She saw Erma stare at the mesh separating them from the front, and heard Annabel whine, "I did nothing wrong. Nothing!"

Ingrid reached out to her. The cuffs grabbed her back, the crisis showing her the essence of her staff she'd have to keep together. Ryoji and Erma: passive (if not submissive) in defeat. Annabel the good girl: now more naive than innocent. Trish, a slave to her emotions, swinging from rage to sorrow. Ingrid herself doing a slow tilt toward rage, fists clenched into the bite of cuffs gobbling at her wrists, raging at Pierson and Bobbie driving up in vans festooned with *Massage World*, then cutting across the street with their *don't-give-a-shit* attitudes. "*Bad girl. Caught greasing the meat, huh Ing?*" Frustrating her fury stream was pony girl Janice. Then Annabel sobbing in counterpoint to Trish shouting curses until the cop pushed his lips against the grill. "*Sound like a bunch of squawking ninnies back there for Christ sakes shut up!*"

JACKSON COBB

Felt like royalty. He was in a third-floor VIP room submerged up to his neck in a bubble bath. On his head he wore a cone-shaped red-and-white-striped party hat held in place by a rubber band under his chin. He stared vacantly at CNN images flickering on a wall-ensconced TV—its sound turned down—between parlor palms and ferns bathed in green tinted light, which lay like a sheet over the vibrating massage table in the room's center, glanced off novelties on a marble-top brass stand. A rubber ducky, bottles of herbal remedies, aromatherapy, spices, ship's lantern—all complementing the Captain's Quarters/Pirate Ship motif, complete with Old Spice mirrors and a painting of a pirate ship and pirate flags over a hologram of the ocean at sundown.

Through the speakers poured old Donna Summer songs (Gudsikes inspiration there), over the sound of Cobb sloshing around in the tub, getting comfortable. Two masseuses knelt beside the old four-legged tub and pampered him. Rochelle scrubbed and massaged around his neck, shoulders and chest, cooing *rub a dub dub*. Goofy fed him caviar on Ritz crackers between sips of champagne. "Door's locked? Yeah. Well, all I need is for Janice to come barging in on my first VIP at Massage World. That's enough caviar, Goof. Light up my stogie and slip it in. That's what she said. Or said the president said, right? What a scene we crossed, huh. That little Jap fuck looked like he was going to bawl with his girlfriend after they were caught balling. Would have liked to see her as the cops did: without a stitch, right. A looker I'm telling you. You know you may not believe this, but I once had a run-in with him in Japan. Just a few months ago. Totally by chance."

"A run in with who?"

"With that Jap fuck."

"What happened?"

"Fucker came at us swinging his blind man's cane. Snapped the damned thing against a sailor, big fucker too, who wanted to kick the shit out of him."

"Out of who?"

"That Jap fuck! I actually saved his ass, just outside some *soaplando* in Kawasaki. Wonder if he remembers me, my scent."

"How strange that he showed up here," Rochelle said.

"Talk about a coincidence, I know."

"Wonder how it was for him today," Goofy said, "not being able to see, cuffed, taken off to jail."

"Probably pretty dark," Cobb said. They laughed.

"You see Ingrid?" Rochelle said. "She was looking at the new paint job on the vans like this." Moving her head back and forth, Rochelle let her mouth drop open, eyes huge. A stupid stare.

Goofy stuck the cigar in Cobb's mouth, saying, "How about Erma? She didn't know what the hell hit her either."

"And Annabel *fanabell*—"

Rochelle interrupted, "I'll bet good money she's still a virgin."

"Swan Fuck herself ain't no virgin," Cobb said.

Rochelle said, "*Betchya* she ain't getting any, though."

Cobb said around his cigar, "I'd like to give her some. Then sit back and watch her melt. All that tension. Shit. Turn her into a new woman. Love slave. Under my command."

Goofy said, "Like you did to Janice."

"Fuck Janice," Cobb said, irritated by the memory of spying on her through the one-way, watching her spread for some stiff, legs open on the massage table there. The end of Janice and Jack.

"Never forget the red-headed dyke."

"I know! Jumping up and down screaming like a chimpanzee."

"See that skinny ass moon she shot at the cameras?"

Around the cigar, between puffs, Cobb said, "That media bitch sure didn't look bad."

There was a knock on the door. Freezing, the three of them shut up, not moving their heads but their eyes cutting back and forth. A woman's hushed voice came through the door, "Let us in."

Rochelle looked at Cobb. "It's just the Officer."

"And who else?" Cobb shouted.

"Me. Kevin," said Kevin.

His arms submerged in soap suds and hot water, Cobb inclined his head toward the door, saying around his cigar, "Go ahead and let her in. But tell the fag to take a hike."

Rochelle nodded. Bare foot and bare breasted, she crossed the palatial VIP room wearing nothing but a mini-skirt, unlocked the door, then opened it just enough to slip out. She came back in a minute later facing the Officer who slipped in, closed the door, then told Cobb, "Don't worry. Janice thinks you went home."

Cobb scowled, irritated, "*Fuck Janice.*"

The Officer said, "You already did."

"About a hundred times," Goofy said. "You know she keeps saying she's going to have it."

"She'll abort. Or else I'll help her. Anyway, she's gotten to be too much of a nag. Tomorrow she goes back to the Near East." He watched the Officer unbutton the crisp white shirt of her uniform so as to match the other masseuses—all topless. "You give her the order."

"With pleasure, sir." The Officer grinned, saluted him.

"Kevin's pissed off you wouldn't let him in," Rochelle said.

Cobb scowled, watching the Officer unsnap her bra, large breasts rejoicing as both swung freely. "Little fag's the last person I want in here drooling over my cock." He liked the way she sauntered over, knelt beside the tub between Rochelle, who resumed massaging his back, and Goofy, who was pouring him more champagne. The Officer took Cobb's cigar from his mouth. "Here, let me tend it for you."

"That's what she said."

Cobb grunted, tipping his head back, parting his lips to receive another sip of champagne from Goofy. He swallowed. Then opened his mouth. On cue the Officer slipped in the cigar. Cobb raised a soapy hand from the bath in order to fondle the Officer's breasts, first the right one then the left one, sweetly larger. "You've got *tits, no question.*"

In a squeaky little girl's voice the Officer pleaded, "Let us give you a Turkish, Mr. Cobb."

"Three way," Rochelle added, then nibbled on Cobb's neck and slid her hands deeper into the bath down over his belly and tickling closer toward his manhood's swelling.

Control could be lost if he acquiesced. He clutched Rochelle's hands underwater then directed her strokes back up toward his chest, grunting, "Maybe later." He took a few puffs before rolling the cigar toward the side of his mouth then back to the center. Lifting his jaw, his teeth made the cigar rise and fall. Tiny flakes of ash trickled onto the suds. On cue the Officer removed the cigar from his mouth then flicked ashes into the tray. He cut her a glance, grunting, "Mess cleaned up downstairs yet? Stage two begins tomorrow you know. Can't wait to frost ole Swan Fuck again. Ho!"

INGRID

Gasped at what she saw in front of Massage World.

After bailing all of them out and having the others chauffeured home, Ms. Colladay had Ingrid dropped off at Massage World. "It looks like a riot scene, Ingrid," Colladay cackled.

Some forty members of the Uptown Neighborhood Association were picketing Massage World, pacing the front sidewalk with placards. *Not in Our Neighborhood. What is the World coming to?* As if in reply, some joker had spray painted *FUCK WORLD 5655* in five foot red letters across the mansion's front wall.

"There's the madam herself," some weasel-faced man yelled, pointing at Ingrid stepping out of the limo as if he wanted to lead a lynch mob.

On her way to the mansion they shouted at her. "You know, Ingrid Swanson, we all have children." Some house frau told her, "This is a residential neighborhood, Ingrid."

"No place for a whore house," added a man in dungarees and a jean jacket. "Read here, Ingrid." He pointed up to the words on cardboard tacked to lath. "Whose *World* is it anyway?" *World* written in the red Massage World logotype, over the Uptown Neighborhood Association's logo UNA, in bold capitals and circled.

Ingrid stopped before them and tried to explain but was interrupted.

"If it's not a whore house then what is it!?" Two dozen men and women surrounded her, stabbing her with accusations. "We read in the paper, see on the news, you there and ten others. Arrested for solicitation. If that's not proof that you're running a brothel..."

Her explanations only upset their ire, so she pushed through then continued up the steps. Inside, Pierson was busy at the desk, giving orders, taking and making phone calls, giving Ingrid a curt nod as she stood before him in a defiant stance meant to communicate that she wouldn't budge. A full five minutes later, after several phone calls—"How much? When? You'll meet me there? When? Fine. Tell them she no longer works here. Now just a second, Bob"—he rested the receiver against his clavicle, raised his eyebrows at her. "Swanson," he said, exasperated, "in case you haven't noticed, we're in crisis mode. In ten seconds or less spill it."

"I want you out of here." She ran her arm across the desk, sweeping it clean of everything: schedules, note pads, pen holders, files, telephone—all crashing to the floor.

Still seated, clutching receiver against a taut cord, he said, "Oh, that's just great, Swansdown. You get carted off to jail in cuffs and a paddy wagon. Leave me here with a nightmare of an image problem. Redneck neighborhood associations and media breathing liquid fire up my ass. Then throw a tantrum in front of clients and staff. Just fucking great." He took a deep breath. "Now you get the fuck out of my face before I blow big. Yeah, Bob, you still there? No, just Swan River cleaning my desk. Now she's on the verge of tears. Yeah. I know. What can I do?"

Wounded, holding her stomach, Ingrid walked over, in careful steps, to the wheelchair. She sat down heavily, fighting an impulse to weep. Luckily, she found that she had a hanky in her pocket. Grabbing it out and unfolding it she had an idea and tied it around her head like a babushka, then slipped on her sunglasses. Wheeling backward in the wheelchair, she inched even closer to the desk. She listened to Pierson retrieve the phone and accessories then sigh, then take a deep breath, then announce, "Time, Bob, to go into holistic PC new age mode." He made another call. "Yeah, Dick Pierson of Massage World. Got a pen or a computer? Start jotting on the order form. I'd like to order one Watson-Hudson Isolation Tank, three Nordic Tracks, at least three good bodywork chairs for my lobby here, you got four in stock? Give me all four. I'll need a few body cushions as well. As in three, yeah. And some rock climbing apparatus to stack all the way the heck up to my skylights here. You'll have to do the measuring yourself, sir. Next: a dozen eye pillows. Four Oriental Natal Charts. Thirty pair of Birkenstock sandals, thirty gis, in all sizes, yeah, three tarot decks, and throw in some Chinese astrology handbooks if you have any around. You know, with the bestiary and all that? Half dozen each of chakra candles and chakra meditation scrolls. Seven crystal pendants with chakra gemstones, one magnetic energy kit, the kind with polar power magnets, right, good. One magic mirror spiritual toolbox, seven strings of affirmation beads that can double for the other kind of beads that feel heavenly being tugged sweetly from the backside. Catch my drift? Four wave-makers. Six rain sticks. A dozen bamboo flutes, shakuhachi style. And I'm not talking about b.j.'s. Forget it. Just a Japanese joke. Onward... A dozen scents of essential oils. A ouija board, too. Oh yeah, and a sweat tent. Got it? Charge it to the Massage World account. Steven knows me. Yeah. Anything I'm forgetting? An electromagnetic field detector? How much? Throw it in. Send it along. Oh, and I need some jungle sounds. Rainforest rain. Leopards and lions roaring. Monkeys chattering. Insects chanting. That sort of thing. On CD. Ciao."

He hung up. Then the phone rang. "Dick Pierson's Massage World. Oh, yes, the reporter from the Border City Times? Right. That's all changed. We're under new management now. That's right. The masseuse lady who ran the show before was—how should I put this?—a little on the liberal side. We're strictly a holistic outfit now. A straight shop in other words. Right. Body work pure and simple. That's right. No dirty pool. Or pocket pool. Strictly straight pool. Oh, you talked to Mr. Poarch? Manager of the Uptown Neighborhood Association, and proud of it, right? No, I didn't know the gentleman was working up a petition. Sure you can come by. Give you a tour myself. Photographer, too? I don't see why not."

* * *

Disguised in a babushka, shades, and in the wheelchair, Ingrid pumped across the salon after Pierson. Who was currently forging a false connection with the nearby hospital, in stethoscope, surgical greens, and then a touch of dash with his hair in a ponytail, he was ready to play the role of doctor for a tour, one staged for the Uptown Neighborhood Association and the media, as Ingrid had learned via eavesdropping. Out front, Pierson got the mob to give up their pickets before he'd start the tour.

A tiny woman, eyes as alert as a hare's, piped up with a question. Turned out she was the reporter from the daily, accompanied by a photojournalist, in blue jeans and vest, a flash-equipped digital Nikon looped around his neck.

"Are you a doctor, Mr. Pierson?"

"A doctor of sorts. Think of myself more as a healer, mam, and holistic health practitioner, if it's a title you're after." He paused as she jotted down notes. "I completed over two thousand hours of formal training, equivalent to certain m.d.'s. For that, most folks call me doctor." His fingers scratched the degradation of quotation marks around the word doctor. "I have written numerous articles for prestigious medical journals, plus a book on such arcane specialties as the Chinese *qi gong*, which is *ki kou* in Japanese. In English, qi gong is best rendered as *the body's vital force*. My master's thesis probed this ancient Chinese exercise system, which invigorates the body's life force, as I said, q-i in Chinese, k-i in Japanese. The path coefficient between regular ki stimulation and longevity is remarkably high. The essence of the discipline centers on *wujishi*—"

"Could you spell that, please?" the reporter asked.

"Certainly. W-u-j-i-s-h-i. It's Japanese, meaning timeless beginning. On a more practical level, wujishi has been proven to ameliorate posture and calm the mind, simply by aligning the feet, torso, head. and abdominal breathing. When a mind is connected to the body's center of gravity the rejuvenating effects are astounding. If I could get all of you to park your pickets for a moment, I'd like to give you a tour of the facilities."

The photojournalist aimed, focused, and shot photos of the neighbors leaning their pickets against the fence, as Pierson continued, "I'll have you know that I very much want to be a part of the neighborhood and am going to give a twenty percent discount to anyone in the UNA. As you know, I have an Olympic-sized swimming pool out back. Come summer we're going to roast a pig there then do a little barefoot hot coal walking. I'm trusting Mr. Poarch'll see that you're all invited to the soiree. Now, about the pool. When I was a teenager I lost a friend to the ocean. His drowning was a result of not knowing how to swim. When do we learn to swim? When we're kids, right? To get to the point, I'm willing to loan my pool to the neighborhood for x number of hours a week, *free*, that is, if you can coordinate with a swimming instructor. How many of you have kids? A show of hands please. Nine, ten, fifteen, seventeen. Okay. The pool will be yours for lessons." Excited whispers swirled through the crowd. A lot of eager nodding at this generous offer. Pierson, confidently motioning the way, said, "Now let's get on with the tour."

The Officer, in full uniform, greeted them just inside the door with a nifty salute. Pierson introduced her as "an actual lieutenant in the United States Marine Corps, my second in command."

Deeper into the salon Pierson's masseuses stood erect in a straight line, as if for inspection. Off in her wheelchair, inconspicuous, Ingrid couldn't believe the show Pierson was putting on. The camera flashing, capturing uniforms of white karate-style shirts open to *Massage World* emblazoned t-shirts and birkenstocks. In unison, a hearty, "Welcome to Massage World!" A deep bow. *Flash*. Mechanical sounds of film winding.

The Officer was standing at attention at a forty-five degree angle from the troops as Pierson went down the line, advancing a step with each masseuse he introduced. "This is Rochelle, an expert in acupressure, deep breathing techniques, and meditation. Any insomniacs? Yeah? Then see Rochelle." She bowed. "Now here is one of the seven dwarfs, Goofy. She goofs up just about everything but a massage, folks, an absolute virtuoso in helping clients find their roots and wings. Meaning: she helps realign and balance the body, untying those nasty little knots of tension. Here's Kevin, a tui na practitioner himself. What else can I say about Kevin?" The tour group laughed at Kevin's devilish grin. "Tess here gives a dynamite Swedish. Our Swedish clients swear by her."

The reporter piped up with another question. "What exactly is Swedish?"

"Swedish massage," Pierson explained, pivoting around, and continuing, "mainly uses hot oil and *effleurage*. The fingers are kept together like this." He held up his hands, fingers tight together. "The flat of the hand makes continuous motions at approximately the same speed and rhythm, but with more pressure applied mid stroke, followed by a kind of tapering off. It's a smooth flowing stroke, then, effleurage, and proven to promote relaxation. It also paves the way for other strokes. Most practitioners use effleurage as a way into and out of a massage, appetizer and dessert if you will. But lovely Tess here serves it up as the main event and clients can't get enough. Now we come to my four friends from that sweet pearl of the Orient, Thailand, a most special place for me in all the world." *Flash*.

Four Thai girls simultaneously offering the delightful Thai greeting, the wai. Beaming, they placed their palms together and raised the tips of their fingers to nose level, making a subtle bow while bending at the knee. "Look at those smiles, folks. You won't find four sweeter massage technicians. I proudly present Joom, Oi, Sumala, and Suntaree. Each has undergone a formal apprenticeship in the ancient art of Wat Po massage, taught to them by Buddhist monks in ancient temples in Chiang Mai, Northern Thailand. Wat Po originated in China several centuries ago. And let me tell you, folks, you haven't lived until you've had a Wat Po massage. Later we'll have a demonstration to wrap up the formal part of the tour.

"Now here's Fay. Look at the size of her hands, folks. Clients call them stress busters. Fay's thing is sports massage. And she goes deep. Two thousand leagues under the sea if you know what I mean. These burly weightlifter dudes come in like this, all pumped up." Striking a gorilla pose, Pierson did a Hulk Hogan imitation. "You should hear them howl under Fay's grip. *Huuwee!*" Pierson hooted, making a pained expression. The crowd laughed, eating his act up, as was Ingrid, spellbound by the whole transformation under Pierson's command, taking an odd and rag-tag assemblage of "masseuses," disciplining them somehow to pull off this snappy presentation, then taming the neighbors in the same stroke. For the time being, Ingrid had no choice but to give him free reign.

"Here's little Cindy Windy from the windy city. Don't let her size fool you, folks. You should hear her pummeling and hacking and cupping, like the percussion section of a jazz band." Sucking in her lip, Cindy posed as an eager-beaver, demonstrating hacking strokes, karate chopping the air. Then she bowed, stepping back in line.

He kept going, introducing the rest, then concluding, "At ease, everyone." The neighbors applauded. The technicians took a bow. "Now let's continue on to the back. As I said, we're under totally new management. We're strictly holistic now." He shot a glance at Ingrid pumping the chair along, "The masseuse lady who ran the place before is no longer employed here. The police ran her out. Thank god. Types like her give us all a bad name." He managed a coy wink. Retaliating, Ingrid raised a middle finger to her chin, pretending to scratch an itch, whispering, "Fuck off, Pierson." What would happen if she started screaming?

"Poke your head into the massage rooms along here and you'll see that they're all done up thematically. Now, to our Oriental Room. Time to get down and do a little Wat Po. Right, girls?" Pierson did a little jig, as if doing the Twist, and everyone laughed. He then addressed Scott Poarch, a mole faced man in his early fifties who led the neighborhood brigade. "Mr. Poarch, would you like to volunteer? I guarantee your body will feel the better for it. And it's free. Oi, could you?"

"Please, sir. Take off shoes. Lie down on the futon here."

He gave his wife a deferring look. "You know my back could certainly use it."

His wife blushed, made a shooing motion before her face. "Just as long as it's not like before." She shook her head several times to exaggerate the disbelief. "My goodness."

"Oh, no," Pierson said, gesturing with both hands. "Actually, clients are given pajamas to wear during a Wat Po massage. But you can go ahead as you are, Mr. Poarch."

The Thai girls ushered everyone in. The photographer was shooting the session from different angles, lying along the futon, then standing on a chair in stockinged feet, camera getting in close and winding away between flashes. The hare-eyed reporter was taking dutiful notes, asking questions as to the benefits of different moves. The spine of Scott Poarch was bowed over one of Oi's knees as her other leg was bent back around in a kind of archer's stance. Poarch's mole eyes, his face upside down, flickered up at the gallery of neighbors, Oi explaining, "This good stroke. Break stress all over body. Calm mind, too. We hold for thirty seconds."

Pierson leaned against the wall, arms crossed, grinning. "How's it going there, Mr. Poarch? Enjoying ourselves are we?"

"Ohhhh my goodness," Poarch cooed, "just lovely, Dr. Pierson. Just lovely. My back has never felt so good."

Just then Pierson gave Ingrid a wink which made her break out into an itchy sweat all over. She scratched at her side, then at her temples, her nose, and her neck, wanting to curse quite loudly his audacity.

ANNABEL

Closed her eyes in session, against the laser beam drill of light Pierson shot at her through the one-way. "He's a special client," Pierson had said earlier, "with a special problem."

"What problem?"

"Benign prostatic hyperplasia."

"What do you mean?" she asked. "Speak English."

"A noncancerous enlargement of the prostate gland. You treat it by a gentle milking motion, like this." He illustrated by making an obscene jerking gesture.

"I don't believe it. I've never heard of such a massage."

But Pierson had walked away, irritating her now by shining his pen flash in her eyes. She sensed him on the other side of the mirror, through which the ray gun beam bored, stabbing at the little bump in the drape, her client's penis.

Her client was in his fifties, had a steel gray flat top and a big head. Annabel just wanted to give him a massage, and she kept shaking her head at Pierson's command to undrape Peterson and give him a handjob. This communication done by directing the light beam from the forbidden zone then to her eyes. To his thing then back to her eyes. Back and forth. Harassing her.

She walked around the table, turning her back on the mirror. But he reflected his wicked beam off the mirror ball. The light jumped wildly off her hands and eyes and around the room in a mad oval.

In preparation for his blatant trespass on her session, the autocratic Pierson had told all the technicians that he'd be looking in on them from time to time, saying in a singsong tone that contradicted the evil of the idea, "Just to see how you're all getting along." To demonstrate, he led a dozen of them through a trick panel in the wall, down behind the juice bar that opened to a long narrow passageway running the length of the inner massage rooms. In this peekaboo tunnel, the skeleton of walls was exposed in two-by-fours and rough drywall, over a raw plywood floor, was the blackened back of a 3x4 inch mirror every ten paces or so. On each mirror back the paint was scratched off in jagged-edged circles like right out of a comic strip. "Should I want you to do a *prosterate* on a special client you'll see my light flash." He held the beam against the glass and flashed it on and off, a red glow (the flashlight's perimeter plastic) blinking on and off. "Like this. That's the signal to go into tease mode. Ease your hands in and around the dong, without touching any dong mind you. When he groans and can't take it anymore you ask if he's interested in the full massage. Total relaxation. The sweet escape into release land and happy ending. If he asks you to spell it out for him, don't. Only cops ask dumb questions. If he says, yes, then you must explain the extra charge of forty dollars, if he's got a moneyed aura, twenty if he doesn't. Never go under twenty. After he agrees to pay, do him. Get him off A.S.A.P. and out the door. Brush off the pubes from the table and get in the next bill of sale. Remember these little mirrors here are my windows on your sessions and dare I say your souls. Don't even think of skimming. I'll catch you out every time. If I don't then a dummy client will. As I said, I'll be sending dummy clients around randomly. They're good friends of mine and will tell me everything. It's termination time if you're caught skimming." He made a guillotining motion across his neck.

A call came through on his cellular. He pulled the ringing receiver from a lab coat pocket. The lab coat, together with a stethoscope clamped around his neck and a too-busy-to-be-bothered comportment, gave him the aura of a doctor. "Yes, this is Dr. Pierson. I'm due at the hospital when? What!? When exactly did he go into remission? Be right there," he said.

He pocketed the cellular. "Remember, ladies, the doctor will be looking in on you. Ciao ciao." Before Annabel could call his bluff he had dashed off, as if on ice skates, the hard soles of his boots sliding across the floor.

Fighting an urge to walk out of her session now, Annabel closed her eyes to the vexing pen flash blinding her, shivering at the rapacious feeling of Pierson's cold eyes raking her back. Heard the *tink tink* of his ring rapping at the mirror glass. When she opened her eyes in order to reorient her strokes the light hit her hard in the pupils. She couldn't take it anymore.

Walking over to the mirror, she held out a hand to block the light stream. Heard his underwater voice yelling something until she was so fed up she pounded at the glass. "You're sick! You're sick! You're sick!"

"What's wrong, miss? Who's sick?" She felt the client take a hold of an elbow.

"The new manager's sick. And I can't finish your session. Goodbye." Annabel picked up her purse and coat then ran out the door, through the salon, and stuck her head in the break room long enough to yell "*I quit!*" to Bobbie. Annabel then threw open the door, ran down the steps of Massage World, her hands balled into fists, her head shaking, Bobbie yelling after her, "Leaving like that, don't you ever come back!"

INGRID

Watched the tour group disband. The neighborhood association and journalists had finished the tour of the isolation tank, sweat tents, sample massages in bodywork chairs in the salon, saunas, and jacuzzi. They shook rain sticks and held sticks of burning incense. They polished off the last of the finger sandwiches and carrot juice before clearing out. As soon as the door closed on the stragglers leaving, Pierson said, "Listen, all. If any of you so much as says boo to those squares there about a pig roast, fire walk, or swimming lessons, you're fired. Now let's party!"

"Party time!" Kevin yelled, trotting to the barbershop. He switched CDs, from rainforest sounds to New Order's True Faith, flooring the volume, inspiring spontaneous dance and victorious exchanges.

"See that Poarch shrew sponging a Thai massage?"

"Fucking photographer practically sticking his camera up Oi's ass. Know where he gets off."

Goofy asked, "Dr. Pierson, what's effleurage?"

"Flower sewage," he said, lifting his keychain out of his lab coat, jingling them up for all to see, half facing Ingrid in the wheelchair still, then heading for the front door.

"Free show time," Tess said. "Don't go and leave."

"You're going to miss these." The Officer yanked up her Massage World T-shirt, breasts swinging in bra cups. Others followed, whooping, stripping off gi tops and t-shirts, slipping off their undergarments now thrown pell mell in the air, brassiere after brassiere. Masseuses danced on chairs, across the juice bar, and few even boogying on the pool table.

Rummaging through the drawers, Ingrid found the spare keys for the new Massage World van. Following Pierson, she sprung up from the wheelchair at the door, hoping to learn something to help her, in this eleventh hour, to thwart his takeover. As he was pulling away in his old van she ran down the steps. Bolting across the street she watched him turn out of sight at the corner. Unlocking the door with the key clicker, she jumped into the van and started it up. Accelerating through a U-turn, she thought she had lost him but then saw his van drive up a rise on Wing. She made sure to stay a half block back heading east on Monroe, then south on Grant.

In a tough waterfront district of sailor bars, t-shirt shops and junk yards, he took two quick right turns, the second down an alley. She slowed and pulled in, braking between two old buildings. Pierson was thirty yards up the alley heading into the back entrance marked by an old merchant's sign. A pair of praying hands painted gold, pointing to the name of the questionable establishment, *The Golden Hands.*

Her own hands trembling at the wheel, she felt her chest constrict and pound blood into her face and a deep blush of pure humiliation. Should have known. How could she not have known? *How could I have been so stupid?* She threw the van into park, switched it off, grabbed her purse and took out her smartphone and called Erma.

Ingrid explained everything to Erma, but Erma cut her off. "You may never speak to me again, Ing, but I have known for a long time."

"You what?"

"Listen, I wanted to tell you. But. He threatened me. It's too, too dirty to tell. Trish knew too."

"Trish knew?"

"And Ryoji said that Cobb and he had fought in Japan once, but he couldn't say anything because Pierson, or Cobb, had broken up the fight, saving Ryoji, some kind of Oriental thing—"

"So my loyal staff just sat back watching him take over—"

"If you had heard his threats, Ing—"

"Threats and what else, Erm?"

Erma started to explain how she needed the money but Ingrid cut her off and slipped her phone back in her purse. Back in the van she cranked up the engine then jumped at a sharp rap on the window. Someone yanked her door open. Pierson. *Cobb.* Growling like a dog. She wanted to scream. "Don't you scream, Swan Song. Relax your splenius now like a good girlie wirlie." He massaged her neck gently. "*Now relax.* Doing this for your own good. You'll see later."

She held her breath, draping her arms over the wheel as cushion and brace. The numbness of fear was seeping in. He eased her head down until it gently touched the steering wheel, his voice husked in the breathless desperation of lunacy. He told her to raise her head then he caressed her cheek. Tweaking her chin, he said, "Look at me, Swanski. You've just stolen my new van. Could have you sent up for grand theft auto. A felony that."

"Like stealing my spa," she blurted, wanting to pounce and scratch out his eyes. Fingers of deep emotion pulled and stretched at her face. Twitching, blinking, she willed herself not to weep, not to bend, but to withstand his torment and wait. Wait for a chance.

"I knew if I chimed my keys long enough in the salon you'd put your detective's hat on and follow. Figured you had to know sooner or later that Dick Pierson is none other than the big bad wolf. *Woof woof.*" He growled up into her face then unbuckled her seat belt. "I want you in the passenger seat. Buckled up like a good girlie wirlie. Then we're off." They switched places awkwardly.

She glanced at him, then to her door knob, calculating escape. "Off where?"

"Off to the races. Off to see the wizard. Off our fucking rockers." He lurched at her, ponytail swinging around before his face, half obscuring a gaping mouth's cavity silver, saliva and tongue, then punched her door lock down. "Don't even think about it." He backed the van out, tires spinning, grabbing, chirping, leaving some tread and smoke as they swung out into traffic.

INGRID

Wanted to untangle herself from the seat belts and Cobb's kidnapping and jump out of the van the first few miles out of the city, but there wasn't a single red light. Reading his mood, she no longer sensed an immediate threat of violence. But he kept blabbing business schemes (torturing her with a different kind of pain). They were out on a desert highway, heading east before she asked yet again, fear in her voice, "Where are you taking me?"

He ignored her again, giving voice to his own thoughts. "I was right again. Painting the vans with the logo and telephone number paid off already. Ten fold. The outcall biz is booming. Pretty boy Kevin's raking it in for us. More than anyone. If your little twerp Ryoji wasn't blind and could drive I might even keep the twerp around. But I'm gonna can him, along with the rest of your dim-wits." He raised a hand over the wheel, making a flinging motion across the dash. "All out on waivers. Without their noise pressing in on my ears I can concentrate on developing the outcall biz. The sudden demand there comes down to a keeping-up-with-the-Joneses thing. One neighbor hag sees big old Massage World logo on van parked next door. Figures that something so bold and open can't be criminal. And since neighbor Myrtle is getting her tired old ass cheeks massaged by that pretty-boy Massage World technician they see on all my commercials, then, well, she's gonna have the same. You wouldn't believe how many rich old bags have requested"—here Cobb made his voice sound as if he had just snorted helium—*"that cute little blond boy. Don't you send me anyone else but that cute little blond boy I see on television."* That little fag has got something, Swan Thighs, I tell you..."

He kept babbling. "My next venture should pan out like gold. Gonna buy me a panel truck. Painting it red and white. MW colors, right." He held up a hand, dramatizing *Massage World* in the glow of marquee lights. "Logo and phone number broadcast all over. Damned right. It'll have one of them sliding doors. Client can hop right up in back. Won't be intimidated by the male thing that way. Driver's gotta be a man. No question. A bouncer's build. Packing at least a taser in case the client gets too big a hard-on for the masseuse. Or should I say stripper? Anyway, it works like this: the panel truck's equipped with everything, cellulars, CB's, CD's, fuzz busters, the works, right. Whoever's at the Station One desk at MW Central routes the call through. To either of the vans, The Golden Hands, The Near East, or the panel truck. If the client requests a panel show then she'll switch the call direct to the driver's cellular. Driver slash bouncer can make his maleness known up front like. Which could head off a whole heap of shit."

"What kind of *shit*?" Ingrid asked, blinking as a bug smashed into the windshield.

"Shit like masseuse-jackings. If the client thinks it's an all-femme revue. I'm serious. Dig this. The driver immediately puts the client at ease by telling him he'll go wherever the hell he needs to, to pick him up. Far corner of a supermarket parking lot near the Goodwill Box, in front of an auto parts store at the strip mall. Top of a parking deck. Down the street from his house. Around the corner. Through the woods. Or straight up the drive to grandmother's arse. Anywhere. Just so as he knows his uptight neighbors don't have to see him looking both ways before boarding our strip show on wheels, dig. Now, the second the panel truck pulls up to him, the masseuse in back throws open the door with a winning Dallas Cowboys' cheerleader grin and tits shaking all over his blues. Hooks him like a little bluegill. He hops in. She swings round, bends over, sticks her ass up into his face fishing out his beverage. Beer, wine, cooler, champagne, g & t, marg, whatever. Spins the tuneage of his preference, asks him what sweet nothings he'd like to see her in. She draws a curtain and changes, comes out strutting, gripping a kind of ceiling pole thing for balance. As the truck swings around. She skins the cat. Shoots the beave and moon. Client, meanwhile, has been handed an instamatic and is free to snap away at her sweet snatch as he fans himself all he wants. Can't touch the merchandise, though. Driver's right there behind the curtain, see, ready to step in and throttle the hanky from the panky. He's also there with a little conversation after the wad has been shot and mopped up good and proper. Sports scores, stats on the Super Bowl, zoning referendums, the drought, earthquakes, any of that shit. Client has front seat privileges, right. You know how lonely some of these characters get. After they unload in their laps the last person they want to look at is the bitch in back—"

"I can just imagine," Ingrid cut in, *the bitch in back* being mauled by these morons, and your gorilla driver shooting his own wad, crashing into the bus of school kids on the scenic route. I do like your eloquence, though, Cobb. A real way with words. But tell me, why are you telling me all this? Unless you have plans of getting rid of me, as I sit here like a dope and we drive deeper into Death Valley." She looked at him, repulsion mixing with fear and anger. His schemes were sick. He was sick, pulling off an elaborate con job on the neighborhood association then…kidnapping her.

He cut her a glance. "Swanny. You're not *worth* getting rid of. Not my style besides."

"Then why are you carting me out here?" She motioned around to the view of the sage brush and mountains going by at seventy five miles per hour. She pushed out at her seat belt. "All strapped and locked in, what gives, Cobb?"

He guffawed. "Your luck, if you don't shut up."

"What luck?"

Pensive, he stared out at the road, at the stripes rushing under the van rushing toward a gap between two mountains. No other vehicles were in sight. "You're in line for the interest payment on a plumbing project I did several years ago."

"A plumbing project?"

"I laid some serious pipe in the Far East once. Made the mistake of turning in the marker before going into takeover mode."

To face him, Ingrid turned as much as her seat belt would allow, glaring. "I have no idea what you're talking about."

TRISH TOTT

Awakened late for work. She didn't care. Work was nothing but continuous hassles of *a nasty little massage war.* She still felt dirty then angry from being busted: yanked around by the leash of handcuffs, media scrutinized as a whore, cuffed and pushed into a paddy wagon then taken to a holding pen, fingerprinted, photographed, cuffed back to a paddy wagon, then hauled out to a desert jail run by brutal female rent-a-cops throwing an ugly orange prison jumpsuit into her face. More terrible, she now had a record. She was a criminal. It felt as though nothing mattered anymore, and that there was nothing to keep her from going out and committing a real crime, one of vengeance.

In the early evening light curling around her window shades, Trish stared at her lover's face in the shadow, pushing Elizabeth's brown locks from her eyes and freckled cheeks, listening to her breathing on the pillow. She looked at the clock. She had the night shift and just the thought of having to go back there wrenched loose guilt and anger and all kinds of unwanted thoughts that steered her into the rut of depression. She hadn't told Ingrid about Pierson. That Pierson wasn't Pierson but Jack Cobb, corrupt proprietor of Golden Hands and worse. Cobb had burst in on her with client, a friend from the Blood Jet, saying that her session was over, balling up Gloria's clothes, handing them over as she shrieked, and was pushed out into the hall naked. "Sessions over. Hit the showers."

As soon as she left he closed the door then swung around to stare down Trish with his evil glare. He dug out a switchblade and flicked it open and thrust the business end of it at her a few times, getting closer and closer to her face. "*Like cutting clams from the shell.* Say a word to Swansky and you're history." She squeezed her eyes closed and backed up but he had the door. She trembled, not knowing what to do. When he left he slammed the door and she could only stand there breathing deep.

Now the phone rang in the kitchen. She put on her robe, and went to answer it. "This is Trish."

"Trish, they take my room again."

"Who took what room, Ryoji?"

"Thai girls. They tell me go away. Goofy take Annaberu's room. I heard Annaberu quit, though. Officer take your room, Trish. Where we give massage now? All rooms full. Bobbie-san hire too many techs. I tell Bobbie-san that I no make money if I have no room to give shiatsu massage. That I gotta eat. You know what Bobbie-san say?"

"What did she say, Ryoji?"

"She say, *So sorry.* That all she say. *So sorry.*" He paused. "Trish? You there?"

She let her head tap the wall. Once, twice, three times. Drew a deep breath. Exhaling, she said, "I'm here, Ryoji. I'm just so pissed off that I can't see straight."

"Pissed off? Can't see straight? You dizzy, Trish. You all right?"

Her anger concentrating her mind, she spoke precisely, "So pissed off I can't see straight means angry, enraged, wrathful, furious, livid, mad, Ryoji. Understand?" She hung up then dressed. Buttoning her shirt, she crossed the room in a beeline for her pile of motocross armor.

Elizabeth had awakened, pulling at her night gown, stretching, yawning. "What's wrong?"

"Nothing," Trish said, raising her arms over her head to get into her chest protector. "Go back to bed."

"I can see you're upset. What—"

"Nothing!"

"Then why are you shouting?"

"I'm not shouting! Now get out of my way!"

INGRID

Watched the road, listening to Cobb's prattle.

"Just remember that you've no business savvy, Swan Song, and that your former swannery Massage World wouldn't have made it under you. Remember that. Massage is an entrepreneur's game, and you're no entrepreneur, swan river everlasting."

Ingrid felt more giddy than afraid as they turned off the highway, saying, "And you're no Jack Kennedy." All the fear felt flipped over and she guffawed deliriously as they pulled into a gravel parking lot before a grand Japanese restaurant, roof ornately tiled and upturned at the corners. They walked over stepping stones planted over rows of raked gravel toward the grand entrance of red doors, which were offset by bonsai trees and fox statuettes. Cobb opened the door for her. "Hope you're hungry, Swan Shot."

A Japanese hostess, in a light blue silk kimono, bowed demurely, welcoming them. Surprising Ingrid, Cobb bowed back to her and said something in Japanese. The hostess led them past a waterfall and deeper into the dining room, partitioned with shoji screens around tatami mats and lacquered tables. Ingrid wasn't surprised to see the Japanese woman, Motoko Ogawa, sitting on her legs both crossed acrobatically on the same side while nodding deeply to Ingrid as Cobb acted like a Japanese, bowing and speaking to Ms. Ogawa in Japanese.

"Ingrid. Happy you come. We have nice *runch*. My treat. Sit down *prease*." She motioned to the pillow across from her.

Ingrid hesitated, glanced at Cobb, the ice-gray of his eyes. He said, "First things first." Ingrid, still standing, said, "Maybe I want it explained now."

Cobb, sitting himself, replied, "Remember your manners, Swan-hopper. Look around. You're in Japan now."

"I hope that I wasn't kidnapped and brought here because someone wants to make another stupid offer. As a result of a certain Corn Cobb Pipe's curious plumbing project."

His eyes were chunks of ice staring at her. "Listen up and obey and you may come out of it all right. Now sit down." He motioned more insistently.

Ms. Ogawa told Ingrid the same, her hands pressing downward. "Now *ret's* enjoy nice runch."

Hair in a bun, but for some loose locks curling around her ears, a striking Japanese lady wrapped in a beige and red kimono approached their table with yet another welcome and bow.

Cobb ordered for them in Japanese. The waitress bowed, left, then returned with two flasks of sake, setting one between each pair of diners. Cobb picked up a flask. "It's customary to pour for the other person, Swan Boat." He filled Ingrid's cup then set down the flask.

Unsettled, wanting closure, Ingrid picked her way through several delicate courses, but wasn't hesitant with the sake. When the flasks were finished two more were ordered. Ogawa was now saying something in Japanese. Cobb nodding, looking at Ingrid, interpreting for her, "Now is the time to discuss more important matters, honorable Swan Mussel."

Ms. Ogawa spoke again and Cobb interpreted. "It is the wise person who knows his strengths, his weaknesses"—a theme she had just heard—"and recognizes opportunity, and the fool who doesn't."

Then she spoke to Ingrid in English, "I knew Jack-san when he was good boy, Ingrid." She lifted to the table a green silk scarf tied around a bundle of something. She untied the knot and let the folds fall away. "Jack-san wasn't always bad. Sometimes one helps bring out some of the bad in someone." In this knowing look given to Ingrid, the jelly of her dark brown eyes melted into a film of tears. "He bring you here, that good, Ingrid. All that money yours now."

Ingrid looked at Cobb. She felt vexed that the cops had been right. She hated herself for her gullibility, not foreseeing Pierson as Cobb as twin tendrils connected to the underworld and the police department via Gudsikes and who knew who else in the corrupt sewer they inhabited. They had used her to get the spa started, and now she had no use for them. Growing deep within her were flames of anger burning up through her insides. Breaking the quiet, she said, "What a show of conscience from all sides. Mr. Cobweb Disease included."

A wrinkle fluttered crossed Cobb's brow. "You're in an incredibly delicate position, Swans down. Don't push. Take the money, sign the papers. Run."

Ingrid glared at him, "Maybe I don't want to, Cobby."

"You don't get it, do you? We're talking about swan-upping

and—" Anger blinking in his eyes (Was it possible that this filth had a conscience?) Cobb blurted, "You're saying that you're giving us the swannery. *Free.* There won't be a good god damned thing you can do to stop us. I try to be a nice guy. Sing this swan song of chivalry. And the Swan Potato snubs me—"

"Oh shut up, Cobb Coal!" Ingrid didn't know what to do, blotting them out by closing her eyes, listening to water falling on water. She had to make a decision. Take the money. Or fight for the spa.

RYOJI

Heard a truck skid to a stop out front of the mansion. Its door opened and an empty beer can hit the street. Sitting in a barber's chair, Ryoji knew such an abrasive entrance had the redneck's signature scrawled all over it. The one they called Johnny. Erma's loser man. Who didn't bother to switch off the engine or close his door as he got out of the car and veered up the steps, boot heels scratching concrete, now stomping over tile. Booze in his voice, he bellowed, "Whore bait!" Now yelling into the break room, frightening masseuses cowering there. "Back from jail or still locked up? After all the goddamned work I put in here she goes and pulls tricks like that."

Ryoji heard one of the masseuses say something, but he could only make out the inflected word *gun*.

"Yeah, I got a gun," his voice tapered off from a boom, concentration elsewhere. Ryoji heard him pulling at something, maybe a plant strung to the ceiling, the way its hook was clanking against its eye.

The Officer asked, "What do you think you're doing?"

"Think I'm gonna shoot your ass if you don't back the fuck up, lady."

"I'm calling the cops."

"Call 'em." This Johnny grunted, straining to pull the pot down from the sound of its clattering. It finally came down, hook clanking against the tile. Ryoji heard him jerk in the rope, then let it out, the hook cutting circles in the air, whipped around in wider arcs until he screamed, "*Got it!*" As if on the toilet, he kept grunting, pulling at something. Pulled harder. Bobbie yelled, "You're gonna topple that..." Ryoji heard the base of the statue wobble over the tile like a giant chess piece. "Here we go—"

The statue fell against the fountain rim, crushing it in a huge gush of water spilling, in a sound of river water pouring through a dam, out across the salon floor. He was dancing and rejoicing in cowboy catcalls, ignoring the women yelling at him. He ran out to the pool as Bobbie, the Officer and Rochelle were screaming after him as Ryoji just sat there, tilted back in the barber's chair, listening to the place come apart.

INGRID

Was ready to give them her answer but Cobb's cellular phone rang. Cobb nodded an apology to Ms. Ogawa, pulled out the phone. "Yeah? What!? God, I hope you're kidding. No? Why don't you stop him? Still there? Throw something at him then. Christ. Tell the Officer to kick his ass. He just shot at the Officer? Don't let him... I just heard another shot. Bobbie?! You there? Bobbie!?" He hit the cellular against the table, then lifted it back to his ear. "Bobbie!? Shit, the line went dead. Gotta go."

"You can't go, Cob Rot. Who's going to translate?" Ingrid asked, watching Cobb stand up.

"I will, in all of ten seconds."

"Jack-san, you go?" Motoko asked, pausing from piling still more stacks of bills on the table, pulled from her big brown purse this time.

"Here's the deal, Swan Spectrum: You're being offered a hundred grand for Massage World, something that I was planning on taking for nothing. Thank your lucky stars and take it."

"Yes," Motoko Ogawa said. "Hand over keys to castle, Ingrid-san. Best that way."

"I already got the keys," Cobb said, shaking his key ring. "All I need is a signature and I don't even need that. Jesus, I hate feeling charitable. Makes me feel weak. Pity—I swear—is the pissest poor of emotions." In rapid Japanese Cobb spoke to Ogawa, nodding and busily pushing glasses and plates aside to clear a place for more stacks of bills she was setting down. A contract was produced from her purse then set down and wrinkles were ironed off by her old hand. She proffered a pen.

Cobb tapped an impatient finger on the line. "Make your swanmark here, Swanimote!"

Crossing her arms, she hesitated. "Maybe I don't feel like it now, Mr. Cobola Cobego Cobelligerency Cobhouse."

"Don't be a mugwump, Swanskin. Either sign now or the offer's off. You loose the place for nothing, and the place may not be worth anything, given what's going on with some cowboy jerk shooting it up." Cobb formed pistols out of his hands and waved them around.

Ingrid resisted the pressure, sensing an advantage in the urgency. She didn't want to sign. Didn't like their ordering her to sign and set the pen down.

"Damnit, some jerk is shooting at my sister and sundry and throwing shit in the pool, playing fuck all with the statues and fountain. Now are you going to sign, Son of Swan, or what?"

Ingrid said, no, she wasn't, adding, "You're such a liar, you,"—she pointed at him—"squirming cob-nosed, cobless, cobbles, coblenzian Cobb! Fob. Banana nana fo fob—"

"I don't believe this swanning around you're giving me."

Enjoying his squirming urgency, "Oh, Cobb. How do I know this isn't just another conus?"

He shook his head, left in a huff, ignoring the old Japanese woman telling him to wait.

"I'm not going to sign anything and take any money!" Ingrid shouted after him, her shrill voice bringing the waitress around, now bowing around the shoji. "Everyding aright?"

"Think for a moment," Ogawa said, leaning over the table. "Think of your strengths, your weaknesses—"

"I already heard that line," Ingrid said, then excused herself. She sauntered over to the waterfall, and sat on the stone ledge ringing the pool and closed her eyes, getting closer to the sound of tumbling water. Letting it flood her mind over the question turning over and over.

JOHNNY

Picked up a lounge chair in each hand then heaved them together into the deep end of the pool. They hit water and sank slowly, landing upright but blurred by ripples and the depth. Embarking on a course of more serious damage, Johnny jumped up and grabbed the upper trunk of the biggest potted tree, walking it down in his hands, then dragging it to the diving board. He walked to the end, pulling branches well over deep end water until the huge pot plunked in over the lip of the pool. A swirling snake of water rushed around the pot in a gurgling sound. It slid down the slope to the bottom until the tree stood straight, squids of muddy water bubbling up through the branches. Then the leafy treetop swished above the surface in a spray of droplets.

Johnny jumped up and grabbed the top of another potted tree, grabbing it by its tip and a handful of branches, then heaving it in a spinning motion. It too splashed and sank. He did two more the same way. Inky water and gritty sand bubbled up from down around the drain. The buoyancy of wood and leaves left the trees pointing at the sky weighed down by anchors of pot, soil, root—all made wobbly by water.

He saw someone rushing him. Some sailor in a uniform with two bitches behind her. He responded by throwing potted petunias at them. They broke into shards at their feet, stopping two of them, one yapping on the phone. The bigger one kept charging. "Drown your hillbilly ass!"

He drew his pistol. Raised and aimed the weapon the old way (with one hand), singing, "Johnny's got a gun."

Rochelle screamed, "Stop, Officer! Can't you see he's gonna shoot!"

JACK COBB

Drove the van at ninety-two miles per hour down Highway 8, heading for Massage World. Bobbie giving him the play by play on the cellular, "He just ran out, Jack. The Officer's lying on the concrete bleeding... Sirens blaring up. Gotta go."

He yelled for her to wait, but the line went dead. He threw the phone onto the passenger seat and pressed harder at the pedal, passing in the express lane a line of four cars in the slow lane then a semi-truck holding them all up. He honked and flipped off the truck driver while swerving in front of him all the way over to the exit ramp, in one death-defying swoop.

JOHNNY

Repeated the chorus, which had no effect on slowing down her charge. Aiming down the barrel, Johnny fired a shot, hitting the Officer in the shoulder, knocking her to the concrete. But the bullet seemed to have gone clean through in a sharp zing which ricocheted off the concrete before proceeding to tear through some bushes, and thumped into the trunk of a eucalyptus. In the region of her left greater pectoral, blood pumped a heart-shaped splotch across her white uniform. He stared at it, thinking of a time as a child, shooting a snowman where his brother had lodged a tomato juice can. Her face was like a raspberry between finger and thumb.

"Don't you go and cry on me," he said. "And you jabbering on the phone there, *Shut the fucking fuck up!*"

Angry, she held blood-dabbed fingers before her eyes. A gunshot wound confirmed.

"Yeah, you've been shot." He watched her toss back her frizzy hair and frantically climb to her feet, elbowing off her friends.

Johnny shook his head. "Charging again, huh?" He aimed lower, squeezed. The Officer screamed as her right leg folded, her body crumpling. Her head cracked against the pool slab, shocking her as if with electrical current, her body shaking all over.

Gun back in its holster, watching them dragging their wounded inside, Johnny sauntered over to the wall and picked up an armful of flower pots then lobbed them up high, one after the other, like free-throws splashing into the net of the jacuzzi. Then he went back and did three more, this time spiking them, pots exploding into shards on the concrete then shards, roots, soil, all, skidding into the water. He stepped on the start button then kicked any remaining shards into the water, which he stared at, fascinated by the circular streams turning muddy and bumping around flowers, stems, and roots. The jacuzzi, a mud hole with filters and jets fouled, groaned then quit altogether, the motor issuing a frustrated hum.

He headed back toward the salon then stopped to consider the round robin of a pig iron table surrounded by three pig iron chairs. He nodded once, indicating settlement of course, this closure of rampage, then hefted the pig iron table over his head, taking a moment to get its round top adjusted just right on the backs of his forearms over his head, his legs now quivering with the weight as he lifted it higher, his fingers, walking like upside down spiders, pursuing the optimum grip for maximum thrust. He grunted and heaved. The pig iron table crashed through the French window and its metallic panes. Breaking loose screams from inside.

He slapped his hands together, said calmly through the jagged hole and lace curtain's billowing, "I'm through now. Done took back all the work I put in this shithole." Sirens were whooping closer up the street as Johnny sauntered through the salon, tipped his hat, and said to the women peeking at him from behind furniture, "Look like a bunch of scared animals."

Hustling down the stairs he pulled his hat brim down over his eyes, climbed in his pickup and drove off just as the squads and ambulance pulled up, giving the cops and paramedics a nifty little salute.

RYOJI

Still sat in the cupped hand of the reclining barber chair, hands behind his head. Not wanting anyone to see him as he listened to the siren wail, the ambulance transporting the Officer the short distance over to the hospital. After questioning everyone and ordering the neighborhood association to disperse, the police officers left with a description of this Johnny who, Ryoji imagined, would repeat his lament of victimhood for judge and jury then be released. America. Americans flitted about from one thing to the next, *like bees*, Ryoji thought, but never quite getting any nectar.

Where was the resonance? After several months he had only two steady clients stepping up to the front desk and requesting his massage. That and no one wanting to accept responsibility for anything. Hierarchy eroding just when it was most needed—he didn't know who his boss was one day to the next. Ingrid had hired him, asserting her authority through orientation and grand opening until her face fell under money problems. Then Bobbie pushed her way in behind stupid Erma, the two pushing out Ingrid while holding the door open for Dr. Pierson or Cobb-san or *Jack*, the barbarian stomping around upstairs now, who he had first encountered at the Donald Duck Conversation Lounge, who then later the same day saved Ryoji from a beating by kicking his legs out from under him and restraining his friends from stomping Ryoji, a gesture—translated into the currency of *giri*—that restrained Ryoji from stepping in and helping Ingrid. As if it would have mattered anyway.

Cobb ruled as he pleased, early that afternoon stinging Ryoji after Ryoji had found him in Ingrid's old office (located by his underarm odor of rancid coconut). *"A mistake, Dr. Pierson. Thai girls push me from my room."*

Cobb-san sneered. *"No mistake."*

Ryoji was shocked, asking where he should work then.

Cobb lit a cigarette. *"You can work anywhere you want, blind man, just as long as you don't work here."*

Banging his cane on the floor, speaking in Japanese, *"You treat me worse than dog. I am no dog. You are dog, like your friend bragging he fucked my sister. Why you do this, you who smells worse than dead animals?"*

Cobb responded in Japanese, *"Don't try to insult me in a language you didn't think I understood. Coward."* Cobb paused, inhaling another puff, as if considering, then exhaled, speaking at the same time. *"So that was your sister, that's why you were upset. Some family, Nakamura, a blind masseur and a soapland whore."*

Ryoji was silent, shaking with rage, trying to plot the path he'd take to whip Cobb with his cane.

Reading his thoughts, he said, *"Don't even think of it, unless you want to go back to jail. By the way, that cute girlfriend of yours go back to Japan?"* He sucked on his cigarette, making a loud smacking sound as he clipped off smoke then blew it back at Ryoji, who recoiled, waving it away from his face. Shaking, struggling to hold on, and knowing Cobb's intention, he uttered, *"Bakayaroh."* Then for good measure in English. "Sonofabitch."

Cupped in the cold vinyl hand of the barber chair, Ryoji felt the crackle of Cobb's anger two floors up now. He knew that Cobb was stewing over the destruction, pacing back and forth in Ingrid's old office, repeating seven swear words, but with pauses and different stresses, *"Goddamn... sonofabitch... motherfucker... shithole..."* Then in a booming voice tumbling off the walls, down the stairs, he shouted, *"COCKSUCKING COWBOY BASTARD!"*

Ryoji grinned, delighting in the angry stomp of Cobb's heels vibrating through the mansion. Hearing something else, Ryoji sat up. A sharp noise cutting toward the plane of Cobb's anger, a larger anger like the buzz of an electric knife going to work on a roast. He pulled the chair lever forward and stood. He ambled into the salon, cane tapping, and guard hand out against wreckage.

The floor felt wet and slippery (he heard in his mind's ear again the fountain busting, gushing its waters). His cane tapped against something the size of a boulder he now touched with his toe. Knew what it was already but knelt to feel its stony texture. His fingertips feeling giant nostrils. Cool stone sockets of eyes. Tracing around the cornucopia of the fallen warrior's ear, bringing its whole shape to mind. His long thick legs he remembered massaging up standing on the fountain rim, helped up by Ingrid giving him that first tour, when the air of Massage World held the magic of promise. A job with a future.

His hands ventured farther down the statue now. Felt its pieces, arms and torso split, but still joined by chalk-powdered iron, its skeleton.

The buzz got closer. He stood and knew, from the aura's edge touching him here, the source of the buzzing belonged to Trish, hacking up side streets and down. Closer. He nodded, relishing in the feelers of her larger wrath. In a whip-saw whine and roar, the voice of her 1200 led thirty others, Ryoji figured, his ears twitching, working like a pair of tweezers separating out each engine's voice over Cobb's boots, now stomping down the stairs. Stomped almost down to the salon landing when he swore under his breath one sharp "*Shit!*" then quickly turned around to clomp back upstairs, trying to outrun his karma, the swarm of motorcycles buzzing closer, climbing harder, Cobb tensing in fright. Ryoji felt his cold wave of fear and swore in English, "Shithead!" *So that was your sister, that's why you're upset.* "Coward!" *You can work anywhere you want, blind man, just as long as you don't work here.* "Cocksucking cowboy bastard!"

Ryoji started across the salon after him.

TRISH

Gunned her motorcycle past Cobb's van parked in the drive. Trish bounced up the front stairs of the portico then waved the others to follow, a stream of thirty some motorcycles whose engines and riders issued disparate war-cry shrieks echoing between houses and walls and pillars and porticoes on Melon Street. She drove her bike straight into the salon, looking for Cobb, seeing Ryoji point his cane upstairs.

She saluted. Remembered he couldn't see her, and told him to stand back. She circled the wrecked fountain and statue, her feet out, careful not to slip on the slippery wet tile. Bikes streaming in and around like a bee swarm. Trish buzzed through a gap, downshifted to first and throttled up, ears tightening to squeeze out the thunder deafening her as she bumped up the stairs chopping at her tires. Engines winding up behind her. She glanced in the rearview and counted four, five, six of her club on motocross Yamahas and Suzukis racing up the slack behind her.

Swung right, headlight rushing down a hall empty but for half tables of flowers and ferns, she gunned down the corridor then had no time to duck. An arm—his arm!—shot out of a door and clotheslined her off her bike, hitting just under the neck. She leapt, rolling out from under the hog.

A flurry of hair before his face, he threw himself into a diving tackle at the lead bike's rider behind her. Trish charged, tried to spear him with her helmet hard into his back and take him down in the same stroke. Saving himself he made a matador move to avoid an oncoming bike, then swung around to push Trish aside, then he swung the other way to push Nancy from her motocross. Pivoting, he kicked at Trish. His boot lanced the side of her knee and she toppled, steaming her helmet shield with curses.

JACK COBB

Grabbed up a 250 and ran it two steps then hopped on, clutch starting it on the stairs. Standing on the footrests, Cobb rode straight into the path of motorcycles screaming up. Helmetless, he pinned the horn with his thumb, shouting, "Fuckin' biker bitches!" Cutting through streams of riders faceless behind dark shields of black helmets clanking against the wall, leaving there wild streaks of black paint over the white, bikes ditched left and right, riders diving from toppling motorcycles, gloved hands clutching railings, legs kicking up at him snapping off a mirror, then his back tire crunching someone or something. The bikes toppled down like boulders, exhaust sputtering, stair creases crunching metal, leaving the front tires spinning.

The bikers rode hard circling the fountain's rubble then accelerated straight at Cobb screaming down the last few stairs. Cobb hit bottom and fishtailed, terrorized, tires staining black on the white of the checkered floor. He was on his way to the door. He rode out and down the steps, standing on the footrests again so his seat wouldn't slap at his ass, the adrenaline clapping through his heart as intense as the engine screaming as he cleared the gate behind him. They'd have his balls. His life, he knew. If they caught him.

TRISH

Picked up Lori's 250 and horsed it around. Facing the stairs she jumped on, jump starting it in the same stroke. She could hear motorcycles revving on all three floors, the mansion itself an angry hive's buzzing, as she bumped down the winding staircase slowed only by the first gear friction. She lurched into a break in the stream of bikes rushing out after Cobb. Cut off the sidewalk to the street to make time, throttling, kicking up to a very high third and gaining, taking another way into the lot to swing right in behind him, just close enough to try to knock him off his bike in a leap.

COBB

Saw her handlebars dip trying to smash her front tire against his leg, so he accelerated, popping a short wheelie and the front of the bike went up a sharp curb that marked the far corner of the block the hospital took up, seven floors of lighted windows looming like a ship across the parking lot. Slashing across a patch of grass then hitting the asphalt, tires still spinning then grabbing, she was still right there. He shot across the fifty feet of open lot for the labyrinth of cars parked in arrow-headed formation. He zig-zagged, vexed to see her still *there*, practically riding up his asshole's puckering, bouncing through tight spaces and over concrete logs of parking protuberances, the hand of adrenaline getting in there around his heart and twisting some new terror through his torso and limbs.

Took seventeen swoops to break their ranks, riders riding back at each other like a football teams in a brawl, blinded by the canyons of minivans and trucks. The sign for Emergency Room (This is an emergency!) was close, and with Trish thirty feet behind, he rode hard at the automatic doors opening to the step of a paramedic running out to see the sound of Daytona racing at the hospital. The same paramedic jumped back from Cobb, who was steering his stolen 250 onto the black mat of the door that swung open to warm air carrying a faint whiff of feces cut with an odor of antiseptic, pressing into his face a dozen alert orderlies and nurses rushing at him waving hands and expressions grave as they come. Yelling something, a pissed off doctor, red faced, bald domed, gray haired but suddenly much alive, broke through the ranks, his lab coat a swirling shroud, cocking an arm back preparatory to hurling his clipboard side-arm style at the demon storming into the Emergency Room on the thunder of a trail bike. "This is a hospital!"

Cobb shouted, "This is an emergency!" And then, "*Cardiac arrest yourself.*"

Dropping an angry flurry of papers, the metallic clip winked, and a thin slab of brown press board sailed an inch above Cobb's ducking head now ducking right to avoid a wild-ass side arm the doctor threw as a follow up. Cobb went back with the bike, riding a wheelie like an axe through white uniforms bumping back against carts and jostling the sharp point of instrument glint. There was an old black man sitting up on a cot, expression hang dog indifferent, sagging eyes and lips, hand holding open his cubicle curtain as the wheelie ended in the front tire banging against the rubber mat signalling another door to be thrown open.

In low second Cobb rode into Sherman Hospital at large, kicked up a gear passing the entrance for X-ray and some pimply faced nerd of a transport aide heading in, black name tag pinned to a white smock, dirty blond hair hanging over black-rimmed glasses, one minute pushing an empty wheelchair, and the next second looking as fierce as a lineman steering it sharply into the path of Cobb who was left with no choice but to swerve at the pimply face hero now hugging white tile, screaming over engine yowl. Cobb swerved back and accelerated, going down the straight-away of the corridor, buzzing with the engine echo, and allowed a glance in the rearview which showed the tenacious image of none other than Trish.

Bitch. And then two, three, four bikes swooping around the wheelchair. The transport aide was still pressed against the tile, like a spastic, humping the wall with each motorcycle's passing. On the other side of a long wall of windows, their black aluminum frames slashing at courtyard evergreen under spotlights, the corridor went right. He followed the path, passing a snack shop, waitresses, and customers clogging the door to see what was happening. Blowing by them to an elevator bank, the doors of one lift were closing as Cobb gunned it, managing to slip his front tire into the crack and, with the kind of precision timing the Japanese were known for in their just-in-time assembly line feeding, goosed open the doors with a back and forth jerk of the handlebars.

A patient, a very old man, gaunt and sickly with pasty hospital pallor in robe and slippers, newspaper tucked under arm, leaned against a walker and listened earnestly to Cobb. "Going up to give my sick brother his birthday present. A surprise." A good egg, the old guy, perhaps not having life enough left in him to object, did his best to scoot his contraption aside, not an easy move, given what he had to do—a kind of lateral lift and shuffle.

Cobb let the engine die. Walking the motorcycle in diagonally, he said over his shoulder, "Seven please. And I'd really appreciate your help, sir, to make it a surprise. Bro's dying see."

Then he turned to face Trish and her contingent riding up. Motorcycle leaning against his leg, in the gap of the door's closing he held up his hands, both of them, showing Trish five fingers plus two fingers, mouthing *seven* over the engine din, adding so she'd be sure to get it, "As in floor." Flipped her off for good measure when she nodded.

TRISH

Felt wings of fright flapping in her chest. Kept swallowing as the elevator went up. Her fingers trembled, trying to tighten her helmet strap. Then the bell rang and the doors parted. She glanced back and forth, wheeling the bike out, and looked all the way down the hall, past a nurse, holding a metallic tray, cutting from one room on one side of the hall to another room opposite. She saw Cobb at the far end, sixty meters down, waving his hands over his head like a signal corpsman, then giving her a swashbuckler's bow, one hand at his waist, the other behind his back. Standing upright now, one foot in a contra position in a bull fighter's pose, he did a magician's trick, yanking up a bed sheet, revealing the motorcycle. The sheet went sailing to the ground as he bowed again. Returning the insult, she flipped him off when he mounted. Facing her sitting astride her ride, he gave her a thumbs up sign before kick starting his bike. Beside a cot against the wall, she did the same, feeling the blood leave her fingers as he gripped the clutch and throttle. The engine racket was drawing patients from their rooms, heads poking from thresholds, looking up and down. *What gives?*

A stream of nurses ran from their lounge, four heading one way down the corridor toward Cobb, three up at Trish. Taking a deep breath and accelerating at the same time, she kicked the bike hard into first, her tingling fingers popped the clutch into raising the front tire into a six inch wheelie, coming back down to tear up through second, bouncing up and down, passing an old man with a whiskery face wheeling an I.V. stand from his room, tubes leashed to his wrist, head swinging one way then back the other at the sources of these great sounds rushing together like bullets, hospital gown upset in the breeze of her passing, passing nurses who were now flattened against the wall like paper dolls, faces pinched tiny as birds but gashed with fright.

She clicked into mid third, gunning up into high engine wind where she'd keep it, not wanting any fourth gear slack to rupture her engine's screaming. With her upper body bent, eyes driven like nails at Cobb in his crouch, whose face was puckered like a chipmunk's rocketing toward her, she felt calm. The fear leaving her in this game of chicken. Five feet, four feet, three. She saw his teeth framed in the pucker of his lips' war cry, hearing the sound tunnel by her as if ribbed in hoops rushing down the hall. Then the crunch of a giant aluminum can, front fenders tearing at each other like mad beasts, glass breaking, gasoline sloshing from tanks buckling, handlebars curling under and around like in a wrestling game played back to back, arms entwined, bodies slapping together over wreckage, engines sputtering, dying.

INGRID

Sat buckled into a 747, the jumbo jet taxiing toward the runway and Sweden. She was heading home after thirteen years. The pilot made his welcoming announcement over the loud speaker. "...We hope you have a nice flight and remember Atlantic Airways."

After takeoff, the aircraft banked over Border City, heading east. Over Uptown, Ingrid looked down the wing, locating Massage World by the pit of shimmering turquoise that was its swimming pool beside a mansard roof of oxidizing copper.

The turmoil that befell the spa behind or rather below her, Ingrid, staring out the window at the mansion grounds, delighted in remembering her little speech before signing the business over to Jack Cobb, then practically running out the door, silk-wrapped lucre in hand. Motoko Ogawa bowed deeply to her. Wise old eyes moist with tears, the Japanese woman squeezed Ingrid's hand, following Ingrid's speech. Which went like this:

"With a thank you to our charming friend Jack-san, I realize that I lack the entrepreneurial skills and inner resolve to make a go of Massage World. That I am, and always will be, a freelancer who works best alone. I humbly accept your offer, Ogawa-san. Finally, I look forward to returning to the old country. I can see myself already, behind the wheel of a rented Benz driving up from the airport. Dropping in on family and friends. Then in my hometown near Stockholm opening my own little place, calling it Ingrid's Massage, and hiring no one."

THE END

OTHER ANAPHORA LITERARY PRESS TITLES

The History of British and American Author-Publishers
By: Anna Faktorovich

Notes for Further Research
By: Molly Kirschner

The Encyclopedic Philosophy of Michel Serres
By: Keith Moser

The Visit
By: Michael G. Casey

How to Be Happy
By: C. J. Jos

A Dying Breed
By: Scott Duff

Love in the Cretaceous
By: Howard W. Robertson

The Second of Seven
By: Jeremie Guy

CPSIA information can be obtained
at www.ICGtesting.com
Printed in the USA
BVHW03s0115280818
525275BV00002B/1/P